To Melissa,

It is a cliché to say that
without you there would seem
book, but in this case you
know it is true. Thanks for
your patience + generosity,

with gratitude and affection,

Lauren

Choke

Creek

a novel by
Lauren Small

Bridle Path Press, LLC
8419 Stevenson Road
Baltimore, MD 21208

www.bridlepathpress.com

Direct orders to the above address.

Printed in the United States of America.
First Edition.
ISBN 978-0-615-22011-6

Library of Congress Control Number: 2008907367

Designed by Giordana Segneri.

Cover photographs © Bryan Eastham/istockphoto.com and
Diane Cromartie/bigstockphoto.com.

Printed on paper containing 30 percent postconsumer waste fiber.

Bridle Path
Press

To Don

A place is what it is, partly, because of the deep strata
of stories that are still being laid down,
and will continue to be, presumably forever.

Elliott West

One

The ranch sat in a hollow in the land—house, barn, a tin-roofed shed that once had been a bunkhouse. Nearby trickled a creek. The house was low and squat, hunkered down on the line of a low ridge. The barn, on the other hand, was spacious and soaring, with an airy loft that stretched beneath a high rounded roof. Inside the barn was room for a dozen horses, two rows of box stalls on either side of a long concrete aisle. The feed room sat at one end of the barn, the tack room at the other. In the middle was a ladder, leading up to the loft, along with a washroom and two wide doors, set directly across from one another.

The barn doors were open now, letting in the warm spring air, letting out the scratchy thin sound of a radio playing big band dance music, golden oldies from the 1940s. A pair of barn swallows busied themselves building a nest in the eaves, fetching mud and straw from the haystack. The haystack itself was not far away, just behind the barn, alongside a row of long, rectangular paddocks that held horses needing turning out for their exercise. In front of the barn, beside an oval riding ring, a pump dripped cold spring water into a mossy tin trough. A pickup truck and flatbed horse trailer with red slatted sides sat by the house, at the end of a long drive. Far in the distance, across the broad plain, the mountains hugged the horizon in a blue-tinged haze.

It was early morning, the time that has always been best for exercising horses and always will be. A seventeen-year-old boy was in the ring now, riding a roan colt. He was tall and wiry, with rangy limbs and the clear-eyed look of a boy who was still young enough to believe he knew what he wanted—to believe he knew what was right. He wore his cowboy hat low on his forehead, his flannel shirt tucked into his jeans, his raw leather chaps buckled tight. Just outside the ring a man stood watching. He was tall like the boy and had the same broad shoulders and trim waist. But his face was lined and weathered, his hair stone grey, and he held himself with the rigid bearing of a man who'd seen too much and wished he'd forgotten more.

The colt was acting up, acting unruly. He clamped down hard on the bit, his withers wet, his jaw flecked with foam. The boy put his leg on him, giving him a gentle squeeze, but the colt reacted by taking off, lunging and bucking across the ring. "Get after him, Eason," the man shouted. "Goddamn it boy, use your spurs."

The spurs came nowhere near the horse. Eason rode the colt in an easy manner, his body following the horse's movements with a fluid grace. At last he brought him to a halt. "He just needs more time."

The man shook his head. "You can't always gentle them." But the look on his face had softened. "Try him again."

Eason nodded, put his leg on the colt, and once more the horse took off, skittering across the ring. This time when he brought the colt to a halt, his father wasn't watching. He had his eye on the creek. Eason followed his gaze and caught sight of a girl, riding towards them on the creek trail. He could just make out the blood-bay coat of her gelding, the black mane and tail. She was wearing blue jeans, along with English riding boots and a long-sleeved sweater. Her hair was fashioned into a braid, which hung long and dark down her back. Much of it had come loose, so that from time to time, as her horse picked its way down the creek trail, she reached up with an absentminded gesture to brush the stray strands out of her eyes. Eason gave his father a questioning look.

His father wasn't in the mood for answering questions—or didn't have any answers to give. He shook his head and with a grimace pressed a hand against his hip. Then he jerked his chin at the colt.

"What are you waiting for? We don't have all day."

Eason readied himself, put on his leg, and once more the colt responded by leaping and crow-hopping across the ring. This time when he halted his horse, the creek was empty, the girl gone. Confused, he cast about with his eyes. The creek bed was wide and shallow, the banks low, affording no place to hide. She couldn't have just disappeared, could she? She couldn't have just been swallowed up by the earth. With a sense of relief that surprised him, he found her standing on the ridge-line that ran between the house and the barn. His father was studying her, too, the grimace on his face deepening to a frown.

"You have some reason for being here?" his father said.

The girl glanced at Eason then at his father. "No, sir." She rode down to them, the dark hair matched by equally dark eyes. "I was just riding."

"Just riding." The older man made no attempt to hide the sarcasm in his voice.

"Yes, sir."

She brought her horse to a halt and crossed her hands over the pommel of her saddle in a casual way—in a way that implied ease, or a sense of belonging. This, as Eason expected, only increased his father's irritation. "Do you know where you are?"

Once more the girl glanced at Eason before answering. "Not really."

"For one thing you're on private property. This is the Swale ranch, my ranch." Eason's father put a hand on the rail, drawing himself up. "I'm Cyrus Swale. Do you always make a habit of trespassing on other people's property?"

The girl shook her head. "I've never been out this far before. But I like it." The wind was blowing down the ridge behind her, and she turned her face towards it, tilting her head. "I like the way it sounds."

"You—what?" Astonished the two men looked at each other.

"The wind. I like the way it sounds." She turned her face to it again, listening. "It's different at home."

Curious, Eason cocked his head and listened to the wind, but all he heard were the familiar sounds it always made—the ones he'd been hearing all his life. There was the faint rattle of cottonwood leaves by the creek, the whispery call of the willows, the keen note of emptiness the wind always conjured when it blew across the plain.

The girl noticed him listening and smiled at him. Her smile made him feel warm, but his father would have none of that. He gave his son a sour look and turned back to the girl. "You have a name?"

"Evie." The smile withered under his father's stern gaze. "Eve Glauber."

"Glauber. Like *The Sun*?"

She nodded.

"Jase Glauber's girl."

"Yes, sir."

"And you live there." He pointed westwards down the creek, towards the city. "In Danvers."

"Yes."

The older man considered this. He took his time, his fingers kneading the muscles of his hip. "So you like to ride, do you, Eve Glauber?" he said finally.

Evie nodded again, but with an air of uncertainty this time. Her eyes found Eason's, but he responded with a slight shrug, as if to say, *Don't ask me.*

"Then maybe you'd like to ride this colt."

The remark surprised them both. Startled, Eason turned to his father, who dismissed him with a wave of his hand. "Eason can't make any sense of him," he said with an air of nonchalance. "Might as well give someone else a try."

Eason's face colored, and he shot his father a look. "Don't," he said. He didn't know if he meant the warning for Evie—*Don't ride him*—or his father—*Don't let her*—or both. It didn't matter. Neither was listening to him. Their eyes were locked on each other as if he weren't even there.

"Okay," Evie said.

"Okay—what?" the older man said. For the first time that morning, Eason saw a hint of doubt come into his father's eyes.

"Okay, I'll ride him." She got down from her horse.

This, Eason knew, was the last thing his father had expected. He'd only meant to get rid of the girl—to scare her away. But one glance at Evie—and the set of her jaw—convinced Eason there was no turning back. They'd both misjudged her. She wasn't the kind of girl to be scared off easily—to be scared off, Eason guessed, *ever*. "You don't want to do this," he warned her, but he knew it was too late. She was already coming towards him, and there was nothing left to do but hand her the reins.

Evie eased herself into the saddle. She'd never been in a Western saddle before, and it felt strange to her, deeper and stiffer than her English jumping saddle, encumbered by the large horn. Eason's legs were much longer than hers, and her feet wouldn't reach the stirrups. But she didn't know how to shorten them, and didn't want to admit she didn't know. She just slipped her feet into the stirrup leathers on top.

She took up the reins automatically with two hands. All at once she remembered that Western riders reined with only one hand. She let her hand drop, but then she didn't know what to do with it, and it dangled awkwardly by her side. Stupid, she thought to herself. *Stupid, stupid.* She was always getting herself into dumb trouble like this, especially when it came to horses. She'd seen the colt and knew what he could do. She'd never ridden anything as wild as him before. Still there was nothing to do about that now. She'd just have to trust herself to figure him out. She settled herself as firmly in the saddle as she could and turned to the Swales.

"Make him trot," Cyrus said, his face impassive.

Eason's eyes met hers, and then he glanced away. There was still time for her to back out of this—if her pride would let her. He wasn't about to make her.

She turned back to the colt. He seemed to have lost interest in the whole proceeding. He was dozing lightly in the sun, breathing softly, his eyes closed. Good, she thought, maybe he's tired out. She clucked to him cautiously, and he heaved a sigh and ambled towards the rail. His gait felt odd after her horse, stiff and leggy, his withers narrow, dropping precipitously away. He held his head high as he walked, jerking it from side to side.

"Trot," the rancher repeated, a note of impatience in his voice.

Instinctively she reached for the reins with both hands, then forced herself to let her left hand drop. She clucked to the colt, a little louder this time, but he just continued his sleepy walk. She tried clucking one more time, and then she put on her leg.

Instantly the colt broke into a dead run, his head down, his back arched, his body twisting and lunging. She tried to pull his head up, but it was no use—the reins were jerked cleanly out of her hands. She lurched backwards then forwards, jamming her stomach hard against the saddle horn, losing her wind. As she gasped for breath—for some way to hold on—the colt charged across the ring, heading straight for the rail. It was a high fence, a good four feet, too high for him to jump. He wouldn't make it, he'd get hung up, flip, or fall, crushing her beneath him. But he was going to try it anyway—she knew it just as she knew there was nothing she could do about it. He was completely out of her control.

Panic rose in Evie's throat. She'd bitten her tongue, and the taste of blood flooded her mouth. She'd lost one of the stirrup leathers. Stupidly, she tried to regain it—reaching for it blindly with her foot—when she remembered the reins. At the last second she managed to grab them and by yanking hard on one side with both hands, turned the colt. He swerved along the rail and back to the middle of the ring. Then he stopped.

For a moment she sat there, catching her breath, swallowing down the taste of blood and bile. Then she bent over and found her stirrup. As she settled herself back in the saddle, she glanced over at the rail. Eason looked like he would be sick, but his father's face was unchanged. "Trot," he said.

This time she ignored convention and took the reins with both hands. She clucked to the colt and headed him towards the rail. Before she put her leg on, she braced herself, gripping hard. She managed to hold the reins for a few seconds before the colt yanked them from her. Then he was off as before, lunging for the rail.

Once again she managed to stop him, but not before he'd scraped her knee hard on the fence. As the pain hit, tears came to her eyes.

Evie blinked hard, fought them back. When she turned to the rancher, there was a faint look of disgust in his eyes. The blood rushed to her face. She took the colt to the center of the ring, gripped the reins with both hands, and readied herself to hold on. Just as she was about to put on her leg, something came to her mind. She'd been wrong about needing to trust herself. What she needed to do was trust her horse. She looked down at the colt. "You want to act crazy? You want to jump that rail? Get us both killed?" She hissed the words at him so that he heard but no one else. "Well, then, c'mon. Let's get on with it. Let's go."

She lifted both legs and kicked the colt as hard as she could, the loose stirrups banging against his sides. Startled, the colt took off across the ring, twisting and lunging as before. But this time Evie didn't even try to stop him. She let go of the reins and held onto the saddle horn with both hands, whooping and hollering the whole way.

They reached the rail. At the last second the colt reared back and swerved. Stunned, he came to a stop on his own. He was trembling, confused. He wanted time to think about it, to figure out what had happened—what had gone wrong—but Evie didn't give in to him. She loosened the reins, kicked him hard, and made him do the charge all over again. The third time she kicked him, he didn't even bother to run. He broke into a stiff, jerky trot. She picked up the reins and rode him a full circle around the ring, trotting all the way. Then she took him over to the rancher.

"He trots okay."

"Son of a bitch." The rancher looked at her for a long time, and then he shook his head.

Evie's tongue was burning, and her knee hurt like hell, but she broke into a grin. She couldn't help it. Her grin widening, she looked for Eason. Only he wasn't there. His spot by the ring was empty, and in the distance, the screen door on the house was flapping shut.

Two

That night when Evie came down to the kitchen for dinner, her father was already at the table, reading through a typewritten report, a thick black pencil in his hand. "You left your boots on the floor," he said. He was still dressed in his clothes from work, his shirt sleeves rolled up, his tie loosened, his suit jacket hung on the back of his chair. Frowning, he drew a line through a series of words on the page and replaced them with others he penciled into the margin. Evie rolled her eyes but picked up the boots she'd dropped in a heap by the door when she came home from riding. She dropped them into the boot box, noting with satisfaction the way her father jumped when she let the lid slam. Then she walked to the oven without washing her hands—an infraction of the rules that went unremarked this time—and removed the plates Ruth had left warming there. She set one at her place, the roast beef and mashed potatoes steaming lightly, the green beans gone grey in the oven's heat, and the other by her father.

In the middle of the table sat the pile of newspapers her father read each day, *The Danvers Post*, *The Wall Street Journal*, and *The New York Daily Times*, with *The Rocky Mountain Sun* occupying its usual position of honor on top. As Evie sat down, she gave the headlines on *The Sun* a cursory glance. They were about the war in Vietnam, but then that was nothing new. It was the spring of 1966, and it seemed as if all the newspapers talked about anymore was the war. She shoved the newspapers aside and began to eat.

Outside it was dark, a thin veil of light from the street lamps shining through the yews onto the windowpane. In the kitchen the pale yellow cabinets glowed, but shadows crossed the green-flecked tile floor. Her father's head was tipped down as he read, putting his face in shadow, too, but Evie didn't need to see his face to picture every furrow, mark, and wrinkle on it—earned, as he liked so often to say, by a lifetime of honest work. Only his eyes made her wonder. They were hazel and changeable, switching with unexpected fluidity from green to brown, as if to warn her against putting too much stock in the appearance of things. He still hadn't eaten. She cut into her roast beef and said, "Dad."

Jase glanced up, a distant look in his eyes. "What is it?" He saw the plate and smiled at her in a fond way. "Oh, thanks, my girl." He took a bite of his dinner then picked up his pencil and began reading again.

"I rode Bird today."

"Did you?" He drew a circle around a set of words, crossed out another.

"I rode another horse, too."

"Another—" Jase paused, the pencil wavering in the air.

"A colt. A roan one. He was kind of wild." She touched her knee, which was still sore, so that when she pressed on it, it hurt. But she didn't want her father to know that, so she shrugged in an idle way. "He was okay."

"Evie." Jase's eyes narrowed. "Did you ride in the creek?"

"To a ranch. They raise horses there. It's owned by a man named—"

Jase cut her off. "You know I don't want you doing that." He busied himself again with the report he was reading.

"Why not?"

He shuffled the pages in an important way. "When I bought you that horse, we agreed there would be limits."

"I'm not twelve anymore." Evie's voice rose in exasperation. "I'm practically sixteen, old enough to drive. You can't expect me to ride around here forever."

"You won't be sixteen until next winter, and that's still a long ways off." Jase put the report down. "And don't even think about getting your driver's license if you don't bring your grades up. Did you finish that social studies paper for school?"

Evie cast her eyes down. "No."

Jase lifted the pages he was reading and tapped them in an aggravated way on the table, putting them together with a snap. Then he sighed and put the pages down. "I know Bird is a wonderful animal." He reached across the table and took her hand. "But he can't teach you about the things that matter in life." He slid *The Sun* over to her with an encouraging smile. "Your future is in this newspaper, Evie. One day you'll see that everything you need is in its pages."

Evie gave the newspaper a sour look. "You're the one who says I have to run *The Sun* when I grow up, not me." She stood up, leaving the paper where it was. She'd hardly touched her dinner, but she didn't feel like eating anymore. The idea of spending her life the way her father did, locked in an office all day like a jail, turned her stomach. She carried her plate to the sink and washed it up, recklessly flinging the plate under the stream of water so that it banged against the side of the sink with a clatter. Then she grabbed a dishtowel and turned around to face her father, her eyes fierce and glowing with pride. "You should have seen me ride that colt. I made him trot. No one else could, but I did."

"I know you're a good rider, Evie." Jase raised his hands in a conciliatory way. "And riding is a fine hobby when you're young. Plenty of girls enjoy it." His tone sharpened. "They also outgrow it—at least the sensible ones do." He picked up *The Sun*, holding it once more out to her. When she refused to take it, his face darkened. He shoved his chair back and stood up. "No more riding in that creek. You obey the rules I've made."

"I'm not a little girl anymore. I'm old enough to decide things for myself." Evie wrung the dishtowel back and forth. "Old enough to know what I want."

"What *you* want—" The color rose in his face, and he shook the newspaper at her so that the pages jerked and almost flew from his grasp. "What about this paper, and this family, and your responsibilities to it—"

"What family? I don't even know where my mother is."

All at once it grew very still in the kitchen. In the silence they heard the humming of the refrigerator, the tick of the oven clock. Outside the wind was blowing. The swing on the porch rattled, and the yews tapped against the pane. Jase crumpled the pages of the newspaper into his fist. "You know I can't tell you that."

She met his eyes without backing down. "Why not?"

He slammed his fist on the table. The sound startled them both. The newspaper flew apart and scattered across the floor. "You're not old enough. When you are—"

"I'm not a baby, and I'm tired of being treated like one." But now the tears were coming, and that was the last thing she wanted him to see. She flung the dishtowel to the floor and fled the room.

Evie slammed the door to her bedroom and threw herself onto her bed. She bit down hard on her lip to make the tears stop, and once they had, stood up and walked to her window. It was open, letting in the cool night air, which was scented with the irises from her father's garden and the early spring grass that was still greening up. She leaned against the sill, breathing hard. At the bottom of the yard the creek flowed by, and when her breathing had quieted down, she could hear it, the thin stream of water trickling through the sand. On the far side, in the darkness, loomed the stable where she kept her horse: the barn, turn-out paddocks, and fenced-in field where her father expected her to confine her rides. Past the stable, the lights of the city glowed, the mountains rising in dark swells against the starry sky.

The wind was still blowing down the creek, and beneath the willows a white shape glimmered in the sand. It was nothing, Evie knew, a bit of paper or trash, but she found herself thinking about the creek lady anyway, an old ghost story about an Indian who wandered the creek in a white dress, clutching a baby in her arms. When Evie was little the story had terrified her, keeping her awake far into the night. She shook her head. What would her father think if she told him she was thinking about ghosts? She was far too old for that kind of nonsense now.

She turned around and walked to her dresser. It was heaped with the detritus that accumulates naturally in the rooms of teenaged girls: hair bands and erasers, beads and pencil stubs, pins, paper clips, a watch-band missing its watch. Her desk was piled high with schoolbooks, their spines barely cracked, and school papers in various states of disarray, none of them done, including the social studies report her father had spoken of, which was on the geology of Iceland. Evie glanced at it with disgust. What did Iceland have to do with her? She'd never been there, and based on what she'd learned so far, never wanted to go. Above the desk a shelf was crammed with pleasure books, most of them stories about horses, all of them showing signs of being well-thumbed and read. Another shelf held her horse collection, figurines made of spun glass, porcelain, and brightly painted molded plastic.

She bent over and opened the bottom drawer to her dresser. Digging through to the back, past clumps of balled-up socks and old T-shirts, she found a cigar box. She glanced towards the door, making sure it was still closed. Then she pulled out the box and carried it to her bed. On the top was a picture of an Indian, a solemn figure with war paint on his cheeks, dressed in a striking headdress made of flowing feathers. Evie ran her fingers across the Indian's face, but it made her think of the ghost again, so she lifted the lid, hiding it away. As she opened the box, the faint scent of tobacco and wax came into the air. When she was little, she'd kept her crayons in the box, but now it held scraps of paper, each one folded over and over until it resembled a tiny square, no bigger than a pebble or button. She pushed the papers aside, making a whispering, rustling sound, and reached for a photograph that was nestled in the bottom. Then she put the box aside.

She changed into her nightgown and, carrying the photograph, crossed the hall to the bathroom. Then she locked the bathroom door and held the photograph up to the light. The picture, which was black and white and grainy, had been crushed and crumpled, and creases ran through it like white lines. But Evie could still make out the image of a woman standing by a low stone wall on a wide expanse of grey sand beside the sea. She was a young woman who appeared to be on the cusp of things, not old enough to be married, perhaps, but old enough to be married soon. An eager look graced her face and an air of hopeful expectation, although Evie also thought there might be a hint of sadness in her eyes. She couldn't be sure. The sun was coming from behind her, casting her face partly in shadow.

Evie had found the photograph a few days earlier, tucked into the back of a kitchen drawer. Apparently her father had forgotten it, just as, Evie suspected, he wished he could forget everything about her mother. He never talked about her. All Evie knew was that she had been a baby when her mother left them. Over the years she'd tried everything she could think of to find out what had happened to her, but nothing worked. Everyone she asked either didn't know or wouldn't say. Once she'd asked Ruth, the housekeeper who had taken care of her for as long as Evie could remember, but Ruth had looked at her with genuine astonishment and said, "I have no idea. You mean you don't know?" Just last winter Evie had gone to the *Sun* building and visited the archives. She looked through the newspapers published after she was born, but found no stories about deaths, divorces, or missing women with the last name Glauber. All she could conclude was that her mother was still alive. Afterwards she'd run into Harold Simmons, the newspaper's solicitor and one of her father's oldest friends. Pulling him aside, she'd asked if he knew what had happened to her. But he'd only given her a sad look and said, "Those were such hard times."

She had a grandmother, she knew that; she'd even met her once. Her name was Agatha Wickham, and she wrote an art column for *The New York Daily Times*. From time to time Evie read the pieces Agatha published in the New York paper, but she could never make sense of them. She couldn't even imagine the art her grandmother described with such fervor, paintings made of spots and squiggles, sculptures constructed out of old car parts. Once Agatha had paid them a visit, and Evie still remembered the day, even though it had been years earlier, when she was only eight. She'd found her grandmother strange and frightening. Agatha had been dressed entirely in black, she wore her hair in a severe style, and she spoke in a commanding, nasal voice. The visit had gone badly. Agatha and her father had argued, and in the end she had left in a huff, storming out of the house. The fight, Evie assumed, was because of her mother, although at the time she'd been too young to understand. In any case Agatha had never come back, and the one time she'd asked her father why they didn't go to see her, he'd given her a sharp look and said, "Because I don't want to waste my time."

Still Evie had never forgotten the strange woman who was her grandmother, and one day, a few years after Agatha's visit, had summoned up her nerve to call her. She found the number for *The New York Daily Times* in the masthead and dialed. When the receptionist answered, she asked for Agatha, and a few moments later her grandmother came onto the line. Agatha was surprised to hear from her, but to Evie's relief, chatted in a friendly fashion. At least whatever Agatha was angry about didn't include her. Finally Evie hazarded a word about her mother. Agatha's voice dropped, and she abandoned her breezy tone. "Oh, dear," she said. The line grew silent, as if Agatha were considering. Then, "I'm sorry. I can't talk about that. I gave my word." Agatha concluded the call by promising to write, and made Evie promise to write, too. But later, when Evie picked up her pen, she didn't know what to say. She never heard from Agatha again, so she decided her grandmother must feel the same way.

Evie put the photograph down by the sink. She undid the band at the bottom of her braid and ran her fingers through her hair, loosening it. Then she brushed it until the waves from the braid were gone, and her hair hung straight and dark down her back. Once more she lifted the photograph, this time holding it up to her face. In the picture, her mother's hair was pulled straight back, revealing a pronounced widow's peak. Evie pulled her hair back, studying the line of the identical widow's peak that emerged there. Then she let her hair go.

She could hear her father coming upstairs, the heavy tread of his footsteps on the stairs. Clutching the photograph tightly to her chest, she slipped back into her room, making sure the door was tightly shut behind her. Digging through the heap of books on her desk, she came up with a notebook and a pencil. She tore out a scrap of paper and carried it to her bed. She positioned the photograph beside her so that when she looked down, she could see her mother's face. Then she closed the cigar box, and using the top as a writing surface, spread out the slip of paper. Grasping the pencil, she wrote:

I rode Bird in the creek today. I rode all the way to the Swale ranch. I wasn't supposed to, but I did anyway.

She spun the pencil between her fingers, a gesture which, although she didn't know it, closely resembled one her father habitually made. She glanced at the photograph. Then she wrote:

He still won't tell me what happened to you. I asked him straight out, but he wouldn't say a word.

She thought for a moment and wrote something down. Then she frowned, erased it, and wrote:

Am I like you? Will I ever know?

She gave the scrap of paper one last look, ensuring that it was the way she wanted. Then she folded it tightly until it resembled the other squares in the box. *Like snowflakes*, she thought with a feeling that was both sad and satisfying as she placed it with the others, each one outwardly similar, but inwardly entirely unique.

The wind was blowing harder now, coming through the window, bringing a chill into the air. She shivered and walked to the window. Far down the creek, she knew, on the broad, wide plain, lived a tall, rangy boy with clear grey eyes and a wild roan colt. Her father would be furious if he knew she was planning on riding to the Swale ranch again. She closed her eyes and imagined herself back on the roan colt, cradled deep in Eason's saddle, feeling the thrill again as the horse twisted and lunged across the ring. *Eason.* It was such an odd name. She wondered what it meant. She said the name out loud, liking the way it felt in her mouth, the long drawn-out first syllable rolling easily off her tongue. Then she opened her eyes. In the creek, the white shape was still there, shimmering in the starlight. She turned her back on it and turned off the light.

Three

Saturday morning Evie woke early, but when she came down to the kitchen, her father had already left for work. The news, he liked to remind her, never took a day off, and so neither did he. She ate a quick breakfast then saddled up Bird and rode to the Swale ranch. As she came up the ridgeline, she caught sight of the rancher in the distance, hauling feed in his pickup to the herds in the fields. Eason was by the barn, saddling up the roan colt. It was a clear day, sunlight silvering the branches of the sagebrush, gleaming in white patches on the tin roof of the old bunkhouse. Overhead the sky was deep and cloudless, pinned to the mountains like a bright blue cape, flowing to the horizon. She rode down to him. "How's that colt doing?"

"He's all right." The tips of Eason's ears reddened, and he took a sudden interest in the roan's bridle, adjusting the reins. Then he turned his back on her and in a stiff and businesslike fashion, hoisted the saddle onto the colt.

He was mad at her. She didn't understand. Then she remembered. After she'd ridden the colt, Eason had disappeared into the house, slamming the screen door shut behind him. All she'd wanted to do was impress him. By making the colt trot when he couldn't, she'd wounded his pride. "I'm sorry," she said. "I never should have gotten on him. It was a dumb thing to do."

Eason remained busy with his horse, bending the stirrup back over the seat of the saddle, pulling the leather cinch strap through the ring.

Then he turned back to her and tipped his head, accepting her apology. "Anyway, he trots better now."

There was the hint of a smile on his lips. She smiled back, and the next thing she knew, the two of them were grinning at each other. "I've been thinking about your name," she said. "It's so unusual. What does it mean?"

Eason kneed the colt gently in the belly until he let out the air he was holding. "It doesn't mean anything. It's just been in my family for a long time." He circled the leather strap through the ring a second time and yanked the cinch tight.

"But it must come from somewhere."

The colt was getting fidgety, and Eason rubbed his ears, quieting him down. Then he turned back to her, only this time with a serious and appraising air, as if he were judging her, taking her measure, the way he might judge a filly, trying to imagine the mare she would one day become. "You always this stubborn?"

"I don't know." Evie's face turned warm. "I guess so."

Eason nodded, as if her answer had satisfied him—as if stubbornness were the trait he admired most. "Come on." He put his foot in the stirrup and lifted himself into the saddle. "I'll show you."

They rode into the creek, heading eastwards, deeper into the prairie. The spring run had ended just a few weeks earlier, and the creek bottom was still damp, boggy in spots. The air was cool and fresh, thick with the musky scent of sage. Water trickled through the greening sedges, past stands of shrubby willows and clumps of cattails, which grew along the sandbars. Here and there the stream collected into small pools that looked up at Evie like dark eyes, or split apart into smaller rivulets, which curved and curled through the sand like strands of her braided hair.

The colt was jittery and jogged fretfully down the creek bed, scenting the air with wide nostrils, his eyes white and rolling. His nervousness infected Bird, who trotted beside him with his head held high, his muscles quivering. Evie felt jittery herself, her heart pounding, her head light. She'd never known a boy like Eason before. In comparison the boys at school were silly and childish, all wrapped up in schoolyard games and rivalries. Eason had an air of direction about him, a straightforward clarity in all his actions. He even rode the colt in a purposeful manner, keeping him firmly to the trail while he gentled him with his seat and hands. He looked like the kind of person who would accomplish meaningful and important things. Being around him made her think that maybe one day she would, too. *There must be more to life*, she thought with a sour shake of her head, *than running a newspaper*.

He wasn't particularly good-looking, and she found herself feeling glad about that. Pretty boys were always so much less interesting. His nose was too wide and his jaw too square, his eyes deeply set beneath a broad forehead. But overall he gave a pleasing appearance. She liked it. She liked everything so far about this boy.

In time they came to a low bluff which rose alongside the creek with a sharply-eroded face, scalloped and bare. Root tendrils emerged from the weathered soil, tender and white. Eason rode his horse to the top of the hill, and Evie followed, discovering a pleasing new vista from that height. In the distance, the mountains shouldered out of the earth, sharp and muscular. Everywhere else the plain sloped gently away, running flat and empty to the horizon. Eason dismounted, and Evie did the same. For a time they walked along the bluff, leading their horses by the hand, while Eason studied the ground with an intent look on his face, as if he were searching for something. Evie stared at the ground too, trying to be helpful, although she had no idea what they were looking for. As far as she could tell, there was nothing to search *for*, the ground was hard and dry, the way the prairie always was, stony and studded with thin clumps of grass. Now and then Eason scuffed at the soil with his boot, and Evie dug her toe into the ground too, for good measure. All at once he bent over and picked something up. He brushed it with his fingers, scrubbing off the dirt, and held it out to her.

"Take a look."

It was a piece of mottled stone, milky white in color, with a flat bottom, pointy top, and chipped facets on the sides. She took it from him and examined it in the palm of her hand. The facets were smooth and glossy, the tip surprisingly sharp. When she tested it against the ball of her thumb, it left a dot of blood on her skin. "Is it an arrowhead?"

Eason nodded. "From the Battle of Choke Creek."

She looked at him in amazement. "The Battle of Choke Creek was here?"

"On our land."

Astonished, she shook her head. "I didn't know it was so close to home. I thought it was much farther away."

She ran her fingers one more time across the arrowhead then held it back out to him, trying to give it back. He waved it away with a casual air. "You can keep it. I have a whole collection at home. I have metal pieces, too. Bullets and buckles."

"Thanks." She fingered the stone a moment longer in awe, then tucked it into her pocket.

"So you've heard of the Battle of Choke Creek?"

He spoke with an air of nonchalance, but she could tell he didn't mean it. The battle meant a lot to him—more, maybe, than anything else in the world. "Sure. Everybody has. We learned about it in school."

"What did they tell you?"

She frowned as she thought about it. "Let me see." They'd studied the famous battle in history class, just a few years ago, but history had never been her strongest suit. Now she found herself wishing she'd paid more attention. "It was Stevenson." She smiled with relief as it all came back to her. "Colonel John Quintius Stevenson." She spoke with a rush, repeating the formula her teacher had made them memorize. "He fought the savage Indians and made the plains safe for humanity and civilization."

"What about Stevenson's daughter? Did they tell you how she was raped by an Indian?"

Evie swallowed hard. "No."

"I bet they didn't tell you anything about the Wyngates either."

"The Wyngates?"

"A ranching family. Lived just south of here. Father, mother, children, the youngest still a baby. All of them scalped and killed by Indians."

Evie's face paled. "They didn't say anything about that."

"I'm not surprised." Eason shook his head in disgust. "Nobody talks about the things that matter anymore." The colt had dropped its head to graze among the sparse spring grasses, and for a time Eason watched him, shooing away a harrying fly. Then he turned back to her with the same nonchalant air. "I can tell you the story if you want."

"Okay."

He grinned, then grew quickly serious again. He took a length of rope from his saddle and hobbled the colt, leaving it to graze on its own. "See that trail?" With a broad sweep of his arm, he indicated a crease in the land to the south, a slight dip that might have once been a trail. "They came from there. Stevenson and his men, the cavalry and the volunteers." His voice dropped and his words took on an air of portent. "It was late November, freezing cold, snow on the ground knee-high to the horses. They rode up silently, in the dead of night. They had to. It was their only chance, using the element of surprise."

He studied her with a searching expression on his face, as if he were curious about how she was taking his story. Once again she had the feeling he was judging her, taking her measure, trying to decide whether or not she was worthy. She held her breath, trying to look appropriately interested and impressed, hoping she passed muster. Apparently she did, because with a curt nod, he continued. "The Indians were camped there, by the creek, at the bottom of the bluff, their lodges spread out over two miles." Another sweep of his arm indicated their position. "Hundreds of warriors, armed to the teeth, led by seasoned war chiefs. Lying in wait. They'd even dug in rifle pits for defense." He pointed out some spots in the earthen bank where shallow depressions still marked the face of the cliff.

"The attack came at dawn. Stevenson assembled his men here, on the top of the bluff. First came the cannons." A look of growing excitement came into Eason's eyes, and he trembled as if he could hear them firing. "Then the rifle barrage, companies firing on either side." He swung his arm to the left, indicating the expanse of land beside her, then showed her the right. "The Indians returned fire, driving the men back." He stumbled backwards. "Then Stevenson rallied them and they advanced, firing." Holding his arms out in front of him like a rifle, he dashed forwards, dropped to one knee, then rose and advanced, spinning, feinting, and ducking as he fired. At last he stopped, his hands dropping to his sides. "The fighting lasted all morning with blood shed on both sides." He said this with evident satisfaction. "But in the end Stevenson won." He turned to her, his eyes shining. "He whipped those savages, killed over five hundred, and half a dozen of their chiefs."

All at once she burst out laughing. She couldn't help it. "I'm sorry," she said. "It's just so funny, the way you tell it. It's like a movie, the cavalry charging and all that." Then she saw the look on his face. She'd wounded his pride again, perhaps fatally this time. Her laughter died away. "Oh, Eason," she said. "I didn't mean it." She felt awful. "It's just that—well, it happened so long ago."

"Maybe so." He nodded, conceding the point, his face still showing a tender dignity. "But that doesn't mean it isn't still important."

He turned away from her, occupying himself with the colt, brushing away some stray strands of grass that had gotten tangled in its tail. She didn't know what to say. Silently she cursed herself. She was always so reckless—so reckless and so *stupid*. Once again she'd managed to ruin things. Maybe forever.

"My great-grandfather fought in that battle," Eason said at last, his voice still carrying vestiges of his wounded pride. "He was in the cavalry, first lieutenant under Stevenson. His name was Thomas Eli Eason."

"Oh," she said. *Eason.* At last she understood. No wonder he cared so much about that old Indian fight. It wasn't just some silly old battle from history. It was *his* battle, his family, and his name. "Is that why your family settled here?"

"My great-grandfather homesteaded this place after the Indian Wars. It's been in my family ever since. We've always taken care of it, and we always will." His face was fierce and determined, although there was also a hint of defensiveness in his eyes, as if he thought she might laugh at him again.

Laughing at Eason was the last thing she wanted to do now. She looked out over the bluff, trying to see it the way he did, wanting to picture that people had fought there and even died. She couldn't imagine it. It was all too peaceful, the creek meandering in lazy curves across the ground. Even the air felt serene, a hush lying like a weight over the land.

"My father was a soldier, too." Eason said. "He fought with the Marines in the Pacific. He got wounded there, a bullet in the hip. That's why he can't ride anymore."

"What about your grandfather? Did he go to war?"

"No, not him." Eason studied the colt's bridle, making an unnecessary adjustment to the bit. "He was different, that's all." He let the bridle go. "But I'm enlisting next year, as soon as I turn eighteen. I promised my father I'd wait until I'd graduated. My friend Billy's there now. He joined up last winter. He was only seventeen, but his parents signed for him and he got to go. Now he's in Vietnam. He sent me a letter all about it." He reached into his shirt pocket, pulled out a small square of blue paper, and opened it. "He says, 'Don't worry, Eason. I won't kill all the gooks before you get here. I'll save some for you.'" Her questions seemed to have mollified him, and he grinned at her in a shy way. Then he folded the letter and put it away.

Gooks? Vietnam? She didn't know what to say. It had never occurred to her that the war they wrote about in the newspapers was actually being fought by real people—by people like Eason. No wonder he looked so purposeful and directed. He was going to be a soldier. The thought of watching him go off to war one day made her feel both proud and sad. She'd only just met him, but already she felt as if saying good-bye to him would break her heart.

Just then the wind picked up, blowing across the plain, shimmering through the sagebrush. Evie turned her face to it, expecting to hear the same low keening note she'd found so beautiful the first time she rode out to the Swale ranch—so haunting, enticing, and sad. Instead she found herself growing wary and frightened, as if the wind were bringing her a message of warning, or danger. The horses heard it, too. They snorted and lifted their heads, their eyes wide, their muscles trembling. Evie shuddered and pulled her arms around herself. "Don't go."

"Don't—what?" Eason gave her a surprised look.

"Don't do it. Don't go to Vietnam."

"Why not?"

"Because it's dangerous. You could get hurt. You could even get killed."

He fell silent, and for a moment she thought he felt what she did—the aura of danger in the air. Then his face broke into a smile. "You should talk." He came over to her. "You're the stubborn one, remember? You could have gotten killed riding my horse, but you got on him anyway."

She was so confused. She'd never been so close to him before. She could see the way the spring sun had reddened his skin, the deep set of his clear grey eyes. He had a musky scent that overwhelmed her, as deep and clear as the sage. She dropped her eyes to his hands. He was so gentle when he touched the colt. She found herself wishing he'd touch her, too.

He must have known. He put his hands on her shoulders, drawing her to him. Then he tipped up her chin. "You don't need to worry about me." She closed her eyes, and he kissed her. When she opened her eyes, she saw that he was studying her again, but that he was done judging her. He knew what she was made of. "Don't worry," he said again, his face serious, his eyes hard and direct. "I'll be back."

Four

On Monday, when Jase came down to breakfast, he found his daughter hunched over the kitchen table, scribbling in a notebook. She was already dressed in her school uniform, the white blouse, green pinstriped skirt, and black-and-white saddle shoes. Scattered around her were several volumes of the encyclopedia, some mimeographs from school, balled up clumps of discarded paper, and a half-eaten bowl of cereal. She glanced up at him. "I'm almost done with that school report. There are about a million volcanoes in Iceland."

"Is that so?" He gave her a fond smile, put the coffee on to perk, and walked to the window. It was a beautiful day, the sun shining through the yews. He glanced back at Evie. He'd hardly seen her since Friday. For weeks now the printers had been threatening a strike, and on Saturday he'd been called into the office for an emergency meeting with the union. When he came home, she was out riding. The negotiations resumed early Sunday morning and lasted until the evening. This time when he came back, Evie had left him a note. She'd gone to the movies with her friend Bobbie and had been invited to stay for dinner.

He poured himself a cup of coffee and sat down, watching with secret delight as she wrote, pulling in an absentminded way on her lower lip, the way she had since she was six. His heart filled with warmth, and love. She thought she was all grown up, but he knew better. She was still his little girl. She got so angry with him sometimes, but that was normal for girls her age, wasn't it? At least everyone said so. Teen troubles and all that. In the end everything would work out, he was sure of it. He was the fourth generation to run *The Sun* and she would be the fifth. The thought made him smile with pleasure. It was the reason he'd named her Eve—the first woman in their family to take the helm.

He smiled again and shook open *The Danvers Post*. A moment later a scowl crossed his face, and he jabbed a finger at the editorial page. "That Andy Zeitler," he muttered. "If he thinks for one minute that I ... "

His voice trailed off as he continued to read. For some time now, the owner of *The Post* had been taking potshots at *The Sun*, but this time he'd gone too far. Zeitler thought *The Sun* was treating its printers unfairly, did he? Well, Jase would see about that. He'd take it up with Harold when they met that morning. If there was one thing he was sure of, it was that Evie would inherit a newspaper that was treated with respect. Frowning, he turned to *The Post*'s front page. A few minutes later it seemed to him that Evie had spoken. Or had he just imagined it? He looked up, forcing the smile back onto his face. "Yes?"

"I said," she repeated with a note of exasperation in her voice, "what do you know about the Battle of Choke Creek?"

"Choke Creek?" He looked at her with surprise. That battle was ages ago. Why was she bringing it up now? "Why? Do you need something for your report?"

"No." She toyed with her pencil. "I've just been wondering about it, that's all."

He thought about it. "Well, it was Stevenson, of course. He was the hero."

"I know that." She gave the table an impatient tap. "I mean the other things. The ones people don't talk about anymore."

"Don't talk about?" Puzzled, he studied her. She had shoved her report aside and was looking at him expectantly. "Evie, is there something you're trying to tell me?"

"No." She glanced down, and her voice took on a stubborn tone. "It's just that I've been there. I've seen it."

"You mean the battlefield?"

"Yes. I rode there on Bird."

So that was where she'd been all day Saturday. With a growing sense of irritation, he turned back to *The Post*. "I thought we agreed you wouldn't ride in that creek anymore."

She ignored that remark. "It's on the Swale ranch. The owner's name is Cyrus, and he has a son named Eason—"

Startled, Jase looked at her. "Eason?"

"Eason Swale." She was looking exasperated again. "I tried to tell you before, but you wouldn't listen. He's the one who showed me the battlefield. He said his great-grandfather fought there. His name was Eason, too. Thomas Eli Eason."

"Thomas Eli Eason?"

She nodded, waiting for him to go on, but Jase's mind was whirling. "Evie." His voice tightened. "What exactly do you know about the Swales?"

She gave him a puzzled look. "I know they raise horses, and—"

"Do you know that Cyrus used to be a judge?"

"A judge?" She shook her head. "No. Why?"

"Because years ago some Indians tried to come onto his land, and he chased them away with a rifle. The sheriff got called out, and Cyrus spent the night in jail. After that he couldn't be a judge anymore."

She was taken aback. She fell silent, and he could see her thinking about it. Then her face grew defiant, and her voice took on the obstinate tone again. "So?"

"So now you know why I don't want you going out there anymore. That man's reckless and a danger. You could get hurt."

"You don't know anything about it." Evie swept the unfinished pages of her report into her book bag and stood up. "And you don't know a thing about me." She jerked the kitchen door open. "I have to go now." Her voice took on a hard, sarcastic edge. "You don't want me to be late for school, do you?"

"Evie." Jase shoved back his chair. "Wait—" There was a note of pleading in his voice, but it was too late. She cast a last, withering look in his direction and left the house.

Why did things between them always have to end like this? Jase slumped in the doorway and watched his daughter go, her bare bird-like legs striding beneath the pin-striped skirt of her school uniform. The wind was blowing from the north, and as she walked up the street she leaned into it, pitching forward slightly at the waist, her long hair whipping back. Even from a distance he could see how angry she was. All he wanted was what was best for her. Why couldn't she see that? She kept riding in that creek, even after he expressly forbid it. Now she was talking about the Battle of Choke Creek and some boy named Eason. He sucked in his breath. What had that boy said to her? And what in God's name did she mean by the things people didn't talk about anymore?

He glanced at his watch. It was late and Harold was expecting him, but right now Andy Zeitler and the demands of the printers' union seemed like the least of his troubles. He picked up the phone and dialed his secretary. "Margaret?" he said, when she came onto the line. "Tell Harold not to wait for me. I'll see him later, when I get in."

Jase hurried out of the kitchen and into the front hall, which stood at the center of the house, a long spine connecting two wings. On one side stood an enclosed sun porch and octagonally shaped living room, which doubled as a home library, with shelves holding the family's books, including the encyclopedia Evie had been reading from that morning. The other wing contained the kitchen and dining room. At the front, a wide door gave out to the street. Opposite it, a curving staircase led to the second floor, and beneath the stairs, tucked into the paneling, so at first glance to be all but invisible, were the outlines of a small, inconspicuous door.

He walked to the door, his shoes sounding dully on the black-and-white tiles. Overhead the frosted globes of a chandelier gave out a pale, flickering light, a poor imitation of the gas jets they had once replaced. The entrance to the hidden room was low, and he ducked down to pass through it, but straightened up on the other side. There the ceiling was high, and the room, while narrow, was long enough to serve as a small office. On one side stretched a row of filing cabinets, accompanied by a set of bookshelves with cupboards at the bottom. The other side of the room held a desk, topped by a warren of cubbies. Straight ahead, at the far end of the room, a small window provided a sliver of light and a glimpse of the creek.

The air in the office smelled of disuse, of neglect and decay. Originally it had belonged to Asa Glauber, Jase's great-grandfather and the founder of *The Sun*. A paranoid, irascible man, Asa had been distrustful of enemies and fearful of natural disasters. Having lost two *Sun* buildings—the first to flood, the second to fire—he'd insisted on keeping his most important records at home. The house itself he had built of massive blocks of stone, fire- and flood-proof. And the office he set exactly in the middle, his castle keep, his newspaper's beating heart.

There Asa had often worked during his declining years. But the very features that had made this room feel so safe to him—the thick walls and cramped space—had the opposite effect on the rest of the family. They found it unbearably claustrophobic and stifling. As far as Jase knew, no one else had ever used it. The newspaper's first twenty years were archived in the filing cabinets, and he had a vague memory of his grandfather going to them to refer to an old document or look something up. Perhaps once or twice his father had done the same. Otherwise Jase's father had avoided the room beneath the stairs, preferring instead to work at home at the kitchen table—a habit that Jase had acquired from him and still maintained.

In any case, as the years passed by and the age of the documents stored in the little room increased, their relevance declined. As a working newspaperman, Jase had never once needed to enter Asa's office. Still he distinctly recalled passing many pleasurable hours there as a child, when the secretive nature of the room had appealed to him, as did the advanced age of the things it contained. He'd spent many afternoons at Asa's desk, rubbing his fingers over his great-grandfather's waxy stamps and seals, testing the sharp nibs of his pens, and examining his ink pots, with their shrunken, bone-dry clots of ink. He rummaged through the desk drawers and spent hours searching through the filing cabinets, reading the headlines of newspapers written long before he'd been born.

Much of Jase's love for *The Rocky Mountain Sun* came from those hours spent playing in Asa's office as a boy, so naturally he'd been pleased when one day he noticed his own daughter entering the tiny room beneath the stairs. He could still see her now, a little girl of six or seven, sitting serenely at Asa's desk, pretending to be a newspaper editor like her daddy. The sight had gladdened him and made him proud. He remembered feeling so confident then about the future of *The Sun* and his daughter's role in shepherding it into its next era. But that had been ages ago. When was the last time Evie had begged him to take her with him to work? Not since she'd started riding horses.

At the thought of Bird, Jase scowled again. He should just sell that damn beast and be done with it. But Evie was already so angry with him. It would only make things worse. She'd never forgive him. He pressed a hand to his eyes. Surely this infatuation with horses was just a phase. Little girls and their horses. Everyone knew about that. Eventually she would get over it. He just needed to be patient and let it run its course.

He turned now and glanced about the room. *Eason*, she'd said. He hadn't thought of that name for years. What had he done with that briefcase? He'd left it here somewhere, but that had been so long ago. Where could it be?

He began his search with the desk drawers. The first one contained the old seals and pots of ink he remembered from his childhood, along with piles of documents, some secured in binders, others rolled into tubes or tied with string. He pushed them aside. The next drawer held more papers, certificates which crackled under his fingers and gave off a moldy scent. These he sifted through and left in place.

The other drawers were equally fruitless, as were the cubbies on top. He tried the filing cabinets. When they didn't yield what he wanted, he searched the bookshelves, looking carefully among the heavy leather bindings. Then he bent down and methodically went through the cupboards. The first held nothing but boxes and folders. The second was full of miscellaneous trays of type. By the time he'd finished looking through the third, he was all but overcome by frustration. Where was it? What had he done?

It was cold in the room, but despite that he was sweating. He wiped his brow, straightened up, and scanned the room. There was nowhere else to look. Or was there? He frowned and concentrated. For a moment he stood perfectly still, hardly breathing. Then seized by a sudden burst of certainty, he reached behind the books on one of the shelves and retrieved Asa's briefcase from the place where, over thirty years earlier, he himself had hidden it.

He carried the briefcase to the desk. There was a lamp, but he left it unlit, choosing instead to rely on the slanting window light. He sat down and examined the briefcase, which was old-fashioned, made of cracked, worn leather, secured with a tarnished brass clasp. The clasp was broken and opened easily under his fingers. Inside were more papers, more documents, and records. They weren't what he wanted, but he took his time searching through them anyway, studying each item with care. He found stock certificates to non-existent railroads. Deeds to properties in ghost towns. Claims to worthless and long-defunct mines. A small white envelope containing a package of seeds.

The ghost of a smile flickered across his face. Asa had been a brilliant newspaperman, but a terrible businessman, easily seduced by promising-sounding ventures. All of them, save the newspaper, had failed. Even his attempt to grow wheat on the banks of the creek— to demonstrate once and for all the fertility of the land—had come to naught when the climate proved unsuitable for agriculture. *Choke Creek.* Jase shook his head. People said the name came from the choke-cherry bushes which grew along the creek's banks, but as far as he was concerned, it might as well refer to the lives of the people who'd tried to earn a living beside it—only to give up, choked on dust and bile.

He searched further through the case. Finally he extracted two letters, still in their original envelopes, bundled together with twine. He put the rest of the documents away. Then he set about untying them. The knot was tight, unyielding to his fingers, as if the string had congealed into place over time. Minutes passed until Jase gave the knot a final twist, and the letters fell free.

At last he allowed himself the lamp. In its cool, bluish light, he separated the envelopes. He took out the first letter and put it aside. Then he pulled out the second letter and skimmed down to the signature at the bottom. There it was, just as he remembered: *Thomas Eli Eason.*

For a moment he closed his eyes, remembering back to the day he had discovered them. He had been just a boy, playing in the office, when he had come across the briefcase. Excited, he'd taken the letters to his father. His father had looked at them and then given him a hard stare. "So now you know," he'd said. "And now you will put those letters back and never speak of them again."

Jase had burned with indignation—a secret, so enticing and thrilling, and he couldn't even share it! But he'd known better than to defy his father. He'd put the letters back into the briefcase and hidden them away behind the books so that no one—not even his father—would know where they were. If he couldn't talk about them, no one would. Over time he'd forgotten all about them, until the day his father died. Jase had been a young man then, only recently graduated from journalism school. He'd expected his father to have years left as editor-in-chief of *The Sun*, but instead he had died suddenly, felled by a stroke. On the day they buried him, Jase found himself thinking again of the letters. But by then he was old enough to understand why his father—and his father before him—had insisted they remain a secret. He let them be.

Now he opened his eyes and held the letter with Thomas Eli Eason's signature up to the light. It was written on a plain piece of lined paper, most likely torn from an old ledger or notebook. The paper was frayed along one side, yellowed at the edges. The black ink was faded, turning nearly to brown. But the words were still readable, clear and crisp on the page.

My dear Sir:

You will be undoubtedly surprised to receive this letter, and perhaps will be inclined to dismiss it, coming as it does from one of my station, but believe me, Sir, when I tell you, that circumstances conspire to give me no choice but to address myself to you, in hopes that some measure of fairness, of Mercy, that may still lodge in your breast, some desire for the Truth that is so often your expressed desire, will lead you to consider the words of a most unfortunate man ...

He scanned quickly down to the end of the page. He had forgotten how disturbing the man's words were. Once again he pressed a hand to his eyes. The question remained: What had Eason told her? What did Evie know?

In a rush of clarity, it came to him. She didn't know anything. Eason hadn't told her. He couldn't have, because he didn't know himself. No one did. Not even the boy's father, the discredited judge. The letters had been buried too long, more than a hundred years. They'd been completely forgotten.

A wave of relief surged through him, surprising him with its strength. He fingered the letters. He ought to destroy them, put an end to it, the way he'd wanted to put an end to Evie's infatuation with that horse. He was just about to tear through them when he hesitated. He'd done nothing wrong. No one in his family had. Certainly not Asa. As a matter of fact, he'd been the only one in the entire sorry affair to do what was right. And who knew what the future would bring? Maybe one day they'd need them to prove their case.

He slipped the letters back into their envelopes and put them away, the briefcase hidden firmly behind the books. With growing confidence, he decided that one day he would even show the letters to Evie. But first he would wait until she was old enough to understand. In time she would learn to respect the role her family and its newspaper had played in safeguarding their city—in safeguarding the life of Thomas Eli Eason. He stood up to go. As he left the room, he caught a glimpse of the creek through the window. His breath caught in his throat, and he was seized by a sudden wave of sorrow. One day he'd tell Evie about her mother, too. But not now. She was already so angry with him, and she was all he had left. What if she didn't forgive him? He couldn't risk losing her, too. He'd just have to keep doing what was best for her, and hope that one day she would understand. He ducked through the doorway and closed the door behind him. Surely one day she would see that he was right.

Five

Three days later the printers went on strike, and on Saturday when Evie came down to breakfast, her father was just leaving for another round of negotiations with the union. She poured herself a bowl of cereal and ate it standing at the counter. Then she put on her boots and walked to the barn.

It was still early, the light muted, the air pleasantly cool from the night. A few days earlier it had rained, and the grass by the stable was thick and green, smelling of springtime and damp earth. She slid open the door to Bird's stall and led him, yawning and with sleepy eyes, into the aisle, where she picked out his hooves, curried his coat, and combed out his mane and tail. As she brushed him, she crooned in a low voice, "You, you, you are the best horse, yes you are, the best horse that ever was, the best that ever will be." Outside the world warmed, and the air took on a bright, golden hue. Evie pressed her face against his, taking in the sweet alfalfa smell of his breath. Then she saddled him up and rode him into the creek.

In the city the banks of the creek were high, rising steeply on either side. The willows were lush from the rain, the sedges bursting, the thin trickle of water widened to a shallow stream. For a time she rode past houses like her own with well-kept gardens and neatly fenced back yards. Now and then a storm culvert emerged from the dark earth like a shadowy cave, while bridges crossed frequently overhead, rumbling with traffic. In time, however, the banks of the creek grew more shallow, and the neatly kept houses gave way to run-down farmhouses and vacant lots. She rode past an abandoned truck rusting in a weedy yard. Farther on a broken-down cattle chute stood behind the remains of a brickyard, an old tin shed surrounded by piles of shattered brick and lime. Gradually the bridges grew more widely spaced. The last one she came to was for a railroad. As she rode under it, she looked up and caught glimpses of the sky, bright, retreating strips of blue lodged between the iron rails.

Now the land around the creek grew desolate and bare. Bunches of yucca and prickly pear studded the earth. Tumbleweeds rocked in the wind. In the distance a set of wagon ruts cut across the prairie, a braid of creases in the earth. For a time a dirt road paralleled the creek, a line of junked cars sunk into the side to make a levee. Then the road swung away and vanished on the horizon, converging in a point. Far away a windmill rose on the plain, spindly arms swinging on top of a gangly frame, like a thistle gone to seed. Closer by, a cottonwood was blooming, its lower branches green and leafy, its upper branches as dead and dry as a stone.

Soon she came to the Swale ranch. As she rode up the ridgeline, she saw the rancher in the distance, working in the outer fields, but there was no sign of Eason. She checked around the barn just to be sure. Then she rode back to the creek and followed the trail eastwards as she'd done with Eason the week before. It was getting warmer now, and Bird's neck was damp with sweat. Evie was sweating, too. Using the back of her hand, she pushed away the sticky strands of hair that had come loose from her braid. The sun was strong and hard on her eyes, shining down from a piercing blue sky, whitening to a haze on the horizon. She rode past a stand of willows and then a clump of chokecherry bushes which grew at the creek's edge. In their shadow lay the skeleton of a horse. Had it been there before? She didn't remember, but it must have been. The hide was already gone, hanging in shreds and tatters off the bone. The neck was twisted, the head cocked as if to bare the throat for sacrifice. She rode past it with a grimace, skirting the bushes, keeping her distance from the bones.

At last she came to the place where the low bluff rose beside the creek. She watered her horse in a pool that had collected beneath a pile of deadwood, clucked to him with her tongue, and rode him to the top. Eason wasn't on the battlefield, either. She raised her head and gazed out far to the north, and then in a complete circle around her. In every direction the land was empty. There was no horse coming towards her in the hazy light, no boy on the creek trail.

She sat with her hands resting on the pommel of her saddle. Then she dismounted and walked across the bluff, leading Bird behind her, studying the ground as Eason had before. From time to time she bent down and scratched with her fingers at the soil, unearthing some small stones, but none of them looked like arrowheads to her, and she let them drop.

Finally she stopped. As Bird grazed, she reached into her pocket and pulled out the arrowhead Eason had given her. She examined it from all sides, curling her fingers around the edges. Once more she looked up, gazing in all directions around her. Then she shook her head, put her hand on her saddle, and prepared to go.

All at once the wind picked up, blowing across the bluff. Evie turned her face towards it and listened. At first she heard nothing unusual, the rustle of the cattails in the creek, the rattle of the yucca, the swoosh of a dirt devil swirling across the ground, but gradually it seemed to her that a new sound had come into the air, a low vibration or hum. She closed her eyes and concentrated on it, her muscles tight and straining. Suddenly she began to tremble. A deep shudder passed through her, and she cried out in anguish. Startled, Bird reared back and jerked the reins out of her hands, skittering away. Evie's eyes sprang open, and she gazed about herself wildly, unseeing. Then she blinked and saw her horse, staring back at her with fearful eyes. She went to him and reached for the reins. As she opened her hand, she saw that it was bleeding. In her fright she had clenched her fingers into a fist around the arrowhead, and her palm had been pierced by the pointed tip of the stone.

Cyrus Swale was standing at the pump, filling buckets for the horses in the barn, when he looked up and saw the Glauber girl coming towards him on the creek trail, riding from the east. That was strange. There was nothing past the barn, just pasture for the horses and empty rangeland. What did she want out there?

Something must have happened to her. She rode down to him at a fast trot, chased by an air of urgency. "Where's Eason?"

She brought her horse to a halt. Her lips were dry, her face pale. Cyrus turned the water off. Then he jerked the pump handle up again and let the water flow. "Eason's not here."

"When will he be back?"

"He's not coming back."

"What do you mean?" There was a note of panic in her voice.

"I mean he joined the Army. Three days ago." The bucket was full. Cyrus slapped a hand on the pump and jammed the handle down. Then he pushed the bucket aside and stood another in its place. "Gone for a three-year stint."

"That's impossible!" Her voice rose to a wail. "He said wasn't going until next year."

"He changed his mind." The second bucket was full now, and Cyrus leaned on the pump handle, shutting it down. He gave her a hard look. "You seem to know an awful lot about it."

"He told me last week when he took me to the battlefield."

"Choke Creek?"

She nodded.

Eason hadn't said anything about that. Well, it didn't matter much. He was gone, and even if the girl had taken a liking to him, she'd just have to get over it. Cyrus carried the water into the barn and exchanged the buckets in the stalls. When he came back out with empty ones, she was still there, looking upset. "Look," he said. "Something came up." He cleared his throat. "A friend of his died."

"Billy?"

He nodded. So Eason had told her about Billy, too.

"Oh," she said. "I'm sorry. I didn't know." A sad look came into her eyes. "I still don't understand. How could Eason have gone into the Army? He wasn't old enough. He was only seventeen. He—" Her voice took on an accusing tone. "You signed for him, didn't you? Just like Billy's parents did. You let him go."

Cyrus bristled. "That's none of your business." He shoved the empty buckets under the pump and filled them, hauling the water back into the barn.

"You shouldn't have done that." Her words followed him down the aisle, echoing on the concrete aisle. "He thinks going to war is a good thing, but he's wrong."

He turned back and found her staring at him with the same angry look, the color high in her cheeks. "What makes you say that?"

"Because they told me." She opened her hand and showed him her palm, which had been bloodied by a sharp wound. "I heard their voices on the battlefield."

"You—what?" He dropped the buckets. He didn't even realize he'd done it until he felt the water sloshing onto his boots and saw it spread like a stain on the floor.

"The people who died there." She was speaking calmly now, but with conviction. "You can hear their voices in the wind. I should have known last week when I was there with Eason, but I didn't understand then. Now I do."

"They spoke to you?"

She nodded.

"You mean the Indians?"

"I don't know." She paused, considering. "Eason said blood was shed on both sides. Could have been the soldiers, too."

"What did they say?"

"It wasn't like that. They didn't say actual words. It was the way they sounded."

"How was that?"

"Like they didn't deserve it." A look of defiance came into her eyes. "You can say I'm crazy if you want. I don't care. I know what I heard."

Cyrus's hand came up and settled on his hip, the fingers working into the joint. "I didn't say you were crazy."

"Okay then." Her eyes lost their combative edge. "I wanted to tell Eason about it. Do you think he's heard them, too?"

Cyrus pursed his lips. "If he has, he never told me."

Evie swiveled in her saddle and gazed with longing at the ridgeline, as if she still thought Eason might appear there on the roan colt. Then she turned back to him with a resigned air. "I'm not even supposed to be here. My father told me to stay away from you. He thinks you're dangerous. He said you chased some Indians off your land with a rifle."

Cyrus's back stiffened. He picked up the buckets and carried them back to the pump. His hip hurt, and he limped as he walked.

"Well, did you?" She was waiting for his answer, the stubborn look in her eyes.

"Don't you ever give up?"

"My father says I'm worse than a bulldog."

A smile twitched at the corner of his lips. He set the first bucket under the pump. "You like horses?"

"More than anything."

He didn't even have to look at her to know it was true. He heard the passion in her voice. He filled the buckets then jammed the pump handle down. When he turned to her again, his face was set in the familiar frown. "I have work to do. I can't have you bothering me every time you come out here."

A look of surprise came over her face. Then, as she realized what he was saying, it turned to gratitude.

"If you're going to keep riding on my land, you'll have to earn it. You can start with that roan colt." He picked up the buckets. "He still needs some work, and now that Eason's gone, there's no one left to ride him."

Spring deepened, and the irises in Evie's garden gave way to roses, then dahlias and zinnias. Every Saturday now she rode out to the Swale ranch. At least her father didn't try to stop her anymore. She figured he'd given up trying, or maybe he just was too busy to notice. After weeks of hard work, he had finally resolved the crisis with the printers' union, but after that other problems arose, equally demanding of his attention. A shortage of newsprint. A scandal with one of his reporters, who'd faked his sources. And the ongoing rivalry with *The Danvers Post*, which Evie knew consumed him, although he'd never admit it.

She didn't always see Cyrus. Sometimes he was busy, working in the fields. Other times he was simply away, buying feed, or hauling horses back and forth to auction. She remembered what he'd said about not bothering him, so she let him be. But whenever she had the chance, she asked him about Eason. The answer was always the same. Eason's fine. The rancher repeated the two words without variation, like a mantra, as if saying them would ensure it stayed so. For a long time Eason was in Texas, undergoing basic training. Then one day, after the usual reply, Cyrus added, "His unit just got called up."

"What does that mean?" She imagined a bunch of recruits, clustered by a telephone, waiting for it to ring.

"It means he's going to Vietnam."

Then she didn't know what to say, and afterwards every time she asked about Eason, her words were accompanied by an anxious jolt. What if something awful happened to him? What if the answer were the unthinkable? Cyrus always reassured her, saying Eason was fine, and she shouldn't worry. He knew how to take care of himself. But secretly, she knew, the rancher felt the same way. Eason's absence had taken a toll on him. He had aged since his son had left, becoming thinner and more frail, his limp more pronounced. A heaviness in the air followed him wherever he went.

She always made sure to ride the roan colt first, fulfilling the bargain she'd struck with Cyrus. Afterwards she stayed on to lend him a hand with his chores. Anyway, she liked working with the horses. She carried grain to their stalls, filled their buckets, and swept down the barn aisle. Cyrus kept about thirty horses on his ranch, two stallions, the rest divided roughly equally among yearlings, two-year-olds, mares, and foals. It was far too many horses, Evie thought, for one man to handle by himself, especially one with a bad hip. But he never complained. He had plenty of land, but most of it was hardscrabble with scarce grazing, so he had to buy feed to supplement the herds. The only money he had came from selling horses at auction or training them, like the roan colt, to sell as cow ponies. It wasn't much. Evie wondered how he made ends meet. There were no extras on the ranch, no frills or luxuries. When things broke down—when the pump needed repairing, like it often did, or the barn roof leaked or a fence rail came down—Cyrus stopped what he was doing and fixed it himself.

As soon as Evie was done with her chores, she got on Bird and rode to the battlefield. When she reached the bluff, she dismounted and led her horse across the bluff by hand. People had died there—she understood that now with the fullness of her heart—and approaching the battlefield on foot like a penitent felt like the right thing to do. As she walked, she studied the ground, holding the arrowhead Eason had given her in her hand. She didn't find any more like it, and she didn't hear the voices again either, even though she often tried, turning her face to the wind whenever it blew. Still the memory of what she had heard—the sound of people keening, their voices rising and falling in anguished wails—never left her. Just as she never forgot Eason, or the kiss he'd given her. She didn't tell the rancher, but that was the real reason she'd been so grateful when he'd said she could come back and ride Eason's colt. Now that Eason was gone, that, and the arrowhead, were the only tangible links to him she had left.

One afternoon as Evie was riding the colt in the ring, black clouds massed over the mountains. The wind began to blow, and soon rain began to fall. She hurried the colt into the barn then ran back and got Bird, who was tied to the rail. Wet and dripping, she unsaddled both horses and rubbed them down with rags. Then she put them into stalls and prepared to wait out the rain.

The rancher had left earlier that morning, hauling some yearlings that he had culled to auction. For a time she stood by the barn door, watching the rain come down, the drops raising puffs of dust as they hit the ground. Then she decided she might as well put the colt's tack away. The rain was taking too long, and she wouldn't bother riding him anymore when it was done.

She slipped the colt's bridle over her shoulder, lifted his saddle, and carried them down the aisle to the tack room. She put the saddle on its rack and the bridle on its hook, a horseshoe that had been bent up and nailed to the wall. There was a window in the room, and she glanced out it at the sky. It was still dark and threatening. Through the window came the scent of the rain, rich and sharp.

She would wait out the rain and then head home. Bored, she sat down on an old tack trunk and pushed her hair out of her face, idly tapping her fingers on her knee. She'd never given the Swales' tack room a second thought—it was just an old tack room like any other, full of equipment for the horses—but now she found herself growing curious. She stood up and opened the box she had been sitting on. Inside were winter blankets for the horses, stacked and folded. She reached in and fingered the coarse wool of the one on top. Then she put the lid of the box down.

She walked about the room, lightly touching things, the braided reins of bridles, the stiff horns of saddles, the bristles of brushes and cool metal hoof picks. The room was dusty and smelled of leather, of rubbing alcohol and camphor and neatsfoot oil. She opened a cabinet and examined the supplies inside: brown bottles of Epsom salts and liniment, bandages, hoof tar, greasy tubes of ointment, a rubber worming hose. Another cabinet held the rancher's records, ledgers detailing over forty years of feed purchases, stud fees, and auction sales. She ran her fingers down them, noting how few of the years had been profitable, and how little money had been made in the ones that were. In a thick black binder she found a chart of bloodlines for the horses, all of them dating back to a lone sorrel mare. Another binder held a list of foals that had been born, lived, and died long before she was born. One of the more recent entries was for the roan colt. It had been born three years ago, the name listed simply as "Eason's foal."

She closed the binder with a snap. She had a bad feeling—the feeling that she was trespassing. Cyrus wouldn't want her going through his things. She glanced out the window. Still no sign of his truck. She shook the feeling off and began working her way through the rest of the trunks. Most of them were innocuous, no more interesting than the chest of blankets. She found a tangle of tack needing repair—halters with missing buckles, broken reins, lead lines without clips. Another box held saddle soap, sponges, and rags. The next one had chaps inside.

She was about to slam the lid shut when all at once she hesitated. The chaps looked familiar. As she lifted them up, she realized why. They were Eason's. Everything in the box was his—the boots and denim jacket and riding gloves. She ran her fingers across the chaps then held them to her cheek, burying her face in the worn leather. Just holding them there brought it all back to her, the way he'd looked when they'd ridden to the bluff, the way his voice had sounded when he'd talked. Even the kiss seemed real to her again, soft and warm against her skin. She lifted her head. She knew what she would do next. She glanced out the window. The rancher's truck was still nowhere in sight. She craned her head, peering far down the drive, just to be sure. Then she dropped the chaps back into the trunk and snapped the lid shut.

Outside it was still raining, but the storm was beginning to taper off, bits of clear sky appearing among the black clouds. Evie dashed through the last of the rain to the house. Her boots echoed with a hollow sound as she climbed the porch stairs. At the door she hesitated. Trespassing in the tack room was one thing, but what would Cyrus say if he knew she'd gone into his house? She tested the door. It was unlocked. Well, that was no surprise. Even her father didn't lock their door at home. She cast a last furtive glance behind her then slipped into the house and closed the door.

It was cold in the house, much colder than it had been outside. It was darker, too, the ceilings low, intensifying the gloom from the rain. Now that she was inside, she realized how small the house was, not much more than a log cabin with a few attached rooms. She had come into the middle of the house, a square-shaped room which served as the main living area. On the far side a hearth burned with a slow fire, giving out little heat. To her left was the kitchen, to her right a narrow hallway, which led to the bedrooms. All together the house had a rough, cobbled-together feel. The ceiling was higher in the front, the wide-planked floor sloping to the back. The logs in the walls were scarred and worm-eaten, chinked with mud and sand. They gave the air a scent of dry rot, magnifying the smell of the rain.

The house reminded Evie of a story her history teacher had told them in school the year before. When the first settlers came to Danvers, the teacher had said, wood was in such short supply, they built sod-roofed dug-outs to live in. Later, whenever one of them left—driven out by the unrelenting harshness of frontier life—the others descended on his house, tearing and picking it apart, cannibalizing the wood to use in their own homes. Was that the way this house had been built? It looked as if it had been built out of other people's failures. As if it had been constructed out of defeat.

She glanced about the room. A wing chair stood by the window, alongside a small round table topped by a worn lace doily and a copy of the day's Sun. Beside it stood a bookcase filled with books on horse breeding and ponderous law volumes, which dated, Evie supposed, to the rancher's judging days. A sofa sat across from the chair, facing a small black-and-white television, which looked distinctly out of place in the room, like an automobile in a carriage house.

In the corner a glass cabinet held a dark blue coat with brass buttons, along with a long rifle. Was that the gun Cyrus had used to chase the Indians off his land? She tried to open the door, but it was locked. She peered inside at the coat. It was hung carefully upright as if at any moment the Swales expected the owner back, the pitted brass buttons gleaming dully in the dim light.

She left the cabinet and went to the mantelpiece, which held an array of photos. The first was Thomas Eli. She lifted it up to study it closely. He was wearing his cavalry uniform—the same coat she recognized from the cabinet. He had a broad forehead and thick beard, and wore the expression people in old photographs so often did: a bit frightened, as if he feared the camera might capture not just his likeness but also his soul. But there was no mistaking Eason's ancestor. They shared the same deeply set eyes.

She put the photograph down and examined the other pictures on the mantelpiece. One showed a younger version of Cyrus, dressed in

World War II battle uniform, standing with one foot resting on the bumper of a jeep. The sun was full on his face, illuminating the eager look in his eyes and the surprised grin on his lips, as if he couldn't believe his good fortune in being there. At the bottom of the picture, inside the glass, was a medal attached to the ribbon.

"Purple Heart," Evie said, whispering the words out loud. She'd never seen one before, and the sight awed her. A small piece of twisted metal sat inside the glass beside it. For a moment she stared at it uncomprehending. Then she remembered. It must be the bullet that had wounded the rancher, putting an end to his riding days.

The frame next to Cyrus's photograph held the picture of a woman. She was standing in a field, and it must have been a windy day because with one hand she was holding down her dress. She had a shy smile on her face—Eason's smile. A small brass plate attached to the bottom of the frame read, *Elaine 1923–1955*. So that was why Evie had never seen Eason's mother. He had been only six when she died. A pang of sympathy coursed through her for this boy who, like her, had grown up without a mother.

The next photograph surprised her. It was of Eason, although it took her a moment to realize it. It must have been taken when he joined the Army. It showed him in his uniform, and she recognized the pride and determination she'd seen in his eyes when he took her to the battlefield. But his face also seemed to hold a glimmer of resignation. She touched the glass as she wished she could touch his face. Why had Eason left so suddenly for the war? Why hadn't he waited until he turned eighteen like he said he would? *Something came up*, Cyrus had said. He'd meant Billy's death. But had something else happened—something even Cyrus didn't know?

She put the photograph back. The only person missing in the photo gallery was Eason's grandfather. Maybe that was because he hadn't been a soldier. What was it that Eason had said about him? *He was different, that's all.*

She left the room and traveled down the hallway. She figured the first bedroom belonged to Cyrus. It held a double bed, a nightstand,

and a tall wardrobe chest. The next room was the bathroom, which she passed without stopping. The door to the third room had been left ajar—neither quite open or closed. She pushed it softly, widening the gap. Then she slipped in.

It was Eason's room. On the far wall, beneath the window, stood his dresser, bare except for a small electric clock. His bed was to the side. Opposite it stood a cupboard with white painted shelves. A poster of Gary Cooper and Grace Kelly in *High Noon* hung on the wall, and a BB gun stood in the corner. Evie was surprised to see how neat and orderly the room was, everything tucked precisely away, in its place. She figured Cyrus must be keeping it like that—keeping it ready for the day his son would come back home. She knew he meant well, but she couldn't help thinking it was a mistake. The room had a closed, airless feel, like a museum or mausoleum—a place for someone who had died.

She shook her head and chased the thought from her mind. Then she walked to the cupboard. On the top shelf was a row of baseball trophies and a lone baseball scrawled with signatures. Turning the ball, she found Eason's name written in blue ink, the letters neatly marked in capitals. The next shelf held his Boy Scout handbook, a papery grey wasps nest, a shoebox filled with tin soldiers, and a bowl of Indian-head pennies. Beneath that was a well-worn chess set, the black queen missing, replaced by a pebble, and a row of books, a few for reading, like Jack London's *White Fang*, the rest textbooks for school. Algebra, Chemistry, Physics, American History. She recognized his French book, the same one she had used in school the previous year.

On the bottom shelf a wooden box held the collection of arrow-heads Eason had told her about. She sifted through them, finding several that were like the one he'd given her, others made of different kinds of stone. There were metal pieces, too, just like he'd said. She lifted out a bullet and rolled it thoughtfully in her fingers. Was this one of the bullets Eason's great-grandfather had fired from his rifle? The thought chilled her, and she put the bullet away.

She looked about the room, struck by how neat and orderly it was. Even the blanket on the bed was tightly tucked in. In the military, she'd once heard, soldiers had to bounce quarters off their beds. She sucked in her breath. It wasn't the rancher who kept this room so tidy—it was Eason. All along he'd been readying himself for the Army, practicing for military life. She opened the top drawer of his dresser and peered inside. It was full of pants, each pair precisely creased and folded. The next drawer held shirts, the collars all buttoned up and facing the same way. Even Eason's socks were in neat rows, color-coded from dark to light. The last drawer held his undershirts. These were folded in piles, the grey separated from the white. She reached in and pulled out a grey shirt, cradling it in her hands.

The sound of an engine in the distance startled her, and she glanced out the window. The rain had stopped, and a light wind had blown the sky clear. Cyrus was coming back, the pickup pulling the flatbed horse trailer up the drive. She sprinted from the house and into the barn. By the time the rancher got out of his truck, she was saddling up Bird. "You're still here?" he said.

"I waited for the rain to blow over."

He nodded and set about unloading the trailer, which held a new mare. She waved her good-byes and rode Bird into the creek, heading home. It wasn't until she was safely out of sight that she allowed herself to pull out the grey shirt, which she'd stolen, hidden beneath her blouse. Raising it to her face, she breathed in its sweet scent, which reminded her so strongly of Eason. Eason had finally gotten what he wanted. He'd become a soldier. So why did she feel so sure he'd gone to war for reasons he couldn't even begin to understand?

Six

Each week that Eason was in the Army, he wrote a letter home.

"Well," he wrote that spring, "I'm here now. I've finally arrived in Vietnam. They've stationed us on the coast for now, by the sea. Everyone says this is a fine place to be in, quiet and safe. They say I'm lucky to be here, that nothing bad ever happens to anyone here."

He wrote the letters to his father in the evening, before it got dark. He used paper and a pencil that he kept in a plastic bag in his pocket. When he was done writing, he put the letter in the bag. Later, when a transport helicopter came in, he handed the letter over. Then he stood on the ground and watched as the helicopter lifted it up into the deep blue sky and flew it away.

"The other guys here are all real nice," he wrote one day. "I'm the youngest and nobody says so but I can tell they're all looking out for me. Liver—he's been here the longest—can be hard on you sometimes, but he doesn't mean anything by it. He's just trying to toughen you up. Everyone says what a smart guy he is and how lucky I am to have him for my friend. So I try not to mind it when he's hard on me, and I try to remember that."

Sometimes he took his pencil and his paper down to the thin strip of sand by the sea. He sat there and wrote with the paper on his knees. From time to time he put the pencil down and turned around to gaze at the mountains. The mountains in Vietnam were nothing like the ones he knew at home. The Rocky Mountains were steep and dramatic, a jagged line against the horizon. Even at the height of summer, their peaks were white with snow. These mountains were softer somehow and more peaceful, painted in every shade of green imaginable. He figured there must be names for the colors, but he'd never been any good at coming up with things like that. Somewhere out there, he knew, soldiers were risking their lives, fighting and dying. One day soon it would be his turn to join their ranks. But he didn't want to think about that. So he turned around instead and looked back at the water. The sea always brought an ache to his heart. He supposed that was because of the long expanse of it, because of the fact that it went on forever. It reminded him of the prairie, the only other place he'd ever known where you could look all the way to the horizon without stopping. Where the very sight of it made your breath catch in your throat and your heart soar.

The sea made him feel at home and made him feel homesick all at once. But he didn't write about that. Instead he wrote, "Is that spotted mare still acting colicky? Did you get that dun filly sold? I hope that patch on the tin roof is holding up." He signed his name, and then he remembered something and added a postscript. "You might want to check the fences in the northeast quarter again. They got hit bad in that storm a few years back and the rails are looking splintery and thin."

Sometimes he finished his letter in only a few minutes. He closed it up and then sat looking at it, wishing he had more to say. Other times he sat down with a full heart, certain he had pages and pages to write. But when he was done, he was surprised to discover how little he'd written, that he'd composed only a few lines.

"The weather here's not too bad," he wrote. "The days are hot, but it gets cool at night. We had one whole week without rain, which everybody says is unusual for this time of year. Mostly they say it rains."

That was the one thing Eason couldn't get used to about Vietnam— the amount of water there was everywhere. Not just in the sea, but in the air and on the ground. The first river he saw took his breath away: it was so deep and wide, he couldn't see the bottom of it. He felt as if he couldn't see a thing. Even when it wasn't raining, the humidity stuck to him, to his face and neck and back. It made him feel stupid and slow. He hung a pair of socks out to dry, and days later they were still moist, musty, and damp. Nothing seemed to fit in the dampness, nothing seemed to work. Everything swelled and warped. Sometimes the rain was so thick, just breathing it made him feel like he was drowning. He wondered if a man could drown in the air. But he didn't write that. Instead he wrote, "The rain's not so bad. You get used to it. I guess it's true what they say, that a person can get used to just about anything."

During the day there wasn't much to do. Sometimes they went out on training exercises. They practiced their grenade throwing and their marksmanship. They learned how to handle mines. Most of the time they just sat around, waiting. Nothing ever happened. He told himself that what he was doing was important. He told himself it meant something. He reminded himself to remember everything because later he would want to know. Later he would want to have stories to tell, when people asked him, *What did you do in the war?*

But what would he say then? What would he have to say? There were no stories in Vietnam, at least not as far as he could see. All he did was follow along with the others, doing what he was supposed to, marching, training, looking for ways to pass the empty hours.

"Last night," he wrote to his father, "I couldn't sleep. I lay in my bunk and thought about you fighting in the Pacific. And then I thought about Thomas Eli Eason, fighting in the Indian Wars. I want you to know that I know everything. I found out the night Billy died. But it doesn't matter. I don't blame you. I came here anyway, to be a soldier. I came here to make it right."

When he finished the letter, he sat for a long time looking at it. He folded it neatly in half, and then in quarters. And then he tore it into pieces, into tiny bits of paper that no one would ever be able to put back together, no matter how hard they tried. He took out a new sheet of paper, picked up the pencil, and wrote, "Yesterday a couple of us got together and made ourselves a chess set. We whittled the pieces out of wood and have a piece of painted canvas that we use for the board.

We've had some good games since then, and I guess I can say I'm holding my own."

When he was done writing his letters, he checked his gear. He made a point of keeping it in order. Everything was in its place; everything was neat and clean. Taking care of his gear made him feel useful, as if he were doing his part. He was taking the war seriously—giving it its due. He packed and repacked his rucksack, checking that everything was as it should be.

Sometimes he got so caught up with maintaining his gear, he forgot to write. A day would go by and then another, and then in a rush he would remember that he was overdue for writing. It bothered him when he forgot to write because he wanted to keep up his schedule. He thought it was important to do so, just as he thought it was important to keep his letters cheerful so that his father wouldn't worry about him. He made sure to put in enough detail so that his father wouldn't think he was hiding anything. But not too much detail, because he didn't want to give himself away.

He liked to think he was keeping his chin up, keeping a stiff upper lip and all that. He kept his gear in order and did everything he thought a soldier should do. That, he believed, was what it meant to be brave. Although truthfully, he hadn't come across anything yet that required bravery. Keeping your gear in order and marching from place to place was a good thing, but not exactly brave. He knew that, but he tried not to think about it. Instead he opened his rucksack and took everything out. And then slowly and carefully he checked through it and put it all back in.

"Some of the guys have girlfriends back home," he wrote. "Liver has a wife but he never talks about her so I guess he misses her a lot. One of the guys has a sister, and he said I could write to her if I wanted to. He showed me her picture, and she looked real pretty and nice. But I haven't written to her yet, because I can't think of anything to say."

One day he got a letter from a girl he'd dated at home. The letter was written in a way that was cheerful and friendly, but also perfunctory and dry, as if she were trying too hard. Eason could just imagine people saying to her *You should write to him. He's in the Army now.* It wasn't like it hurt his feelings—he was genuinely grateful that she'd taken the time to write. But he figured he'd be doing both of them a favor if he didn't write back.

The truth was, the only girl he ever thought of writing to was Evie Glauber. He couldn't help thinking about how fearless she'd been the day she rode his horse. Later, when he'd taken her to the battlefield, she'd laughed at him, but then she'd listened when he talked about his family and its history as if she'd understood. Maybe if he wrote to her and explained how things were, she'd understand. He shook his head. She hardly knew him. What would she think if she got a letter from him saying, *I'm sorry about all those things I told you. I didn't know they were lies.*

The days passed by, and every one of them was the same. The men passed the time talking about things that reminded them of home, things like music and sports and movies. Most of them admired John Wayne, but Eason insisted Gary Cooper was the greatest hero there ever was. He took on a gang of bad guys in *High Noon* all by himself, even though everyone wanted him to run away. Liver listened to Eason defend Cooper, and then he laughed out loud. He should have known, he said. Eason had that same dumb look, like he thought it was his job to save the world.

Otherwise nothing ever happened, and while Eason was very much afraid that something would happen, after a while he began to be just as afraid that it wouldn't. What would he have to say afterwards, if this was what his war was like? What kind of stories would he have to tell?

He began to feel as if the war were a question and he had been sent there to answer it. But how could he answer the question when he didn't even know what it was? And so he spent his days cleaning and arranging his gear. He stood on the sand when he could and looked out over the water. He listened to the wind as it blew down from the mountains. Sometimes the sound it made was so lost and plaintive, just hearing it made him sad. It reminded him of the way the wind sounded at home when it blew across the plain. The day he rode with Evie to the bluff, the wind had frightened her. *Don't go*, she'd said to him. *Don't go to Vietnam.* At the time he'd thought she was being silly, but now he wondered. What had she heard in the wind's empty tones? Did she know something he didn't? He shook his head and cleared his mind. There was no point in worrying about that now. He was in Vietnam with a job to do. And so he readied himself for it, doing what every soldier had done before him and what every soldier would likely do after him. He waited for his war to begin.

Seven

"What do you know about the Battle of Choke Creek?"

Bobbie gave Evie a puzzled look. "Nothing. Why?"

It was a Friday night in late May, and the two girls, still in their school uniforms, were sitting on the floor of Bobbie's den playing gin rummy. Recently Bobbie's mother had remodeled the den, and the carpeting, which had a bright burnt-orange color, gave off a faintly chemical smell. A low Formica table with an avocado-green top stood on one side of the room, flanked by two brand-new plaid armchairs in orange and green. Bobbie had her back pressed against one of them, her legs, pale with russet freckles, sprawled out in front of her. She was one of Evie's oldest friends and the smartest girl Evie knew. Her father was an accountant, her mother a librarian, and Bobbie had inherited their talents in equal measure. She was a whiz at math and got straight A's in everything. If anyone would remember what they'd learned in school about the battle, Bobbie would. "Seriously, Bobbie," Evie said. "What do you know?"

Bobbie was in the middle of studying the two of spades Evie had just thrown down, doing some kind of hidden mental calculation, trying to decide whether or not to take it. Now she put her cards down and ran her fingers through her red hair, a thoughtful expression in her wide blue eyes. "Well, it was during the Civil War, of course, after the Gold Rush." She frowned, concentrating. "That would make it the early 1860s." She broke into a smile as it came back to her. "Eighteen sixty-four. Colonel Stevenson fought a decisive battle on the plains, defeating the Indians and securing the economic future of Danvers."

"What else?"

"There isn't anything else." Bobbie reached for her cards. "That's all they taught us." She picked up the two and tossed down a three of hearts. Then she looked at Evie, her eyes narrowing. "Why do you want to know?"

"No reason," Evie said, trying to put a casual lilt in her voice. "I just think about it sometimes, that's all."

Bobbie wasn't buying it. "Something's been bothering you for weeks, Evie. Even I can see that. Are you telling me it's that old Indian battle?"

"No, of course not," Evie said, although she didn't have the heart this time to disguise her true feelings. Bobbie studied her with a doubtful air. It wasn't that Evie didn't want to tell her friend about the experience she'd had that day on the bluff—about the voices she'd heard—it was just that she didn't know how. She didn't know how to tell anyone. The only person she'd told so far was Cyrus Swale, and even they had never spoken of it again. "I met this boy," Evie said.

Bobbie's eyes lit up. "Do tell."

Evie gave her an exasperated look. "It's not like that. It was weeks ago. His name's Eason. Anyway, he's in the Army now and—"

"The Army?"

"He's seventeen. He enlisted early because ... " Evie's voice trailed off. That was precisely the problem. Why had Eason gone off so suddenly to Vietnam? She still didn't know. "He lives on a ranch outside the city—on the land where the battle took place. His great-grandfather fought in it."

"In the cavalry?"

Evie nodded. "Under Stevenson. He took me to see the battlefield. We rode out there together."

"So that's why you want to know more about it."

"Yes." Evie leaned towards her eagerly. Maybe Bobbie would understand after all. "I can't help feeling as if something awful happened at that battle—something no one talks about anymore. I want to see if I can find out what it is." She reached for her book bag. "Yesterday I went downtown to the library, and I got this book."

"You went to the library?" Shocked, Bobbie dropped her cards, scattering them across the rug.

Evie gave her a sour look. "I like to read."

"But *history*?" Bobbie shook her head in disbelief. "This boy must really be getting to you."

Evie ignored that. She pulled out a thick tome titled *The History of Danvers* and flipped the book open, releasing the scent of dust and old glue into the air. "It even has some stuff in it about my great-great-grandfather." She skimmed through the pages until she'd found the one she wanted. "*The first Danvers newspaper was founded by Asa Glauber, who arrived in the burgeoning mining town on the banks of Choke Creek in the spring of 1859, on the eve of the Gold Rush, with his printing press in hand.*" Just talking to Bobbie was raising her spirits. She stabbed the book in delight. "That's only the half of it. Did you know he bought that press with money he took from the pockets of a hanged horse thief? My father told me." Without waiting for Bobbie's response, she continued, "*Soon* The Rocky Mountain Sun *was known throughout the region as the voice of Danvers, and Asa Glauber as the city's premier booster.*" She put the book down with a thoughtful air. "Do you think he knew Colonel Stevenson?"

"I don't know," Bobbie said, "but I suppose so. There weren't that many people out here back then. They probably all knew each other." Her interest, Evie could tell, was piqued now, too. "What else does it say?"

"All sorts of things." Evie flipped through the book. "For one thing, it says that by the time the Battle of Choke Creek took place, the Indians had been making war on the whites for years. *Every year it was the same,*" she read out loud. "*In the autumn the Indians signed peace treaties. In exchange for food and firearms, they agreed to move to reservations—to lands the government set apart for them in safe places. All winter long they lay in wait. Then in the spring they rode out, and the depredations began again.*"

"What kinds of depredations?"

"Robberies, mostly, and theft of cattle." Evie ran her finger down the page. "But in the spring of 1864 the Indians murdered a whole family."

Bobbie raised her eyebrows. "Why?"

"It doesn't say." Evie turned the page. There was nothing in the book about the rape of Stevenson's daughter, but the murder of the Wyngates was there, just as Eason had described it.

Bobbie nodded. "Go on."

"*Over that summer the Indians cut telegraph wires and waylaid freight trains. By the time the autumn came, the people of Danvers were in a state of panic. Winter was coming and they were cut off, hundreds of miles from civilization. There was danger of starvation. Food prices soared. Meanwhile word came that the tribes were assembling out on the plains for the final attack, which would mean an end to them all.*"

Evie put the book down and tried to imagine it, the peril the settlers faced, how they felt. How her great-great grandfather felt. For the first time in ages, she felt a pang of sympathy for him—and a faint note of pride. Asa had been a brave man. No wonder her father felt so strongly about their newspaper. Maybe she shouldn't be so angry with him for wanting her to take it over after all. "*The citizens of Danvers sent word back to Washington of their precarious situation,*" she continued. "*But there were no federal troops to be had. They were all preoccupied, fighting the Civil War. So they called on Stevenson, the colonel who had served them so well a few years earlier, when he defeated the invading Confederates at Gloria Pass and saved the gold fields for the Union. Stevenson was a war hero, a Christian minister, beloved and respected by all. He assembled his cavalry,*" including, Evie thought with a thrill, Eason's great-grandfather Thomas Eli, "*and the other courageous men of Danvers, who lined up to form the Volunteer Third. Then they marched out of Danvers to engage the enemy.*"

Bobbie reached for the book. "I remember this part." She skimmed ahead. "They met in battle in November, on the banks of Choke Creek. Afterwards they found the scalps of white men in the Indian tipis. There was even a blanket fringed with white women's hair." She grimaced and gave the book back. For a moment both girls were silent, thinking about it. Then Bobbie said, "So what does all this have to do with Eason?"

"I don't know." Evie closed the book, feeling suddenly tired and defeated. The book hadn't helped her at all. Nothing in it explained why Eason had gone away so suddenly. "He just wanted to be a soldier like his great-grandfather, I guess." She put the book away.

Bobbie was still thinking about it. "Maybe you should tell me what it was like when you went there."

"To the battlefield?"

Bobbie nodded. "What does it look like?"

"It doesn't look like anything. It's just a piece of land—a part of the prairie. You can't even tell a battle was fought there anymore. Only ... " Evie's voice trailed off.

"Yes?"

"Later I went back there by myself, and I had the strangest feeling."

"Like what?"

Evie looked away. For a long time she was silent. Then she said, her voice small, "Like I could hear the voices of the people who had died there."

She gave Bobbie a furtive glance, trying to gauge her friend's reaction. Bobbie was studying her with a thoughtful air. Evie had the feeling that Bobbie was engaged in a hidden mental calculation again, only this time she—not the cards—was the focus of her reckoning. "Has anything like this has ever happened to you before?"

"No."

"Then forget about it." Bobbie busied herself, picking up the cards.

Evie looked at her with surprise. "Forget about it?"

"Sure." Bobbie shuffled the cards with a confident air. "It's not real, so why waste any more time thinking about it?"

Evie gave Bobbie a dumbfounded look.

"Look, Evie." Bobbie dealt the cards with a flick of her wrist. "Dead people can't talk, can they?"

"No," Evie said with a doubtful air. "I suppose not."

"Then it was just a trick of your imagination. You thought you heard something, but you didn't." Bobbie picked up her cards, fanned them out, and looked at Evie with an expectant air. "Ready to play?"

That night when Evie got home, her father was at the kitchen table, working on his Sunday morning editorial. It was one of the most important pieces of writing he did each week, and she didn't want to disturb him. She crept upstairs and went to her window. Outside, starlight was shining on the roof of Bird's barn. A light wind stirred the air.

Evie raked her fingers through her hair, revealing the dark widow's peak. She should have known better than to tell Bobbie about the voices. Bobbie was relentlessly logical. What would she think if Evie told her about the white light that had been glimmering outside her window every night since she started riding to the Swale ranch? She looked down to the creek and sure enough, there it was. Recently the light had begun to move, wandering up and down the creek bed in strange and unpredictable ways. Now it moved as she watched, flitting first up the creek bed and then back towards her.

Evie turned away from her window. She wished she could be like Bobbie, dismissing everything that didn't make sense. She walked to her dresser, knelt down, and opened her sock drawer. She pulled out the cigar box, took out the photograph of her mother, and put it on the dresser. She put the arrowhead beside it: along with the other things she'd collected in her trips to the battlefield, a rattling black seed pod, a dusty brown pebble that revealed startling bright colors when she moistened it with her spit, the tail feather of a magpie, the tooth of a coyote. She'd taken these things without knowing why, just feeling moved somehow to put them in her pocket. Maybe it was because they came from a place where Eason had been. They were like talismans, things she used to keep him close.

She bent down, reached into her sock drawer, and took out Eason's shirt. She had been saving it for last. It was too big to fit inside the cigar box, so she kept it folded neatly in the back of the drawer. She fingered the soft cloth before lifting the shirt and pressing it to her face.

Breathing deeply, she took in its familiar scent. Taking the shirt and photograph with her, she sat down at her desk. She spread the shirt and photograph out in front of her. Then she tore a scrap of paper from her notebook and wrote:

Did you ever have feelings you couldn't explain?

Outside the wind was blowing harder now, coming down the creek bed. She could hear it, along with the faint murmur as the thin trickle of water wended its way steadily westwards. The patch of white glimmered steadily in the night.

Did you ever hear things other people couldn't? Is that why you went away?

When she was little, she had made up stories to explain her mother's disappearance. She imagined her mother as a fairy, flitting from house to house, bringing children dimes like the ones she found under her pillow every time she lost a tooth. Or she pictured her mother as a princess, locked in a tower or asleep in a castle. When she grew older and tired of make-believe, she told herself that her mother was too talented for an overgrown cow town like Danvers. She'd moved to Hollywood to become a movie star or to New York to paint or sing in the opera. Still later, she'd thought with glum fatalism that the most likely reason for her mother's disappearance was that she'd fallen in love with another man. No wonder her father didn't want to talk about her anymore. She closed her eyes and clutched Eason's shirt to her cheek. More than anything she wanted to have him beside her, so that she could touch him, talk to him, and kiss him, like once she'd done on the prairie.

What did it feel like, the first time you fell in love?

The woman in the photograph looked up at her as if she would answer if only she could.

Did you ever fall in love with someone you hardly knew?

She didn't care what Bobbie thought, and she didn't care what people wrote in history books either. Something had gone wrong at that Indian fight—something no one talked about anymore. Not even Eason. And it was up to her to find out what it was and tell him what she knew.

Eight

In May the weather turned hot, and an early summer hovered in the air. For weeks there was no rain, and the creek subsided to its usual shape, a shallow stream of water trickling through the sand. The willows were still thick and green, but around them the ground was hardening, drying out. When Evie rode Bird to the Swale ranch, his hooves raised puffs of dust on the ground. In the shallows cattails bloomed, pushing up feathery brown spikes. As she passed by them, she ran her fingers down the spikes, turning them into fluff, releasing a sharp peppery scent in the air.

A few days after her card game with Bobbie, Evie had returned the Danvers history book to the library. But she remained determined to find out what had happened at the Battle of Choke Creek. Surely somebody must know. Ruth, she recalled, came from a family that had lived in Danvers for generations; her grandfather had famously made a fortune in the gold mines and lost it in gambling saloons the same year. One day after school, Evie asked her. "What do you think happened at the Battle of Choke Creek?"

Ruth was in the pantry, putting jars of homemade jam away on a shelf. "The same thing as everybody else." She gave Evie an odd look, as if she thought she were out of her mind just for asking. Then she set the last jar on the shelf and bustled out of the room.

Evie knew better than to bring the topic up with her father again. Riding to the Swale ranch was still a sore point with him. But thinking about *The Sun* reminded her that, despite her disdain for newspapers, they were actually useful sources of information. One night after dinner as her father worked on some financial reports, she crept out of the kitchen and into Asa's office. She opened the filing cabinets and dug through the drawers, searching for the newspapers from 1864. Finally she found the papers from the time of the battle, but they only repeated what the history book had said. *Great Battle with Indians*, the headlines crowed. *The Savages Dispersed!*

The next day she decided to ask her history teacher at school. He was even more surprised by her question than Bobbie had been. "Why, Evie," he said, his face full of delight. "You've never shown an interest in history before!" He launched into a description of the battle, which was so long-winded it made her late for lunch—and which didn't tell her anything she didn't already know.

If anyone would know about the battle, she reasoned, Cyrus Swale would. After all, his grandfather had fought in it. One afternoon, after she'd finished riding the roan colt, she put the question to him. The answer he gave her was the most baffling of all. "Every single one of those men did his duty," he said, speaking with an air of grave dignity—and a hint of affront. "I don't care what anybody says."

The frustration of not knowing was almost more than she could bear. Often she had the feeling that the answer was right there in front of her, if only she could see it. Like the pictures of Indians. She'd never noticed them before, and then all at once she did. Apparently Indians were in great demand. They were featured on everything imaginable, from butter boxes and cornstarch tins to old nickels and pennies. The Indian on her cigar box was particularly grand, with a forbidding air and fierce gaze. As she looked at him, Evie wondered what the Indians at Choke Creek had been like.

This question was even harder to answer than the one about the battle. The history book she'd consulted with Bobbie had had a great deal to say about Stevenson, but almost nothing about the Indians he had fought. The fact that they were worthy adversaries seemed sufficient. She found an article on Indians in the encyclopedia one afternoon, but it was generalized and abstract. *The Indian was a great hunter*, the writer intoned. *The horseman of the plains.*

Later, as she was walking across the creek to Bird's barn, it occurred to her that she'd never once, in her entire life, seen an Indian. That was strange. As far as she knew, there weren't even any left in Danvers. Where had they gone? Surely Stevenson hadn't killed them all. She figured they must be on a reservation somewhere. But which one? She had no idea.

The next day after school, she rode the bus downtown—her second trip to the library that year. There, at the information desk, she found the librarian, a young woman in a blue print dress. "I want to know about the Indians who fought at the Battle of Choke Creek," Evie said.

"Indians?" The woman said.

"Their name," Evie explained. "Who they are. Where they live."

"I see." The librarian gave her a thoughtful look. "I don't know. There were Indians at the battle, of course, but which ones ... " She frowned, and then she brightened. "Let's see if we can find out."

She led Evie to a room filled with government documents and reports where, in a dusty folio, they discovered an old census of Indian tribes. A name was listed for the territory encompassing Danvers. "That must be it," the librarian said with a smile.

Evie studied the name. "Where are they now?"

"Now?" The librarian frowned again.

"Yes. The Indians. Where do they live?"

The librarian's frown deepened. "Well, now, I can't say ... " Her voice trailed off. Then her manner became brisk and businesslike. "Follow me."

She took Evie to the circulation desk where an elderly woman with stooped shoulders was checking out books. The two librarians conferred in whispers, then the older one disappeared into the stacks. A few minutes later she returned with another bound government volume, this one of more recent issue. She opened it for Evie and pointed to the page. "They're on a reservation. There."

Evie looked at the address. "But that's nowhere near here! It isn't even in our state."

The elderly woman shrugged as if such things were beyond her purview. "I'll copy the address for you, if you'd like."

Evie rode the bus home with the address in her pocket. She took it up to her room and put it on her desk. Then she sat down, tore a blank piece of paper out of her notebook, and wrote, "I am a fourteen-year-old girl who lives in Danvers, and I want to know what happened at the Battle of Choke Creek. Not what people say. What really happened. The truth."

She signed her name, found an envelope and stamp in the kitchen, and addressed the letter according to the librarian's instructions. Then she mailed it, and waited. For the first time in months, she felt a measure of hope. Surely the Indians would know what everyone else didn't. But as time passed by and no reply came, she sank into despair. She would never know. They would never write back. And why, she reflected with bitter irony, should they? After all, they knew no one cared about them. Like pirates and knights, they'd been relegated to the land of make-believe, to some kind of mythic, storied past. There was nothing left of them but legends, pictures used to sell cornstarch and tobacco. In the eyes of the rest of the world—the world she was inextricably a part of—they didn't even exist.

The Danvers Academy, the private school Evie attended, was an old-fashioned institution, the kind in which a belief in the salutary nature of fresh air was enshrined. All year long, rain or shine, for thirty minutes after lunch, the children were put outside to get a healthy dose of it. During the winter they huddled in the schoolyard in miserable masses, swaddled in parkas, mittens, and hoods. But as the weather warmed, they took to the playground with a joyous air.

One afternoon in mid-June, as the sun shone down from a clear, summery sky, the fourth-grade girls took advantage of the recess to jump rope on the blacktop. The seventh-grade boys started an impromptu game of baseball on the playing field, while the third-grade boys chased each other across the grass. Evie's classmates, the ninth-graders, were in especially good spirits, reveling in the knowledge that in a few short weeks they would be graduating, leaving the academy behind for high school. The girls stood in clumps in the schoolyard, laughing and chatting, while the boys engaged in friendly shoving matches nearby. But Evie found it impossible to share in the joyous mood. Soon Bobbie would leave for summer camp. Usually Evie went away to summer camp, too, to one that specialized in riding, but this year she'd persuaded her father to let her stay home. She'd promised to use the time to catch up on her studies, and had even made another trip to the library to bring home a stack of books. Most of them were on dry, deadly subjects like French and math. Seeing the books, her father had been delighted and had agreed to her request.

Secretly she'd planned on spending the summer at the Swale ranch, riding the roan colt and walking on the bluff, where she always felt closest to Eason. Now she wondered. She had to stop fooling herself. The truth was, Eason was at war, thousands of miles away, and despite all her efforts, she had nothing new to tell him. It was time to accept the fact that she never would. Bobbie was right. Dead people couldn't talk. The things she'd heard on the battlefield had been nothing more than her imagination, playing tricks on her. Nothing untoward had happened at the great Indian battle—there were no hidden secrets about it, no mysterious events. No one talked about it because there was nothing more to say. Every day when Evie went home, she looked at the stack of books on her desk with growing despair. It was beginning to look like a long summer indeed.

Just thinking about it made Evie feel as if she were coming down with a headache. She pressed a hand to her forehead and glanced about the playground. The teacher who had recess duty that day—a thin, angular woman who was named Mrs. Fogarty, but was known to generations of children at the academy as the Old Fogey—sat on the stone steps to the school, yawning. The school itself, a tall, imposing structure built of red brick, looked as if it had fallen asleep in the sunshine, its window shades drawn down against the light. Even the creek, which ran behind the school, looked sweetly innocent, sunlight glimmering in a frank and cheerful manner on the sparkly grains of fools gold embedded in the sand.

"Hey," one of the girls standing near her—a tall, long-legged girl named Ella—suddenly whispered. "Want to see what I have?"

They were standing together in the shade of a maple tree, Evie, Bobbie, Ella, and three girls from Ella's crowd. Ella was a rebel, one of the most popular girls in their class, famously known for skating perilously close to the line. After school she hung out by the bike rack smoking, and she had already been suspended once for kissing a boy in the hallway.

Bobbie glanced at her with disdain. She had no sympathy for Ella's outlandish grabs for attention, but the other girls were delighted. They drew closer, forming a knot around her, shielding her from the Old Fogey's gaze. Even Evie allowed herself to be drawn it. She had no idea what Ella was up to, but at least it would be a distraction from her gloomy thoughts—something else to think about for a while.

Ella thrust her hand into the center of the circle, revealing a shiny gold lipstick. Make-up was strictly forbidden at school; just last week the Old Fogey had forced a seventh-grade girl to scrub the eye shadow off her face with soap and water in a public humiliation. Bobbie rolled her eyes. "Put it away before we all get into trouble."

"What's wrong?" Ella asked with a smirk. "Afraid of a little lipstick?"

Bobbie's face reddened. Evie hurt for her friend. Bobbie might be the smartest girl Evie knew, but in many ways she was also the dumbest. She had no idea how to fit in. It wasn't just make-up. She had no clue about fashion or style. Evie tried to help her, giving her little tips on how to dress, but Bobbie refused to listen. It doesn't matter what people look like, she insisted. As if to prove her point, she stubbornly wore the skirt of her uniform down to her knees—the way it had come from the store—while everyone else in the class rolled their waistbands up until their skirts crept up their thighs. Ella's skirt was the smallest, so short she could hardly sit down. Even Evie rolled her skirt up, although to more modest levels. She knew what Bobbie meant, but she wasn't about to look like a fool either.

Bobbie frowned. "C'mon," she said to Evie. "Let's get out of here."

She turned her back on Ella and walked away from the tree, her arms folded over her chest.

Normally Evie would have followed, but she was still feeling miserable. Her headache had gotten worse, and now she felt queasy, too, as if she were coming down with the flu. She wanted to rest a moment in the shade until the feeling passed. She leaned against the trunk of the tree. "In a minute," she said to Bobbie.

Ella gave the group a triumphant smile. Then she flicked the top off the lipstick and wiped a sheen of color across her lips. She put a hand on her waist, wiggled her hips, and made pouty, kissing motions with her mouth. The other girls giggled and squealed, "Let me try it, Ella. Let me."

Evie closed her eyes. It wasn't just her head. Her heart was pounding, too. She felt a surge of anxiety, as if something bad were about to happen. She opened her eyes and glanced about the playground. Everything was calm and placid as before, the children cheerfully engrossed in their games. Even the Old Fogey, who was notoriously known for zeroing in on rule-breakers, seemed lulled by the bright sunlight and showed no sign of being aware of what they were doing. "Shh," Evie warned Ella, just in case. "She'll hear us."

The girls quieted down and passed the lipstick around, each one taking a turn. Ella smacked her lips then wiped the lipstick off with the back of her hand, admiring the bright red smear it left on her skin. Meanwhile the first-grade girls swung on the rings, and the second-grade boys played marbles, the brightly colored orbs of glass spinning and glittering in the sunlight. One of the boys ran along the fence, rattling a stick in the chain link. The sound felt painfully loud and jarring to Evie, as if the boy were rattling the stick against her head. She pressed a hand to her eyes.

The lipstick had finally made its way around the circle to her. She took it and pulled the cap off the bright golden tube. As she twisted it up, she heard a whoop on the grass. The third-grade boys had organized themselves into a game of cowboys and Indians and were chasing each other in circles. The Indians howled and beat the palms of their hands against their mouths while the cowboys shot at them with their finger guns. All at once one of the boys came to a stop on the grass. "I don't want to be the Indian anymore," he wailed, with a pouting look on his face. "I was the Indian last time. It's your turn now."

Evie sighed. No one ever wanted to be the Indian. It never changed.

She had forgotten the lipstick, but Ella hadn't. "Are you going to take your turn or not?" she asked.

"Sorry." Evie lifted the lipstick to her lips, but before she could put it on, shouts came from the blacktop. Two of the fifth-grade boys were fighting over a ball. One of the boys grabbed the ball and pushed the other boy, hard. Moving with surprising swiftness, the Old Fogey leapt up from her seat on the steps. "You there."

The girls froze. Evie closed the lipstick, thrust it into her pocket, and spun around. The teacher wasn't looking at them; she was glaring at the boy who had done the pushing. "Stop that right now."

The boy made an elaborate show of pointing to himself, miming in a surprised way. "Who, me?"

"Yes, you." The Old Fogey kept her eyes on him until the boy backed down, turning the ball over to the other boy. The Old Fogey eyed the two boys a moment longer, letting them know she meant business. Then she sat back down.

The girls laughed in relief. Ella was delighted, as if she'd personally engineered the joke. Evie thought she would be sick. She might as well give the lipstick back to Ella. She just didn't feel well. Maybe she should go inside.

She pulled the lipstick out of her pocket, but before she could give it back, she was overcome by another wave of anxiety. The feeling was even stronger this time. Something awful was about to happen—something right there, right now. She turned towards the grass, where the boys were still playing, the Indians attacking with their tomahawks, making chopping motions with the side of their hands, while the cowboys galloped around them, whipping their horses, smacking their palms against their thighs.

"Hurry up, Evie," Ella said, the annoyance plain on her face. "It's your turn."

Evie didn't answer. She detached herself from the knot of girls, a frightened look in her eyes.

Bobbie looked over at her. "Evie? Are you okay?"

Ella stuck her hand out for the lipstick. "If you're not going to use it, at least let someone else have a chance."

Evie ignored her. Taking the lipstick with her, she walked towards the third-grade boys.

"What is it, Evie?" Bobbie said, coming towards her. "What's wrong?" She put a hand on Evie's arm, but Evie shook her off.

One of the cowboys aimed his finger-gun at an Indian. "Bang bang," he hollered. "You're dead."

Writhing in agony, the Indian fell to the ground and clutched his heart.

"Stop it," Evie said. She was halfway to them, on the grass.

"Evie." Bobbie's eyes widened in alarm. "Come back."

Another cowboy shot his gun, and a second Indian tumbled to the ground, making choking sounds in his throat.

"Stop it," Evie said, louder this time. She was almost on them. "Don't do that. Stop it, right now."

The girls playing jump rope turned and looked at her. The boys looked up from their marbles. The four-square ball dribbled away unnoticed across the blacktop.

The Indians ran in a tight circle around their fallen comrades, stamping down hard, beating the earth with their feet. The cowboys pursed their lips and blew the smoke from their guns.

"Don't do that!" Evie shouted. Her eyes were rolling, and her face was twisted in terror. Her body trembled, her hands jerked open, and the lipstick fell to the ground. "I said, stop it. *Stop it right now.*"

The cowboys and Indians came to a halt. The cowboys' arms swung loosely at their sides. Breathing hard, the Indians struggled to their feet.

All across the playground, the children stopped moving. The swings stopped swinging, and the rings hung empty. A puzzled look on her face, the Old Fogey stood up. Shielding her eyes from the sun with her hand, she looked out at the schoolyard, but nothing was amiss. Nothing, that is, except Eve Glauber, one of the ninth-grade girls, who was standing alone in the middle of the playground, her body rigid, her face contorted, and her hands clenched at her sides as she screamed, "*Stop it stop it stop it*," over and over again.

Jase Glauber walked into the Danvers Academy, climbing up the same steps Mrs. Fogarty had sat on just a few hours before. It was late in the afternoon, the schoolchildren gone for the day, the air inside the building stale and still. He walked down the empty hallway, his footsteps echoing on the tile. A pale light leaked in from the windows, shining dully on the long rows of metal lockers on either side. From one of the classrooms came the sound of voices, two women talking and laughing. They fell silent as he walked past, and then the sound started up again, hushed and whispered.

The door to the headmaster's office was ajar. He was about to knock on it when the man inside stood up and came forward, his hand outstretched. "Mr. Glauber. Thank you for coming in." He was tall and thin with an undertaker's stooped bearing. "You have no idea how much I appreciate it. I know how busy you are."

"Jase." He took the hand. It was soft and warm, slightly damp.

"Yes, well." The headmaster cleared his throat. "Jase." He looked distinctly uncomfortable as he said the word. He rocked for a moment back and forth on his heels. His suit, loose and ill-fitting, rocked with him. "Well, then," he said again. He held a hand towards the chair in front of his desk. "If you'll just ... "

Jase sat down. The room was hot, too hot, but the windows were closed; the curtains were closed, too, so that only a narrow band of light slipped through, falling uselessly to the patterned carpet. In the corners, the bookshelves, replete with thick cloth- and leather-bound volumes, retreated into shadows. The chair he had taken bore the school's crest, as did a shield on the wall. The air smelled of ink and dust.

The headmaster sank into his seat on the far side of the desk as if he were relieved to have something so large and solid between them. He took off his glasses, polished them on a white handkerchief he removed from his pocket, replaced the handkerchief, and put the glasses back on. He ventured a smile. "I don't suppose you have any news about our boys over there? Any inside scoop on what's really going on these days in Vietnam?"

Jase didn't return the smile. It was one of the things he hated most about running a newspaper, the way people assumed he knew things they didn't—all kinds of secrets, conspiracies, and lies. Even worse was the way they assumed they would want to know about them if he did, when half the time they couldn't even deal with the things he did put into print. "No."

The headmaster cleared his throat again. "Yes, well." He reached for his glasses then smiled in an embarrassed way and dropped his hands to the desk. "It's about Eve."

"I figured that." He was such a stupid man, faintly sanctimonious with an underlying arrogance. Jase could hardly bear to be in the same room with him. Why did such stupid people always end up in positions like these?

The headmaster's voice changed, becoming businesslike. "You heard about the playground then."

"That teacher called. Mrs. ... "

"Fogarty. Renate Fogarty. She had recess duty today."

"That's what she said." A look of distaste came over Jase's face as if he'd just been forced to swallow something unpleasant. "I don't see where losing your temper is a cause for getting in trouble."

"No one's in trouble here. I want to be clear on that."

"Then why am I here?"

"It's just that ... " The headmaster removed his glasses, held them up to the light, and peered through them. Then he put them on the desk and dropped his eyes, as if overcome by the difficulty—the delicacy—of proceeding. "It's not just the playground."

"Then what is it?"

"There have been other things."

"She screamed in school before?"

"No, no, nothing like that." He put the glasses back on. "In fact, I would say it's just the opposite. If anything, Mr. Glauber—Jase," he corrected himself, "lately Eve has had a tendency to be a little too quiet."

"Too quiet."

"Yes." The headmaster looked at him hopefully, as if he were relieved they had finally found something on which they agreed.

"This is the first time I've heard of anyone getting into trouble at school for that."

"Please, Mr. Glauber." He didn't bother correcting himself this time. "No one's in trouble. I thought I made that clear." He cleared his throat. "It's just that we're concerned about the way Eve conducts herself. The way she appears. I'm sure you know what I mean."

"I do not."

"Well, some students daydream in class, especially at this age. I'm sure you're familiar with that."

"She's in trouble for daydreaming?"

"No, sir, not at all." The headmaster removed a file from one of his drawers. It was a plain, nondescript yellow manila folder, the kind Jase used himself at the office for filing, but at the sight of it, his mouth went dry. The conversation, he understood, had taken a turn from a simple discussion between concerned adults to an official school meeting about Evie, with everything that implied. The headmaster opened the folder. "The way her teacher tells it, lately Eve has been acting like she has something on her mind. Like something's troubling her."

Jase glanced at the folder then back at the headmaster. More than anything he wanted to dart forward and grab that folder off the desk, read what was inside. But he swallowed hard and restricted himself to repeating the headmaster's words. "Troubled."

The headmaster nodded. "After recess today Renate took Eve directly to the school nurse. She examined her and found nothing wrong. Nothing physical, that is. I assume you'll want your own doctor to do a follow-up ... "

His voice trailed off with an expectant air. Jase didn't answer. The headmaster waited a moment longer then drew himself up. "As you know, Mr. Glauber, at the Danvers Academy we are strict with our students. Perhaps," he conceded, "at times too strict. But I like to think that we are not unfeeling. As educators we've learned that our job requires more than just looking after the academic progress of the children who have been put into our charge. We need to be aware of what goes on inside them—in their minds, so to speak."

"I'm not a mind reader. Are you telling me you are?"

"Of course not." The headmaster consulted the folder again. "But the nurse thinks the incident on the playground today might be an indication of other, deeper things." He closed the folder and looked at Jase directly. "I understand there is no mother?"

Jase stiffened. "That's none of your business."

"No, of course not." The headmaster opened another drawer and removed a small slip of paper. "I've taken the liberty of writing down the name of a psychiatrist I know." He held it out to Jase. "He's worked with children before."

Jase looked at the paper and then at the headmaster's face. "You brought me in here to tell me that?" His voice rose in anger. "Psychiatrists don't do anything. All they do is talk, talk, talk. What's the good of that?"

The headmaster was taken aback. He put the paper down. "Eve will be in high school next year," he said, changing tack. "She won't be with us, in the protected halls of this academy, anymore. In high school, as I'm sure you know, things can get more complicated." He spoke in a grave tone, with a dignified look on his face, one that Jase wouldn't have guessed was within his capability. "I understand she will be attending North High?"

Jase nodded.

"A public school." The headmaster looked as if he had something more to say about this—as if, of all the choices available for Evie, this one was undoubtedly the worst. Then he retreated, like a man who had learned over time to choose his battles. "I'm only trying to be of help."

This only increased Jase's anger. "If you want to be of help, you might want to think about the reading, writing, and arithmetic that gets done around here. Last I heard, that was your job, wasn't it?"

The headmaster shrugged in an apologetic way. "I want you to know that I like Eve. She's a bright and creative child, engaging in her own way. We think the world of her." He held out the slip of paper again, and when Jase still refused to take it, put it down with a distinct air of regret. "There is one thing I wanted to ask you about."

"Yes?"

"At recess today, Renate pulled Eve aside. She wanted to calm her down. Afterwards she asked her why she was so angry and upset. Eve said, 'Because it isn't a game.'"

"Isn't a—what?"

"Cowboys and Indians. Some of the younger children were playing it on the playground. Eve said they shouldn't, because it wasn't a game. Do you have any idea what she meant by that?"

Jase fell silent. He glanced down at his hands then stood up and met the headmaster's eye. "If there's nothing more?"

"No. There's nothing more." The headmaster pushed back his chair. "Children go through many phases. I'm sure that in time, Eve will be fine."

"She *is* fine." Jase turned to go, but as he reached the door, he heard the headmaster's voice again.

"Perhaps ... "

He turned around.

"It's not in Eve's official file." The headmaster tapped the folder on his desk with his finger. "I never report anything that isn't directly observed by a teacher. But perhaps you should know ... " The headmaster paused as if considering, then nodded to himself and went on. "Eve had a problem the other day with one of our other students. A kindergarten girl. The kindergarteners are still allotted play time." His voice took on a defensive tone, as if he were still smarting from Jase's earlier remark on reading and writing. "They are given toys to play with. The girls often choose dolls. This particular girl happened to carry her doll into the hallway just as Eve's class was passing by."

"A doll?"

"An Indian doll. I'm sure you've seen them. They're quite popular with the little girls nowadays. I suppose they always have been. This one was quite authentic. It showed an Indian woman dressed in native costume. You know. Braids. Moccasins. Beads. I believe it even had a small papoose on the back." He allowed himself a small smile. "It was quite charming, actually, but apparently your daughter didn't think so. The girl reported it to her teacher. She was quite upset over it, crying."

"Evie made someone cry?"

"I'm sure she didn't mean to," the headmaster hastened to add, "but the girl was quite little, and your daughter was rather harsh."

"What did Evie do to her? What did she say?"

"Your daughter told the girl that she shouldn't have a doll like that. She told her to put it away and never touch it again." One last time the headmaster lifted the paper with the psychiatrist's name and held it out to Jase. Jase sunk his hands deep into his pockets. "It's not in her record, Mr. Glauber, but I thought you should know. Eve told one of our kindergarteners that she shouldn't play with dolls of people who had died."

Nine

In June the rumors began to fly. Any day now the men would move out, leaving the coast for the central highlands—for the war. In preparation, Eason joined a squad with four other men, Liver, Page, Music, and Nye. The men lived and worked together, learning to depend on one another, growing as close as the five fingers on one hand. "Like five fingers balled into a fist," Liver said, punching Eason affectionately in the arm. "Those slopes won't even know what hit them."

They called him Liver because of the birthmark that stained his face from neck to cheekbone, a dark purplish patch that floated against the backdrop of his skin like the map of a lost continent on an ancient sea. Nye was Nye because that was his name, and that was the way he liked it—and because, the others quickly learned, he was the kind of person with whom it was better not to argue. Music carried the radio. Page was Page because—well, the truth was, nobody knew why. Not because of books. "The one thing the Army has to recommend it," Page liked to say, "is how little it requires you to read."

They named Eason "Cowboy" because he knew about horses and knew how to ride. And because of his great-grandfather. "A goddamned Indian fighter," Liver said, giving Eason an admiring glance. "You just watch him kill gooks. It's in his blood."

They were out on patrol one morning, one of their last days by the sea, when they came across a water buffalo. A light rain fell, turning the sky into a misty damp grey that reached down to the ground. Nye was the first one to spy it. It was standing by itself in the distance, in the middle of a field, a swampy patch of ground. It looked weak and abandoned, knock-kneed and bone-thin, the skin hanging in deeply wrinkled folds. "Man," Nye said, "that is one sorry-looking animal." He shook his head, a burly man who wrestled in high school and whose body still bore a wrestler's thick and compact build.

Page nodded his agreement. He was the tallest man in the squad and the thinnest, and his voice had a way of breaking when he talked, as if he hadn't finished growing up. "One sorry-looking son-of-a-bitch."

They stopped walking to admire the buffalo, which slowly raised its head, regarding them with wary eyes. "You gotta wonder about something as ugly as that," Music said. But then Music was always wondering about things. He had a dreamy, sweet quality to him that led him to forget he was a soldier—making him do things like comment on how pretty the sunsets were, or how nice it was when the moon rose over the water.

Usually Nye made fun of Music's comments, but Music's dreamy mood had caught him, too. "It's gotta make you wonder."

Eason just shook his head and scuffed his boots in the mud.

Liver was the one who came up with the idea to ride it. Ride it and have a rodeo. They all looked at him. "You know, ride 'em cowboy," he explained. "Yahoo!" His voice had a hopeful lilt that carried them along. But first they had to catch it. They sent out Eason. Well, he was the cowboy, wasn't he?

What did he know about water buffalo? Eason thought about that as he trudged across the field, the muck slopping into his boots. At least the rain was lifting now, the air lightening as the sun rose higher in the sky. In the distance a dark line of trees took shape at the edge of the field. Behind him the men were talking, their voices rising and falling. They were laughing, making fun of him. The thought thoroughly depressed him, but what could he do? He stopped and turned around. "Ride 'em cowboy," Liver called out to him in an encouraging way. He smiled and waved his helmet, circling it high in the air above his head. "Yahoo!"

The buffalo monitored Eason's progress across the field. So far it hadn't moved or in any other way betrayed its intentions. As Eason got closer, a musty stink came into the air, the smell of shit and decay. One of the buffalo's eyes was fused shut by oozing gunk. The other regarded him warily beneath a drooping lid.

Once more Eason turned around. Grinning, the men waved him forward with their hands, as if they were shooing barnyard fowl. He approached the buffalo from the side, his hand outstretched with the palm up, the way he caught horses. To his surprise the buffalo accepted his hand, twisting its head and shoulders just far enough to root in his palm with its nose. Finding his hand empty, the buffalo lifted its head and looked at Eason with sad, disappointed eyes.

It was starving. Even Eason could see that. It was basically half-dead. It must have been too old to eat grass anymore. Probably didn't have any teeth left. Rotting from the inside out. *He sure smelled like it*, Eason thought. The stench was much worse there, fetid and thick. A few stray flies buzzed about the gunk in the buffalo's eyes.

Behind him the men had fallen silent. They huddled together in the remaining tatters of mist watching him. Liver regarded him with a grudging respect. A wary feeling had come into the air, a hint of expectation. They were waiting to see what he would do next.

Eason had no rope, nothing to use as a halter. He considered using his belt, but it was far too short to reach around the animal's massive neck. He studied the buffalo. The buffalo looked patiently back at him, its eyes watering and oozing. Maybe he imagined it, but Eason swore there was a measure of trust in the buffalo's gaze now, a glimmer of hopefulness. He considered his options. He shrugged, grabbed the horn that was closest to him, and tugged. The buffalo heaved a sigh, as if this was what it had been waiting for all along. It followed Eason back across the field, lumbering alongside him as tamely and obligingly as a dog.

Once Eason had succeeded in capturing the buffalo, the men seemed to lose interest in it. "Forget it," Music complained. "He stinks."

Nye wrinkled his face and turned away.

"C'mon," Page said. "Let's go." He picked up his gear and prepared to move out. Shrugging slightly, the others did the same. Eason shouldered his pack, feeling strangely relieved, although he had no idea why.

Only Liver didn't follow suit. He was lost in thought, contemplating the buffalo, his head cocked to the side. "Hey." He had just noticed that the others were leaving. There was a look of surprise about him, a faint aggrieved air. "We can't go yet. We haven't had our rodeo."

They decided they would take turns riding him. Music, who had a stopwatch, would time them. The one who stayed on the longest would win a prize. The prize remained undisclosed, although Liver led them to believe it would be something fine. But then Liver often led them to believe things would be fine, even when they weren't. And yet they went on believing him anyway.

Eason would go first.

Once more he approached the animal from the side. This time he got close enough to press his belly against the buffalo's hide. Nye, who was strongest, stood in front of the buffalo, grasping its horns, steadying it. Eason hopped up and down on the ground. In one swift, fluid motion he flung himself across the buffalo's back and swung his leg down the other side. He sat upright, his hands grasping the wrinkled skin of the animal's neck. The buffalo groaned and staggered backwards. For a second Eason was afraid that the animal couldn't take it, that it would collapse. Then the buffalo straightened itself and accepted the weight, blinking at the men with patient, wounded eyes.

"Hey," Music said with a surprised voice. "He likes it."

"Maybe he's used to it," Page said. "Maybe he gets ridden all the time." He turned to Nye. "They ride water buffalo, don't they, the gooks?"

Nye shrugged. "How the hell should I know?"

Liver, as usual, kept them organized, the momentum moving forward. "All right!" he called out. He grinned happily at the men. "It's rodeo time."

Nye released the horns. The men stepped back, a short distance away, giving Eason some room. Eason waited, but nothing happened. The buffalo didn't move. It seemed to be waiting, too. As it breathed, its bony sides bellowed out between Eason's legs, collapsing inwards like an empty sack. Its head dropped and its one good eye closed, as if it were falling asleep.

"Hey," Liver complained, "let's go! This is a rodeo, remember?"

Eason tapped the buffalo's sides gently with his heels. The buffalo murmured and swayed its head from side to side as if it were dreaming. Eason rapped the buffalo again, more sharply this time. The buffalo grunted and stumbled forward a few steps. Eason slipped to the side, in danger of losing his seat. The men whooped and cheered. But then the animal came to a stop, and Eason regained his balance once more.

"All right!" Liver hollered. "Ride 'em cowboy. Yahoo!"

The men whooped and hollered, flapping their arms like giant birds, circling their helmets high above their heads. At the sight of all this commotion, the buffalo snapped up its head, snorted and spooked, trotting with jerky steps across the field. This time Eason was prepared and had no trouble staying on. Finally the buffalo stopped. Panting slightly, it turned and faced the men, looking out at them with mournful, endlessly suffering eyes.

The men dropped their arms and fell silent.

"Aw, hell," Page said.

Nye turned away in disgust. "Some rodeo."

No one wanted to admit it, but they had all been hoping that the buffalo would buck Eason off. Otherwise what was the point?

Music took his disappointment out on the buffalo. "That thing's too dumb to ride."

"Too dumb to live," Nye said.

"Anyway, it sure as hell smells bad enough."

Once more the men turned to gather up their gear. From his perch on the buffalo's back, Eason watched them, making sure that they really meant it this time, that they really were leaving. Finally the others were ready, standing serious and businesslike in the field with their packs and their gear. "C'mon," Page said. He glanced at his watch. "Let's go."

Only Liver was still watching the buffalo, with a thoughtful look on his face. *I can go now*, Eason thought to himself. *It's over. I can get off and join the others.* But for some reason he didn't. He knew it wasn't over yet, that in fact it was only just beginning, and that he had a crucial role to play in what came next. He was pinned to the buffalo's back by Liver's eyes.

Meanwhile the buffalo had lost interest in the proceedings. Its head nodding, it appeared to be falling back asleep. All at once a crack reverberated behind Eason, echoing from the trees. The buffalo grunted and jerked up its head, its eyes open wide in surprise. And then its knees buckled, and it crumpled to the ground.

At the last second Eason managed to extricate himself from the falling animal. He twisted loose and jumped to the side, looking down at the buffalo. A small red wound had opened on the side of the animal's head, right below its ear. Its eyes were glassy now, blankly staring. The flies had already settled on them and were feeding on the gunk.

Eason turned around and looked at Liver, who looked back at him, his eyes curiously blank, his rifle in his hand.

Somehow Eason covered the ground between them, and then he was rolling in the muck with Liver beneath him and then on top of him, rolling and punching and sobbing, "You son-of-a-bitch you could have killed me what the hell were you thinking it could have moved and you could have killed me you goddamned son-of-a-bitch."

A few nights later they packed up their gear. The next morning they moved out, and Eason's war—the one he had been both dreading and desiring ever since he arrived in Vietnam—finally began. The first time things got really bad—the first time he got caught in a firefight and men around him were falling and dying—Eason discovered that it wasn't fear so much that seized him but madness. He was sure he was going crazy, losing his mind. Even when he was safely back in his bunk, he felt himself slip away as if he were still on the water buffalo, feeling its knees buckle and fall, its muscles jerk and quiver between his legs.

After a while Liver came over and sat beside him.

It was late at night, and the other men were asleep. "You've got to forget about it," Liver said. "It didn't happen. It's not real. None of it is. It's just a game we're playing, cowboys and Indians, like you played when you were a kid. You're a cowboy, remember? An Indian killer just like your great-grandfather. You got it now?" Cool and quick he put his finger gun to Eason's forehead. "Welcome to Indian Country," he said. And then he grinned and shot it off.

Ten

Summer came, school let out, and soon Evie was riding to the Swale ranch every day. Most mornings Cyrus caught sight of her on the creek trail before he finished mucking out the stalls, and she didn't head home again until long after evening feeding time. She rode the roan colt faithfully each morning, putting him through his paces, and under her care he steadily improved, until the rancher began to believe he might be worth something after all. When she was done with the colt, she always offered to help Cyrus with his chores, doing whatever he needed, filling water buckets, tossing flakes of hay from the loft into the mangers, measuring sweet feed into the grain boxes. Now when he drove bales of hay out to the pastures, Evie rode with him, sitting on the tailgate of his pickup, hopping off to open and close the gates as once Eason had done at her age. She was a hard worker, surprisingly strong for a girl of her size; with a twist of her body, using her legs for leverage, she could heft an entire bale. And she was a willing worker, too, never complaining, even when he asked her to do the most tiresome, boring tasks: scrubbing water troughs, washing brushes, raking the ring.

In the afternoons when she had finished her chores, she always left for the battlefield, riding eastwards on the creek trail. He wondered what she did day after day on that empty piece of rangeland. Did she still hear the voices of the people who had died there, as once she'd claimed she did? If so, they brought her no pleasure. She had a grim look to her when she left for the bluff and an equally grim look when she came back. Sometimes he had the feeling she was being drawn there against her will, by some kind of fear or compulsion. She had always struck him as an odd girl, with a look of wildness and neglect, loose hair from her braid falling into her face as if it had a mind of its own. Now she looked unsettled, too, and was dogged by a troubled air. What, he wondered, had become of the girl who had ridden the wild colt so fearlessly? Something must have happened to her, something that had changed her. She had the air of a person who was haunted, who'd seen something she shouldn't have. Who'd seen a ghost.

He could tell she was worried about Eason. She never failed to ask about him. Cyrus always answered her truthfully, saying, *Eason's fine*, and afterwards the air always seemed a little lighter around her. One day he asked her if she didn't want to write to him; he would be glad to give her the address, but she just shook her head with an air of regret. She'd often dreamed about it, she said, but the truth was, she had nothing to say.

To his surprise, he discovered that he'd grown fond of her. He hadn't expected that. He wanted to ease her troubles but didn't know how to. What did he know about teenaged girls? Not for the first time he wished his wife were still with him. She would know what to say. But Elaine had been gone for eleven years now, and there was nothing to be done about that.

At least Evie liked being around the horses. They soothed her soul; even he could see that. Watching her with them reminded him of the old saying *There's nothing so good for the inside of a person as the outside of a horse.* She befriended the wary yearlings, who surged forwards when she visited their pasture to lick the salty sweat from her hand. On more than one occasion he found her standing by the paddocks, watching the stallions at play. She spent hours with the foals, watching as they cantered about on their gangly legs, or lowered their heads to nurse. Often he found her just sitting in the barn, where she seemed comforted by the shadowy presence of the horses in their stalls, the soft huffing of their breath, the tangy scent of their manure and hay.

But one day when he came into the barn, he found her in distress.

She was on her knees in the roan colt's stall, fumbling through the straw. Alarmed, he said, "What's wrong?"

"I lost it," she said, flinging the bedding aside.

"Lost what?"

"My arrowhead. The one Eason gave me. I had it just a minute ago, and now its gone." Her hands were stained with manure; bits of straw clung to her hair. She looked ready to cry. He fetched a rake and helped her look, cleaning the colt's stall down to the dirt floor, but they never found the arrowhead. That day when she left for home, she rode away with a miserable air.

The lost arrowhead gave him an idea, and that night he took out his own collection of arrowheads, the one he had assembled in his childhood. He kept the arrowheads in a mahogany box with trays lined with velvet and partitions to separate the stones. The next morning as she dismounted from her horse, he presented the box to her with a stir of pride. "Take one of mine," he said, holding it out to her. "Whichever one you want. Take two."

To his surprise she refused, turning away from the box with a look of disappointment on her face. He tried to understand but couldn't. What was the difference? They were all arrowheads from the same place. But she wouldn't explain. Even when he pressed her, all she would say was, "It's not the same."

Then in early July he sold the roan colt. He thought she would be happy about that, especially when he offered her a share of the proceeds. "You earned it," he said, handing her two hundred dollars in an envelope. "I never would have sold him if it weren't for you."

This, apparently, was an even bigger mistake than the arrowhead. She pushed the money aside, and her eyes darkened with anger. "How could you! That was Eason's horse."

The vehemence of her reaction startled him, but later that night, as he thought about it, he thought he understood. He'd given up being attached to horses long ago; he'd seen too many of them come and go over the years. They were nothing more than commodities to him, living animals to be sure, to be treated fairly and with kindness, but nevertheless to be bred and trained, bought and sold. She, on the other hand, was just a young girl, naïve and inexperienced. She'd grown fond of the colt. Well, there was nothing he could do about that now. The colt was gone.

He offered her a filly to ride instead, a dappled grey mare. He knew it was a poor act of substitution, but at least she accepted. When he insisted, she even took the money, although she did so with a begrudging air, as if it were tainted with blood. After that she rode the filly every day, training it with the same care she had given the roan colt, but he didn't even have to ask to know that, in her eyes, it wasn't the same.

It was a dry summer, dryer than usual. Weeks passed by without rain. Over time the trickle of water that made its way down the creek bed shrank in on itself, retreating into the earth, for long distances entirely disappearing. The leaves of the willows hung heavy with dust. The cottonwoods looked pinched and parched. When the wind blew, the yucca rattled with a throaty, gasping sound. Dust burrowed deeply into the horses' coats, defying the most vigorous brushing. It coated the rancher's boots, his skin, his lips. As he went about his work, unloading bags of feed, stacking bales of hay in the loft, he felt it dry his mouth.

The pump took the opportunity to become balky, working and not working in spurts. One afternoon in late July as Cyrus was fiddling with it, he looked up and saw a storm brewing over the mountains. Soon the sky darkened, the wind picked up, and a chill came into the air. He gave a loose bolt on the mechanism a last turn with his wrench, gathered up his tools, and hustled back to the barn. Rain began to fall just as he got inside. He stood in the doorway, looking out towards the creek. Evie was on the battlefield—she'd ridden there hours ago—but he figured she'd come galloping back at any moment; she could see the storm coming as well as he.

Only she didn't come back, even when the wind turned freezing and the rain changed to hail, icy pellets that pounded the roof of the barn and bounced like shot off the hard ground. Inside the barn the noise was so thunderous, he felt like the air was throbbing. The wind had a biting smell, as sharp as the ice. It bent the willows in the creek and flattened the grasses on the prairie. A piece of tin tore off the roof of the old bunkhouse and flew with a clatter against the side of the house. In their stalls, the horses skittered with fear. Cyrus shivered in the doorway, his eyes trained anxiously on the creek. Where was she?

Just as he was about to go after her—he'd get in the truck and force it somehow across the plain—the storm subsided, passing over as quickly as it had come. The sky cleared and the sun came out, making the hail-strewn ground glitter like a carpet of glass. As the air warmed, the hail began to melt, turning into puddles that seeped into the soil. As the last of the puddles disappeared, he saw her riding back to him on the creek trail.

She was wet and bedraggled, her horse soaked and shaking. As she came down the ridgeline, he was weak-kneed with relief, but by the time she had dismounted, he was beside himself with anger. "Are you telling me you didn't see the storm coming?"

She shook her head. "I saw it." She led her horse into an empty stall and pulled off his saddle. Then she fetched a rag from the washroom and began to rub him down.

He was speechless with fury. And her father thought he was reckless! He'd never once in his life endangered himself—or an animal—like that. "You—" he said. His eyes were burning. "Why in God's name didn't you come in?"

Her face paled, and he thought she would collapse. With what must have been a great effort of will, she kept working on her horse, rubbing his flanks and shoulders. "I wanted to hear it," she said finally. Her voice was small.

He had no idea what to say to that. Dumbfounded, he watched as she went into the feed room and prepared a warm mash for her horse. She sank down on a stool outside his stall while he ate, her face blank, her eyes vacant. Now and then a shudder passed through her. But with this, as with the other things, she refused to explain herself, even when bruises from the hailstones blossomed like petals on her bare skin.

July passed into August, and after the hailstorm, there was no more rain. In the fields, the grasses withered and died. Cyrus used up the money he had set aside for summer hay and dug into the funds he was saving for the winter to buy more feed. One afternoon as he was loading his pickup with bales for the herds in the fields, he heard the low whine of an engine in the air. He looked up and saw a plume of dust in the distance. Then a truck came towards him on the drive.

It was black and battered, an old pre-war model, the kind people who couldn't afford better still kept on the roads. A man sat behind the wheel, an older man beside him. Two boys rode in the open bed behind. Cyrus glanced at the creek. Evie had gone to the battlefield, but it was growing late, and he expected her back soon. He brushed the loose hay from his shirt. "They're lost," he said, whispering the words to himself. "They've taken a wrong turn." But even as he said it, he knew he was wrong.

The truck came to a standstill a short distance away, its engine running. The man behind the wheel kept his gaze averted, as if it would be rude to do otherwise. The others in the truck did the same, even the boys. Then the engine stopped, and the driver stepped out. He stood by the truck, his eyes trained on the horizon. Cyrus glanced one last time at the creek then walked towards him.

They met midway. The man spoke in an undertone. Cyrus answered the same way. In the truck the older man kept his eyes averted, but the boys stared with open curiosity now. Once the driver raised his hands, as if he were pleading. The rancher shook his head. A hint of disappointment crossed the man's face. He swung about to face the truck, then turned back to the rancher, his hand pointing eastwards down the creek. There was a tone of urgency in his voice. Cyrus pinched his lips closed and once more shook his head. The man fell silent. For a moment it looked as if he would ask again, then his shoulders dropped almost imperceptibly, and he turned away.

The truck was halfway down the drive, the tail of dust still hanging in the air behind it, when Cyrus realized he wasn't alone. He turned around and saw Evie riding towards him, cantering down the ridgeline.

"I saw them." She jumped down from her horse. "I came as fast as I could. They were Indians, weren't they?"

He discovered that he didn't want to talk about it. He turned away from her, busying himself with the truck, loading in the last of the bales.

"What did they want?"

"Nothing that concerns you."

She didn't let that stop her. "They wanted to go to the battlefield, didn't they?"

Cyrus shrugged and swung a bale into the truck.

"Why didn't they?"

"Because I didn't let them." The bed of the pickup was full. He clanged the tailgate shut.

A look of surprise crossed her face. "Why not?"

"Because they have no business being there." He reached in his pocket for the keys.

"No business—?" Her eyes flashed with anger. "You chased them away, didn't you? Just like my father said you did before."

He didn't answer. He wrenched the door to the truck open and climbed inside.

"You shouldn't have done that." She moved her horse around in front of him, blocking his way. "They have as much right to go there as you do."

"Right?' His voice sputtered. "You don't know what the hell you're talking about." He jerked the door open and jumped out to face her. "That land is sacred. People died there. Good people. Indians have no business setting foot on it. Not now or ever."

Her face was tight with fury. "You can't really believe that."

"I'll believe what I want."

For a moment longer she glared at him. Then, to his surprise, her eyes filled with tears. "You could have at least let me talk to them."

"Talk to them?" He was taken aback. "Why?"

"So that I could ask them what happened there. Not what people say. The truth."

Shocked, he stared at her. She was crying freely now, the tears wetting her blouse. His voice softened. "You still hearing those voices?"

"No. Not even that day in the hailstorm." She wiped her nose with the back of her hand. "But I've seen other things."

"Other things?"

"At school. On the playground. These kids were playing cowboys and Indians. At first it was just a game. Then it wasn't anymore. It was real."

What did she mean by that? It made no sense. "Does anyone else know about this?"

"My father. He got called in to school, and they told him."

"What did he say?"

She sniffed, and he saw a hint of stubbornness come back into her face. "He says there's nothing wrong with me. He thinks it's all the school's fault. He says they're much too rigid and oppressive. He says it's enough to drive anyone ... " Her voice trailed off. When she spoke again, it was with an air of resignation. "I'm going to a new school in the fall. North High. He says I'll be happy there."

Cyrus nodded. "I see."

"There was one more thing."

He wasn't sure he wanted to hear it. "Yes?"

"Have you ever heard of the creek lady?"

"Creek lady?" Puzzled, he shook his head.

"It's an old ghost story about an Indian woman who walks the creek with a baby in her arms. I saw her."

"You—what?"

"Saw her. A few nights ago. She was in the creek behind my house."

No wonder she looked so troubled. The girl was disturbed. A sorry case. "Look," Cyrus said. There was nothing more he could do for her. "I'm sorry. I never should have let you come out here. I didn't know it would affect you like this." His hip was hurting, and he pressed a hand against it, trying to ease the pain. "I don't think you should come here anymore."

The crying started up anew. "What about Eason?"

Was that what all this nonsense about Indians and ghosts was? Some kind of superstitious way of trying to keep Eason safe? "Don't you worry about that." He forced himself to speak with confidence. "Eason will be fine."

She nodded, but with a doubtful air. Then she moved her horse so that he could leave. At least she had stopped crying. She put her foot in the stirrup, mounted her horse, and turned for home. He watched her climb the ridgeline. Sending her away was the right thing to do, but he couldn't help feeling sorry about it. "Are you going to be all right?"

"Maybe I am crazy." She twisted in the saddle to look back at him. "Maybe I have lost my mind. But you never should have chased those Indians away. Something happened on that battlefield, something that wasn't supposed to. And now we'll never know."

Luck in ranching goes in spurts—good and bad—and for the rest of that summer Cyrus had nothing but bad. A mare got colic and had to be put down. A yearling foundered. Then the pump broke down so thoroughly he had to pay for a new one, digging into funds he didn't have. With Evie gone, he returned to his old routines, doing his chores on his own as he had in the weeks after Eason left. But he didn't feel up to it anymore. At the end of the day, he ached. Sometimes he had trouble telling which ached worse, his body or his heart.

The ranch felt emptier to him now. Even the horses had a forlorn air. In her paddock, the dappled filly languished with no one left to ride her. One afternoon late in August he found himself thinking about that. It was feeding time, and he was on his way to fetch grain when he found himself going into the tack room instead for his saddle. Then he fetched the filly and saddled her up.

It took him a while to find a position on her back where the pain was bearable. He ended up sitting hunched to the side, with one foot in the stirrup, the other hanging down. At least the filly didn't seem to mind. She took his weight willingly, and when he turned her southwards walked without hesitation across the plain. It was late in the day, the sky windless and clear, the sun hanging low over the mountains. For a time he rode across a waterless stretch of prairie, unbroken by land-marks or trees. The land was dry and stony, studded by greasewood and rabbit brush, which clung in grey-green clumps to the soil. In the dis-tance flocks of plovers and longspurs were feeding, foraging for seeds. Without wind the air felt heavy and weighted. Even the tumbleweeds rested like stones on the ground.

Soon he came to a low hill which emerged like an anomaly from the plain: a buckle in the land which had occurred eons ago, he supposed, when the ancient seas that had once covered that place had dried and contracted. At the top of the rise a weather-beaten picket fence marked out a square plot of land. He dismounted with a groan and, stiff and aching, trudged on foot up the hill, leading the filly behind him. When he reached the fence, she lowered her head, snuffing along the ground for something to eat. There wasn't much. The soil on the hill was thin, scoured by wind. A few stunted, misshapen stands of sagebrush grew from the earth, seizing it with knobby, exposed roots, lending the air their musty, pungent scent.

The place needed some work. He felt bad about that; he didn't come there as often as he should. Inside the fence, scattered among the scrub, were a half-dozen gravestones, grey and listing. A lone stone stood on the far side, just outside the fence line. The fence itself showed signs of once having been painted white, but now nothing remained of the paint but a few peeling strips, faded to the same dismal grey as the gravestones. In one spot a picket had worked loose from its crosspiece, and he bent over, holding the board in place, while he pressed the nail back in with the heel of his hand. The repair held for a moment then sprang loose. He shook his head, dropped the filly's reins over the pick-et, and walked to the stone that sat alone, outside.

Ornen Swale, the stone read, *1871–1918*. He took off his hat. The preacher had said his father didn't deserve to rest in hallowed ground, but Cyrus had never understood that, not then, not now. Wasn't death lonely enough without the strictures of the church to make it worse? "I don't blame you," he said, looking down at the grave. "There have been times when I wished I could do the same." He tugged the gate open and went inside. The graveyard was on the highest piece of land on the ranch, and the view never failed to affect him, making him feel curiously empty and light. He could see in every direction, from the snowy peaks of the mountains, which crested on the western horizon like white-capped waves, to the curve of the earth, where the land vanished into the sky. It made him think of the first time he saw the ocean, on the deck of a troop carrier, steaming out to the Pacific. Then, as now, he'd felt larger than himself and smaller all at once, as if the vast spaciousness of the planet had flowed into him, expanding his heart, making it hard to breathe.

He steadied himself by resting a hand on the fence. Then he walked to the first gravestone. This one bore an engraved symbol at the top, a rifle crossed with a saber. Beneath that, carved in plain block letters, stood the name *Thomas Eli Eason* and the words, *First Lieutenant, Second Cavalry*. His grandfather had been a man of fifty-three when he died, only twenty-four at the Battle of Choke Creek. *So young*, Cyrus thought. His own son, who'd been soldiering since the spring, was younger still. "Too young," he said, inadvertently speaking the words out loud. The thought brought a stab of guilt to his heart, and he chased it from his mind.

The cavalryman's wife was buried beside him, the marker stained and flaked by weather. For a time he studied it, then he wandered across the graveyard to another stone, a small one, which lay half-sunk into the earth. It belonged to a stillborn baby that had been born some time after him. He remembered the birth, although he had no idea whether it had been a boy or a girl. They never named it, but before his mother died, she made him promise to bury her beside it anyway, so that it wouldn't be alone.

The largest stone was at the back of the graveyard. This one was wide enough to hold the names of two people, and its surface was still new enough to retain its polish. On the right side stood his wife's name, followed by the dates. Cyrus stood before it with his head bowed and his hat clasped in his hands. Then he bent down and scrabbled through the earth with his fingers. He chose a pebble, which he rubbed between his palms, smoothing off the dirt. Then he placed the pebble on the headstone. He remembered the first time Eason had seen him do that. "What's that for?" he'd asked.

"So she'll know I've been here."

He didn't know if his son had understood him, but later, when he visited his wife's grave again, he found another pebble on it. Then he knew Eason had been there, too.

The other side of the gravestone bore his name, followed by the date of his birth and a dash. It was all ready to go; all they had to do when he died was add the date. Eason wasn't happy about that—he found it gruesome. But to Cyrus, it looked just right. After Elaine died he'd felt half gone anyway, the better part of himself resting in the soil.

The wind had picked up since he arrived at the graveyard. He turned his face to it, but nothing came to him. The sound was as empty as an abandoned well. He opened his eyes and shook his head, laughing in a short, bitter way. "You foolish old man," he said out loud. "Do you think you're going to start seeing ghosts now, too?"

He put on his hat. On his way to the gate, he stopped by the grave of his mother. "You knew, didn't you?" His voice was soft, but the rancor in his heart surprised him. "You knew all along what happened there, but you never told me. You were afraid of the truth, and so you let it die with you." Stray bits of litter and chaff had settled at the bottom of the marker, blown by the wind. He swept them away with the back of his hand and rode home.

Darkness fell as Cyrus returned to the barn. He put the filly away and fed the horses, which had grown impatient waiting for their feed. Then he went into the house and made his own dinner, a simple skillet of chopped sirloin and canned corn. When he was done cooking, he discovered he had no appetite. He put the food away.

He sat in his chair and paged through the newspaper, but the news from Vietnam depressed him, and he put the paper down. He'd stopped watching television months ago, after Eason left; the screen had a way of bringing the war too close. He shifted in his chair, trying to ease the pain in his hip, which had grown sharp after the long ride. Then he stood up and drew his bath. For a long time he soaked in the tub, the water as hot as he could stand it. As the heat worked on his body, easing the stiffness, he closed his eyes so that he wouldn't have to see the things that were missing around him: Eason's comb, his toothbrush, his razor, the baseball cap he used to leave hanging at night on the hook by the mirror.

When the water had cooled, he stood up and dressed in his night-clothes. Then he pulled on his boots and walked to the barn. He made his last check on the horses and returned to the house. Lately the nights had gotten cold enough to merit a fire. He bent before the hearth, building one. His wood came from the high country—he bought it from a man who brought it down—and when it burned, it gave off the scent of the mountains, the smell of snowy damp earth and pine.

He walked into the kitchen and took down a biscuit tin from the shelf. Inside he kept Eason's letters. He took them out and counted them. More than twenty so far. He counted them again, as if doing so would increase their number. When the number reached one hundred fifty, Eason would be coming home.

The fire needed stoking up. He put the letters back in the tin and returned it to its place on the shelf. Then he tossed a log on the flame. The wood snapped as the fire took hold. He swept the spent ashes to the side with a hand broom. In the morning he would collect them in a tin bucket he kept outside the door for that purpose. He would carry them to the barn and throw them on the manure pile. When his wife was alive, he had saved the ashes to mix into the soil of her garden in the spring. Ashes were good for that. But he'd never been able to make a garden grow without her. The earth wouldn't stand for it. It shook off his seeds the way the horses shook off flies.

He walked back to the kitchen and took a pencil and piece of paper from one of the drawers. Then he sat down at the table and smoothed the paper out. Slowly and laboriously, choosing his words with care, he wrote:

I made the second payment on that pump. If I can sell a few more year-lings at the fall auction, I'll have enough to get through the winter.

He looked at what he had written. The words looked back at him like an accusation. He tore the paper up. Then he fetched a new sheet from the drawer and wrote:

Today I rode to the graveyard. I went to the grave of your mother and laid out a stone.

This wasn't at all the direction he had intended. He crumpled the paper and threw it on the fire. Outside the sky was clear, stars shining brilliantly across the plain. The Milky Way was a brush of light against the darkened sky. Was that the wind? He closed his eyes and listened. Then he shook his head. It was only the fire. The wind had died down hours ago.

He sat back down, spread his hands on the table and studied them, the thickly ridged nails and cracked skin. His father's hands. When had he gotten those? He picked up the pencil.

When I think of you at war, I remember your namesake, the cavalryman Thomas Eli Eason, the first man to take up soldiering in our family, the one in whose shadow we still stand.

A vision came to him of his mother, standing at the window as the wind blew. Her lips were pinched together tight, her eyes dark with a haunted look—the same look that haunted Evie's eyes. He closed his eyes again and listened. Still no wind. He shook his head. What difference did it make? He wouldn't hear it anyway. It had been more than twenty years.

He pushed the paper aside and took a clean sheet. In the hearth, the sap sputtered and sang. Outside there was nothing, just another empty night. In the silence Evie's words rang in his ears. *Something happened on that battlefield, something that wasn't supposed to.* He pressed a hand to his hip. *And now we'll never know.* Suddenly, with great energy and speed, he wrote:

There is much that I have told you, but much more that I have not. All along I have had reasons for my silence, and at the time they seemed right to me and prudent. But now I wonder.

He wouldn't stop himself any longer. Either he didn't want to, or he simply lacked the strength.

These are the things I wanted you to know from the beginning, even before you went to war.

He wrote long and hard, with an urgency born of grief and desire, swept away by the need to unburden himself.

I tell you this because I want things to be different. Not for me, but for you.

He wrote until he was exhausted and could write no more. Then he folded the letter, put it in an envelope, and left in on the table so that he would be sure to post it in the morning. His hip had stiffened up as he sat. With great pain he made his way to bed. As he lay down, he heard the wind. It was unmistakable this time, blowing down the creek, swirling about the house. He closed his eyes and listened, every muscle in his body tense and reaching, angled towards the darkness outside. Surely this time he would hear it, surely now, when he needed it most ...

His eyes snapped open. Convulsed with grief and rage, he stumbled to the kitchen and snatched the letter off the table. Furiously he tore the envelope to bits and tossed the scraps on the fire, where they withered into spark and ash. No. He wouldn't do it. He wouldn't burden his son with the weight he'd borne his entire life, the shame and fear. No, he would give his son the chance to be the soldier he deserved to be. Eason would have his war. And when it was over, God willing, he would come back home.

Eleven

Fall came and the creek registered the change in seasons, the shorter days and colder nights. The grasses in the creek bed withered and died, fading to shades of silver and bronze. Seedpods nodded like sleepy heads on the spindly stalks of the cattails. The light was softer and gentler without summer's harsh glare. The cottonwoods and willows shivered in the wind.

On the Swale ranch, Evie knew, the pregnant mares would be rounding out, their gait slow and languorous, their heavy bellies swaying from side to side as they walked. The yearlings would be anticipating the coming winter, their coats thickening by the day until they looked as foolish and fuzzy as bears. Even the foals would be changing, leaving behind the milk of their mothers for spiky fronds of hay and alfalfa, sweet molasses and corn. But she tried not to think about that. Ever since the day she'd watched Cyrus chase the Indians off his land, she'd tried very hard not to think at all about the Swales.

She'd done what the rancher had wanted, and hadn't returned to the ranch. She'd spent the rest of the summer confining her rides to the vacant lot behind Bird's barn and to short jaunts up and down the creek, never far from home. The truth was, she was sick of it. Sick of Indians and voices, battles and ghosts. She had stopped taking the cigar box out of her drawer; she didn't even touch Eason's shirt. What was the point? He was in combat now. His fate was out of her hands.

Then September came, and she started at a new school, North High, on the far side of town. Instead of walking to school each day, she and Bobbie rode the bus. The first time they went to the bus stop, they found Ella already there, along with a group of other kids from their neighborhood. Ella seemed to relish the prospect of attending public school. She had taken advantage of the lack of uniforms to dress in hip-hugging bell-bottom pants, an embroidered peasant shirt topped by a fringed leather jacket, and beads. She had put her hair in braids, and she was wearing enough make-up, Evie thought, to give the Old Fogey a heart attack for sure.

Evie had decided to wear jeans and a long-sleeved blouse to school—her riding clothes. That way when she got home in the afternoon, all she would have to do was slip on her boots, and she'd be ready to ride. Bobbie, as usual, had given no thought at all to her clothes and was wearing the skirt from her old school uniform, although at least she'd changed her top. Clearly Ella knew what was in style. Most of the other kids at the bus stop were dressed just like her—like hippies—in fringes and headbands, the boys with long hair parted in the middle, the girls in braids and beads.

The bus came, and Evie and Bobbie followed the others on board. Ella, who had made a point of ignoring them all morning, took a seat in the back next to a boy in a letter jacket. The girls took a seat together up front. Bobbie chattered with excitement about the math class she'd be taking; they'd placed her ahead into Pre-Calculus. But Evie had trouble paying attention. "What is it?" Bobbie said finally. "What's wrong?"

"It's those kids," Evie said, swiveling in her seat to look at them. "The way they're dressed." Her voice was full of irritation. "The beads and headbands. What do they think they are—Indians?"

Bobbie gave her a stricken look. "You're not going to start with that Indian stuff again, are you, Evie? You're not going to freak out like last time?"

Evie slumped in her seat, her eyes downcast. "No, Bobbie, don't worry, I won't." She put as much conviction as she could in her voice, but she knew Bobbie didn't believe her. Why should she? She hardly knew if she believed it herself.

It took Evie only a few days to decide that North High was a decidedly unpleasant place. The building was built like a prison, with grey cinderblock walls and narrow windows beneath a low, flat roof. It even had a chain link fence around the perimeter, surrounding a parking lot of broken asphalt and a weedy concrete basketball court. Inside the air had a foul smell, a mixture of the greasy food they served in the basement cafeteria and the disinfectant they used to clean the bathrooms. During passing periods the school erupted into noise and chaos as lockers slammed, and students used the five minutes allotted them to rush from class to class. Otherwise the hallways were eerily silent and deserted.

In one sense, Evie soon discovered, her father was right about public school. The students had a lot more freedom there. None of the teachers seemed to care what their students did as long as they didn't disrupt their class. At the Danvers Academy, whenever she lapsed into one of her spells of daydreaming, a teacher was bound to come by, put a hand gently on her arm, and recall her to the present. But daydreaming at North High was fine. Some of her teachers even seemed to prefer it. Sitting in the back row, Evie passed the hours undisturbed, gazing out the window, her mind miles away.

From time to time her thoughts still wandered to the Swales or to Eason at war. But as time passed, she found it easier to think about other things. One morning in early October, she found herself studying the back of the head of the boy who sat in front of her in history class. His name was Tyler Foley—they were seated alphabetically—and while she'd never paid particular attention to him before, she knew he was on the swim team; when he came to class, his hair was still damp and smelled faintly of chlorine. The teacher handed out a paper for the class, and as Tyler turned to pass it back to her, she noticed that his eyes were warm, and his mouth, pliable and full, was smiling at her. Smiling *at her*? She'd never noticed that before.

Over the next few weeks she found herself noticing a lot of things about Tyler Foley. He was tall—tall enough to pick out easily in a crowd—had broad shoulders, and had a thick thatch of unruly wheat-brown hair. He was goofy, but in an endearing way. Once she saw him put his arm around another boy in what seemed like an impromptu hug—only to finish the gesture off with a playful punch to the boy's shoulder. Afterwards she found herself wondering what it would feel like if Tyler put his arms around her. And he liked her. At least she thought he did. He always chose her group when the class divided up to work on projects. And he kept stopping her after class to ask about the homework—even though she knew for a fact he'd already copied it down. Why had she never noticed that before?

In early November, the teacher announced that the class would be taking a field trip to the State Capitol building. The bus would leave from the school parking lot early the next morning, and the students should be sure not to be late. That night Evie stood by her window thinking about it. Outside it was snowing—the first real snowstorm of the season—and the creek bed was already turning white, although the water had not yet frozen, and still trickled in a steaming dark line through the sand. In the mist, the white light glimmered, flitting back and forth like an animal in a cage. For a minute Evie watched it, then she turned around and closed the shade. She'd made up her mind. She would make things go back to the way they were before she met the Swales. No more ghosts, no more voices, and above all, no more cowboys and Indians. She needed to feel safe again—she needed to feel *normal*. And that, she decided, meant she needed Tyler Foley.

The next morning Evie lined up with the other students for the bus. It was freezing, and while most of the storm had passed in the night, the sky was still overcast, errant flakes of snow slicing through the wind. Even with her hooded parka on, Evie felt the cold. She craned her head, looking for Tyler. There were about twenty students in their group, including Ella and her latest boyfriend, a skinny boy named Jack who had a ponytail, a denim jacket, and black leather boots. The history teacher, a stocky older man with a crew cut, scanned the group with an important air, a clipboard under his arm; in addition to teaching history, he ran the school's ROTC program for boys who wanted to join the military. Finally Evie saw Tyler—or rather the familiar back of his head. He was ahead of her in line. She watched as he boarded the bus, the tips of his ears turning pink in the cold. She held her breath, and when her turn came, saw to her relief that he was still sitting alone. She made her way down the aisle to him, then stopped and said the words she'd been practicing since the night before: "Is anyone sitting here?"

Tyler looked up at her and smiled, sliding over to make room. "Sure. I mean, no." The tips of his ears turned even pinker. "I mean, yes, please, you can definitely sit here." His cheeks were turning pink now, too. "I mean, if you want to."

"Thanks." Evie took a deep breath. She wondered if he had any inkling of what this meant to her. Then she returned his smile and sat down.

The State Capitol was on a high point of land in the center of downtown, the most prominent building in the city. No matter where Evie was in Danvers, she saw its famous gold dome hovering above the skyline, with the mountains as its backdrop. As they drove towards it, Evie kept her eyes trained straight ahead, but she was acutely aware of how close she was to Tyler—so close, their bodies jostled against each other every time the bus hit a bump. Tyler was aware of it, too. She could tell, even though he didn't say anything. She inched subtly closer so that they would touch more often. Everything was working out just as she had wanted—just as she had planned. The thought made her glow with pleasure.

Outside the wind was icy, but inside the bus the air was close and warm, smelling of diesel and damp wool. They drove through neighborhoods of small brick houses, each one surrounded by a patch of snowy yard. Now and then a commercial block broke the monotony, a line of stores containing a pizza parlor or diner, grocery store or pharmacy. As they reached downtown, the streets narrowed, and the buildings rose higher on either side. They passed through the financial district and by hotels and department stores. Soon the *Sun* building appeared; the boxy yellow brick structure was only a few blocks from the Capitol. Tyler glanced out his window at it as they passed by. "Does your family really own the newspaper?" he asked.

This was most definitely *not* in her plan. Evie nodded, then shrugged as if it were no big deal, hoping Tyler would drop the subject. He showed no signs of doing that. "I want to be a sports writer some day," he said with an edge of excitement in his voice. He shoved his hands in his pockets, his eyes downcast in an embarrassed way. "At least I think I do." He ventured a smile. "It must be cool to know that one day you'll run *The Sun*."

"I guess so." Evie slunk down in her seat. The newspaper was the last thing she wanted to think about. She could practically hear her father's voice echoing in her ears, scolding her about her poor schoolwork and her lack of attention to her *future responsibilities*. Then she straightened up, chiding herself. She shouldn't blame Tyler. It wasn't his fault. Asking her about the paper was only the normal thing to do. And didn't she want to be normal? She cozied up next to him and smiled back.

As the bus pulled to a stop in front of the Capitol building, the students spilled out, gathering together on the sidewalk. The massive grey granite building sat above them on the crest of a snowy hill, its gold dome floating against the windswept sky. Evie had never been inside it before, and she found herself feeling a budding sense of curiosity. Tyler seemed to feel it, too. Together they gazed up the hill. The rest of the students showed little interest. Made miserable by the cold, the girls huddled together, the hoods of their parkas up, their backs to the wind. Jack and Ella stood off by themselves, with carefully composed looks of boredom on their faces. And the boys dashed across the hill, scooping up snow with their bare hands, tossing it at one another in an impromptu snowball fight.

"Hey, Foley!" one of the boys hollered. He sprinted across the lawn and dumped a handful of snow on Tyler's bare head.

"Cut it out, Hoffman," Tyler grumbled in a good-natured way as he brushed the snow out of his hair. But despite the provocation, Evie noticed with a warm sense of satisfaction, he didn't leave her side.

The teacher stepped off the bus and frowned. "Now then, enough of that." He clapped a hand on his clipboard. "You there, you boys." And then, more loudly, "On the double, right now, *here*."

Reluctantly the boys settled down and gathered by the girls. Just then a man emerged from the front door of the Capitol and came down the steps. He was dressed in a cowboy costume—leather chaps, a pearl-button shirt, fringed vest, and bolo tie. His boots were hand-tooled, decorated with roweled spurs, and he was wearing a large, white Stetson. "Welcome, welcome," he said with a broad grin and a tip of his hat. "Or should I say—" He waved the hat wildly above his head. "Howdy!"

The students laughed, not all of them kindly. Evie shook her head. She'd never seen a more ridiculous looking cowboy in her life. That man had probably never even been near a horse. The teacher frowned and clapped his clipboard again. "That's enough, settle down." He raked the group with his eyes until the last of the laughter had died away.

"Today," the cowboy guide said, speaking with a pompous air, "you young men and women are in for a special treat: a tour of our State Capitol." The teacher put his hand on the shoulder of a boy who was whispering loudly, imitating with exaggerated gestures the cowboy guide's every move. The boy's face reddened, and he grew still. "This building," the guide continued, "resounds with history. It is, so to speak, a living remembrance to the people and events of our past. Understand it and you will come a long ways towards understanding who you are and where you come from. Do you follow me?"

History? Evie thought. *A living remembrance to the past?* Despite herself, she found her interest piqued. Then she shook her head. She'd had enough of history, enough of worrying about the past. It was time to dwell in the present, in the here and now. In Tyler. She smiled at him and was rewarded by a broad smile back.

As the students squinted through the snowflakes at the building on the hill, the guide continued his talk. "Our State Capitol," he said, "was built to resemble the house of Congress in Washington, D.C. Like that building, it is laid out in the shape of a Greek cross, topped by a towering dome. But with the dome," he added, speaking more dramatically now, "the resemblance to the house of Congress ends. The congressional dome, as I am sure you know, is quite impressive and stately. But our dome, as you can see, is gilded in one hundred percent, genuinely pure gold. The gold, of course, is meant as an homage to the gold fields, in which the origins of our state reside. It is the crowning jewel of our city—indeed, if I might say so, of the entire region—the grace note that has justifiably earned this building its name as 'The Pride of the People.' Let's see the congressional dome top that," he concluded, his face broadening again into a grin. "And now, if you will follow me, I will take you to something else of which I am sure you will be justifiably proud."

The cowboy led them across the lawn to a statue of an old-fashioned nineteenth-century soldier, cast in bronze, standing on top of a high marble pedestal. The soldier, who had a determined look in his eyes, held a rifle in a pose of eternal vigilance. His shoulders were brushed with snow.

"This statue," the guide said, "is our War Monument. It commemorates the men who fought to establish and safeguard our state. Now I know I don't have to tell you about the man this statue represents, since he is famous throughout our city. I'm talking, of course, about Danvers's finest son, John Quintius Stevenson, the colonel who led our troops in the battle of Gloria Pass, defeating the Confederates, and securing the gold fields for the Union. Colonel Stevenson is most famous, of course, as the hero of the battle fought on the banks of our very own Choke Creek. But more about that later.

"Now," he continued. "I'd like you to turn your attention to the statue that we call 'The Closing Era.'" With a broad sweep of his hat, he indicated a bronze figure, which stood on top of a granite pedestal on the other side of the lawn. This statue showed an Indian hunter with a spear, killing a buffalo. "For centuries," the guide said, "the Indians of the plains subsisted on the buffalo, which they hunted. But eventually the great animals of the prairies were hunted to near-extinction, and the Indians moved to reservations, where they were fed by Uncle Sam." The guide winked at the students. "That's the ticket, isn't it?" he said with a grin. "Now," he added, "you may spend a few more moments looking around on your own outside, and then you may join me inside."

The guide turned and walked back to the Capitol, his spurs clinking in the damp air. Anxious to get out of the cold, most of the students straggled after him. A few of the boys, including Joey Hoffman, hung back to fight a war with the bronze soldier. Even Tyler joined in this time, dashing through the snow, shooting at the soldier with an imaginary rifle. Left on her own, Evie studied the statue of Stevenson. Was that really what he had looked like? She pulled her parka closer around her. Something was making her feel uneasy. The statue. It was making her think of the battle again. She turned her back on it and walked away.

Tyler was busy throwing snowballs at the statue of Stevenson, and she didn't want to go inside without him. While she waited, she wandered over to the statue of the Indian. It was cast in a dark-green bronze, dusted with powdery snow. Across the bottom lay a dying buffalo, its great horned head lowered to the ground, its legs splayed out in an attitude of defeat. Over him stood the Indian with one foot on the buffalo's back and one hand held high, thrusting a spear into the buffalo's heart.

The sculptor had clearly taken pains to make his work as detailed as possible. The buffalo's coat was thick and curly, his horns sharp and curved. The line of every joint and sinew was distinctly visible in his body. The Indian was similarly well defined. He was wearing an authentic-looking costume, moccasins and a loincloth, and had three feathers stuck at a jaunty angle in his hair. His naked torso, like the buffalo, was finely sculpted, with the muscles and ribs accurately portrayed. But when it came to the Indian's face, the sculptor's imagination must have failed him. It was flat and expressionless, sculpted without understanding, and even though Evie spent a long time looking into it, she could read nothing in the statue's blank, unwavering eyes.

"Hey," a voice said all at once. "Are you all right?"

Startled, Evie turned to find Tyler gazing at her with a questioning look in his eyes. How long had he been standing there? "No," she said, her face warm. "I mean, yes, I'm fine."

"You look upset."

"Upset?" She forced her face into a brittle smile. "Why?"

"I don't know." Tyler took her question seriously. "Because of the statue, I think."

"The Indian? That's impossible." Her face reddened, and she looked away, feeling distinctly annoyed with him. No, that was unfair. Not annoyed with Tyler—with herself. After all, he'd only spoken the truth. The statue *had* been upsetting her. She'd been looking for something in the Indian's face—for answers to questions she'd told herself to stop asking ages ago. She turned back to Tyler, forcing herself to concentrate on his warm mouth and tousled brown hair. "Who cares about Indians?" she said playfully. She scooped up a handful of snow and threw it at him. And then screaming in delight, she dashed up the hill, letting him chase her the entire way.

They joined the group just as the last student slipped through the bronze doors and into a grand lobby, decorated with columns and pilasters, a carved plaster ceiling, and rose-colored marble walls. The guide took a moment to point out the lobby's features, then took them on a tour of the rest of the building, down one sweeping corridor after another, up and down staircases with shiny bronze railings and balustrades. Along the way he explained the legislative bodies that met in the building, the state committees and judicial courts. Tyler and Evie walked naturally together, side by side, close enough that they occasionally touched, shoulders, hips, hands. *As if they belonged together*, Evie thought, with a warm rush of pleasure. And they didn't have to be as overtly obvious as Ella and Jack, who hung together at the back of the group, their arms around each other's waists, studied looks of disdain on their faces.

The guide took them to the Hall of Presidents and past a marble statue, which depicted the founding trio of their state: a homesteader, miner, and cowboy. He showed them the plaque in the floor which marked the spot that was 5,280 feet above sea level—a mile high. The boys made a point of jumping up and down on the marker or scuffing it with their shoes, but the girls tiptoed across it in awed silence.

"Our State Capitol building," the guide told them, "is a full quarter

mile around. The materials used to build it are native to the state: granite, sandstone, marble, and onyx." On his way down one of the staircases, he paused to rest his hand on a lead ball, which was fixed to the
top of a newel post. The ball was roughly fist-sized and had a gleaming,
pockmarked surface like a small moon.

"This, boys and girls," the guide said, his voice hushed and filled with
portent, "is an actual cannonball, taken from the Battle of Choke Creek.
I've heard people say that touching it will bring you luck. Now, I don't
know about that," he added with a sly grin, "but I don't see where it
can hurt." He rubbed the cannonball vigorously with his palm. All the
students who filed after him did the same. When his turn came, Joey
Hoffman rubbed both his hands on the lead ball in an ostentatious
display. Even Jack and Ella, Evie noticed, made a point of touching the
cannonball, the bored looks on their faces softened now by smiles. Tyler was modest in his approach, touching the sphere lightly with his
hand. But just as Evie reached for it, her hand froze.

"Aren't you going to touch it?" Tyler asked.

"Maybe next time." She was feeling uneasy again, and light-headed,
too, a pain throbbing behind her eyes. Touching the cannonball would
only make it worse. She slunk past it with her hands in her pockets,
even though she knew her behavior wasn't normal. And even though
she knew Tyler was watching her with a puzzled look in his eyes the
entire time.

The students followed the guide through a narrow oak door and,
counting out loud, up the ninety-three steps of a winding stone staircase to the observation platform that circled the dome. It was much
colder outside, and snowing harder. The students were freezing, their
faces reddened, their hair whipping in the wind. But the view excited
them, and no one asked to go inside. They darted about the platform,
pointing out the landmarks of the city, their homes and their school.
Evie showed Tyler her house and the barn where she kept Bird. She
made out the shape of her old school and the line of the creek, cutting through the city. In the distance the foothills, coated with snow,
crouched beneath the back ranges, whose tips were hidden by clouds.

To the north lay the industrial center of the city, the stockyards and railroads that brought cattle to the slaughterhouses. Even in the cold Evie could smell the packing houses, the familiar salty-sweet scent that permeated the city whenever the wind blew from the north. At least she felt better outside; the cold air had cleared her head. She shivered deliciously in the wind, using it as an excuse to huddle up to Tyler.

"Here," he said, putting an arm around her and drawing her close. "Is that better?" She nodded happily because it was. He was so warm—she couldn't believe it. She could even feel his warmth through his coat. It was an amazing feeling, comforting and exciting all at once, just one more amazing thing she was learning about Tyler Foley. And she liked everything she learned.

"Now, ladies and gentlemen," the cowboy guide said. "If I could have your attention, please." The teacher clapped his clipboard and the students quieted down. "I would like you to take a moment to think about what this place looked like in the days before the pioneers came. See that road there?" He pointed to one of the city's central avenues. "And that building?" He indicated a flat stucco structure.

"That's the Danvers Dry Goods Store," one of the girls said. "My mother shops there."

"Of course she does," the guide said, smiling his approval. "How many of you boys and girls live in houses that you can see from this dome?"

Most of them raised their hands.

"And how may of you have fathers that work inside the city?"

Again a show of hands.

"How many of you get your heat and light from the public service utility? Your food from one of our local grocery stores? How many of you have parents who keep their money in one of our local banks?"

The students were excited, chattering again, and the guide gave them a moment to quiet down. "I would like you to imagine what it was like to live here before there were any of those things," he said finally. "Before there were banks, grocery stores, houses, and roads. I am talking, of course, about the settlers, the first people who came to this place, back when there was nothing, just a barren, empty wilderness. Imagine, if you can, how difficult their lives were. Think about how hard they worked, and against what odds, to create everything you see here.

"They said it couldn't be done," the guide continued. "Important men of the time, like Daniel Webster and the great explorer Stephen Long. They doubted anyone could settle this place. They despaired of ever putting it to use. They said the land was worthless, a vast wasteland of whirling winds and shifting sands, inhabited by wild savages and beasts. They said it would never support human life. They called it the Great American Desert. They warned people away.

"But the pioneers didn't listen. They came anyway. And so," he concluded, "think for a moment about the debt we owe them. A debt which we can never truly repay." His voice grew thick with emotion. "It is not, perhaps, too much to say we owe them our lives."

All the students were silent now, gazing at the cowboy. Even Ella and Jack seemed to have been taken in by his story and for once were listening respectfully to everything he said. The cowboy guide let them stay that way for a time, adding to the reverence of the moment. Then he gathered himself together again. "If you will follow me back inside, I will tell you more about the pioneers and their brave deeds, which still inspire us today."

The guide led the group back inside, down the winding stairs. The students followed one by one. Evie and Tyler were among the last to leave the platform. Evie stood by the dome, lost in the view of the prairie, which unfolded to the east in a flat white haze. Her thoughts had drifted to the Swale ranch, and despite herself, she found herself closing her eyes, listening to the sound the wind made as it whipped about the dome.

"Evie?"

She opened her eyes and found Tyler looking down at her.

"Are you okay?"

She wasn't okay—her headache had come back, and now she felt frightened, too, just as she had that day on the playground. But that was the last thing she wanted Tyler to know. "I'm fine," she said, speaking the words fiercely, as if just saying it would make it so. "Really, I am." Just to prove it to him, she reached up and kissed him. As her mouth met his, she felt his amazing warmth flow into her, working its way from her lips to her toes. The kiss took them both by surprise, and they paused to gain their bearings and find their breath.

"We better go," Tyler whispered, his eyes soft and shining.

Evie gave Tyler her hand and followed him down the stairs. Being with Tyler Foley, she was rapidly discovering, had its own rewards. Her headache was receding again, along with her fears. When they reached the bottom, they discovered they had been left behind. The last of the students had disappeared, and all that was left of the group was the sound of their voices, echoing down a hallway. Suddenly giddy and giggling, they ran hand in hand after them, catching up just as the cowboy guide led them into a new place.

Twelve

"This is the rotunda," the guide said, as he led them into the new room, "the exact center of our Capitol. It is, you might say, the heart of our city, the very soul of our state."

The rotunda was a perfectly round chamber situated beneath the dome. One by one the students followed the cowboy inside, falling into a hushed silence as if they had entered a cathedral. Evie and Tyler caught their breath, their laughter dying away. They craned their heads and looked up, past the ornate marble columns with gilded tops, past the coffered curved walls and elegantly turned balconies, to the dome itself, which rose impossibly high above them, a dizzying arc of vast, inspirational space.

Evie's heart rose in her throat as if drawn to the vaulted heights. The feeling she had was of excruciating humbleness: how small they all were in the face of such majesty! She also found herself overcome with pride in this wonderful place—her State Capitol—and in everything it represented, her city, and her state. Now, for the first time, she understood how much her dark preoccupation with the past had led her to ignore the pleasures of the present. The guide had said the building was a living remembrance, a testimony to all the people who had come before her. *He meant people like my great-great-grandfather*, she thought with a rush of awe. Asa Glauber had been one of the settlers the guide talked about on the dome platform, a man who came to Danvers armed with an unwavering belief in the ability of newspapers to civilize the wilderness.

The thought brought a renewed sense of warmth flowing through her, as if she were kissing Tyler again. *Maybe it would be all right after all*, she thought with a sudden surge of optimism. Maybe it would even be, as Tyler said, *cool*, to run *The Rocky Mountain Sun*, and make her mark on Danvers as well. She stepped closer to him, smiling up at him, intensely grateful to have him beside her, so they could share in this moment together.

"Take a minute," the guide said, "to explore this room on your own. When you are finished, we will gather together to hear the story that makes this such a special place."

The students broke off into groups of two and three to view the chamber, tiptoeing about, their voices hushed and whispering. The apex of the dome was embedded with windows, which captured the light and concentrated it, so that it seemed brighter inside the rotunda than out. But it was a cold light, and the room was cold, too, rent by drafts as the wind found cracks in the walls and slipped through, swirling across the stone floor. Evie huddled closer to Tyler to stave off the chill, her hand tucked securely in his.

Slowly they circled the room. The walls of the chamber were divided into sections, each one partitioned from the others by a column. In all there were eight panels, each one containing a mural. A cursory glance at the panels told Evie that they had all been executed by the same painter. The colors were bright and bold, the figures almost cartoonish in their simplicity, giving the murals a childlike quality. But the overall effect, especially when viewed from a distance, was charming and surprisingly powerful.

There was an order to the murals, too, Evie realized gradually, as she and Tyler walked past them. Viewed properly, they told a story—the story of Danvers. In the first mural, the painter showed the landscape that the city had risen from, the mountains and the plains, pristine and unpeopled, with the creek flowing gently to the river. In the second picture, two prospectors squatted by the creek, shaking wide metal pans in the water; in the bottom of one could be seen a distinctive gold sparkle. The next painting showed a small mining camp resting at the .

confluence of the river and the creek, with smoke rising peacefully from the chimneys of the cottonwood cabins.

In the fourth panel the mood of the paintings changed. The sky turned dark, and the sun was obscured by threatening, thunderous clouds. This mural showed a street scene—the main street of the mining camp depicted in the previous painting. On either side stood simple frame stores with false two-story fronts. In the middle was a wagon, pulled by two dark horses, carrying the corpses of a family—father, mother, three small children—their faces bleached white in death, their throats gashed, their heads lying in awkward angles to their bodies.

The Wyngates, Evie thought. *They're telling the story of Choke Creek.* Sure enough, the next painting showed a group of men and horses standing on a low bluff overlooking the creek. At the center of the picture, Stevenson stood beside his horse, a tall man in resplendent nineteenth-century Army uniform. He had penetrating eyes, a full beard, broad shoulders, and a thick, muscular chest. Gathered around him were other men in uniform, some on horseback, others on foot like their commander, all carrying rifles like the one on the War Monument. Still other men, at the edges of the group, wore the garb of clerks and farmers and miners, and held antiquated-looking muskets or simple pitchforks and rakes. With one hand the colonel gestured towards the creek bottom, where a sleeping Indian village lay, smoke rising lazily from the tops of the tipis.

In the sixth mural a pitched battle raged in the creek bed, the soldiers and citizen-volunteers against a band of heavily armed Indian warriors. The painter had divided the scene into several groups, in various poses of victory and bloody defeat. At the center of the painting Stevenson stood like a giant, holding his rifle aloft like a lance, urging his men on.

In the seventh painting a cowboy sat easily on horseback gazing over a herd of cattle, which grazed peacefully on the plain.

And in the final mural a modern-day city could be seen rising in the shadow of the mountains, with the State Capitol building at its center, topped by the sparkling gold dome. "Danvers," a plaque at the base of this mural read, "The Princess of the Plains."

"You will remember what I told you," the guide said, gathering the students around him, "when I first met you outside on the lawn. This building, and especially this place—" he swept an arm around the rotunda "—is a living monument, a testimony to who you are and where you come from. Nothing in that history is more important—more key, I might say—than the Battle of Choke Creek." His voice took on a singsong, storytelling tone. "I know I don't need to tell you about the brave deeds of Colonel John Quintius Stevenson, and his band of hardy men. But imagine yourself for a moment with them, on that cold November morning, over one hundred years ago, on that bluff by Choke Creek, overlooking the tipis of that Indian village."

The students gathered in closer to the guide, listening with rapt faces to his words. Even the teacher seemed lulled by the guide's tale. He stood at the back of the group, a dreamy look on his face, holding the clipboard limply by his side. Standing close to Tyler, feeling warm and protected, Evie settled in to hear yet another version of the story she knew so well. After all, it was only the normal thing to do. But as she listened, she frowned.

"What's wrong?" Tyler whispered.

Evie shook her head. "Nothing."

"Are you sure?"

"Yes. Just wait here." She returned to one of the paintings, the one that depicted the cavalry gathered on the bluff above the sleeping Indian village. Something was wrong. Her frown deepened as she studied it. Suddenly, just like that, the answer came to her. "It's wrong," she said to herself. Then more loudly, "The picture's wrong."

The rest of the students turned and looked at her. In the middle of telling his story, the cowboy guide hesitated. "Yes, young lady," he said brightly. "You have a question?"

"It's not a question. It's the painting. It's wrong."

"Wrong—?" The guide gave her a puzzled look. "I don't think I understand."

"The bluff," Evie said, pointing to it. "It's nowhere near that big. And the creek flows the other way."

The cowboy guide fiddled nervously with his bolo tie. "I don't know about that, I ... "

The teacher studied her with a curious look on his face, his clipboard tucked beneath his arm. "What is it, Eve? What exactly are you trying to say?"

"The picture's wrong." There was a note of exasperation in her voice. "I know because I've been there. I've seen it."

"You mean the battlefield?"

She nodded. "Yes."

The teacher pursed his lips. "You've heard of artistic license?"

She shook her head.

"It means artists can change things when they need to, to capture the essence of what they are trying to say. It doesn't matter if some of the details are wrong, as long as the message of the picture is correct." He studied her a moment longer. "Okay?"

"Okay." Evie nodded, but with a doubtful air.

"Okay, then." The teacher turned back to the guide, speaking briskly. "If you will continue, please."

The guide took a deep breath and gave the group an uncertain smile. "Well, boys and girls, as I was saying, the night before it had snowed, and as Colonel Stevenson led his men to the enemy village ... "

Evie didn't rejoin the group, even though she knew Tyler was looking towards her in a puzzled way. She sunk her hands deep into the pockets of her parka and stared glumly at the painting. It was wrong. She didn't care what the teacher said. If the artist didn't know enough about the battlefield to make it right, he shouldn't have bothered painting it at all.

Besides, it wasn't just the one painting; it was all of them. They were *all* wrong. She was sure of it. If she took the time to study them, she was certain she would find errors everywhere. She wandered about the room, examining the murals closely, one after another. But what was it? What else was wrong?

Meanwhile, outside the snowstorm had finally ended. The last cloud was swept away, and the sun came out, shining brilliantly through the windows of the dome. The light was so intense, Evie had to shield her eyes with her hand to protect them from the glare. In front of her the bright colors of the paintings swam in the shimmering light as if the figures had come to life. But the temperature had dropped; she felt the room grow colder, seized in an icy grip. People always said it got colder when it stopped snowing; this must be what they meant. She shivered, and when she breathed out, her breath misted before her face.

The wind was blowing harder now, too; it gusted through the rotunda in freezing drafts that were so strong, they buffeted her from side to side. Somehow it was thundering. How could that be? There were no clouds. But it was undeniable; the noise was so deafening, the floor shook. And it was cold—she was so cold—she pulled her hood up, her teeth chattering, the tips of her fingers turning blue. Didn't they see how cold it was? Didn't they feel the wind? She looked at the other students, but they were still standing blithely together, listening to the cowboy guide's story, while she could hardly hear him, his words were lost in the thunder, like in a gale.

Tyler was talking to her, too, she could see his lips moving, but she couldn't hear him over the wind. He was walking to her, but he was so far away, he'd never make it, the wind was too strong. And it was cold, so cold, she could hardly bear it. Her head was pounding again, the pain worse than before, throbbing behind her temples. Everything shimmered in the light and swayed, buffeted by the wind. The whole room moved like the deck of a ship in a storm. It made her sick—she felt seasick—and dizzy. Then suddenly the light flickered. Darkness came in from the edges of her sight and worked its way in, growing closer, until finally it was complete, and she saw nothing more.

The darkness lasted forever or for only a very short time. Seconds or days. She never knew. As long as she was in it, time went on without her, just as she had no idea where she was. All she knew was that when she finally heard her teacher's voice, she was glad. "Stand back," he said, "give her air. Get back, I say, she needs air." His voice was loud and commanding, the kind of voice that was used to giving orders and seeing them followed. She opened her eyes and looked happily into his face, this commanding man, who was going to fix everything now and make it right.

Then she realized that she was looking *up* at him and he was bent over, looking *down* at her, and that meant she must be lying on the floor, while he was standing over her. Sure enough, when she focused her eyes, she realized she was on the floor. There, in the distance above her, was the dome. Somehow the storm had come back, and the sky was grey and cloudy as before. The air had warmed up; her breath no longer misted in front of her face. But her head hurt, the back of her head hurt a lot, and as she reached up a hand to touch it, she groaned. "What happened?"

"You fainted."

"I—what?" As she struggled to sit up, something warm gushed on her face.

"Fainted." He pressed his handkerchief to her nose. "Your nose is bleeding, and you banged your head on the floor when you fell, although luckily you had your hood on, or it might have been worse." He studied her. "Don't try to sit yet. Just lie there."

She lay still, holding the handkerchief to her face, probing gently with her fingers at the back of her head, where already she could feel a lump, bruised and tender, emerging. The rest of the students had stepped back as they were ordered to, but they still hovered in a group around her, staring down at her. Tyler was there, too, looking at her with worried eyes. She groaned and glanced away.

She felt so foolish. What had she done? She'd never fainted before. And she'd never, ever had a nosebleed. It was all so strange and confusing. She needed to get up, to make sense of it. She struggled to sit up again, and this time the teacher let her, steadying her with a secure hand under her arm. When she was able to stand, he led her to a bench by the wall and sat her down. "Okay now?"

She nodded. "Okay."

The teacher studied her a moment longer. "Keep your head back and sit there until it's time to go."

Obediently she tipped her head back against the wall. Meanwhile a buzz of voices had come into the air. The worst of the emergency was over, and as the tension eased, the students laughed and chattered. The boys got rambunctious and elbowed one another in the ribs, having shoving matches.

"Enough of that," the teacher called out. He waited for the group to settle down. Then he glanced at his watch and turned to the guide. "We have only a few more minutes, so if you'll just finish quickly, please."

The guide nodded. He looked decidedly nervous now. He was sweating, and he took a bandana out of his pocket to mop his forehead. Then he took up his story again, speaking at a rapid pace.

Evie didn't listen. She couldn't. Her head hurt too much. Anyway, she still felt sick, queasy and dizzy. At least the bleeding had stopped. She could sit up now without the handkerchief. Tyler gazed at her with a questioning look on his face, but she shook her head, warning him away. She wasn't ready to talk to anyone yet. She sank her head in her hands and closed her eyes.

Meanwhile the guide proceeded quickly through his story, omitting nothing, his voice high and strained, like a record playing too fast. Soon he reached the part where Colonel Stevenson ordered the charge against the enemy warriors. "And so," he said, "the cavalry, poised on the bluff, mounted their steeds, and with the volunteers standing in reserve, galloped towards the creek, their banner flying, and ... "

That's when it came to her, everything at once, the things she'd seen when she fainted. No, what she'd seen *before* she fainted, while the light shone so brightly, the room was so cold, and the wind blew with such a thundering force. As the memory came to her, she shuddered and cried out, her voice full of anguish and horror.

"It wasn't like that." She pulled herself to her feet, unsteady, facing the guide, her voice ringing in the room. "The battle wasn't anything like that—or like these paintings." She came closer to him, waving a hand at murals. "It wasn't just warriors who died that day, it was women, and children, old people, too. And they weren't even armed. They were murdered. He did it." She pointed to the portrait of the colonel.

"Stevenson and the rest of them. Afterwards, they went to the bodies, and ... " She broke off, her face deathly pale, her eyes fixed and bright.

The guide wavered between the teacher and Evie, a frozen smile on his face.

"Now, Eve," the teacher said. "You've had a bad shock, and I'm sure you're upset."

He took her arm and tried to lead her back to the bench. But she shook him off, her eyes on the cowboy guide. "You're not telling the story right."

The guide glanced nervously about the room, mopping his forehead.

One of the girls stepped out of the crowd. "My great-grandfather fought at Choke Creek. Are you saying he was a murderer?"

"My grandmother's uncle was killed there," Joey Hoffman said, fixing Evie with an accusatory glare. "Her father almost died. He wouldn't do anything like that."

Another voice spoke up in the group. "None of them would."

"She's crazy." Ella said, looking at her with disdain. "She freaks out like this all the time. I've seen her do it before."

"Crazy as a loon."

"Loony."

"Loony tunes."

They were all speaking at once now, staring at her in embarrassment or disgust.

"Now, now, enough of that." The teacher banged on his clipboard. "I said enough!" His voice echoed in the room, bringing a reluctant silence in its wake. He pinned the students with an angry gaze, glaring at each and every one of them in turn. Then he turned to Evie. "You," he said. "Sit back down. I don't want to hear another word from you. Understand? Not one more word." He waited until she had taken her seat again as ordered. Then he turned to the guide. "And you. Get on with it. Finish up—for God's sake, just get it over with, whatever you have left to say."

The guide nodded and returned to his spiel, speaking in such a rapid, high-pitched voice, no one understood a word of what he said. But the students didn't stop him, and they didn't care. They just stood awkwardly in their places, waiting for it to end.

Evie pressed the heels of her hands into her eyes, pushing until it hurt, to keep the tears away. When she looked up again, she found Tyler gazing at her, his face hurt and confused. She stifled a sob and turned away. What was the point? She had no chance with him. She wasn't normal, and she might as well get used to it, because she never would be. She tipped back her head and gazed up at the dome, but it had lost its magic now, and she saw it for what it was. There was nothing majestic or awe-inspiring about it at all. It was just a pretense—the glory and the gold—a huge wasted effort, containing nothing.

Thirteen

That night the last of the storm finally passed over and the sky cleared. As darkness fell, the creek froze, the thin line of water turning to a ribbon of gleaming ice in the sand. Then the ice disappeared, vanishing without a trace beneath drifts of blowing snow. Inside the house, the furnace was on, and Jase basked in its warmth. He was sitting at the kitchen table, working in a contented way on his weekly editorial, when the doorbell rang. Startled, he looked up. "Evie?" But Evie was in her room and didn't answer. He cast a last, lingering glance at his work, then went into the hallway and turned on the porch light. When he opened the door, an elderly woman greeted him on the other side, blinking owlishly in the sudden light.

There was something judgmental in the way she looked at him—something accusatory—and naturally he began to apologize. "I'm sorry. I left the light off. I wasn't expecting anyone."

Apparently she had little interest in his apologies. She was a small woman, not much larger than a child, with a sharp, birdlike face, and pronounced widow's hump. But as she spoke, she drew herself up so straight, the widow's hump all but disappeared.

"Mr. Glauber?"

"Yes?"

"I'm Virginia Hoffman. My grandson Joey goes to school with your daughter, Eve."

"Hoffman." Jase mulled it over, trying to place the name. "You mean like Hoffman Bakeries?"

He ventured a smile. In his experience people usually liked it when he succeeded in placing their name, especially when it was an old, venerated Danvers family name like Hoffman. Mrs. Hoffman would have none of that. "That," she said, "has nothing to do with it."

"No, of course not." Jase's smile faded. Light glinted off the frozen drifts in the yard with a pale blue glow. Now and then a gust of wind swirled the fallen snow into a fine mist, which hovered briefly in the air before subsiding. The gusts stirred Mrs. Hoffman's hair, which was white and thinning, revealing glimmers of her pink scalp. The color in her face was similarly pink, her cheeks flushed; but that, Jase feared, had nothing to do with the wind. He decided to give it one more try. "Well, Mrs. Hoffman." He stepped to one side and held out a welcoming hand. "It's awfully cold out tonight. Won't you please come in?"

Freezing to death, apparently, was preferable to placing one foot inside the Glauber household. "What I have to say doesn't require that." She drew herself up again, pinning him with her eyes. "My grandson Joey came home from school today and said ... " She took a deep breath, as if she needed to brace herself before she could go on. "He said you're calling what happened at Choke Creek a massacre."

Jase gave her a startled look. "What?"

"At school today. They had a field trip." When he looked at her blankly, she added, "To the State Capitol. Anyway, that's not important." She waved her hand impatiently in the air. "What's important is that your daughter said innocent people died at Choke Creek."

"I'm sorry. I don't think I understand." Jase passed a hand over his face. "If you'll just slow down a minute and explain, I'm sure—"

Slowing down was the last thing Mrs. Hoffman had on her mind. "My father fought in that battle," she said, her voice rising. "He was a decent, God-fearing man. Are you saying my father killed defenseless women and children?"

Jase stared at her, uncomprehending. "Of course not."

"Are you saying my father was a monster?"

"Please, Mrs. Hoffman, I—"

"He lost his brother in that battle. And he when he came home, he had lead shot in his arm. It was still in his body when he died." It was hardly possible, but the woman managed to draw herself up even straighter. "There are other newspapers in this city. I don't need to be reading one founded on lies."

"No, of course not, nobody says—"

"You can cancel my subscription tonight." She paused to make sure he had heard her. "I don't want to find that paper on my doorstep in the morning."

Jase passed his hand over his face again. "If you would just hear me out—"

"I paid a month in advance."

Jase looked at her in stunned silence.

"Today's only the twenty-sixth. I figure that's forty cents you owe me."

"Now, let's be reasonable, I—"

"Forty cents, Mr. Glauber." She held out her hand.

Jase reached into his pocket and counted out the change.

She pocketed the money then looked up at his face. "Frankly, Jase Glauber, I'm surprised at you. I thought I could expect better of you. I know I could have expected better of your father." She turned around, her face bright and shining in its righteousness. And as she walked away, there was not one iota of relenting in her rigidly held, upright back.

Jase was still standing in the open doorway, looking after her in astonishment, when the phone began to ring. The ringing came to him as if from a long distance, working its way slowly to the forefront of his consciousness. He slammed the door shut and hurried to the kitchen, a bad feeling rising in the pit of his stomach.

"Arnie!" His face broke into a grin of relief when he heard the voice on the line. "Thank God it's you. How's that new retriever puppy of yours? Christ, Arnie, you can't imagine how good it is to hear your voice. The strangest thing just happened, and I ... "

His face fell. "Yes?"

"Oh, Arnie. Now, don't tell me that you've been caught up in this nonsense, too. Of course I know what the Battle of Choke Creek means to this city, and no, I'm not trying to dredge up old rumors and accusations ... "

"Yes, I know you need to sell cars and I know you can't do that if people don't trust you."

"We've been running ads for you—for how long now? Hell, Arnie, The Sun ran ads for your father. You know that."

"I never said that, Arnie. I would never say anything like that. Now be reasonable. You know me. Would I ever ... ?"

"Well, what does it matter what people are saying? What matters is ... "

He sighed. "Yes, I'll take care of it. And no, it's not too late to get the ads pulled out for Sunday."

He hung up the phone. The Battle of Choke Creek. Why in God's name was that coming up now? Evie said—Evie said—what? He sucked in his breath. Had that boy Eason told her after all? He shook his head. Impossible. He knew for a fact she'd stopped riding to that ranch months ago. Then it must be—the only way ...

He rushed out of the kitchen to the office beneath the stairs. With a quick glance to make sure Evie was still upstairs, he slipped into the room and pulled the books from the shelves. There was the briefcase, hidden in the back, just as he had left it the spring before. No one had touched it. He took a deep breath and put the briefcase back. Gradually the pounding of his heart slowed. It must be a mistake. Nothing more than that. He would talk to Evie, and she would explain.

The phone was ringing again, and automatically he hurried back to the kitchen to answer it. But just as he reached for it, his hand froze, hovering in the air. Once, twice, three times more the bell jangled, echoing off the tile floor. When it reached ten, he understood that it would make no difference if he didn't answer; the phone would never stop. He could feel the anger coming through the wire at him as if through a living thing. By the fourteenth ring, he felt as if the bell were sounding inside his skull, jarring his bones. He lifted the receiver and gazed blankly at it. Then he put it down on the counter and left it off the hook.

He took the stairs slowly, giving himself time to calm down. Upstairs the hallway was dark, and the door to his daughter's room was closed. He hadn't seen her all day. When he'd come home and called her down to dinner, she'd said she wasn't hungry. He'd eaten alone, frankly glad to have the opportunity to get a head start on his editorial. Now he stared at the door. There was no light beneath it, no sound from within. Seized with a sudden foreboding, he knocked. No response. He knocked again, louder this time. Then he turned the handle and pushed the door open. "Evie?"

"Go away."

The voice came from her bed, muffled by the covers. The room was dark, the shades drawn. His anxiety rose with a jolt. "What's wrong?"

"Nothing."

"Are you tired? Are you going to sleep?"

There was a moment of silence, followed by her voice, sounding thin and small. "No."

"Then you won't mind if I turn on the light." He flipped the switch, and as the light came on, he felt as if he'd flipped a switch in himself, too, pushing his anxiety away, getting it under control. He drew himself up. *No reason to be upset.* This was merely a problem, and he would solve it just like he solved every other problem that came his way. Evie sat up, her hair messy, her face puffy, her clothes in tangles. He chose not to comment on all that. *Prioritize. Get to the root of things.* These were the principles that had always served him well in crises before. He'd relied on them countless times at the newspaper, and he would rely on them now. "Joey Hoffman's grandmother came to the house tonight."

"So?" Her eyes were downcast, her face sullen.

"She cancelled her subscription to *The Sun.*"

Evie shrugged in an idle, uncaring way. "A lot of people are doing that nowadays."

It was a dig at his rivalry with *The Post.* Just that morning he'd had a meeting with the circulation director over the alarming loss of subscribers. His face reddened, and he felt himself grow angry. Then he took a deep breath and told himself to calm down. Losing your temper never helped—another principle he swore by. "You want to tell me what's going on?"

"I told you. Nothing." She lay back down in the bed and rolled over, turning her back to him.

"Mrs. Hoffman said you had a field trip today."

This brought no response.

"To the State Capitol."

There was still no answer, but her body stiffened in a stubborn way.

"Well, did you?"

"It's a stupid place."

"That may be, but still ... " The time had come for tact. He chose his words with care. "Mrs. Hoffman is under the impression that you think the Battle of Choke Creek was a massacre."

"So, what if I do?"

He bit down hard on his lip, once more reminding himself not to lose his temper. "You must have some reason."

All at once she sat up and threw off the covers. "Choke Creek, Choke Creek. I'm sick and tired of hearing about that stupid battle. It's all anyone ever talks about. Stevenson this and Stevenson that." Her voice rose with anger. "Why don't they just declare him the greatest hero that ever lived and be done with it!"

Jase fell silent, giving them both a moment to compose themselves. "Do you want to tell me what happened?"

She had grown sullen again. "You wouldn't believe me if I did."

The feeling of foreboding had returned, and a vague sense of shame. What had he been thinking? This wasn't a problem to solve. This was his daughter—his precious Evie—the person he loved more than anyone in the world. She didn't need some kind of executive decision from him. She needed his support, his guidance, and his love. He sat down and took her hand. It was cold and clammy, as if she were coming down with the flu. When he spoke again, his voice was soft and fatherly. "Why don't you try me."

She glanced at him as if she weren't sure she could trust him. Then she pushed the hair out of her eyes and lifted her face to him. "I saw it."

Her words alarmed him. Not what she said, but the way she said it, her face full of passion, her eyes burning and bright as if she'd been seized by a sudden fever. "You—what?"

"Saw it. The battle." She leaned towards him, speaking eagerly as if she'd been waiting a long time to tell him—to tell anyone—what she had experienced. "It was while we were at the Capitol. They took us to into a room that had pictures of Choke Creek. But the pictures were all wrong. Nothing in them was right. And then I realized it wasn't a battle at all, it was a massacre."

"You mean ... " He reminded himself to go slowly, to choose his words with care. "You looked at the pictures, and they were so lifelike, they seemed alive to you ... "

"No. Not the pictures." She shook her head in an impatient way. "They weren't lifelike at all. They were terrible, like cartoons. Besides, I told you, they were all wrong." A note of exasperation came into her voice. "I only realized the truth afterwards."

"After—?"

"After it started snowing, and the wind was blowing, and it got so cold—"

She was confusing him, and he shook his head as if to clear it. "You mean when you went back outside?"

"No—*inside*." She wrenched her hand away from him. "Aren't you listening to me?"

"I'm trying to, Evie, honestly I am." He looked up at her. "If you'll just explain again."

"Never mind." She stood up and went to her desk, which was a mess as usual, the books and binders and papers lying in disorderly heaps. "You wouldn't believe me anyway. No one does. They all think I'm crazy." For a moment she busied herself, straightening the books and papers, sorting them into piles, her fingers flying through the mess. Then she stopped, her hands frozen at her sides as if she'd suddenly realized how futile it was, as if she'd never be able to fix it—she'd never be able to fix *anything*. She flung her hand across her desk, sweeping the books and papers to the floor, where they scattered about her, helter-skelter.

Her hair had fallen back into her face, but she ignored the tangles, staring out at him from the middle of the mess she'd made, her body shaking like a sapling in a storm. "You do, too, don't you? You think I'm crazy, even though you never say so."

His voice rose. "You know that's not true."

"Then what's happening to me?" She burst into tears.

He couldn't bear to see her cry. He never could. He put his arms around her, feeling helpless and unbearably awkward. "There, there." He led her back to the bed and sat down beside her, letting her cry herself out with her face pressed against his chest. "Shh, shh," he said, soothing her with little pats. "Nothing's happening to you. You're fine. You're just tired and overwrought. It's hard starting a new school."

"You said I'd like it." Her voice took on an accusatory tone. "You said things would be better there."

"And they will be. You'll see. You just have to give it time."

She sniffed but didn't answer.

"Better?"

She nodded, although he had a feeling she didn't mean it.

"Good." He gave her a moment more to settle down. "Now do you want to tell me the rest?"

She averted her eyes. "There isn't anything else."

"I see." For a moment longer he studied her, then he stood up. "Then we'll just stop talking about Choke Creek, won't we?" He gave her an encouraging smile. "Because you know I love you, and everything I do is for you."

She didn't smile back. Instead she looked up at him, her face dark and scowling. "You don't care about me."

Startled, he stared at her. "What?"

"All you care about is *The Sun*. You don't want me talking about the massacre because you know it will make people mad at you and then they won't buy it anymore."

"Evie—don't you ever—don't you dare—" His anger was rising again, and this time he let it build unimpeded—an antidote to his fear. What had he been thinking? This wasn't a problem he could solve with executive skill or fatherly charm. It was spinning dangerously out of control. "You will not talk about that battle anymore, you hear me? You won't even think about it. It's making you sick. It's making you—" He bit off the words. "You listen to me, Evie. I know what's best for you. I'm your father and I demand that you do as I say."

He surged from the room, carried on a wave of fury. Midway down the stairs his knees buckled, and he clutched the banister for support. *Dear God, what was going on with her?* He caught his breath. *What was she thinking? Was it really all happening again?*

Fourteen

One night in December Eason's squad went out on an ambush. That afternoon the lieutenant gathered the men together in the mess tent for their briefing. Squads from their platoon had been sent out on ambushes before, none of which ever amounted to anything. But this time the lieutenant swore his intelligence was reliable: a meeting that very night of Viet Cong officers—head honchos—in a village nearby. The lieutenant didn't elaborate on how he got this intelligence, or why he believed it to be true when just about every other piece of intelligence they'd gotten so far had turned out to be wrong, a mix of myths, distortions, and downright lies.

"There's only one problem," the lieutenant said, speaking in a deep and sonorous voice, a voice which, Eason suspected, he hoped would impress the men and inspire in them the respect he so sorely lacked. He was the third lieutenant they'd had, and as Page liked to point out— Page always liked to point out anything depressing—they'd only gone from bad to worse.

"Only one problem?" Liver said with a smirk to Eason. "Well, I guess we're getting off easy this time."

The lieutenant ignored this remark. He spread his map out on a table. "The problem," he continued, "is that there are two villages." He pointed solemnly to the two locations on the map. "And we don't know which one the meeting is in."

The men gathered around and studied the map as if by doing so they could make it reveal its secrets and show them which of the two villages the VC would be meeting in that night. As if they expected tiny gook figures, like ants, to emerge from the paper and swarm across the map while they watched, scurrying to their meeting spot.

The lieutenant gave the men time to ponder the situation. Then he hitched up his pants in a slow and deliberate fashion. This was a gesture which, Eason knew, like his voice, was meant to inspire respect. It was also a gesture which Eason once saw John Wayne do in a cowboy movie, and which he suspected the lieutenant learned the same way. "You men," the lieutenant said, "will conceal yourselves here, beside a trail which connects the two villages." With a flourish he indicated the spot on the map. "Get Charlie either way," he concluded triumphantly, "coming in or going out."

The lieutenant's face was flushed—he was so in love with the brilliance of his own war maneuvers. Eason looked at him and then at the other men in his squad. He had a bad feeling about this. They all did. Even Liver was silent for once, his face somber and brooding. But what choice did they have? The Duke had spoken. They shrugged and walked away.

They passed the time until dusk in their tent. For days now it had been raining, and the wooden floor of the hootch was caked with mud, the air reeking of mildew. It was coming on Christmas, and Music had somehow procured some tinsel, which he had hung from the ceiling. But in the dampness the tinsel had grown limp and bedraggled, like everything else they owned, and it didn't look festive at all, it just looked defeated. As they waited for the order to move out, Page sat on his bunk, leafing through a magazine, Music listened to the radio, and Nye gathered his gear together, assembling it with a grim precision: poncho, helmet, flak jacket, clips, canteen. But then everything Nye did was grim and precise, dating back to the days when he grimly and precisely demolished one competitor after another on the wrestling mat of his high school.

Eason had already packed and re-packed his rucksack several times, putting in everything he thought he might possibly need, trying not to think about the weight. He cleaned his rifle—which he had just finished cleaning—a second time, rubbing it down. Meanwhile Liver lay on his bunk and gazed at them with a half-smile, Olympian Zeus amused by the antics of mere mortals.

"If you ask me," Liver said to Eason, "no one can beat John Wayne."

Liver was just baiting him, and Eason knew it, but he couldn't help responding. A general argument broke out over who the greater lawman was, Marshal Kane in *High Noon* or Sheriff Chance in *Rio Bravo*. Page argued for John Wayne, but Eason steadfastly defended Gary Cooper. Nye said he would have been better than both of them, and Liver—finally tiring of the debate—said they were both fools; they should have run when they had the chance.

Music, to everyone's surprise, had the last word. He didn't like westerns, he said, because they were too violent. The other men stared at him. "How can you even think that?" Page asked.

For once Nye agreed with him. "It's downright un-American," he said, giving Music a look of disgust.

After that the argument petered out, and silence fell over the men—a silence filled with foreboding over the coming night. As Eason went back to work on his rifle, Page watched him with a thoughtful look on his face. "Cheer up, Eason," he said. "Maybe tonight you'll finally get one."

Cheer up? Page should talk. He was just about the most mournful person Eason had ever met. He hardly ever smiled, and the only time Eason had heard him laugh was when they had the buffalo rodeo. Page, Eason thought, would probably manage to be depressed the day he went back home—already longing for the shithole he'd left behind. But Eason didn't say this. He just concentrated on his rifle, taking what comfort he could from cleaning it, feeling the weight in his hands, the smooth, cool contours.

Page had caught Liver's attention, and he looked at Eason with some interest. "Yeah, maybe tonight Cowboy will finally pop his cherry."

Eason glanced at Liver then shook his head, choosing not to answer. The rifle was done, but he decided to go over it one more time, just to be sure. As he pulled it apart, he felt Nye's eyes on him. "Leave him alone," Nye said to Liver—to all of them. "Can't you see he's already thinking about it?"

As they left camp, rain sifted down from a silvery sky, which grew steadily darker as night approached, as if it were tarnishing. For a time they marched alongside a river through mazes of elephant grass and bamboo. The grass was tall, towering high over their heads, parting in waves as they passed through it, so Eason felt as if he were tunneling through water. Behind him the grass closed up, knitting itself seamlessly back together again as if he had never been there.

The land was hilly, studded with small valleys that ran between thickly wooded slopes. In time they left the river and turned into the woods, making their way up and down the hills, through a dense undergrowth of heavy brush and tangled vines. The air was damp and cloying and had an unpleasantly fetid scent. It caught in Eason's throat, making him feel short of breath. But then he'd been short of a lot of things since he'd come to Vietnam—things like hot showers, decent food, confidence, and peace of mind—so why shouldn't his breathing suffer, too?

"Ready for another night in Indian Country?" Liver said.

"Whoo—whoo," Page answered, but his voice was listless, and Eason could tell his heart wasn't in it. None of them wanted to go. Eason wished Liver would stop calling it Indian Country—just hearing the words made him feel tired and weighed down, as if someone had just added twenty pounds to his rucksack.

He was tired of everything, especially tired of the way the men teased him, calling him Cowboy, saying *Whoa there, Cowboy, where's your horse?* They never tired of making bad jokes at his expense, asking him about the mares on his ranch and what he did with them late at night when he was all alone. Nye had perfected a galloping sound that he made by slapping his hands on his thighs, and he launched into it whenever Eason came by. *High ho, Silver!* he chanted. *Away!*

But Eason had to admit, Nye was right about one thing. He was thinking about it. It was all he ever thought about nowadays. He was the only man in the squad who hadn't killed yet—the only one, that is, except for Music, but Music didn't count, because he didn't want to. Lately Music had become a pacifist. He wore a peace symbol on his helmet, listened to Bob Dylan and Joan Baez, and flashed the peace sign at everyone he saw. This behavior enraged Liver, who told Music that he couldn't be in the Army and be a fucking peace lover at the same time. But Music just smiled his dreamy smile and said, "Peace, brother." And for once Liver was left speechless, holding his rage inside.

Liver was the first of them to get a confirmed kill—two VC gunned down in the trees when they were dropped in a hot LZ. He still carried the proof of it, four ears, which he wore around his neck on a string, the crumpled pieces of flesh bouncing against the bare skin of his chest like slightly rotten, dried fruit. Nye was next, taking out a gook in a tunnel. Even Page got a sniper once while they were out on patrol, although for days afterwards it only made him even more mournful than before.

That left Eason. "Hey, Cowboy," Liver said now, turning to him with a grin. "What's it like to be a virgin?"

Eason refused to answer. He couldn't spare the breath. Anyway, Liver was right to taunt him—more right than he knew. What would Liver think if he knew the truth? If he knew, for example, that a few nights earlier while Eason was on guard duty, he'd watched a dark figure melt out of the darkness of the woods and move towards the perimeter of the camp. For ages it seemed the figure stood just outside the wire, locking eyes with Eason, while Eason looked back at it, his mind numbly trying to make sense of what he saw. And then it faded back into the darkness and disappeared.

Ever since Eason had left the coast, he'd been plagued by nightmares, by a recurring dream in which he was back home riding his horse across the plain. As he came to the bluff where once Stevenson had battled the Indians, he spied a Viet Cong soldier, standing in the creek. The soldier was in clear view, in range. With great eagerness Eason dismounted from his horse, raised his rifle to his shoulder, steadied himself as he had been taught, and took aim. Meanwhile the Viet Cong soldier waited for him to fire, gazing at him with a bemused look in his eyes, making no effort to fight back or flee.

Just as Eason squeezed the trigger, he realized something was wrong. He looked down at his rifle and discovered it wasn't a rifle at all. It was his BB gun, the one that had been given to him when he was just a boy. The BBs sputtered a few feet away and dribbled across the ground. The enemy soldier put his hands on his hips, reared back his head, and with a mocking smile on his lips, roared with laughter. The laughter was still ringing in Eason's ears when he awoke, his heart pounding, his stomach clenched, and his body bathed in a cold sweat.

Now as he followed Liver and the other men through the woods, Eason's fingers tightened on his rifle. He wished they would stop so that he could sit down and check it out again, take it apart one more time, just to make sure it was clean and in working order. And then he shook his head. That was nonsense. There was nothing wrong with his rifle. He knew it, because there never was.

As the day waned, the men made slow but methodical progress through the woods. At last they came to the trail the lieutenant had indicated on the map. It passed through the hills, between two valleys which contained the villages, one a klick or so through the jungle to their left, the other a similar distance to their right. They spread out along the trail and dug in for the night. Eason flattened himself behind a sodden embankment of earth which ran below the trail. He stifled one last urge to take his rifle apart and check it, then propped it up, made sure he had a good view of the trail, and waited.

Soon the sun set, and the last bit of light bled from the sky. The rain stopped, but the sky was still overcast, and there was no light from the moon or stars. Water dripped steadily from the trees, trickling with a damp stickiness from his poncho to his neck. The air had a foul smell, the odor of jungle rot and decay. There was no wind, and the steady patter of falling water was all he heard.

In time the night deepened, and the darkness became so thick, Eason could no longer make out the trail. Instead he felt, more than saw, a lessening in the darkness, a hint of emptiness, which let him know it was there. He stared towards it, his fingers grasping the rifle. From the darkness to his left came a chuckle and then a low, singsong voice. "Cowboy's gonna get him some."

"Shut up, Liver," a voice hissed to his right. It was Nye, speaking up for Eason again. His tone was amiable but carried the hint of a warning. Liver stifled a curse, then quieted back down. Eason returned to his vigil, his shoulder pressed firmly against his rifle. If only Liver knew how much he wished he were right.

He got his first gun—the BB gun of his dreams—for his birthday when he turned nine. A few days later he was carrying it under his arm, walking down the creek bed with Billy and Dane, his two best friends from school. It was early in the morning, a Saturday in late March. The last of the winter snows had come in February, and now the ground was bare and brown with patches of snow left only in the hollows. The creek was still frozen, but lately the days had turned spring-like and warm, and here and there melted water ran beneath the ice. Eason liked the way the running water looked, the way the brittle, icy surface magnified the tiny waves and ripples in the stream, making a pleasing, rapidly changing pattern. He walked carefully around the ice, wishing to leave it intact, but Dane and Billy indulged themselves in a different kind of pleasure. They ran and jumped and stomped on the ice, just to feel the joy of it breaking beneath their boots and to hear the sharp, crackling sound.

Now and then the boys stopped and took turns shooting target practice with the gun. They took aim at pieces of driftwood and outcroppings of rocks. They shot off the BB gun then backed up a few yards and shot again, testing their accuracy at a distance. They looked with satisfaction at the splatters of dirt the BBs made when they reached their target and listened happily to their hollow pocking sound. Then they walked up close and examined the damage they had done, studying critically the holes in the driftwood, the dents and chips in the rocks.

Overhead the sky was cloudless, the sun strong and warm on Eason's face. In the distance a herd of his father's horses stood sleepily in the sun. Nearby a pair of black-billed magpies flew back and forth from the limbs of a cottonwood, their bodies flashing black and white in the clear light, their wings shimmering with a faint blue iridescence that was followed by the green sheen of their long, streaming tails. The harsh croaking sound of their calls echoed through the thin air.

The boys marched farther down the creek, Dane in the lead, followed by Eason with the BB gun, then Billy in the rear. After a while they came to a place where the creek bottom was marked by what appeared to be a deep cylindrical hole. Dane stopped and held up his hand, bringing the march to a halt. He bent down on one knee and studied the hole, frowning with concentration, peering into it at all angles. Then he stood up and said with an air of satisfaction, "It's a prairie dog burrow. I'm going to get me one."

Eason knew it wasn't—prairie dogs never burrowed into the bottom of the creek. Besides they lived in colonies, never alone. A snake might live in there, or a mouse, but most likely it was nothing, just a random hole, caused by wind or rain. He also knew there was no point in arguing about it with Dane. Dane never listened to anyone once he'd made up his mind. Anyway Eason liked the feeling of being on a hunt, even if it was only an imaginary one. There was something to be said for the idea of a kill, for the prospect of a real, honest-to-goodness death at the end of their efforts, instead of just a pockmark in a piece of driftwood or a chip in a rock.

The boys fell to the ground and flattened themselves on their bellies behind a low rise of earth just outside the creek bed. Dane took the BB gun and leveled it at the hole. Then they settled down and waited silently, barely breathing, for the prairie dog to appear.

Minutes passed. At first they seemed like seconds. Then they seemed like hours. Billy was the first to begin squirming. Dane hushed him, and for a time he quieted down again. The boys concentrated on the hole as if the very fact that they wanted the prairie dog to appear would make him do so. Billy began squirming again, and this time Dane couldn't quiet him.

"He isn't coming," Billy said.

"Not with you making all that noise he isn't," Dane answered.

Eason didn't say anything. He didn't fidget like Billy, but he was beginning to get bored with the wait. He could feel his imagination failing him, and the excitement of being on a hunt that he knew was only pretend was beginning to wane.

Finally Billy stood up. "He isn't coming," he insisted, his voice flat and stubborn. "This is stupid. It's stupid to wait for something that isn't there." He kicked at the hole, scuffing dirt into it.

"Well, he isn't coming now," Dane said. "That's for sure." He gave Billy a disgusted look. Then he stood up, and Eason followed. All three boys stared down at the hole with disappointment.

"Might as well shoot it anyway," Dane said.

Dane took aim and fired at the hole. There was a splash of mud as the BBs hit, and the boys watched it scatter. "I guess we can go now," Dane said. He handed Eason the gun, and they turned back home.

The boys trudged silently on the way back. This time Dane let Eason take the lead. The morning was over, and it was getting near lunchtime. They were hungry and tired from their long march, and they didn't stop anymore to fire the gun. They made steady progress, and after a while the ranch buildings came back into view, the barn and the house and the old tin-roofed bunkhouse gleaming in the sun. The magpies were flying back to the cottonwood, calling out to one another. Eason caught glimpses of their distinctive black and white shimmer as they darted through the air. There was a flurry of activity as they settled themselves down. Then all was quiet again.

Dane held up his hand. "Shh. Look."

He was pointing to the cottonwood. At first Eason didn't understand why. There was nothing special about that tree. It had always been there, for as long as he could remember. It was an ugly tree, more than half-dead—it had been struck by lightning years before—with bark that was peeling off, cracked and grey. The limbs were completely bare; even in summer they had hardly any leaves.

But Dane was still insisting. "There," he said, pointing to the tree. "See?"

At last it dawned on Eason that Dane meant the birds, the magpies. "You could get one." Dane elbowed him in the ribs. "You could do it."

"Yeah," Billy chimed in. "Get one, Eason. Do it now."

Eason looked at the boys and then back at the birds. He didn't want to shoot one. It wasn't that he cared for the magpies, but now that he was faced with the actual prospect of killing something, he felt uneasy. A memory floated into his mind, a picture of his mother in her bed after she had died. His father had tried to keep him from seeing her, but he'd snuck in when Cyrus left to use the phone. Her face was pale and drained of color, pinched and silent, real and unreal at the same time. Eason had never seen anyone—or anything—dead before. The previous spring when one of their horses had had to be put down, his father had sent him away before the vet came. But at that moment, Eason finally understood what death was, and how it brought with it contradictory feelings of fear and longing that could never be resolved.

He would never be able to explain that to Billy and Dane, even if he wanted to. Anyway he knew Dane was right. He could get one of those magpies. All he had to do was take aim and fire.

"Well?" Dane said. There was a note of impatience in his voice that bordered on contempt. "What are you waiting for?"

Eason knew what Dane was thinking. He was thinking that Eason was weak or cowardly or both. He also knew that Dane had never really liked him, even though their families had known each other for generations, and their fathers had served together in the war. The only reason Dane had agreed to come on this hike was because of the gun.

"Go on," Dane said.

"Yeah," Billy added. He didn't have Dane's contempt; he was just eager to see something happen. "Shoot'em, Eason. Shoot'em dead."

Eason raised the BB gun.

He meant to shoot the birds, really he did. But at the last moment something happened, and when he pulled the trigger, his aim—which had been deadly accurate all morning—was off. The gun fired harmlessly into the air. Startled, the birds took flight and with a raucous chorus of voices, disappeared.

"Hey," Billy said, bewildered and surprised. He turned to Eason. "What did you do that for?"

In Dane's face there was nothing but contempt, the full flowering of it. "What did you expect?" he said to Billy, his voice full of disgust. He spit onto the ground, the spittle landing at Eason's feet. "He's a Swale, and everyone knows that Swales can't shoot."

Shortly after midnight, the rain started up again, although there still wasn't any wind. Eason hunched his shoulders and pulled his poncho tighter, trying to keep the rain out of his eyes. He shifted the rifle so that it was better balanced and so that holding it would not tire his arms. As he was settling himself down again, he heard a sound. It came from his left, from deep in the woods, far down the trail. A faint rustling, the barely discernible sound of movement in the night.

"Hey, Cowboy." The whispered voice came from the same direction as the sound: Liver. "Did you hear that?"

"Yeah," Eason hissed back.

He listened intently, his body tight, his eyes peering hard into the darkness. But now there was nothing, just the sound of the rain, slipping through the leaves.

"Just spooks, I guess," Liver said. Eason heard a muffled sound as Liver laughed to himself. "Don't you worry, Cowboy," he said. "You just keep yourself ready. Anything can happen in Indian Country. Sometimes even spooks can die."

Dane says we can't shoot," he said to his father a few days later. "He says we're yellow. He says all of the Swales are. Why would he say something like that?"

They were standing in the barn aisle while Eason helped his father tend to one of the mares. The mare had an infected ear and had gotten touchy about it. Eason held the twitch, keeping her attention, while his father administered an ointment to the wound.

His father turned to him, a curious look on his face. Then he turned back to the mare. "You know better than to listen to Dane."

Well, yes, that was true, he did. But still, it didn't answer the question. Dane hadn't said that he—Eason—couldn't shoot, which was what he would have reasonably expected, given his performance with the magpies. He'd said the *Swales* couldn't shoot, as if this were a condition that affected his whole family, entire generations of it. What would make him say a thing like that?

He never did get a satisfactory answer to his question. After a while it retreated to the back of his mind, where it joined a growing list of other, similarly unanswered questions, which lingered in his thoughts as he grew up, festering like the wound on the mare's ear.

Why, for example, did the blacksmith once say to him, "Your father is a good man, Eason. You have nothing to be ashamed of there."

It was late in the afternoon, a clear fall day on which his father had sent him out to assist the farrier. He was just about to lead a newly shod colt back to its stall when he found himself wondering about the blacksmith's words. Nothing to be ashamed of *there*? As if he did have something to be ashamed of somewhere else?

Then there was his father's Purple Heart. He never did find out how his father got it—he never once told him the story of what happened to him in the war. One winter evening as Eason came in from a last check on the horses, it occurred to him to ask. His father was sitting in his chair by the fire reading the newspaper, and he didn't even look up as he spoke. "Well," he said simply, "that's water under the bridge, isn't it?"

Eason figured his father didn't want to talk about it because the memory was too painful, or because he was by nature a modest, retiring man and didn't like to dwell on his own accomplishments. But there it lingered, another unanswered question, the question of what had happened to his father in the war.

There were the Indians, of course, who came from time to time to the ranch, wanting to go out to the battlefield. Without exception, his father turned them away. Eason still remembered the time shortly after his mother had died, when his father, full of grief and rage, had turned on a pair of Indians with his grandfather's rifle—and ended up, as a result, spending the night in jail. It was the only time he'd ever seen his father turn to violence, but he never forgot it. Years later he still wondered sometimes about what lurked beneath the otherwise placid exterior of his father's face.

Eventually he grew old enough to turn the Indians away himself when they came to the ranch, although he never felt right doing it. One spring morning when he was about thirteen, he stood beside his father as a couple of elderly men came on foot up the ranch road. The air that day was sweet and fresh, one of the first warm days they'd had in ages, putting Eason in mind to ride out to the battlefield himself.

"Why don't you just let them go?" he said to his father. "It's not like they can do any harm."

"Because they have no business being there," his father answered. He gave him a long look. "If you don't understand that yet, it's time you learned."

Eason knew better than to press the issue; the tone of his father's voice was ample warning. He waited by the barn door as his father sent the Indians away. But something about the way the men looked as they walked away, their steps slow and their shoulders heavy, struck him. And he never forgot the look on his father's face—as if there were more to the story than he would say.

As the years went by, Eason noticed that most of his unanswered questions revolved in one way or another around the Battle of Choke Creek. There was the question, for example, of why Thomas Eli Eason had abandoned the battlefield for over twenty years. If he felt so strongly about protecting the site, why had he left Danvers right after the battle, returning only decades later to homestead the land? When Eason asked his father where Thomas Eli had gone in the intervening years, his father answered with complete sincerity that he had no idea. "Gone off prospecting for gold, I suppose," he said finally, "like everybody else in those days."

Then there was old lady Brem, the only child of Silas Brem, who, like Thomas Eli, had been one of Stevenson's lieutenants at Choke Creek. Silas Brem had been killed shortly after the battle, gunned down on the streets of Danvers in a murder that remained famously unsolved to that day. To her dying day Ellit Brem insisted that her father had been killed on Stevenson's orders by one of his own men. And since she had been only a baby when her father had died and had lived, a spinster, for a good ninety-three years, she had plenty of time to make her accusations known.

None of Ellit Brem's claims had ever been proven or substantiated. And yet there was the disturbing question of Stevenson's grave. It was an impressive granite tombstone, decorated with military emblems, located in one of the oldest and most fashionable cemeteries in Danvers. From time to time over the years the gravestone had been vandalized, with vile epithets such as "Murderer" or "Killer" scrawled across it with paint or scratched into the stone. Every Memorial Day the women's league decorated the military graves in the cemetery with American flags, and weeks later the other flags were still flying in the wind, but without fail Stevenson's disappeared within days.

For years people suspected old lady Brem of these desecrations, although it was highly unlikely that anyone as frail and diminutive as Ellit Brem would resort to such violent actions. When the vandalizing continued after she died, people had to admit she couldn't have been the culprit. But who was?

Another incident struck closer to home. When Eason was in the ninth grade, a new teacher was hired to teach American history at his high school. The teacher was a young man, a new arrival in the county, a recent graduate of a prestigious college back East. At first everyone congratulated the principal on having netted such a prize. But soon stories began circulating about things the new teacher was saying in the classroom. He was talking about the Indian Wars, saying it was time to take another look at them, to reconsider old assumptions and beliefs. They might as well start with the battle that had taken place in their very own backyard—in Choke Creek.

The teacher was gone by November, fired by the principal in an action that was backed by a unanimous vote of the school board. The football coach took over his job on an interim basis until a new teacher could be found. Meanwhile the firing was greeted by general acclaim in the county, by parents who agreed that they didn't want some outsider putting crazy notions into their children's heads. They wanted their American history taught right, the way it had been taught to them—the way it was in their textbooks. By the time Eason got to tenth grade, the American history teachers were adhering to their textbooks with care.

There were other, more subtle things, which Eason found equally disturbing and difficult to explain. When he was in the fifth grade, his teacher invited him to bring his arrowhead collection to class. His presentation was well received and won him back some of the respect he had lost in the incident with the magpies. But for some reason, as he showed the class the arrowheads he had gathered from the banks of the creek, he didn't feel proud. He felt embarrassed, and deeply ashamed.

One last question was so distressing, he had never broached it to anyone; he hardly even admitted it to himself. But he couldn't deny the fact that the day he rode out to the battlefield with Evie Glauber, he had been overcome by the strangest sensations. As the wind blew, she had become afraid, and for a moment he had, too. Confusing, contradictory emotions surged through his breast. And he swore he heard the sound of something otherworldly—something dangerously close to a human voice—in the wind.

Eason must have fallen asleep. He didn't remember doing so, but all at once he woke with a start. He jerked to his feet and dropped the rifle, which fell noisily to the ground, crashing through the brush.

"Whoa there, Cowboy," Liver called out to him, his voice calm and reassuring, with a hint of merriment. "You got the jitters?"

Eason's heart pounded in his throat, his breathing quick and ragged. He grabbed the rifle and stood perfectly still, listening, but heard nothing out of the ordinary in the woods or on the trail. "No," he said, finally. "Forget it." He settled himself back down on the ground.

"You bet," Liver said. He laughed. "I sure don't want to bother Gary Cooper when he's waiting for his man."

As a Boy Scout Eason worked hard on his marksmanship—moving up to a .22 rifle—and when he finally received his riflery badge, he told himself he had put Dane's accusation to rest. But he hadn't been called upon to kill anything to get the badge, not even something as innocuous as a bird. He only had to shoot targets.

He began to feel as if there were something unfinished about his world, something unanswered and undone. He felt as if the answer lay with him. No one ever told him this, not in so many words, certainly not his father, who maintained with his usual reserve that what Eason did with his life was up to him. Nevertheless, wherever Eason turned, he was met by this feeling of expectation—this feeling that something was out there, waiting for him. It settled on his shoulders like a weight, like a burden he didn't know how to bear. He began to think that the only place he could lay that burden down was Vietnam.

He'd always planned on doing a stint in the Army, ever since he was a little boy playing with toy soldiers. The military was a tradition in his family, but even if it hadn't been, he would have enlisted. He wasn't patriotic in an unthinking, uncritical way, but he believed that living in America was a privilege. His country had given many things to him, and it was only right that he give something back.

He wasn't the only one. By the time they were sophomores in high school, the boys often talked about their military futures. They drove out to the Air Force base, where they sat at the end of the runway, whooping and hollering while the jets roared overhead with their exhilarating, earth-shaking sound. Afterwards they sat in a local diner, debating the merits of this service over that, the Army or the Navy or the Marines. Billy, whose uncle was an adviser in Vietnam, planned on enlisting in the Army as soon as he graduated. Eason planned on doing the same. His father had been a Marine—in the same company as Dane's father—but Eason favored the Army. The rudimentary simplicity of it appealed to him and seemed closer to his great-grandfather Thomas Eli, who had been a simple cavalryman. Dane never said so, but Eason assumed he would go out for the Marines like his father—and like his older brother, who had joined the service the previous year.

As it turned out, Dane didn't have the chance. He had always had a mean streak, even as a small child, and he just got meaner as he got older. In the fall of their sophomore year, he was arrested for robbing a gas station. Soon after, he was sent downstate to a juvenile detention home. Dane would have to wait until he got out to join the Marines—if the Marines would still have him.

Then Billy was gone. During the winter he received word that his uncle had been killed assisting the South Vietnamese Army. The news changed him. He had always been a cheerful boy, but now he turned moody and dark. In March the first contingent of Marines—including Dane's brother—landed in Danang, and after that all Billy talked about was signing up.

"There's no point in waiting," he said to Eason. "They'll take us at seventeen if our parents sign. Besides, if we wait much longer, the war will be over before we get a chance to do our part. Those gooks aren't real fighters—they're just savages who get lucky sometimes. No better than Indians. They won't last long once they get a real taste of American firepower."

Billy's mother wanted him to wait until he'd finished high school, but he refused. The next winter, he joined up. "I'll see you over there," he said to Eason the night before he left. They were standing in the barn, Billy looking on as Eason rubbed liniment on the sore leg of a filly. The prospect of going off to war seemed to have restored Billy's good spirits. Once again he was the happy, slightly goofy kid Eason had always known. "You and me," Billy said, grinning shyly. "We'll show those dinks." He pumped a fist in the air.

That spring, with Dane gone and Billy gone, Eason worked hard around the ranch. He rode the fences, repairing strands of broken wire and splintered rails. He painted the barn and patched the tin roof of the old bunkhouse. His father's hip was bothering him again, and Eason took over the bulk of the work with the young horses, the fillies and the colts. He helped his father cull the yearlings and haul the culls to auction.

Then a letter came from Billy. He'd finally gotten his wish. He'd been sent to Vietnam.

A few days later, Eason heard that Dane's brother had come back from Vietnam. He was home, people said, wounded by a mine. They also said there was something wrong with him. No one would say exactly what it was, only that he wasn't right. Eason thought about that. He thought about Billy and all the other boys he knew who wanted to go off to war. And then he thought about the burden he was carrying. Sometimes it felt as if he were carrying the whole world.

He was still thinking about it the day Evie showed up on the ranch. The next time she came out, he took her to the battlefield. Later that afternoon, after she'd gone home, Billy's sister drove up to the house, and before she even got out of her car, Eason knew Billy had died.

He spent the rest of that day driving aimlessly through the county. When night came, he kept driving, up one dirt road and down another. He didn't bother putting on the headlights. He sped recklessly through the darkness, gravel flung backwards beneath the truck's tires, mailboxes looming dangerously close in the windshield then whipping away.

After a time he found himself driving by the Air Force base. He parked at the end of the runway and listened as the jets flew overhead in the darkness, their lights catapulting into the night like flaming stars. The noise of the engines was loud enough to feel as if it came from deep inside him, giving a voice to his anger and despair. When he left, he had a destination in mind. He drove to Dane's house and brought the truck to a stop. Dane's father managed a feedlot, and in the darkness behind the house Eason could just make out the pens, the cattle clustered together like a dark stain in the night. When he stepped out of the truck the air was pungent with the stench of manure and hide.

There was a light on in an upstairs window, and a light on downstairs. As Eason walked towards the house, he thought he caught a glimpse of movement in the upstairs window. Dane's brother, Eason thought. He couldn't be sure. The motion was there and then it was gone.

Dane's mother answered the door. She had always been a pretty woman, quiet but lively in her own way. Now her face was drawn, and her eyes were dull, her hair patchy and uncombed. "Why, Eason." Briefly light came into her eyes. She smoothed down her hair and smiled at him with some of the warmth he remembered.

Then Dane's father came to the door, pushing himself past her so that he stood between them.

"It's only Eason," Dane's mother said, worry working in her eyes. "Eason Swale. You remember him, don't you, Hyde?" She put a hand on his arm. "Eason is a friend of Dane's."

Hyde shook off her hand. As she withdrew into the shadows behind him, he looked Eason over, his voice and eyes flat. "Dane's not here."

Eason had always been afraid of Dane's father. They all had been, especially Dane, although he had never owned up to it. Hyde Culbert was a short man, squat and strong, with a thick bull's neck. He took little care with his appearance, wearing clothing stained from the cattle yards, his hair hanging thin and greasy to his collarbone. As Eason felt his eyes on him, fear seized his belly, and he was a boy of nine or ten again, not a grown one of seventeen.

"I know that," Eason stammered. "I didn't come here to see Dane." He took a breath and steadied himself. "I came here to see you."

Hyde had been about to shut the door when all at once he stopped as if he had been struck off balance. He cast an uncertain glance at his wife.

"I want to know why Dane said I can't shoot," Eason said. He paused, correcting himself. "I want to know why people say all the Swales are yellow."

Hyde turned to him with interest. He ran a hand through his hair.

"Don't," Dane's mother said. "Don't do it, Hyde. Leave the boy alone."

A light came into Hyde's eyes, a greedy look. A picture came into Eason's mind of Hyde Culbert moving with a swagger through the densely packed pens of the feedlot, randomly shocking the cattle with an electric prod, so that they bellowed and stampeded, climbing onto one another's backs in fear.

"Leave him alone," Dane's mother said again, her lips dry and her mouth working. "Let Eason go."

Hyde just smiled. "The boy asked. He has a right to know."

The next morning Eason woke early. He took the .22 rifle he still had from his Boy Scout days, saddled up a mare, and rode her to a distant field which contained a large prairie dog colony. He dismounted and hobbled the mare, leaving her to graze. Then he crept towards the colony and flattened himself behind a low rise on the ground overlooking it.

He didn't leave until he'd killed a dozen of them. He left their bodies on the ground to rot in the warm spring sunshine. Then he climbed back onto the mare and rode her home.

That afternoon, when he was finished with his chores, he told his father about Billy. He didn't tell him about the visit he'd paid to Dane's house. He just told his father that he wanted him to take him into Danvers.

On the way into town it began raining. The sky blackened, and drops of rain skittered off the windshield of the truck, creating tiny explosions of dust in the dirt on the side of the road. By the time they reached the recruiting office, the rain had stopped, but the sky was still dark, slicks of oil shining like rainbows on the parking lot.

They went inside where Eason waited while the recruiter gave his father the paper to sign. Cyrus looked at the paper and then at his son. "You don't have to do this."

"Yes, I do." Eason gave his father a long look. "I expect you know that better than anyone."

A few days later they returned to the same parking lot, where Eason boarded the bus with the other recruits. When he looked for his father, he found him framed in the bus window, standing alone on the parking lot, watching him drive away.

Now Eason huddled in the darkness by the trail, grasping the rain-slick rifle. Those prairie dogs were still the only things he had killed. But maybe Liver was right. Maybe tonight he'd get lucky.

It wasn't so much that he wanted to kill, that he was bloodthirsty or evil or seized by the passions that overcame so many of the other men: fear or anger or hatred or even simple patriotic zeal. It was just that ever since he had talked to Hyde Culbert, Eason understood what it meant to be part of a family. It meant being a part of that family's history—of its story. Hyde had told him the story of the Swales as if it were already over, as if the ending were pre-ordained, beginning with his great-grandfather, who was too cowardly at the Battle of Choke Creek to fire his gun; continuing with his grandfather, who sat out the first World War then killed himself on the eve of the Armistice; and on to his father, who—as Hyde witnessed with his own eyes—deliberately courted the "million dollar wound" that sent him home. "Everyone knows you Swales can't shoot anything," Hyde had said cheerfully that night, concluding his narrative with a triumphant grin, "except yourselves."

In one fell swoop Hyde had answered the questions that had troubled Eason for a lifetime, finally making sense of everything that had disturbed him since he was a young boy. Telling him the things that, in a strange way, he felt as if he'd known all along. But Vietnam was Eason's war—the only one he'd likely have. It was his story, and he was determined that the ending would be one of his choosing. So he waited, his ears straining into the darkness. As he listened, he heard a sound in the distance, on the trail. Someone was coming. He was sure of it this time. He willed himself to be still and silent as he waited. Meanwhile the rain increased, coming down in sheets, and the wind began to blow. Eason heard it cascading through the limbs of the trees, gusting with a terrible voice—with Billy's voice—saying, *Shoot'em, Eason. Shoot'em dead.*

Fifteen

With December came the snows. They came in earnest now, rolling in over the mountains, driven by winds that blew so hard, Evie swore sometimes it was snowing up instead of down. For days at a time the mountains disappeared, and the city vanished into a white haze. Even the gold dome of the State Capitol was lost in the foggy clouds. In between the storms the sun came out, shining on the snow with a brilliance that hurt her eyes. But it was a cold sun, and the sunlight only hardened the drifts, solidifying them into an icy crust that waited out the next storm.

Bit by bit the creek disappeared, buried by snow. The willows were gone, the cattails invisible, the cottonwoods shrouded in white. The trickle of water was nothing more than a memory now, a jagged line of ice hidden deep beneath the snow. At night when the wind blew, a fine mist rose from the frozen drifts, gleaming in the starlight. Through the mist the ghost walked, the baby in her arms. Evie saw her every night now. The phantom's dress hovered about her naked feet, only inches from the ground, layers of white on white. Her dark hair flowed behind her, stirred by the wind. Her face was haunted, filled with longing. Whenever Evie looked at her, the ghost looked back with beseeching, pleading eyes.

She couldn't bear to see it. She closed her window and drew the shades down to the sill. She couldn't bear to hear the wind anymore either, the keening, mournful sound it made as it swirled about the house, rattling the chains of the porch swing, echoing in the empty attic. She stuffed a towel under her door to keep the sound out. One day, as Ruth brought a load of clean laundry into her room, she found Evie crouched on her bed in the dark, a pillow stuffed over her head. "Good God, girl, what's wrong with you!" she exclaimed without thinking. "Have you lost your mind?" She clamped a hand over her mouth and fled the room, a frightened look in her eyes.

Ruth wasn't the only one. They all thought she'd gone mad, especially her father, although he wouldn't admit it. He blustered about the house with a false and hearty cheerfulness, insisting there was nothing wrong with her, as if by saying it, he could make it so. But there was something wrong with her, even if she didn't know what it was. She couldn't eat, she couldn't sleep, she had dark circles under her eyes, she was losing weight. When she looked in the bathroom mirror, she saw the face of a stranger. She took to brushing her teeth in the dark, feeling her way to the toilet with the lights off.

One night she fell into a fitful doze only to be awakened by a vicious nightmare. To her great shame, she discovered that she'd wet her bed. She crept downstairs in the darkness and spent hours in the laundry room, secretly washing and drying her sheets so that no one would know. But her father must have found out anyway. The next morning when she left for school, she caught him looking after her with a helpless air, grief and fear in his eyes.

School was the worst. Ever since the field trip to the State Capitol, the disdain with which Ella and her crowd regarded her had spread like a virus through the school, infecting everyone. The kinder students looked away when they saw her, averting their eyes the way people do from the crippled or blind. The rest stared at her with open contempt as she walked down the hallway, hissing in passing, *Loony. Loony tunes.*

Joey Hoffman had made tormenting her his personal mission. He took every chance to taunt her, treating her with outright scorn. One morning when she came to class, she discovered that her history book was gone. Later when she found it in the trash, Joey feigned innocence, but she knew he was the culprit; the pages were defaced with obscenities scrawled in his cramped hand. A few days later at lunchtime, as she and Bobbie were waiting in the cafeteria line, he snuck up behind them. "Hey Glauber," he said, "how's life as a weirdo?" The remark engendered laughter up and down the line, and Joey, emboldened, spun his forefinger around his temple in the universal sign for craziness. "Why don't you and the math freak go back to the nuthouse where you belong?"

Usually Evie ignored him, but this time he'd gone too far. He'd insulted Bobbie, and while she might be fair game, Bobbie most certainly wasn't. Besides, Evie didn't like the way Joey was crowding her, leaning in so close, she could see every pimple on his acne-scarred face and smell the sour odor of his breath. "You know what the worst thing about crazy people is?" she said. She dropped her voice to a menacing growl and advanced on him, step by step, a lion stalking its prey. "The worst thing is ... you never know ... what they'll do next."

She'd backed him up against the wall. With glittering eyes, she raised her hands, her fingers tensed into claws, ready to pounce. Joey's face turned white, his eyes rolled, and he gulped in fear. She couldn't believe it. He was actually afraid of her. How stupid could he be? She dropped her hands in disgust. The line erupted in laughter again—laughing with her this time, not at her—but Evie took no pleasure from it. "C'mon," she said to Bobbie, "let's go."

The two girls left the cafeteria and climbed the stairs together to Evie's locker, where Evie gave Bobbie an old orange for her lunch—all she had. "I told you not to freak out again," Bobbie said in a sad, tired voice as she peeled it. "Why didn't you listen to me?"

Evie slumped against her locker. Bobbie was right, and Evie knew it. She shouldn't have freaked out. She felt bad about the incident in the rotunda, not because of idiots like Joey Hoffman, but because of Tyler. For days afterwards she'd been too embarrassed to talk to him, and out of guilt and shame, had avoided him. For weeks she shuffled through the hallways, her eyes downcast. She even asked their history teacher to assign her to a new seat, so that she wouldn't have to sit behind him.

Then one morning when she came into class, she caught sight of Tyler chatting with a new girl, a fellow swimmer with short red curls. A few days later she saw them in the parking lot, walking arm and arm. Now whenever Evie saw them together, she felt sad, but also secretly relieved. At least she didn't have to worry anymore that Tyler would corner her, asking her to explain something she couldn't even begin to understand.

Meanwhile Bobbie had begun dating a boy who, like her, was a math whiz. One night he came over to her house so that they could do math problems together, and soon afterwards they went to the movies, with Bobbie—who'd just gotten her driver's license—behind the wheel. Bobbie, Evie understood, was adjusting to life at North High. She was growing up and moving on, while Evie hadn't even started driver's education classes yet; good to his word, Jase had refused to let her drive until her grades came up. Even Bobbie, with her freakish brilliance and poor sense of style, was *normal*. While Evie was stuck in the past, which had cast its talons into her and wouldn't let go.

It was the battle. She couldn't shake it from her mind, no matter how hard she tried. Over and over again the vision she'd seen in the rotunda replayed itself in her imagination, images too horrifying to contemplate—or forget. One minute she stood on the marble floor, studying the murals on the wall, and the next thing she knew she was staring at tipis on fire. Bullets rained down like hailstones; the air was choked with earth and lead and fire. She saw a man swing his musket like a club, crushing the skull of a toddler as casually as a melon. The bloodied stump of an arm flying through the air, trailing tatters of clothing and jagged bits of bone.

The snow was stained with blood; the creek ran red. The air was rank with smoke and the stench of burning hide. She saw soldiers slash at throats and rip through bellies, scalping the dead and dying alike. With long knives they cut off fingers to get at rings; they sliced off noses and pocketed ears. One man jigged by with a heart at the end of a stick. Another galloped past like a specter, the genitals of a woman streaming from his hat like a flag. They paraded past her with ghastly grins, shaking scrotums like trophies, swinging long hanks of dripping hair. While corpses littered the frozen ground where they fell, ghoulish fodder for wolves and dogs.

It had all seemed so terrifying to her—and so real—and when she came home she was desperate to tell Eason about it. She sat down at her desk, grabbed a pencil, and began to write him a letter. But as soon as she started, she realized she would never be able to do it. Even if she could bring herself to describe what she'd seen, he'd never believe her. He'd think she was crazy, just like the rest of them. Or worse, a liar who'd made it up out of some perverse wish to torture him.

With shaking fingers, she tore the paper to bits. What was she thinking? That she could just tell Eason that his great-grandfather—his beloved namesake, Thomas Eli Eason—was nothing more than a murderer, the brutal slaughterer of women and children? That they all were, Stevenson, the cavalry, the Danvers volunteers? She dropped her head in her hands. The whole thing sickened her. Everything her city stood for—every value and virtue it claimed to enshrine—was a lie, a shameful fraud, and no one knew it but her. The famous battle of Choke Creek was a perfidious massacre, and she didn't have a single iota of proof.

The night of the field trip her father ordered her to stop thinking about the battle, and in the weeks following, she did her best to comply. After all, it wasn't like she wanted to spend her days haunted by the dead and dying, her nights riddled by nightmares. But the harder she tried not to think about the atrocities, the more insistently they came to her mind. One January night, deep in the winter, she wandered to her window. There was the phantom, standing in the creek, her Indian-black hair flowing behind her, looking up at her with desperation as if she expected Evie to save her. "Forget it," Evie said out loud as if the ghost could hear her. She pulled the shade down tight with disgust. Didn't the ghost understand? Evie couldn't save her. She couldn't save anyone. Not even herself.

The winter made riding impossible, but Evie still went to the barn every day to groom Bird and turn him out in the paddock behind his stall for his exercise. There he stood in the harsh winter light, his back turned to the wind, staring at her with moody eyes as if the bad weather were all her fault.

One Sunday afternoon in February as she came home from the barn, she heard the doorbell ring. Her father was in the kitchen, reading through the day's thick stack of newspapers. She slipped off her boots and went to the door. On the other side stood a woman dressed all in black: black shoes, black pants, a thick black fur coat pulled up to her chin. Even her hair was dyed black as if to match. Only her lips and nails had color, a deep, shiny red. When she saw Evie, her eyes widened, and she breathed in sharply. "My God. I had no idea." She took Evie's face in her hands, pressing her cheeks. "My dear, you're the spitting image, the absolute—"

Just then Evie heard her father come up behind her. As he slipped past her, the woman's hands dropped, and she turned to him with astonishment in her eyes. "Jase! Why didn't you tell me?"

Confused, Evie looked to her father, hoping he would explain, but he wasn't paying attention to her. He had his eyes on the woman, a sharp note of warning in his face. The woman fell silent. For a moment Evie thought she would back down—turn on her black heel and leave. But then she rallied. Her back straightened, she lifted her chin, and she met Jase's gaze head on. The sight gave Evie a thrill; she wasn't used to seeing people stand up to her father. "Good God, Jase," the woman said. "It's positively freezing out here." She shivered and pulled her coat tighter around her. "Aren't you going to let us in?" Then, as if she knew better than to wait for his answer, she pushed past the two of them and marched herself in.

Us, it turned out, was Agatha Wickham and a young man who had been standing invisibly behind her, hidden by the yews. "This is Boo. He's the photographer," Agatha said with the wave of a hand in his direction as if that explained it, although to Evie's mind, it didn't explain anything. Boo was a young man, in his mid-twenties, Evie guessed, dressed in bell-bottom pants, a tie-dyed shirt, and a leather jacket. He had long hair, which he wore parted in the middle, and wide brown eyes, which were filled with a vacant look. As he passed by her, he exuded a musty, peppery smell.

They sat in the living room, a room they used so rarely, just being in it felt like a surprise to Evie—a surprise almost as great as finding her grandmother here again after so many years. Four of the walls in the octagonally shaped room had long, narrow windows. The others held shelves with her father's private book collection along with the delicate botanical prints her grandfather had collected before she was born. In the center of the room stood a sofa, a coffee table, and two upholstered armchairs. Agatha and Boo took the sofa. When Agatha held her coat out, Jase took it, but instead of hanging it up, he dropped it on a bench beneath one of the windows. The meaning of the gesture was clear: *You won't be staying long.* He didn't even bother with Boo's coat, although Boo held it out for him helpfully. Boo ended up balancing it awkwardly on his knees, the vacant look in his eyes giving way to unease. Boo, for one, Evie thought, would be glad to comply with her father's wishes and leave soon.

"So," Jase said, his voice even and pleasant. "What brings you to Danvers?" He smiled at the two of them in the relaxed way that people who didn't know him often mistook for a sign of friendliness, but Evie knew it was nothing of the sort, only her father's way of hiding his true intentions. Boo was taken in by it. He relaxed, sat back, and offered a smile of his own. But Agatha knew quite well what was going on. She sat on the edge of her seat, tense, her foot jiggling.

They had come to do an article on Indian art. The newspaper had sent them. The Indians lived on a reservation somewhere in the Southwest—Agatha waved her hand vaguely northwards. Evie's ears pricked up, but it was a different Indian tribe, not the one she had written to. Agatha would write the article, and Boo would take the pictures.

"You can't imagine what it's like in New York nowadays," Agatha said. "People have absolutely lost their minds. It's the rage everywhere, anything that's been made by an Indian—silver, turquoise, painting, rugs. You can't believe the prices these things are fetching. Especially the rugs—as long as they're one hundred percent genuine Indian."

Agatha sniffed. "Probably come with their own one hundred percent genuine Indian fleas."

As Agatha talked, Evie studied her, this woman who had vanished from her life for so long and then suddenly reappeared, like the fairy— or witch—in a fairy tale. Witch, Evie decided, thinking about it. It wasn't just Agatha's hands, which had been so shockingly cold when they pressed against her cheeks. Everything about her grandmother was sharp and severe, from her body, which was rail thin, to her hair, which was cut straight to her chin in a style which Evie assumed was fashionable back East, but which made Agatha look pinched and pained. She was beautiful in her own way, with full lips, a high-bridged nose, and dark, arching eyebrows, and she had a commanding presence; when she spoke, she dominated the room. Boo paled in her shadow.

They were lovers. Evie hadn't realized it before, then in a flash she did. How strange! She'd never been in a room with people like that before. And there were so many years between them! Agatha must be at least sixty, although she clearly took great pains to disguise that fact. What could Boo possibly see in her? Nothing, of course. It wasn't what Boo saw in Agatha that mattered, it was what Agatha could *do* for him. She was an esteemed art critic with a long tenure at *The New York Daily Times*, whereas Boo would just be starting out. Even Evie knew that plum assignments like this one would be hard to come by without Agatha's help.

She stole a glance at her father, wondering if he knew, too, but his face was impenetrable, guarded even from her. He turned to her with impassive eyes and said, "Agatha would like some tea."

"Tea?" Agatha waved her hand in a flustered way. "No, I don't think so, I—"

Jase kept his eyes on Evie. "We all would."

Evie stood up. "I'll get it."

She went into the kitchen and put the kettle on to boil. In the living room, the conversation had dropped to a murmur. She could hear the guarded tones of her father's voice, Agatha's taking on a melancholy air. She crept back into the hallway to listen, but she couldn't make out their words. Then the kettle began to whistle. By the time she came back with the cups of tea on a tray, Agatha and her father were talking brightly again, about the newspaper business.

"How's Mel Zeitler?" Agatha said.

"Gone. Retired over five years ago. Andy's got *The Post* now."

"Mel gone?" Agatha pressed a finger to her cheek. "How sad. You must miss him."

"Only when I think of him," Jase said, "which is never."

Evie put the tray down on the coffee table—where it was completely ignored—and sat back down in her chair.

"Boo's the most wonderful photographer," Agatha said to Jase. "You really must see one of his shows. He takes the most brilliant pictures of the sky. Don't you, Boo?" She turned to Boo with an eager look, but Boo didn't answer. He wasn't about to sally into the middle of this conversation—into the middle of anything. He was looking uneasy again, as if he wished he were out photographing the sky right now. As if he wished he were anywhere but in Jase Glauber's living room.

Jase studied Boo as if he'd be more than happy to help him along his way. "How's Norman?" he said finally, turning back to Agatha.

"Norman?" Agatha waved a hand in the air as if shooing away a pesky fly. "I haven't spoken to Norman for years."

"I guess it's hard to keep up with your ex's," Jase said pleasantly, "especially when there are so many."

"Only three," Agatha protested. Once again she fell silent. "All right," she said at last, giving him a long look. "Point taken. But let's stop this silly arguing, shall we? The truth is, I came here to see you. Despite what you think, I care about you, Jase. I always have. I care about *both* of you."

A change had come into the air. They were looking at her. Everyone was, even Boo. Evie had become used to being ignored, an invisible presence in the room. Now as she took shape in their eyes, she found her face growing warm.

"Care about us? About *Evie*?" Jase almost laughed out loud. "You have a strange way of showing it."

Agatha bristled. "Let's not talk about the past." She gave him a pointed look. "I'm sure you would prefer it that way."

Evie turned to her father, curious to see what his response to this challenge would be. It was bound to be something remarkable, she thought, strong and biting. She was almost enjoying this altercation between her father and grandmother: it was so astonishing and rare. But to her surprise, her father didn't answer, and his face took on a brooding look.

Agatha took advantage of this momentary victory to turn to Evie. "Tell me about yourself," she said, her voice bright and cheerful. "Tell me *everything*."

Evie was taken aback. She didn't know what to say. The truth was, she was still somewhat afraid of Agatha, especially of the way she was looking at her now, her eyes full of an intense interest. It made Evie feel like a commodity, a product Agatha was considering buying, wondering if it was worth the price. She swallowed hard. "I go to school."

"Do you?" It was a stupid answer, but Agatha acted as if Evie had said something brilliant. "How lovely!"

"I'm in high school now," Evie added. "I just turned sixteen." She snuck a look at her father, hoping he would rescue her from this painful predicament, but he remained silent, his thoughts elsewhere, his eyes moody and dark.

"Sixteen!" Agatha clapped her hands with pleasure. "Imagine that. So grown up! And what would you think about coming back to New York with me?"

"New York?"

Evie was shocked by the question but even more so by her father's response. Agatha had his attention now. He sat up and pinned her with his eyes. "Evie's not going anywhere."

Agatha waved a hand at him with an air of exasperation. "Now Jase, don't start that again. You know as well as I do there's nothing for Evie here. Danvers is a cultural backwater, nothing more than an overgrown cow town. My God, it even smells like cows." She wrinkled her nose as if the odor of the stockyards had followed her even inside the house. "Just think of the things I could show her! The theater, the museums ... . For once in her life Eve could go to a real school, get a *proper* education." The thought made Agatha's eyes sparkle. "She can come to Venice with me in the summer, when I cover the Biennale. Afterwards we'll go on a real European tour—the kind of thing *civilized* people do."

It was a jab at her father, and Evie knew it. As she watched, he stiffened, hardening almost visibly as if he were putting on armor. All at once she realized that the fight her father had had with Agatha years ago hadn't been about her mother—it had been about *her*. Agatha had wanted to take her back to New York with her—to raise her—and Jase had refused. He wasn't about to change his mind now. "Evie's fine just where she is."

"I know you don't want to part with her." A pleading note came into Agatha's voice. "So come with us! There are plenty of jobs in New York. I have connections—good ones—you know that. Just think— you could finally make something of yourself." She must have seen the look on Jase's face, because she changed tack. "Don't get me wrong. *The Sun* is a wonderful paper. Perfectly respectable. You've made it the best anyone could. But be reasonable. What's the use of being a big fish in such a small pond?" She pressed her fingers together. "Who's doing your art reviews?"

"No one."

"No art editor!" Agatha was shocked. "Really, Jase. Don't you think it's time you moved on, put it all behind you—"

Jase shot her a look and once again Agatha fell silent, twisting a loose thread on her sleeve. When she spoke again, she had altered her tone. "Your father's a wonderful newspaperman," she said, turning to Evie. "The best I've ever known. I tried to get him to come to New York from the beginning, but he wouldn't listen to me." She turned back to Jase with a sad smile. "But then you never do, do you, Jase?"

Jase didn't answer. He didn't have to. It was all over, and they both knew it. Agatha turned to Evie with a regretful air. "My dear, I was glad to see you. You are a beautiful girl, and don't you ever forget it."

She shook her head, as if still pining over lost opportunities. Then she stood up and resumed her impatient, commanding air. "Come along, Boo. Time to go."

With a look of utter relief, Boo put on his coat.

Jase fetched Agatha's coat, and with a consideration that signaled a truce—or at least an accommodation—helped her on with it. Together they walked towards the door, Boo following behind.

Evie watched them go. They had been so busy bullying each other, they had completely forgotten her. They acted if she had no say in this—as if it had nothing at all to do with her—when as far as she could tell, it was *all* about her. The thought angered her. She followed them into the hall. They had almost reached the door when she spoke up. "I'll go."

Shocked, they turned en masse and stared at her, even Boo. "What?" he said.

"To New York." She looked Agatha full in the face. "I'll go with you."

Agatha turned to Jase with an air of uncertainty.

"You'll do no such thing," Jase said.

"But—" Evie was about to argue when she saw the expression on her father's face. She'd never seen him look like that before—had never witnessed the heights his rage could reach. His eyes were smoldering, his face tight and pale. "I—" Evie said. "I just thought ... "

"I'm sorry," Agatha said to Jase. "I shouldn't have come here. I didn't realize ... " She glanced at Evie, her eyes full of regret. "Come along, Boo." She swept out the door, Boo in her wake. Evie heard the sound of their footsteps on the drive, then the sound of a car engine, starting up.

Her father was still in the doorway, watching them go, when Evie darted past him. She reached the car just as it was beginning to move and pounded on the glass until the car stopped. The window rolled down. "My mother," Evie said, her voice breathless and her heart hammering in her throat. "He won't talk about her. He won't even tell me where she is."

A deep wave of sadness crossed Agatha's face. She reached through the window and took Evie's face in her hands, only this time her hands were warm, and at her touch tears came to Evie's eyes. "I'm sorry, my dear. I can't help you. I promised your father I wouldn't." Agatha cast a last glance in Jase's direction, but he was unrelenting. Then she released Evie and was gone.

After Agatha's visit a change came over the house. The atmosphere turned frosty and icy as if the winter had seeped inside. Jase stayed at work longer and longer, and when he was home, he all but ignored Evie. He sat at the kitchen table working or staring off into the distance, his face darkened by sorrow. Evie didn't care. She was glad he was suffering. Everything was his fault. *Everything.* He wouldn't tell her about her mother, and he wouldn't let anyone else tell her either. The thought made her speechless with fury.

Just when she was convinced nothing could get worse, the ghost began haunting her in the daytime, too. One afternoon as she was walking home with Bobbie from the bus stop, Evie looked up and saw the phantom, hovering in the creek. It was a windy, blustery day—it had been snowing on and off since morning—and the ghost hovered in the gusts, her long white dress swirling around her, her hair streaming. Evie stared at her with astonishment. "Do you see that?" she said to Bobbie.

"What?"

"There." Evie jabbed a finger at the creek. *How could Bobbie be so blind?* The ghost was unmistakable, floating in plain sight, the baby clutched to her chest.

"There's nothing there." Bobbie shivered. "Come on, let's go. It's freezing."

Bobbie quickened her step towards home, but Evie didn't follow. The ghost was reaching out towards her now, her mouth open as if she had something vitally important to say. Evie stared at her with disgust. *Enough already.* Enough of the haunted looks, the anguish, the pleading, and despair. "If you have something to say to me, say it," she hollered. "Otherwise go away and leave me alone!"

Her voice rang out in the street, followed by a deep wave silence. Evie turned to find Bobbie staring at her with stricken eyes. "I'm sorry," Evie said, "I—" *I'm not freaking out*, she wanted to say. But she knew it was no use. Neither of them believed it anymore.

Bobbie shook her head and turned away with an air of sadness, trudging the rest of the way home alone. Evie watched her go. But she didn't feel like going home herself; the ghost would just be waiting for her there, hovering outside her bedroom window. She decided to take a walk instead. For a time she wandered aimlessly down the street, letting her feet carry her from corner to corner. The sidewalk was icy, the curb crusted over with the grimy remains of months of snow. Icicles hung from the gutters of the houses, and flakes of snow whirled in the wind. Sunset was still several hours away, but it was already dark enough for the street lamps to have come on, casting pale pools of bluish light on the ground. In their glare, Evie caught sight of the ghost. Apparently she had decided to take a walk, too. Her steps dogged Evie's, following a discrete distance behind in the creek bed.

Hardly anyone was out. Once a car drifted by, its windows steamed over, as if it were moving on autopilot, without a driver. Evie passed a woman who was hurrying into her house, her arms filled with grocery bags. In the next yard a small boy was building a snow fort, rolling balls made of snow into a pile. She stopped for a while to watch him. The ghost stopped, too. Evie shot her an irritable glance. "Stop following me," she called out without thinking. The boy gave her a startled look, dropped his snowball, and fled with a fearful glance over his shoulder into his home.

Evie continued onwards, turning her back to the creek, so at least she wouldn't have to see the ghost anymore. She didn't think much as she walked. She tried not to think at all. Eventually, to her surprise, she found herself standing outside the gate of the Danvers Academy. She supposed her feet had carried her there out of habit. On the far side of the playground, past the chain link fence, the ghost floated in the creek. She had made her way there, too.

Evie pushed open the gate, walking past the rings to the old swing set. It was long past dismissal time, and the playground was deserted, the swings coated with snow. She brushed one off and sat down. Scuffing her feet on the ground, she moved slowly back and forth, rocking more than swinging. It was too cold to swing properly. Anyway she hadn't worn gloves and didn't want to touch the cold metal chains.

As she swung, the ghost waited patiently in the creek, wind-blown snow swirling about her, the baby clutched in her arms. Whenever Evie glanced towards her, the phantom took the opportunity to hold a hand out towards her, her mouth open, a beseeching look in her eyes. "I don't know what you want," Evie said, relieved that at least there was no one to hear her speaking to empty air. The ghost responded by shoving the baby in her direction, holding it out at arm's length. "Is there something wrong with your baby? Is that it?" Evie knew it was no use. She might as well be talking to herself. In a way, she had to admit, she probably was.

It was getting late, and as the sun went down, the light took on a deeper shade of grey. The cold turned sharper, taking on a metallic edge. The wind was blowing harder, too. In the creek the ghost wavered in the wind, as if she were having trouble holding on. "Okay," Evie said. "I guess we can go home now."

She left the playground, the ghost following steadily behind. When she got home, she went straight into the kitchen, leaving the ghost to take up her usual position behind the house. She shrugged off her coat and boots and left them in a heap by the door. Then she sat down. On the table sat the usual stack of newspapers, *The New York Daily Times* at the bottom. There, in the arts section, Evie found Agatha's article on Indian art. She'd been looking for it ever since Agatha left. Agatha described the art with barely concealed derision, but Evie thought some of Boo's pictures were pretty, especially the jewelry and rugs.

She put the *Times* aside and glanced at the headlines in *The Sun*. Most of the stories were about the war in Vietnam. Scattered anti-war protests had broken out across the country; draftees burned their draft cards or fled to Canada. Evie shook her head. Even if they did manage to bring the war to an end one day, it would be too late for Eason. He was already there.

She held her breath and turned to the list of war dead, breathing out a sigh of relief when she saw that his name wasn't on it. Then she shoved the newspaper aside. She didn't even know why she bothered. Hadn't she told herself ages ago to stop worrying about Eason Swale? Besides, it wasn't like there was anything she could do about it. His fate was out of her hands.

She went upstairs and walked to her window. As she had expected, the ghost was waiting for her in the creek. The phantom thrust her baby towards her, holding it out in her arms.

"Do you want me to take your baby?" Evie asked. She opened her window so that the ghost would be sure to hear her. "Is that it?" The ghost opened her mouth, but if she said anything, Evie couldn't hear it. Her voice was lost in the wind. "Fine," Evie said. "If you want me to take the baby, I will." She was willing to do anything, if it would only make the ghost go away.

She went back downstairs and opened the back door. It was even colder than when she had taken her walk, the snow thickening, the temperatures plummeting as night came. She glanced towards the creek, where the ghost hovered in the darkness just past the cottonwoods. Evie's coat and boots were still in the kitchen, but the ghost was looking positively frantic now, forcing the baby towards her, as if it were imperative that she take it immediately. "Hold on. I'm coming," Evie said. She would dart out to the creek, grab the baby, and run quickly back inside.

She dashed across the snow, ignoring the cold that stung her cheeks and bit through her socks. As she reached the creek bed, the wind flung snow into her face. She rubbed her eyes and blinked hard. There was the ghost, on the other side of the cottonwoods, clutching the baby, a panic-stricken look on her face. Evie dashed towards her, struggling through thigh-high drifts of snow, fighting against the wind. But now the wind was blowing the ghost, too. She flew away from the trees and was tossed against the bank. Evie doubled back to follow her. Then the ghost was gone again, thrown to the other side. Evie fought her way to her, holding out her arms, reaching for the baby. And that, when he finally came home from work, was how Jase found her: stumbling back and forth in the creek behind their house, half-frozen, and grasping at nothing in the snow.

"Oh, Evie, oh my girl, please don't do that, please stop."

Her father meant stop crying, but Evie was only crying because he was. It was the first time she'd seen her father cry, but he was crying copiously as if to make up for lost opportunities, tears wetting his cheeks and staining his shirt.

They were in her room, on her bed. She was wrapped in blankets, and he was sitting beside her. If only he would stop crying, she wanted to say, she would, too, although she had to admit, she was in an awful lot of pain. Her hands and feet were throbbing, her ears aching as if they were on fire. Jase had found her in the creek and brought her inside, tucking her inside the blankets, holding her tightly through the worst of the shivering. At least, she thought, he deserved an explanation. "I tried to save it."

"Save—what?"

"The baby. She wanted me to take it and I tried to but I couldn't. The wind was blowing too hard, and every time I reached for it ... "

This only made him cry harder. "Shh," he whispered, crooning to her in a soft voice. "Don't talk now. Don't even try. I'm sorry, this is all my fault, I shouldn't have left you alone like that. It's my fault and I'm sorry, I'm so, so sorry. I will never leave you again, I promise, no matter what happens, no matter what ... " He stood up and rubbed a hand over his face. For a long time he said nothing, gazing out the window. Then he left the room. A few minutes later he returned with a mug of hot tea, which he pressed into her hands. "Drink this." He waited while she took a few sips. "Better?"

She nodded because it was. The shivering was slowing now. For a while it had been uncontrollable, but now it came only in short bursts, spasms that racked her body then subsided. He stood beside her, watching until the tea was gone. "You rest now." He took the empty mug. "I'll see you in the morning."

He left the room, closing the door behind him. She sank back into her bed, pulling the blankets tighter around her. The tea had helped, but she was still cold, so very cold. It seemed like ages since she had been warm. The last time she could remember was when she stood on the platform outside the dome of the Capitol with Tyler. She'd kissed him, and his warmth had flowed into her like a spring.

Just like the kiss Eason had given her on the bluff the year before.

Evie stood up, the blanket wrapped around her like a shawl, and walked to her dresser. She took out Eason's shirt, lifted it to her face, and breathed in deeply. It had been so long since she had touched it, she feared it was too late, that the scent was gone. But there it was again, faint but unmistakable: *Eason*. She closed her eyes and breathed him in, feeling herself transported back to the bluff, the warmth of the spring sun on her face, the softness of his lips on hers.

Taking the shirt with her, she went to her window. The ghost was gone, the creek empty. She flung the window open and leaned outside just to be sure. It was still snowing, but a change had come into the air. The wind was blowing, but it had a soft touch now, gentle and mild. The snowflakes were big and fat, without a biting sting. When she held out her hand, they nestled in her palm then melted away.

Her father loved her, she knew that now, loved her with a fierceness that frightened them both. For his sake she'd tried to hold it all in and live the life he wanted for her. But it was no use. She'd never be normal, at least not the way he—and the rest of the world—thought she should be. Soon winter would end, and spring would come. When it did, she would ride back to the Swale ranch. She would find Cyrus and tell him about her vision. Maybe he would understand. After all, he was the only one who hadn't thought she was crazy when she told him about the voices. She'd do it for Eason. Everything he believed in—everything he stood for—came from Choke Creek. She had to know what happened there, and what it meant.

Sixteen

It was a girl, a young girl of fourteen or fifteen, Eason guessed, dressed in the simple clothes of a peasant, in a dark loose-fitting tunic and pants. Liver aimed his flashlight at the ground at her feet, while the men clustered around her, shielding the light with their bodies. The light pooled on the trail, rising to cast a pale glow on her face, on her eyes, which rolled wildly back and forth in terror, on her frail birdlike throat, and on her braid, which a moment ago had been hanging freely down to the small of her back, but which Liver now held firmly in his hand like a lasso.

"Well, well, well," he said happily. "What have we here?"

Liver was the one who caught her, but Eason was the one who heard her first. He had been lying on his belly, his body pressed hard against the damp earth, when he heard her coming. The sound came from his right, from deep in the woods, far down the trail. It was scant and flickering, at times so faint, he felt it more than heard it, the way he felt a lowering in the air on the prairie back home before a storm. Bit by bit the sound grew closer, coming through the rain. His fingers tightened on the rifle. They were coming. The VC officers, the ones the lieutenant had warned them about. It was time for him to do something—time for him to act.

But before he could move, the sound was gone, vanishing in the darkness like a rabbit in a magician's hat. Eason took a deep breath. *Nothing.* He wiped the back of his hand across his face and almost laughed out loud. Liver was right. Nothing but spooks and ghosts.

He had just settled himself down again, his hands relaxing on the rifle, when the sound came back—louder this time, right in front of him on the trail. And another sound, harsh and crashing, which came from his left. There were more of them, coming at him from all sides. His breath caught in his throat, as sharp as a stick, his fingers fumbling for the rifle. Just as he found the trigger, a blaze of light burst in front of him, a bright, blinding flash. The rifle jerked up and fell from his grasp. Then Liver was standing before him, the braid in his hand, shining his flashlight at the terrified face of the girl, and smiling happily as he said, "What have we here?"

Rain dripped through the trees. The men stood on the trail, wet and miserable, their ponchos slung about them dark and shapeless, so that they appeared not so much as soldiers in the night, but as ancient shades who had been drawn to the girl by the light. Only Liver seemed unusually pleased, as if amused at a private joke. He looked fondly into the face of the girl, his eyes full of mirth. The ears on his necklace bounced cheerfully on his throat. He pulled on the braid, tightening the skin around her eyes.

"Hey," Music said. "That's enough. Let her go."

Liver turned to Music, laughter bubbling from the corners of his lips. Then he shrugged and his hand flipped open, releasing the braid. The girl twitched and turned, her eyes raking the darkness, but the men had surrounded her, encircling her like they would a wild horse, and there was no way to escape. She crossed her arms over her chest and withdrew into herself as if she wished she could disappear, her eyes fixed on the ground.

"Shit," Page said mournfully. He dug into the mud with the toe of his boot.

"What the hell is she doing here, anyway?" Nye said.

"How should I know?" Music answered.

Then the three of them were talking at once.

"What are we supposed to do with her now?"

"We can't let her go."

"We can't keep her, either. What if they come looking for her?"

"Better they come looking for her than for us."

"Let her go," Music said. "She's just a girl."

"She can talk, can't she?" Nye said.

They looked at Nye, then back at the girl. She hadn't uttered a word since they had captured her, but they all knew what Nye meant.

"That's all we need—for her to go back and tell them we're out here."

"Tell who?" Liver said.

Page stared at him in disbelief. "The VC," he said. "The officers. You heard the lieutenant. The ones who are meeting here tonight."

Liver gave him a long look. "Don't tell me you actually believe that bullshit."

Page was wrong, and he knew it, but he sullenly refused to concede the point. "If there isn't a meeting, then what are we doing here?"

Now there was chaos again as the men all talked at once. Then their voices died down.

"We'll just have to keep her," Music said. "Until daylight. Then we'll let her go."

Nye took a step backwards, holding up his hands. "Don't look at me. I'm no babysitter."

"Fuck this." Page shook his head.

"Let Liver take her," Music said. "He's the one who caught her."

Eason hadn't said a word. He was still trying to quiet the trembling of his limbs, the wild pounding of his heart. Thoughts coursed recklessly through his mind. I could have shot them. *I could have shot them both. Liver and the girl. Jesus Christ. I almost did.* There was a bad taste in the back of his throat. He thought he would be sick. He turned to the girl. Spittle bubbled at the corner of her mouth, but she was too afraid to reach up and wipe it away. "I'm sorry," he said.

"What the fuck—" Nye said.

"I'm—" Eason held his hands up in a helpless way. "Nothing," he said. "Forget it."

Nye shook his head in disgust. Then he went back to debating the girl's fate with the others.

Eason let them talk. *I'm sorry*, he wanted to say to the girl. *I didn't mean it. I didn't even really want to come here. I just wanted to go to war, and this was the only one they had.*

Finally it was decided. Liver would take her. One by one the men gave the girl a last look, then moved off to take up their positions on the trail.

Eason and Liver were the last to go. There was a thoughtful look on Liver's face now. He had taken hold of the braid again, but lightly. His fingers rubbed the tresses in an absentminded way.

Liver shouldn't have her. The thought rose in Eason's mind, taking the shape of a conviction. *He shouldn't be the one.* Eason knew he should speak up and say so, but he didn't. His eyes locked on Liver, and a flash of understanding passed between them. Liver rewarded him with a grin. "Well, Cowboy, what do you know. I guess you won't be the one losing your cherry tonight after all." His fist closed on the braid, and he shut off the light.

The rest of the night passed uneventfully. Shortly before dawn Eason fell asleep, slumbering on the rain-soaked ground, a sweet, dreamless sleep. He awoke at daylight to the sound of the other men's voices. During the night the rain had stopped, and the wind had died down, leaving behind a deep silence. For a moment he was disoriented and forgot where he was. Then he gathered himself together and joined the others on the trail.

They clustered around the girl, blinking unsteadily in the light. The girl stood among them as before, refusing to look at them or say a word. Only, her lower lip was split open now, her face bruised and bloody. Two long, raking scratches ran down the birthmark on Liver's face. He rubbed them with the back of his hand. "We got along fine," he said, with a quick jerk of his head at the girl. He grinned. "I wouldn't say we agreed on everything."

No one answered him. It had been a long night, and they were exhausted. All they wanted to do was get back to camp. They stepped back, and gave the girl room. But she didn't seem to understand that they were releasing her.

"Well, go on," Nye said irritably. He made a shooing motion with his hands. "Get out of here."

The girl raised her eyes. She took a tentative step. When no one stopped her, she began to run.

At the last second Liver's hand darted out. He grabbed her braid and jerked her head back, baring her throat. The knife glistened in his hand. In one swift motion, he reached out and sliced through her braid. The girl's hands flew up and clutched at her shorn hair. Then she was running as fast as she could down the trail, a long, plaintive wail echoing through the woods behind her.

"What the hell did you do that for?" Page said.

A bad feeling hung over the men, as if in one swift motion Liver had tempted the gods, and their fates. But Liver was unrepentant. He attached the braid to his helmet. "What's the big deal? She's just a gook. Anyway, I let her go, didn't I?" He put his helmet on with the braid hanging down his back. He shook his head so that it swung jauntily back and forth. Then he grinned and shrugged. "Besides, no one said we couldn't take souvenirs."

Seventeen

All winter long Cyrus Swale wrote letters to his son. He sat in the kitchen with a sharpened pencil and a pad of writing paper before him, a pot of coffee warming on the stove. Meanwhile outside the snow lay siege to the house, piling up in scalloped drifts beneath the windows, burdening the roof, lying knee-deep on the plain.

One night he wrote about the dappled mare, which had lost its foal, and about how he hoped to breed her again in the spring. What he didn't write was how he'd found the stillborn one morning when he went to the mares' pasture to put out feed. The foal was lying in the snow beneath a wintry, windswept sky, its tiny body already perfectly formed, the shape of the skeleton visible beneath its gelatinous skin, its eyes pecked out by crows.

He wrote about the creek, which had vanished beneath the snow, and about the watering trough, which had begun freezing over, greeting him each morning with a layer of ice. A few weeks later he wrote about a blood bay mare, which had spooked in her paddock one cold wintry eve. The mare got hung up on the rails, and by the time he succeeded in freeing her, her leg was broken, hanging twisted from the knee. He called the vet and after some discussion, they decided to cast it. Now, he wrote, the mare passed her days in her stall, tethered and sedated, while they waited for the leg to heal.

What he didn't write were the things the vet said to him about his own son, who'd just come back from Vietnam. Once, the vet said, the boy had talked of college, but now all he did was spend his days—and half the night—driving aimlessly around in his car. The vet wound a strip of cloth, soaked in plaster of Paris, around the filly's leg. It was making them both crazy, he added, him and his wife. They were worried to death, but the boy wouldn't talk about it—he wouldn't talk about anything. And what were they to do?

Before he sat down to write, Cyrus took the biscuit tin with Eason's letters down from the shelf. He counted and recounted the letters inside, as if the number might have magically grown larger when he wasn't looking. Then he put the biscuit tin back in its place, picked up his pencil, and wrote.

He wrote about the wind, which had become strangely unpredictable, blowing one day from the east and the next from the west. It swept in broad arcs across the plain, spinning dry clumps of snow into powdery white dust devils, frightening the horses and unsettling their dreams. And he wrote about the blacksmith, who came out one day to shoe the horses. The farrier set up his tin hearth in the snow, and Cyrus lingered nearby as he worked, basking in the heat of the fire. Meanwhile the blacksmith trimmed the horses' feet, shaving off thin slices of hoof, which floated like snowflakes to the ground. He set the new shoes into the fire, removing them with tongs when they'd become glowing hot, then put them on the anvil to shape them, hammering with sharp, chiming blows. When he was satisfied, he plunged the shoes, hissing and smoking, into a water bucket to cool. Then he set them on the horses' feet, each new nail releasing the smoky sharp smell of scorched hoof into the cold air.

The farrier was a garrulous man who liked to gossip while he worked, and after he was gone, Cyrus wrote to his son, filling him in on the news he had heard. The Collins girl had finally gotten married. The Dwyer boy was working at the feed store now; when, the rancher wondered, had he gotten old enough to get a job? Defying all logic, the Lees had left the county and moved to Alaska, leaving stunned neighbors in their wake. Word was—as incredible as it sounded—they'd given up farming for the fishing trade.

What Cyrus didn't write was how, as the blacksmith was leaving, he'd turned and asked, "Heard from Eason lately?" The rancher had looked away for a long time before answering, "No, not for a while." Then the farrier, too, had fallen silent, until finally he said with a cheerfulness neither of them felt, "Well, no news is good news, right?"

For months his son had been a faithful correspondent, and the letters had come regularly, one for each week that he was gone. But all that had ended late in the year. A letter dated just after Thanksgiving came in the middle of December, in reasonable time. After that there was nothing. Not a single letter. Not a single word.

Cyrus told himself not to worry. His son was a soldier now. He had other things to think about, things far more important than writing home. He should be glad Eason was taking care of himself, not wasting his time on frivolous things like writing. Hell, it was ridiculous of him to expect a letter from his son every week. He'd just been spoiled, that was all, by all the letters that had come before.

For a while he considered not writing himself. Maybe Eason wouldn't want to be bothered with news from home. But he rejected that idea. Surely a word or two from his father would be welcome, even if Eason didn't have time to write back. And so, that winter, he continued to write, sitting at the kitchen table, framing his letters with care.

He wrote about the new pump, which was holding up despite the cold. And he wrote about the truck, which had been running poorly until one morning, beneath an icy blue sky, he changed the spark plugs and the wires. A few days later he confessed to his son that he hadn't been out much lately. His hip had stiffened up too much for it in the cold. But, he added hastily, he didn't want Eason to worry. He was fine. And he made sure each day to get his chores done, turning the barn-kept horses out in their paddocks and letting them run until they were tired in the fields of snow.

One night he wrote about the people from the county, who occasionally still stopped by in the evenings. Remembering him from his judging days, they brought him their disputes to settle, grievances that fell short of the court system and the law, but went beyond what ordinary folk could resolve on their own. He refused payment, but the morning after invariably found something left for him on the porch: a jar of chokecherry jam, a sack of cornmeal, jerked venison wrapped in burlap cloth. What he didn't write was how burdened he was by his own fears, and how he wished someone could resolve them the same way.

On Valentine's Day he wrote about a pair of telephone repairmen who'd spent two whole days on the ranch working on the wires. Soon after he wrote about a trip he'd taken into town to pick up groceries and fuel. What he didn't write was how the postmaster looked at him when he stopped in to get his mail. The postmaster set the pile of letters on the counter with his eyes averted and his mouth pinched tight, so that even without looking, Cyrus knew there was nothing from his son.

In late February he wrote about how he fixed the ladder to the hayloft, hammering in a new rung to replace the one that was missing, and how he baited the loft for mice. He'd gotten most of the tack mended, he wrote, and spent one whole evening repairing horse blankets, sewing the torn edges together with thick stitches of white cotton thread. What he didn't write was how lately he'd been waking in the middle of the night from nightmares, shivering and gasping for breath. The dreams all started differently, but ended the same way, with him walking out to the dappled mare's pasture and finding his son lying in the snow, dead like the stillborn foal.

Tired of his own cooking, he drove one night to the truck stop for dinner. Later he wrote about it to his son. He spent a long time describing the road he took to get there, the way the darkness of the county flowed in around him as he drove northwards. Finally the highway appeared before him in the distance, a procession of trucks and cars rolling eastwards and westwards through the night, their headlights glowing like lighted ships upon the ocean, like underwater beasts that moved with gleaming eyes through the murky depths of the sea.

He felt as if he'd been hauled out of the depths himself as he emerged from the darkness of the parking lot into the bright lights of the diner, a nocturnal animal dragged with startled, blinking eyes into the sun. He took a booth at the back of the restaurant, where he had his back to the wall and a good view of the room before him. The food, when it came—chicken-fried steak and gravy—was comforting in a predictable, bland way. He wrote about that, and he even wrote about the waitress, who flirted with him as she served him, and about how he found himself enjoying it, even though he knew she meant nothing by it; it was just her way of cadging a better tip.

What he didn't write was how he'd felt when he emerged from the diner. He stood by the doorway contemplating the long highway, which stretched out before him. All at once he found himself wondering what would happen if he got into his truck, chose a direction, and started driving. He imagined driving all night until the sun came up, emerging from the darkness into a completely different landscape, into a southern forest perhaps, where Spanish moss hung thickly from the oak trees, and the ground was thick with bogs and swamps. Or he pictured himself taking the road until it ended, until he was standing in front of the astounding blue and white expanse of the sea. Maybe in such a place, he thought, he wouldn't have to spend his days clenched in terror each time the phone rang, or an unexpected knock came on the door.

No, he forbid himself from writing about that. Instead he wrote about the days, which were finally getting longer, darkness holding off until six, when beneath their burden of snow the fields vanished in the waning light. And he wrote about the horses, passing the winter months as they always did, dozing quietly in the bleak light, chewing meditatively on their hay, their breath steaming lightly in the cold.

Winter, he often thought, was a kind of limbo for the horses, a time when life was put on hold. There was nothing for them to do but wait patiently for springtime and the changes it would bring to their world. But he didn't tell his son that. Just as he didn't tell him how lucky he thought the horses were. They didn't worry about the future or the past. They knew their spring would come. They felt it in their blood. One day the grass would green up again. The sun would shine warm on their backs, and on a new crop of foals.

He had no such luxury. Each day that winter he felt the pressure of the past bearing down on him, harder and harder to escape. As long as Eason's letters had come regularly, he'd been able to convince himself that everything would be all right—that he'd done nothing wrong by sending his seventeen-year-old son to war. But what if the number of letters in the biscuit tin never grew again? What if the last letter he'd received was—*the last one*? What exactly was happening to his son in Vietnam? And what would he be like, if he ever made it home?

When Cyrus was done writing, he bathed. He filled the tub with water as hot as he could stand, then lowered himself into it with a groan.

As he bathed, steam from the bath water gathered on the window-panes and dripped down the sash. The mirror was laden with moisture. Meanwhile outside the wind blew steadily, making the house shudder and creak. It found chinks in the log walls and worked its way in, its breath as cold as ice. One night in early March Cyrus found himself listening to it. He closed his eyes and held his breath, but he heard nothing but the most familiar, mundane sounds—the rattle of windows, the clicking of a loose board in the eaves.

He opened his eyes and lay back in the tub, resting his head against the cool metal lip. With deep breaths, he kneaded the sore muscles of his aching hip, loosening the joint. The hot water brought a rosy flush to his face. The skin around his wrists and ankles was thin and transparent with age. In the hollows he could see the dusky blue pulse of his heart.

All he needed to resurrect the past was to look at his body. It was like a landscape to him, a roadmap, a book in which he could read the story of his life. The swollen veins in his arms and legs were like the creeks he had explored as a child, the broken blood vessels that branched out from them like the gullies and washes that fed the streams. The insides of his knees were scarred from years of saddle blisters, the skin grown soft and fine and pearly white. He had a chipped front tooth from a colt who surprised him once by kicking a gate so hard, it swung around and caught him in the face. His shins were smooth and hairless from a half century of chafing in boots. One of his thumbs was permanently misshapen from a filly who panicked when he wormed her, crushing his hand between the stall boards.

The skin on his face and arms was dark and leathery, prematurely aged by the sun. But his chest and belly were baby-white. On the back of his skull was the knot he'd gotten when a sorrel mare threw him into the paddock rail. He was only six then, just learning how to ride. "Lucky you hit that fence with your head, boy," his father had said, one of the few times he could remember his father laughing. "Anything else would have broke."

On his calf a lump of twisted, knotted flesh marked the rattlesnake bite he'd gotten as a ten-year-old. He was all alone then, sent out by his mother to gather chokecherries and wild plums in the creek. When the snake struck he fell to the ground in a swoon. After a few minutes he had the presence of mind to cut an X into the skin over the purplish bite with the razorblade his mother made him carry for that purpose. He bent over and sucked out the poison—an act which made him retch and vomit but which, the doctor said later, helped save his life.

He closed his eyes, letting the hot bath water soothe the stiffness in his joints, and imagined himself as that boy again, as a boy of five or six or seven, walking across the prairie with his father, leading the sorrel mare by hand. It was summer, and the sky was clear, a piercing blue. The plains grasses were knee-high on the horse, as thick as water. When the wind blew, it made waves shimmer from horizon to horizon.

His father had seemed like a giant to him then, larger than life. For his fifth birthday his mother gave him a storybook of ancient myths. Every time he looked at the picture of Atlas holding up the heavens, he swore the giant had his father's face.

As he bathed, he saw his father again, kneeling in the grass. He cut through it with his pocketknife, breaking the sod. Then he held up the clump of earth for the boy to see. The dirt was thick with roots, spidery white filaments, which burrowed through the soil like blind white worms.

"There are over twenty miles of roots in a square yard of this soil," he remembered his father saying proudly. "This land is a gold you can count on, richer than the metal they take out of the hills."

His father ran cattle then, hundreds of them, massive animals whose jet black bodies, splayed hooves, and curving horns frightened the small boy. When the cattle moved across the prairie, the ground shook, their bodies flowing across the earth like a torrential dark stream. In his dreams Cyrus still saw them and heard the mournful sound of their lowing, echoing across the plain. His mother was always busy in the kitchen then, preparing platters of food for the hired hands who helped his father manage the herds. At night the boy heard the men in the bunkhouse, a chorus of voices and laughter that spilled out onto the prairie amid a blaze of light.

But his father had been wrong. They couldn't count on the grass. In the end all they could count on was that it would betray them. Year after year they were plagued with locusts, with sandstorms, with hail. Long periods of drought turned the rich green buffalo grasses into brittle brown stalks. The cattle grazed the thick blue grama down to the nub. Winter took its toll on the animals, weeding out the weak, as did the scathing hot summers. Gradually the bunkhouse emptied out until finally it was silent and dark. As the boy helped his father tend to the dwindling herds, he could almost feel the dying plains constrict around him, the prairie tightening like a cage.

The final blow was a blizzard that blew in one winter from the north, a blast of arctic air so cold it split oxen horn to the pith. Far out on the prairie the remaining cattle froze to death in their tracks. In the middle of the night his father blundered out into the storm in a futile attempt to save them. Fourteen hours later, the storm still raging, he stumbled back into the house, more dead than alive.

When spring came, the boy found the cattle. They were in a dry culvert, a line of whitened bones that lay strewn across the ground like a script, like the letters of a language he could not understand. There was no sign of grass on the prairie around them, near or far. Everywhere he looked the soil was dry and dusty, riddled with poison oak and thistles, with cacti and vines. The wind shook loose tumbleweeds, which chased each other across the bare brown ground.

After that his father took to his chair. He had lost two fingers in the storm, and his sense of smell, which he never regained. Meanwhile the Great War raged. One by one the younger men in the county left home, enlisting in battalions that eventually found their way overseas. Plenty of people were left shorthanded, in need of hired help. But his father never budged. For days at a time he sat without speaking in his chair as if he'd been condemned to it. When news of the Armistice came, he took it as a sign of liberation for himself as well. That night, while in homes across the county people joined in joyous celebration in honor of the men who would soon be coming home, he got up. He left the house and walked through the darkness to the barren birthing pasture, carrying the revolver he'd once used to protect the newborn calves from coyotes and wolves. The next morning his son found him there, the way he'd found the fallen cattle the spring before. His father was a man of forty-seven when he died. But his son was only nine.

When the bath water cooled, Cyrus eased himself out of the tub. He dried himself and dressed in his nightclothes. Then he turned off the light and made his way to his bed.

Once the bed had belonged to his father and mother. The nightstand beside it was still covered with the embroidered doily his mother had put there after his father died. His mother had taken in sewing then, and had done embroidery on the side, handkerchiefs and napkins and other such things, which she sold for a few pennies or gave away in trade.

The spring after his father's death, the boy rode the sorrel mare to a neighboring ranch. With the money his mother had saved over the winter, he paid the stud fee to have the mare bred. By the time he was eleven, he'd sold his first colt. He bought a stallion and, the following spring, another mare. By the time he was thirteen, he was managing a small herd of horses. His reputation as a rider spread throughout the county. People brought him their worst horses, their orneriest animals, to break and train.

From time to time he rode to the low bluff beside the wide bend in the creek, the place where his grandfather Thomas Eli Eason had fought beside Colonel John Quintius Stevenson. He had never had the honor of meeting his grandfather, who had died before he was born. But he thought about him as he walked the grounds of the battlefield, leading his horse behind him, looking for arrowheads and bullets, beads and buckles, to add to his collection.

When he wasn't riding, he was in school, a necessity that he respected but never particularly took to. His favorite part of the school day was recess, when the boys gathered outside for games of cowboys and Indians. With painstaking care they re-enacted the battles of the Indian Wars, especially the one at Choke Creek, when the safety of their very own homes had been threatened and then restored. Some of the boys had souvenirs at home, handed down from the battle. One boy had a scalp, which he brought to school in a shoebox. The other boys took turns peering at the thin wisp of curling flesh and long coil of braided hair, nestled inside on a bed of paper. Others boasted of things they claimed to possess even though they were never shown. Ears that had been taken as pocket pieces. Rings and bits of bone. A tobacco pouch crafted from the scrotum of a chief.

One story, never proven, terrified Cyrus as a small boy and haunted him still. He remembered the classmate who told it, a skinny boy with a cleft lip, a shock of red hair, and a propensity for lying. This boy claimed to have an entire Indian head at home, which his father had brought back from the battle. The boy had seen the head often, he said, since his father used it to discipline his unruly children. Later the red-headed boy left the county and was never heard from again. But as Cyrus grew older, he often thought of him. He wondered what kind of man a boy raised in such a monstrous manner would have become. Despite himself, he wondered what the head would have looked like—if it had indeed existed. Would it have been dried up and shrunken, like heads he had heard about, taken in battles between warring tribes in the Amazon? Or would it have retained its original shape, a wizened face with long dark hair and eyes that looked out at you with a fixed and glassy stare?

As a boy, he'd brought his own collection of bullets and arrowheads to school, showing it to great acclaim. But the other boys weren't always so approving of him. At times they were downright cruel. He remembered still with a piercing ache the times when they refused to let him play with them, when they taunted him in the schoolyard, chanting in high, singsong voices: "Swale, Swale, Cyrus Swale, can't shoot a thing on hill or dale."

"Is it true," he asked his mother once, "what people say? That my grandfather was a coward at the Battle of Choke Creek? Is it true he didn't even fire his gun?"

His mother had been in the middle of embroidering a tablecloth, but now, with trembling fingers, she put her work down. "Don't ever speak of that," she said. "A person could get himself killed with talk like that."

Her fear had frightened him, and he'd let it go. In time he outgrew the playground games, but the singsong taunts never disappeared entirely from his mind. After his father died, he discovered a new saying circulating the county, a twist on the taunt of old. The Swales, the saying went, were incapable of using their guns—except on themselves.

The world of his grandfather may have been exciting and thrilling, filled with great danger and deeds of tremendous bravery, but his world, the boy soon discovered, was prosaic and dull, filled with boring, repetitive work, with the endless mucking out of stalls and the unceasing hauling in of feed. As he walked down the barn aisle with his bucket of oats and corn, he cursed himself for having been born so late, for living in a world in which nothing at all dangerous or exciting ever happened, in which there were no more Indians and no more wars.

More than anything he wanted to see a real Indian warrior. He wanted to have it stand before him, this human-creature so wild and strange, resplendent in feathers and hide, in war paint and beads. He wanted to experience the thrilling fear of it, the dizzying rush of blood in his veins, the stopping of his breath. And he wanted to shoot one— he wanted to shoot dozens of them—so that the other boys wouldn't taunt him for being a coward anymore, and would see that he could fire his gun.

How unfair it was, he thought as he looked through his collection of arrowheads and bullets—without a single scalp, without even a single piece of bone inside—that his grandfather had lived through the Battle of Choke Creek and not him! He could shoot and he could kill. He was sure of it.

When he finally saw his first Indian, the experience was so disappointing, he could hardly bear it. On a spring afternoon when he was ten years old, a couple of old men came wandering on foot to the house, coming from God only knew where, dressed in ordinary clothing, without a single feather or bead in sight. Strangers had been coming to the house for as long as he could remember, but he had never realized before that they were *Indians*. Now he found himself examining them with care. They looked like the worst kind of beggars and thieves.

From the safety of the house where she had sent him, he watched as his mother, her face pale, sent them away. Only this time her fear made him angry. He wanted to grab her and shake her, saying, *What are you afraid of? These men aren't Indians. They can't possibly be. Indians are grand. They're fierce and wild. They speak in incomprehensible tongues. They bring danger with them, and death. They come with war paint on their faces, with arrows and hatchets and knives.*

For the old men outside, he had nothing but contempt. How frail they were, how weak and harmless! He despised them for it, for the fact that they had allowed themselves to become so irrevocably defeated.

After that he always watched carefully as Indians came to the house, arriving on foot or on horseback, later in trucks and cars. Eventually he was the one who sent them away, while his mother stayed behind in the house, peering from behind the curtains. And he never felt any compunction doing so, not the least bit of doubt or regret.

As he lay in bed trying to sleep, Cyrus supposed that in some way he'd known all along. The signs were there; all he had to do was take the trouble to read them. Why did those Indians insist on coming back to the Choke Creek battlefield year after year, decade after decade—generation after generation? What exactly had happened there?

It wasn't just the rumored cowardice of his grandfather that made him wonder. There were other things, like the famously unsolved murder of Silas Brem, gunned down shortly after the battle in the streets of Danvers. How was he to explain the absence of his own grandfather from the county for over twenty years? This was a question even his mother couldn't answer, since she had been born after Thomas Eli returned. Then there were the strange, recurring desecrations of Stevenson's grave. Even more disturbing was the way people talked about the battle—or rather, *didn't* talk about it. Everyone agreed it was a glorious victory, but nobody wanted to dwell on the details. They passed on quickly to other things.

The most telling signs of all were the "souvenirs" the boys brought to school. Plaits of hair. Items of women's clothing. Rings so small they could fit only the finger of a child. Where in the context of a battle did these fit in?

He'd heard rumors, of course, that the Battle of Choke Creek wasn't as it seemed—that there was more to the story than people were saying. But what was missing?

The answer came to him one fine autumn day when he was fourteen years old, riding along the bluff. They hadn't just killed warriors that cold November day in 1864; they'd killed women and children, too. It was so obvious, he had no idea why he hadn't realized it before.

The realization left him with a quandary. Either his grandfather was a coward or a murderer—and neither option was exactly inviting. He decided to keep his thoughts to himself. Eventually they slipped from his mind. Anyway, it was easier to believe the same things that everybody else did.

But that winter as Cyrus lay in bed, he couldn't help thinking back to the battle on the bluff. Had his mother known all along about the death of innocents? Did she keep the secret to protect him—even though it ruined her? Was that what Eve Glauber had heard when she rode to the battlefield? Did the murdered women and children call out to her still? If only he could hear them! He wasn't afraid of the truth. He was willing to face it, no matter how painful. But how could he face something when he didn't even know what it was?

Something happened on that battlefield, Evie had said the last time he saw her, *something that wasn't supposed to.* He thought of the letters in the biscuit tin, and he shuddered. It had been over three months since he'd heard from his son. Three long months in which anything could have happened—and in which, he feared, with a growing sense of dread, it already had.

Eighteen

The men marched back to camp with Liver in the lead, still in high spirits from his capture of the Vietnamese girl. He clowned around, flicking the braid he had attached to his helmet suggestively back and forth, wiggling his hips, and prancing with the tight, mincing steps he claimed to have seen in prostitutes in Saigon. The others ignored him. The rain had started up again, and the day was dark and dismal. A bad feeling still hung over them from the night, and they didn't want to take any more chances. All they wanted was to get home. They trudged silently through the woods, keeping their thoughts to themselves and their heads down.

As they reached the river, the rain stopped, and the sun came out, filtering through the trees in a warm and inviting way. The air felt clean and fresh. The men took off their ponchos, and the gloomy air that had dogged them all morning dissipated. They were all right. Nothing bad had happened to them. Even Eason's spirits began to lift. He had made it after all. Maybe one day, he thought, there would even be a story in this. He imagined himself telling it. *And then Liver cut off her braid*, he heard himself saying, *and you should have seen her run.*

He was just about to say so to Liver—*What a story, huh!*—when bullets sliced through the tall elephant grass, whizzing past his head with a piercing, air-sucking sound. He threw himself to the ground, losing his wind, wrenching his shoulder as he fell. For long, agonizing moments he crawled through the brush, seeking cover. A low, moaning sound came into the air, confusing him until he realized it was coming from his own lips. At the last minute he managed to get off a few rounds of his own, shooting blindly into the grass. But by then it was over. Quiet had descended on the river again, and the sun was smiling down on him as before.

He stood up and took stock of his situation. His shoulder was throbbing, but he could still move his arm, so he figured he wasn't too badly hurt. He must have bitten his tongue because the taste of blood was in his mouth. Otherwise he was okay. He looked around, but the other men were nowhere in sight. Like him, they had scattered when the firing began.

Suddenly he heard a rustling in the underbrush. His heart leapt into his throat, but it was only Music, looking for him. Music's hand was injured, hit by a bullet that went straight through. He gazed down at the wound with a bewildered look on his face. "Don't those motherfuckers know I'm a peace-lover?" he said to Eason. Eason helped him bandage the wound, and they set off to find the others. After a few minutes they found Nye, squatting on the ground in a thick stand of bamboo, cleaning his rifle. When Nye dove for cover, he found himself in a swampy patch of earth, unable to fight back. Now he was furious, muttering dark fantasies of revenge. "Son of a bitch. Just let them come back. Give me one more chance, one more *fucking* time."

As they waited for Nye to finish assembling his rifle, Page stumbled out of the grass. He looked lost and frightened but otherwise was unhurt. Like Eason he, too, fired off a few rounds but doubted that he hit anybody. That left Liver. The men waited a few more minutes to see if he would appear. Then they fanned out to look for him.

Eason moved cautiously through the tall grass, still feeling dizzy and sick from the rush of the ambush. His shoulder ached, the pain jolting down his arm. Maybe he was more hurt than he thought. The river was quiet now—unnervingly so. He wasn't used to the sunlight, and he didn't like the way it made dark pockets of shade beneath the stands of bamboo. The shadows looked out at him in a mocking way, as if to remind him that there was more to Vietnam than what he could see.

He wasn't worried about coming across the soldiers who ambushed him; they were long gone by now, vanished into the woods like always. But he was very worried about finding Liver. His imagination ran away with him too easily. He imagined finding Liver intact and perfectly fine, standing tall, like a giant, by the river. In his imagination Liver laughed and clapped him on the back, called him Cowboy, and chided him for being scared. The long braid swung gaily down his back. At the very thought of it, Eason grew giddy with relief. Then he imagined finding Liver another way, and his stomach clenched in fear.

As it turned out, Eason didn't find Liver; Page did. Eason joined the others, who were standing in a semicircle, looking down at the ground where Liver lay facedown, his hands bound behind his back. He had been shot point-blank, execution-style, in the back of the head. The Viet Cong soldiers who had left him there did so with care. They took his ear-necklace, and replaced it with one of their own making, his own ears, which they had cut off and left neatly in his helmet beside him, along with the rest of his gear. Nothing else was missing, not even his rifle—nothing, that is, except the braid. And one more thing, which the men discovered when they turned him over: a long, bloody swath of his scalp.

No one spoke. The men didn't even dare look at one another. Then Music sucked in his breath and said, his voice high and keening, "Jesus."

"Jesus Christ," Page echoed.

"It's like they knew we were here."

"Of course they knew," Nye said bitterly. "What do you think? *She* told them."

Music dropped down on one knee and fumbled with the radio with his good hand.

"What are you doing?" Nye said.

"What do you think I'm doing? I'm calling it in to the lieutenant."

"That asshole? What for? So he can write it up in one of his little reports?"

Music looked at Nye as if he had lost his mind. "What else are we supposed to do?"

The question hung in the air. The men exchanged uneasy glances. All of them avoided looking at the body at their feet.

"It's a message," Page said finally. "It's a fucking message and they sent it right to us."

"Fuck this," Nye said. "I say we send one back."

"What the hell are you talking about?" Music said.

"I'm talking about going back there and finishing off what we were supposed to do last night."

"We were supposed to set up an ambush," Music said, his hand still cradling the radio.

"No, we were supposed to get those gooks."

"Those gooks are long gone and you know it."

A crafty look came over Nye's face. "Do I?" A sly glint came into his eyes. "All I'm saying is we go back and take a look."

"Take a look," Page echoed.

The men glanced uneasily at each other.

"A *long* look."

"This is crazy," Music said. He stood up and turned away. "You're crazy. All of you are."

Suddenly Nye was angry. "It's Liver, man. Look at him. Look at what those savages did to him." He grabbed Music by the shoulders and wrenched him around so that he had no choice but to look down at the corpse. "Are you telling me you can just walk away?"

They couldn't leave him like that. They unbound his hands and covered him with his poncho. Then they set off together through the woods.

They were going back to the trail that connected the two villages, the place where they had lain in ambush the night before. Nye led the way, falling easily into the role Liver once had played. Only he didn't have any of Liver's cheerfulness or affectionate humor. He was all business, his jaw set with determination, his face grim.

The other men trudged behind. Music shook his head, as if he believed they had all gone mad. Page glanced about anxiously. Eason, who brought up the rear, worried about what they would do when they got back to the trail. He wanted to ask Nye what his plan was, but he was afraid to. What if it turned out Nye didn't have a plan? It was better, Eason decided, not to ask. That way he could follow along, believing that Nye had it all figured out.

As they marched through the woods, the sun rose higher in the sky, and the day turned hot. Eason sweated through his shirt. His mouth was dry, and his tongue felt like sand, but he had nothing left to drink; he had emptied his canteen long ago. The air was cloying, hard to breathe. He moved sluggishly, his legs heavy, his shoulder throbbing with every step.

It occurred to him that he didn't want any of this to be happening. It also occurred to him that it was all his fault. If only he had shot that girl like he was supposed to! She had no business being out at night. He should have shot her when he had the chance. Or, barring that, he should have kept her away from Liver. He had known no good would come of it, and yet he hadn't been able to bring himself to act. Just as he hadn't been able to bring himself to fire his gun.

A light breeze stirred the tree canopy, and as Eason listened to it, he heard Dane speak, as if he were marching right beside him. *Don't worry about it*, Dane said. He spoke in a friendly fashion, without irony or rancor. *What did you expect? Everyone knows the Swales can't shoot.*

Eason shook his head and chased Dane's voice from his mind. But he couldn't stop thinking about the prairie dogs he'd left lying on the ground so long ago, their bodies giving off a foul stench in the warm spring sun. Now Billy was dead, and Liver was dead, and it was all his fault. When he'd joined the Army, he thought he was going to Vietnam because he wanted to, but he was only fooling himself. He wasn't here for any reason. He was only one more failure in a long line of failures, stretching from his father to his great-grandfather, riding on the banks of Choke Creek. Eason didn't have free will; he had only the illusion of it. He had no more weight or substance than a leaf from one of these trees, drifting down around him, blown here and there by the hot Vietnamese wind.

When they reached the trail, Nye came to a halt, giving the men a moment to rest. They settled down on the ground and shrugged off their packs. Eason could just make out the place where he had lain the night before, the brush still flattened in the shape of his body. Worms and beetles scurried through the damp soil, doing their part to fuel the engine of jungle rot and decay. A picture of Liver, lying cold and motionless on the ground, flashed into his mind. He was nothing more than food for worms now; they all were. He rubbed his shoulder and willed the thought away.

As they rested, the sky clouded over, and it began to rain again. The rain was warm and heavy and did nothing to clear the air, but for once Eason was glad for it. He tipped back his head and closed his eyes, letting the warm rain wash over his face.

At last it was time to move out again. The men rose to their feet. As Eason lifted his pack, a jolt of pain coursed through his shoulder. He grimaced and gritted his teeth. Then he turned and looked at Nye. There was a flicker of uncertainty on his face, the first Eason had seen all morning. Nye, Eason realized, didn't know which way to go.

None of them did.

The girl had told on them. That much was clear. None of them denied it. But whom did she tell? Which way did she go after they let her free? She came from the right; of that much Eason was sure. He distinctly remembered hearing her coming from that direction on the trail. But which way did she go after they released her? Back to the right, to the village she had come from, or on to the left, to the village she was heading to when they captured her?

None of them remembered. In the chaos of the moment, they simply forgot. They recalled seeing the girl run away, clutching at her shorn hair. They even remembered the sound of her plaintive wails. But for the life of them, they couldn't remember which way she ran.

They looked at one another, a sense of gloom in the air. "Fuck," Page said with a mournful, defeated air.

"Fuck this," Music agreed.

They were waiting for Nye to give up—to agree that there was nothing more to be done about it. They would have to call it in the way Music wanted to in the first place then head back to camp. Music loosened the straps on the radio, preparing to make the call, wincing as he used his injured hand. Nye watched him, a moody look on his face. All at once he headed down the trail, moving rapidly to the right, in the direction the girl had come from.

Dumbfounded the men watched him go.

"What are you doing?" Page called out.

Nye glared at him. "I'm going, that's what."

"Where?"

"You know where."

"You don't even know if that's where they came from!"

"They're gooks, aren't they? You saw what they did to Liver. What more do you need to know?"

Nye stared at them with disgust, then turned and disappeared into the woods.

The men glanced uneasily at one another. A vision hung almost palpably in the air before them, a vision of Liver. They saw the crushed bits of bone at the back of his skull, the jagged, bloody edges of the missing scalp and ears. Music swore under his breath. Then he put the radio away.

The trail ended in a clearing. The men paused at the edge of the woods and peered out. Before them stretched a small valley, studded with rice paddies and fields. A river ran through it, muddy and torpid and wide. A narrow bridge led over the river to a small group of thatched huts, clustered together on the far side. There was no one about. They must have all been inside. Smoke curled from the roofs of the huts. Here and there pigs wallowed in muddy pens, and chickens pecked at the ground. From somewhere came the sound of cattle bawling. In the distance a water buffalo stood in a field, his body blending almost invisibly into the misty air and rainy sky.

It's too small, Eason thought. *They couldn't have come from here. It's impossible. There aren't enough huts. It's not even a real village.*

For the last time he thought about how hopeless it was, and how it was all his fault. Once more he pictured Liver, the motionless body, the bloody swath of missing scalp. This was it, his last chance to shrug off the weight that had burdened his family for over one hundred years. He looked at the huts and then at the other men, taking in their faces one by one. They needed him; they were depending on him. He had failed Billy, and he had failed Liver, but he couldn't fail these men. Not this time.

He remembered a conversation he had with Liver the day before, while they waited in the mess tent for the lieutenant's briefing. It was one of the last times they spoke together alone. Liver, as usual, was giving Eason grief for his adulation of Gary Cooper as Marshal Will Kane.

"If Kane was such a hero," Liver said, "if everything he did was so right, then why'd he throw his badge down at the end of the movie? Why'd he give it all up?"

At the time Eason hadn't replied. The truth was he didn't have an answer to Liver's question; that part of the movie that had always troubled him, too. But now he wondered if Liver hadn't been trying to tell him something or give him a message—guide him even now, from beyond the grave.

Just then a figure stepped out of one of the huts, a small, slight girl. Even from a distance they could see her swollen face and shorn hair. Nye shot the others a triumphant look. "Okay," he said, breathing rapidly in and out. "Okay." The muscles in his jaw twitched and jumped. The girl turned and disappeared inside the hut. And the men stepped out of the woods.

Nineteen

The knock on the door came late one night in March on the cusp of spring, when snow lay thick on the ground, and there was no wind. Cyrus was dozing in his chair by the fire, but at the sound he leapt to his feet, his heart in his throat. It had finally happened, just as he had feared. They had come to tell him about Eason—to tell him he was gone.

He took a moment to prepare himself, breathed in deeply, settled his heart. This, he had decided long ago, was how he would face it, with grace and dignity if nothing more. He turned and made his way to the door. His hip had stiffened up while he was sleeping, and he clutched at the furniture for support as he crossed the room.

He opened the door, his face expressionless, his body rigidly erect. Outside the sky was clear, the stars shining down with a light so achingly brilliant, it blinded his eyes. He blinked, looked again. Only one figure stood in the darkness on the porch. Didn't they always come in pairs? He rubbed a hand over his eyes. This man wasn't even in uniform. He was dressed in old clothes, in thin cotton pants and a worn shirt. The clothing didn't fit properly—the pants were too big, and the shirt was so small, his wrists emerged from the ends of the sleeves. His face was covered in a thick beard, his hair scraggly and unkempt, hanging down to his jawbone, obscuring his eyes. He had no hat. The only thing about him that spoke of the Army were his boots, which were dilapidated and beaten up, but still identifiably regulation issue.

The figure on the porch was gaunt, shivering. Even from the doorway Cyrus was sickened by his odor, a dirty unwashed smell. But instead of disgust, he was filled with gratitude. A wave of relief flooded through him, buckling his knees. He was wrong. He steadied himself against the doorjamb. They hadn't come after all.

As he straightened himself, the feeling of relief ebbed, replaced by a growing sense of anger. It was an Indian, one of the worst he'd ever seen. What right did he have to come here uninvited at this time of night, scaring him to death, robbing him of what little peace he had? He pinned the man with a look of loathing. "Go away. You have no right to be here. Get off my land!"

The man lowered his head with shame, as if he, too, agreed that he had no right to be there. He turned away and shuffled down the porch steps, moving with an air of defeat, his hand rubbing his shoulder. But there was something strange about him—no, something *familiar* in the shape of his shoulders, his hips, the curve of his lower back. Cyrus gasped. "Eason?" His voice was strangled, the word barely audible. The figure shuffled farther away. "Eason—" He managed to get the name out louder this time, his throat choked with emotion. In the darkness the figure hesitated, then turned around. "Oh my God, Eason, it is you, I didn't know, oh my God, my son—"

Cyrus ran down the porch steps, in his eagerness forgetting his hip, which gave way, so that he stumbled and caught himself on the rail. He lurched towards his boy, ready to throw his arms around him, to seize him and caress him—to do all those things he'd been dreaming of for so long. But something in the boy's face gave him pause. "Eason," he said, his body trembling. "Son." He choked on the words.

The boy nodded. "I'm a little tired." His hands dangled loose and empty at his sides. "If it's all right with you, I'll just go inside and rest for a while."

Yes, yes, of course—what had be been thinking? Cyrus led him into the house, practically running, looking back over his shoulder, afraid his son might disappear again or vanish like a mirage into a puff of vapor and desire. He led him to his room as if he feared the boy had forgotten the way, then stepped aside to let him in. He wanted to go in after him, but once again something in the way his son looked at him made him hesitate.

"Thanks," the boy said. Once more he nodded. Then moving gently, as if he didn't want to hurt his feelings—as if he didn't want to hurt anyone anymore—he stepped back and closed the door.

Cyrus stared at the blank door. The shock had begun to wear off, taking with it the numb incomprehension that had settled on him when he'd realized that the man on the doorstep was his son. Yes, Eason was home, just as he had always desired. But he was dimly aware of feeling no joy from this homecoming. Wasn't he supposed to feel joy? Instead he felt even more fearful than before. From inside the room came the sound of the bed creaking, and then nothing. What had happened to his son—and what, in God's name, had brought him home?

He figured they'd talk about it in the morning. Surely his son would have a reason, a logical explanation. It must be nothing more than a mistake, the kind the Army was famous for. They'd sent his son home on leave and forgotten to let him know. But when dawn came, there was no one to talk to. Eason was still in his room, asleep. Cyrus went to the barn to feed the horses, and when he came back, his son was still in bed. He slipped the door open a crack just to make sure. The boy's body was so thin, it barely dented the blankets. Cyrus left the door ajar while he mucked out the stalls and filled the water buckets, but when he came back, Eason was still sleeping the same way.

Only the wind seemed to make a change in him. As the sun rose higher in the sky, the wind began to blow, a sharp, wailing sound. The sound made Eason grimace in his sleep, his body jerking and his limbs contracting as if in pain.

After lunch the rancher drove to the feed store. Foaling season had come, and he needed linseed meal and barley for the mares. He unloaded the sacks in the feed room of the barn then went back to the house. The sun had passed its zenith, and was following its lowering track to the mountains, but the boy was still in bed. Cyrus cleared his throat. Eason didn't move, but something in the air about him made the rancher think his son might be awake and listening. "Can I bring you something?"

There was a moment of silence and then, "No, that won't be necessary. Thanks." The voice, like the words, was excruciatingly polite, as if his son—always a good boy—was determined to show his father that he was a good boy still.

"A sandwich? A glass of milk?"

"No, really, nothing."

"A glass of water then."

"A glass of water." A note in his son's voice hinted at reserve, a conscious effort at control. "Okay."

Cyrus hurried to the kitchen, drew a glass of water, and placed it on the floor at Eason's side. Then he left the house to haul feed to the outer pastures. Later, when he came back, it was almost dark, but the boy was still in bed, the glass of water untouched.

On the second morning, a telegram came from the Army. The rancher read it without understanding. It said his son was missing in action. It said they were conducting an investigation. They would contact him again when they knew more.

Missing in action? He read the words again. It made no sense. Eason wasn't missing—he was right here! Then he shook his head, surprised at his own opacity. As he allowed himself to realize what his son had done, a dull pain settled in his heart, cleaving it in two the way drought cleaved the dry summer earth.

He put the telegram in his pocket and walked down the hallway to Eason's room. The lights were off, the shades closed. In the bleak light Eason slept on his back, his breath shallow. He'd left his boots in the corner and the cotton shirt and pants on the back of his chair. The clock on his dresser was unplugged, the poster from *High Noon* crumpled in the trash.

Cyrus crept into the room. He stood for a time by the bed, looking down at his son's face. Eason had never worn a beard before, and Cyrus was startled to see how much it made him resemble his namesake. In the photograph on the mantel, Thomas Eli wore an uneasy look. Cyrus had always assumed it came from the way pictures were taken in those days: the long wait while the photographer arranged his lens, the shocking effect as the bulb flashed. But now he wondered if, as his grandfather sat for his portrait, he wasn't already dreading the judgments future generations would make when they looked upon his image.

He made sure his son was still sleeping. Then carefully and quietly so as not to disturb him, he lifted up the pants. The fabric was cheap and had a vaguely foreign feel, as if the pants had been passed down to him secondhand or bought for a few pennies off a cart. One by one he turned out the pockets. Inside he found scraps of paper, tickets, receipts, punched-out cards. All were in strange, Oriental writing, in languages he couldn't read. He shuffled through them without understanding.

Gradually a strange feeling came over him. He turned around and discovered his son watching him. Apparently Eason had been watching him for some time. His son's face was impassive, his gaze flat. But there was a hint of violation in the air between them now, and betrayal. The rancher's face reddened. Hastily he stuffed the papers back into the pockets. Then he left the room, with Eason's eyes following him every step of the way.

It made him angry. It made him want to rant and rage. But whom was he to rage at and what was he to say?

That night the creek began to run. Cyrus was sitting by the fire when he heard it, the ice snapping and cracking as it broke apart, the ground groaning as it shifted and thawed. He stood up and went to Eason's room. It was dark inside, and he didn't know if the boy was sleeping or awake. All he could see was the dim outline of his body in the bed. But he decided it didn't matter. He spoke anyway.

"I'll do anything," he said. "Whatever you want. I don't care what it is. I'll help you, no matter what it takes."

"It's a little too late for that now, don't you think?" A bitter, mocking smile flitted across his son's face. "After all, you know what they say about us Swales." Then the smile died away, and Eason turned his face to the wall.

On the third morning Cyrus slept late. He'd been up all night with one of the mares, which was foaling, and hadn't gotten to bed until shortly before dawn. Overcome with exhaustion, he fell into a deep sleep. When he woke, he was shocked to discover the sun already high in the sky. He dressed quickly, and on his way to the barn glanced into Eason's room. It was empty. He believed he felt his heart stop, hanging like a dead weight in his chest. He lost his breath and then his balance, falling to the side, crashing against the wall. "Oh God," he said. "Oh, God. My God." A cold, liquid terror seized his legs. It propelled him out of the house and to the barn. He stumbled through the doorway and stopped, blinking in the light. There, at the end of the aisle, was the wheelbarrow. He had trouble making sense of it. The wheelbarrow was there, at the end of the aisle, and someone was pitching straw into it, pitching straw out of one of the stalls.

He moved down the aisle on deadened legs. When he reached the stall, he saw his son inside. "Eason." The panic was plain in his voice. "What are you doing?"

"Mucking out stalls." Eason shook his head as if he believed his father had lost his mind. "What did you think?"

The boy spent the rest of the day on the ranch, doing chores. He had bathed and shaved, and while he hadn't cut his hair, it was brushed back neatly, the ends tucked behind his ears. He was dressed in the same clothes he'd worn before the war, jeans, a denim jacket, a button-down shirt. The clothes were big on him because of the weight he'd lost, the belt pulled tighter by a notch. But he looked all right. He looked fine. The only difference was the Army boots, which he had put back on, and the fact that he was hatless, as if looking like a cowboy was the last thing he wanted.

In the evening they sat down to dinner. Outside the creek was running, surging noisily through its banks, the cold spring water washing away the winter ice. As the rancher listened to it, his spirits began to lift. The last of the mares had finally foaled that afternoon, giving him a successful crop with no losses. Buoyed by his good fortune, he grew careless. He leaned across the table towards his son. "Why did you come back?" he said. "What happened over there?"

Eason had been hunched over his dinner, but now he looked up and let his hands drop. "Nothing happened. That's the whole point. Don't you see?" He stared at his father in pitying silence then stood up and left the room.

See? See *what*? The rancher pushed his plate away. He fetched a flashlight and went to the barn to check on the horses. The mare that had broken her leg the winter before had a new foal. As he directed the light into her stall, she looked back at him with dark and shining eyes. But all Cyrus could think about was the vet who'd worked on her and the words he'd said about his own son, who'd come back from Vietnam. The boy, the vet had said, was driving them crazy, both him and his wife, but he wouldn't talk about it. He wouldn't talk about *anything*.

It was impossible, but after that, life on the ranch took on a semblance of its old shape, both Cyrus and Eason falling into the rhythm of familiar routines. Eason took up his old chores, carrying feed to the horses in the outer pastures, saddle-breaking the yearlings, caring for the new foals. When the ring finished thawing, he began riding again, working with the two- and three-year-olds, taking up the training of a new filly, a chestnut with white stockings. As long as Cyrus was busy, working with the horses, he was able to keep his mind steady. But at night, when he was sitting still, the thoughts crept in, and his mind began to whirl. His son was a deserter. He'd come home without explanation, refusing all offers of help. The worst was when they sat together at mealtime, sharing the same table. Then the rancher had the feeling that his life wasn't even his own anymore; it was as if he were caught in a play, in one of those absurd scenarios in which the characters wait endlessly for something without knowing what it is, or even if it's good or bad.

Cyrus found himself thinking about that one night as they sat down to dinner, plates of stewed beef, mashed potatoes, canned peas on the side. For a time they ate in silence, Eason hunched over his food. "You're doing a good job with that chestnut filly," Cyrus said at last. "I think I'll get a good price for her in the fall."

Eason didn't answer, his knife and fork working over his plate.

Cyrus turned to his own food, and the room grew quiet again. A few minutes later he cleared his throat. "I hear they're raising the price of hay again, six cents a bale."

Eason nodded without speaking. Outside the wind was stirring. He put down his fork and tipped his face towards the sound. As he listened, a distant look came into his eyes, and he rubbed his hand along his shoulder.

Cyrus studied him then put down his own knife and fork. "Do you remember that girl who came out here last year? She rode that roan colt."

"Evie?" Eason turned to him, a flicker of interest in his eyes. "The Glauber girl?"

"She helped me with the horses while you were away."

A curious look came into Eason's eyes. "What happened to her?"

"I don't know. I haven't seen her since the summer."

Eason hesitated as if he were about to say more. Then he shook his head and cut through his beef.

"She was a nice kid, good with the horses," Cyrus said, "but she was strange, too. She said all sorts of things." He was being reckless, and he knew it, but he couldn't bear the paralyzing silence between them any longer. He would say anything, if only it would make his son speak.

Eason put down his knife. "What kinds of things?" He studied his food as if he'd lost his appetite. Then he carried his plate to the sink and turned the water on.

"She said she saw ghosts. She claimed to hear voices, too."

"Voices?" Eason whipped around to face him. "Where?"

Cyrus fell silent. It was a mistake. He shouldn't have brought it up. There was a hungry look in his son's eyes that frightened him. He'd pried open a locked door without knowing what lay on the other side. "I don't know," he said, his voice withering, his words sounding lame even in his own ears. "On that old battlefield, I guess."

Without a word—without even shutting the water off—Eason turned away from him and left the house. A few minutes later Cyrus saw him on the chestnut filly, riding in the moonlight down the creek trail. Hours later the rancher was still awake, lying wracked with worry in his bed, when his son came back in. The boy went straight to his room and closed the door. In the morning he said nothing about what he'd done or where he'd been. But Cyrus knew. When he looked in on the filly, she was standing exhausted in her stall, her head hanging low, her legs splattered with mud and sand.

A few days later he was leaning on the rail of the riding ring, watching Eason work the filly. It was a beautiful day, the sky flung in a seamless swath of blue from mountain to plain. The spring run, Cyrus noticed, was finally over, and the creek had subsided to its usual self, a thin trickle winding lazily through a broad ribbon of sand. In the pastures the buffalo grass was thickening into grey-green clumps, the prickly pears budding out. The air was clear and crisp, redolent with the musty scent of greening sage. He lifted his face to the sky, feeling the warmth of the sun seep into his bones. In a kind of delirium his spirits lifted, and he felt blessed, as if the events of the past year had never happened—as if his son had never gone to war.

Then the wind picked up. In the ring, Eason brought the filly to a halt. A troubled shadow crossed his face. He put his spurs to his horse and galloped out of the ring, heading for the creek. Startled, the rancher stumbled after him. "Eason," he called, "son, wait," but it was too late. Eason was already too far away to hear his voice, and even if he hadn't been, the rancher knew his son wouldn't have stopped.

Twenty

The thaw came in early March, and by the middle of the month the creek began to run. Day after day Evie crossed to the bottom of her yard, the wet earth sucking at her feet, to watch the water surge by, a muddy torrent of snowmelt that raced between the banks. The current was deep, swallowing up the sandbars and sedges she'd ridden through the summer before, flinging clots of leaves and broken tree limbs past her in its foamy wake. Only the bare tips of the willows were still visible, riding high on the froth like souls in danger of drowning, while day and night the creek hissed and raged, as if it were trying to purge itself, or cleanse itself of memory and sin.

Ever since the night he'd found her half-frozen in the snow, her father had made good on his promise and hadn't left her alone. He was there in the mornings when she left for school and there again when she came home in the afternoons. She tried to enjoy the time they spent together, but she was no longer the little girl entertained by endless games of gin rummy and casino, by listening to him read out loud to her from books, or by working together side by side with him in the garden. His curtailed schedule took a toll on him; he couldn't manage *The Sun* in the minute fashion he liked, and the strain showed on his face, in the pinched line of worry that deepened daily between his eyes. What would he say when the creek stopped running, and she began riding to the Swale ranch again? He had to let her go. One day, when she came home from school, she told him so. He protested, but she insisted, saying he had to stop worrying about her. The winter was over; nothing bad would happen to her now. Even the ghost had disappeared with the last of the snow—although she didn't tell him that—retreating to a small white light that appeared at night outside her window, glimmering harmlessly beneath the willows.

The next morning, when she woke up, he had already left for work, and the following Sunday, when she took her daily walk to the creek, she saw that the spring run was over. Nothing was left of the snowmelt but a narrow streamlet of water, meandering peacefully through the sandbars. She returned to the house and put on her riding boots. Then she braided her hair. As she pulled the long strands back, she glanced in the mirror. Her eyes were deeper and darker than they'd been the year before, her widow's peak even more pronounced, a sharp black triangle that defined her face. What had happened to the innocent girl who climbed so recklessly on the back of the wild colt? She had changed over the winter; she had seen things she'd never imagined.

The creek had changed over the winter, too. The heavy spring run had scoured the bottom, obliterating the old trails, creating new ones. Evie gave her horse his head and let him pick out the way. The sandbars were rough and ragged, not yet smoothed by wind. The sedges and cattails grew in wild stands. In one place a willow, uprooted by the surge, lay lodged across the creek bed. As Bird squeezed past it, the dry, dead limbs pulled at her like fingers. Nearby a shallow pool of water spread across the sand, opaque and reflecting. She glanced down at her image as she rode past, her features blurred and shadowy, marred by ripples. For so long she had waited for this moment, and now that it was here, she was suddenly unsure of herself. She had to tell Cyrus about her vision—about what she'd seen. From the budding cottonwoods came the call of a kingbird, high-pitched and chattering. But would he understand?

She rode up the ridgeline to the ranch, surprised at how relieved she was to find it still there, as if secretly she had feared it had disappeared over the winter, or had been swept away by the surging creek. There was the familiar shape of the barn, peaked and soaring, the low-slung house, the rickety bunkhouse with its tin roof gleaming like always in the sunshine. The stallions were loose in their paddocks, and at the sight of Bird they whinnied, the sound rising and falling through the clear air like trumpeters practicing scales. In the pastures, the mares were grazing beside a new crop of foals, their gait wide and waddling from their full milk bags. The yearlings were dozing in the sunlight, their rangy bodies balanced on long, lanky legs.

The rancher was at the pump washing his hands; Evie caught sight of him with his shirt sleeves rolled up, his hands plunged into the icy stream of well water. She rode down to him. "I have something to tell you," she said.

She'd expected him to be surprised to see her, but he wasn't. He looked at her with steady, appraising eyes as if her appearance were only the latest in a string of such unpredictable, uncontrollable events. "Is it about Eason?"

"Yes." How did he know that?

"Then you can tell him yourself." He shut down the pump and wiped his hands on his pants. "I expect you'll find him on the battlefield." He nodded towards the east. "He rode there over an hour ago."

Eason was home? Her heart leapt, and she clutched her horse's mane as if the earth had shifted, throwing her off balance. "You mean he's home on leave?"

The rancher shook his head.

"Then how—why is here?"

He rolled down his shirt sleeves. "You can ask him that when you see him, too."

She rode back to the creek, her mind whirling. Eason was home? How could that be? She passed beneath the shadow of a cottonwood, its bare limbs studded with long brown catkins. Soon, she knew, the catkins would release their seeds, to be borne aloft on the wind like cotton on silky white threads. She felt like a seed herself, shed from a dry brown husk. Her thoughts raced; her senses bristled with a rawness that was almost painful. Eason was home. *Home, home, home.* The words made a rhythm timed to the beating of her heart. She put her heels to her horse, abandoning all caution, urging him to a gallop. Eason was home. *He was home!* She flew towards the battlefield.

Then she saw him, sitting on the bluff with his horse, a chestnut filly, hobbled, grazing nearby. With a jolt she pulled Bird to a halt, her heart throbbing, her throat tight. Even from a distance she could see how changed he was. His hair straggled to his collarbone; his face, thin and gaunt, was dogged by a hollowness that seemed to come from within. His eyes had grown sharper since she had last seen him and were sunk deeper into the bone as if retreating from things he wished he'd never seen. He was hatless and wore strange lace-up boots that, with a start, she recognized as coming from the Army—she'd seen them in pictures of soldiers before. She looked at him, blinked, and looked again, seeing first the boy she knew and then one she didn't—an imposter who'd come home from the war in his place. It was a vision that set her adrift, and once more she sought to anchor herself by grabbing her horse's mane.

Dear God, she thought. *Cyrus was wrong. Eason hadn't come home. He was still there, fighting the war.* Bird jogged anxiously in place, wanting her to make up her mind, to send him forwards or back. *Back*, she decided, when all at once Eason looked up and saw her, the recognition widening his eyes. "Oh, Eason." She breathed out the words in a rush of gratitude. He was home. He had come back, just as he had said he would. She urged her horse towards him, riding up the bluff. Nothing else mattered, and if it did, she would find a way to make it right.

They sat together on the bluff, cross-legged, side by side. Nearby the horses grazed. Bird kept close to the hobbled filly, cropping at the new spring grasses with his soft lips and delicate nipping teeth. Evie studied her hands, her fingers twisting the hem of her blouse. For so long she had dreamt of the things she would say to him, and now that he was here, she found herself overcome by shyness, at a loss for words. "I never forgot you," she said at last. She stole a glance at him. "I couldn't."

A smile flickered on his face, and briefly he became the Eason she knew—the one she'd fallen in love with so long ago. Then the smile vanished, and a pinched look came into his eyes. "I'm sorry," he said. "I never should have told you the things I did. I didn't mean to lie." He turned and gazed over the bluff at the plain, which unfolded before them in green-brown waves, flowing to the horizon. When he looked back at her, there was an air of wonder in his eyes. "Have you ever seen the ocean? You can't imagine it. All that water, light, and air. It pulls at you, like it's trying to draw you out of yourself. Like it wants you to be greater than you are. It made me think of home." He held his hands out, palms up, as if he would gather the landscape to him if only he could and contain it in his grasp. "It's so beautiful here. I didn't know before. I had to go away to see."

She gazed past the horses, their winter coats puffy and glowing in the warm spring sun, and saw that he was right, the prairie was beautiful. In her absence it had grown more so. In the creek bed water glinted, shaping a shimmering course across the plain. Here and there wildflowers bloomed, tiny lavender petals of blazing star scattered among shoots of golden sunflowers and prickly white poppies. Pigweed grew green and lush alongside banks of yellow-flowered rabbitbrush, while the air carried the rising scent of sage.

Once more she stole a glance at him. How small and unimportant she was beside this man who had gone so far and seen such great things! A gulf had opened between them, so wide, she feared she would never cross it. Then she saw his hands, resting with a quiet gentleness in his lap, and remembered the gentleness with which he had touched her the year before. More than anything she wanted him to touch her again, to feel him close, so that she could hold him, cradle him, comfort him. She tucked her hands beneath her knees.

"I came here a lot last summer," she said. "I was thinking about you. I felt—" She hesitated, trying to find a way to express what she meant so that he would understand. "I felt closest to you here."

"Is that when you heard the voices?"

Surprised, she looked at him. "You know about that?"

"My father told me."

"Oh." Her face reddened. What else had Cyrus told him about her? She studied his face, but there was nothing judgmental in it, just an expectant look as he waited for her answer. "It was last spring, right after you left."

"What did they say?"

He was looking at her intently now, and she closed her eyes, wanting to please him, willing herself back to the day when she'd heard the voices calling to her. The wind was blowing lightly now, shivering through the prairie grasses, and she turned her face to it, listening, but nothing more came to her. She understood it never would. That day had been no ordinary event; it had been a rare and precious gift, a glimpse of another world. She'd been wrong to think otherwise. She opened her eyes and sought his face. "I'm sorry, Eason. I've changed. I'm not the same as I was before. Things happened to me over the winter—things I never dreamed of. This place ... " She groped for the words. "It's not what people say."

"Nothing ever is." He plucked a handful of grass and sifted it through his fingers. "Isn't it strange the way we believe we can make things turn out differently, when they always end up being the same?" A sad smile graced his lips. "I thought I would make a difference if I went to war. I thought ... " He flicked the last of the grass away. "This man I knew once tried to tell me." He reached over and took a gentle hold of her braid. "I didn't understand." He let the braid go.

"Please," she said. She wanted him to go on. She was trying so hard to understand him. She wanted him to touch her hair again. She wanted him to touch her everywhere.

"Have you ever listened to war stories?" He crossed his arms over his chest, hugging himself close. "You know, those stories old men tell when they've been to war. They're so beautiful." The look of wonder came into his eyes again. "Even the most gruesome, awful thing becomes beautiful in the telling, because it was a thing that had to be endured, and they endured it. There were times I wished I would die." He looked to her with amazement. "Just so I could live forever in somebody else's story."

But this was not at all what she wanted, nor what she had intended. "Please, Eason," she said again. "Tell me what happened to you. Why did you come home?"

He took her braid in his hand again, caressing it lightly. Then he stood up and walked to the horses, checking on them needlessly, loosening the filly's cinch then tightening it again. "I thought when I came home I'd have stories of my own to tell," he said at last, resting a hand on the filly's shoulder. "I was wrong. There weren't any new stories waiting for me in the war. Only old ones. They'd been written before I even got there. Before I was even born."

He grew silent then and so did she, thinking about what he'd said, trying to grasp what he meant. Is that what she'd heard when the voices called out to her on the bluff—the anguish of the people who had died there, wanting their stories to be heard? What was left of those people now? Nothing but earth and water, air and wind. Even their bones had vanished, dissolved into dust. She closed her eyes, and her vision of the massacre came back to her, the dead and dying lying mutilated on the ground. Her breath caught in her throat, and she shuddered. "Eason." She followed him to the horses and grasped his arm. "There's something I have to tell you."

In the few minutes he'd been away from her, the Eason she'd known had disappeared, leaving the imposter in his place. She saw it in his eyes. "I saw a dead girl once." He took hold of her hair again, but this time his touch was rough, his fingers tightening on the braid. "She had a braid just like yours. But you couldn't look at her. If you did, she disappeared."

He was frightening her. She tried to twist free, but that only made him clutch her braid harder, pulling until it hurt. "Eason, don't, let go—"

He released her. He tipped her face up and looked with earnestness into her eyes. "Take it out. You should never wear your hair like that." Working carefully, with the gentleness she remembered, he undid the band at the bottom of her braid. Then he raked his fingers through her hair, loosening it, setting it free.

Something was loosening in her as well. Deep inside, she felt a knot come undone. "Oh," she said. "Eason." She closed her eyes, reached up, and kissed him, entering into that sweet darkness she understood was uniquely his. A moan escaped her lips, and she buried her head against his chest. "Tell me what happened to you. Please. Tell me everything."

He took her by the shoulders, pushing her gently away so that she had to look at him. "Nothing happened to me. I thought you knew that. Everything that matters happened here." He thumbed the loose hair away from her eyes. "You shouldn't have come here. I'm not what you think I am. I'm no good for you. Don't you see? I'm no good for anything anymore."

He dropped his hands and turned away from her. "Eason," she said again, "please, listen to me." But even as she said it, she knew he wouldn't. He wasn't capable of it anymore. She put her arms around him and drew him back to her, holding onto him as tightly as she could, because she knew he was right, and she shouldn't have come there. And because she knew it didn't matter. She couldn't stay away.

Twenty-One

Cyrus Swale was sitting in his truck on the street outside the Glauber house when the two girls came around the corner, Evie and a redhead—a schoolmate, he figured, walking her home. It was a clear spring afternoon, the trees leafing out, casting dollops of shadow on the ground like dapples. He took his hat off and stepped outside, resting his arms on the pickup's open door. Evie caught sight of him first, her eyes growing wide with surprise as she realized who he was. She put a hand on her friend's arm, bringing her to a stop. Briefly the girls conferred. The redhead cast a suspicious glance in his direction, but Evie must have persuaded her, because at last she went on by herself, walking past him with a doubtful air. Then Evie came up to him, her schoolbooks slung under her arm, a worried look in her eyes. "What is it? What's wrong? Is Eason all right?"

"Eason's fine." He twisted the brim of his hat. "He doesn't know I'm here."

"Oh." She still looked uneasy. She was wondering why he'd come—what it meant. "Do you want to come in?"

"I don't think your father would care for that."

"No, I suppose not." She was dressed in blue jeans and a cream-colored blouse, patterned with little flowers. Her hair hung loose below her shoulders. He'd never seen it without the braid. The dark tresses seemed to darken the look in her eyes. "There's a swing on the porch. We can sit there."

It was an old porch swing made of slatted wood, hanging down from the ceiling on chains. The porch itself was grounded in stone like the house, white columns supporting a high, flat roof. She sat down, leaving room for him beside her, but he remained standing, thinking it better that way.

"Yesterday," he said, "when you came to the ranch ... " His voice trailed off as he tried to gain his bearings, judging the best way to convey his meaning. "I shouldn't have told you Eason was home."

She nodded, waiting for him to continue. The porch was surrounded by yews, thick, ungainly bushes that had overgrown their plot. Jase Glauber should trim then back, Cyrus thought. Then he corrected himself. Surely the editor of *The Rocky Mountain Sun* had better things to do with his time. With a start he realized his mind had wandered, and he turned it back to his purpose. He cleared his throat. "It was selfishness on my part, pure and simple."

She was holding her books in her lap, her hands resting on top. Now she ran a finger along the spine of one of her notebooks, a coiled spring. "I don't understand."

He fingered the brim of his hat as he spoke. "I thought Eason might tell you what happened to him."

A look of surprise crossed her face. "You don't know?"

"They think he's missing in action." He had brought the telegram with him, and he took it from his pocket and handed it to her. The small square of yellow paper was worn and creased from his repeated perusal of it, as if reading it again would make it change what it said. She unfolded it and studied it. The she handed it back to him.

"No," she said. "I'm sorry. He didn't tell me."

The rancher folded the telegram and put it back in his pocket. "Well, then." He put on his hat. "I'm sorry to have bothered you."

He was stepping off the porch when her voice came to him. "Wait." He turned around.

"Choke Creek. It was a massacre, wasn't it?"

She had startled him. He stared at her in surprise. "What makes you think that?"

"I found out last winter. We took a field trip to the State Capitol and ... " She shifted in her seat, considering, and the chains of the swing creaked. "That doesn't matter." A hint of anger came into her voice. "That's why you chased those Indians off your land, isn't it? Why you *always* chase them away. You don't want to face the truth."

The porch stones were old and cracked, the mortar between them worn and chipped away. He studied one of the gaps, working it with the toe of his boot. He felt tired and chipped away himself, worn out by a lifetime of pretense. "Yes," he said. "I suppose that's right."

"They're murderers." Her voice rose, and he could hear in it the bitterness of someone who had been betrayed. "All of them. Stevenson and the rest. Your grandfather, too."

"Thomas Eli?" He took his hat off, rubbing his forehead. The habitual use of the hat had dented his skin, and it always left a crease like a scar. "No. Impossible."

"I don't believe you."

She raised her face to him, challenging him with her dark eyes. There was a fierceness in the air around her, and it reminded him of the day she'd ridden the roan colt, climbing on him with such wild determination. He'd underestimated her then—he'd underestimated her all along. He'd thought she was just a slip of a girl, a little bit of nothing, the kind of child who could easily be discouraged or frightened away. Now he realized she wasn't afraid of anything. She would keep on until she had the truth, no matter how painful it was.

Standing was making his hip ache, and he pressed a hand to it. "I didn't think you would," he said. Then he sat down.

Down the street someone was cutting grass, and the sound of the mower came to Cyrus from the distance, a tinny whine. Beneath the yews bulbs were blooming, the crocuses giving way to irises and daffodils. What would his life had been like if he'd left the ranch and come into the city, living in place like this where grass grew and flowers bloomed? What would Eason's life have been like? He shook his head. Even if he'd been able to give up the horses, he'd never have been able to leave the land.

"After the battle was over, there were rumors that my grandfather was a coward." Cyrus held his hat in his lap, his eyes studying the crown. "They said he hadn't even fired his gun."

"Rumors or the truth?"

"I have no reason not to believe them."

"Does Eason know about this?"

"I suppose so." He turned to her with a sad, resigned smile. "It's hard not to, growing up the way we did."

She cupped her palms around her books as if testing out a theory. "That's why he went to war," she said, the light of conviction rising in her eyes. "He found out after Billy died. He didn't know before. He would have told me if he had." She nodded to herself. "When I saw him yesterday, he told me that he'd lied. He meant about Thomas Eli." She turned to him. "What happened to your father? Eason said he didn't go to war."

So Eason had told her about that, too? "He died on the eve of the Armistice. By his own hand."

"And you? Were you a coward, too?"

He turned his hat over then rested it back on the brim. "I don't know."

"That's ridiculous."

He gave her a wry look. "It's a long story."

"Then you'd better start telling it now."

In the yard robins were hopping, a bright, jaunty two-step. His hip was stiffening up, and he shifted his weight to ease it, making the porch swing rock, reminding him briefly of the rocking ship that had once carried him across the Pacific. "You know about the war?"

"I think so." She pursed her lips. "Not really, no."

"None of you young folk do." He gave her a thin smile. "You've seen movies, yes? Programs on TV?"

She nodded.

"Good. Then picture this. We were on an island, a rocky thumb of land, jutting out of the sea." He held up his own thumb in imitation. "We were in foxholes, dug in, at the bottom of a ridge. The Japanese held the high ground. They were in fortifications, with clear lines of fire. We were being shelled. I stood up and was shot."

She shook her head, uncomprehending. "You stood up."

"Yes."

"Why would you do that?" When he didn't answer, she added, "You must have had a reason." He saw her trying to imagine it, perhaps thinking back to the movies she'd seen. "You were brave," she decided. "You were going to lead a charge."

"No." A small smile graced his face. "I was a lot of things in the war, but brave wasn't one of them."

"Then you wanted to get shot. You wanted to die, like your father did. You couldn't take it anymore, and you wanted it all to end. You just wanted to be done with it, no matter what."

"No. I wasn't like my father. Not in that way. I didn't want to die."

"Then why—" She stared at him in disbelief. "Why did you do it?"

He stood up and turned away from her, gazing out at the street, where a boy on a bicycle was riding by. He'd put playing cards in the spokes of his wheels, and they made a sharp, rackety sound as he passed by. "I heard a voice." He turned back to her and with a grave dignity put on his hat, as if he what he was about to say demanded his best appearance. "It said, *Stand up.* So I did."

"You—" She was too stunned to make sense of it. "You heard a voice."

He nodded.

"There, on the battlefield, amidst the firing and the shelling."

"Yes."

"And afterwards?"

"They gave me a Purple Heart and sent me home."

She was still trying to make sense of it, an uncertain look in her eyes. "Did it ever speak to you again?"

"No." He raised his eyes and studied the ceiling, where a porch light hung on joists. One of the screws had worked loose and was in danger of falling. Once again his thoughts drifted to Jase Glauber and his neglect of his house. He shook his head and looked back at her. "I can't say there haven't been times when I wished it would."

She touched a hand to her cheek. The look on her face was still dubious, confused. Then slowly it changed to amazement. "So that's why—when I told you about the voices I heard on the battlefield—you didn't think I was crazy."

He nodded. "Yes."

"Oh." She sank back in her seat, and he saw relief flood through her. All along, he realized, she'd harbored the suspicion that what she'd heard had been an aberration, a product of her own confused imagination. Now she realized she wasn't the only one. "Eason." Her eyes widened. "Does he know?"

"No." He passed a hand over his face. "No one does."

"You have to tell him."

"Why?" He sat back down beside her, a bitter smile on his lips. "So that he'll know his father isn't just a coward, but a cheat and a liar, too? That I took a medal I didn't deserve? And that given the chance to go home I did, and was glad for it, even though it meant some poor fool had to go in my place?" He shook his head. "I think Eason has a low enough opinion of me as it is."

She looked up at him, her hands clutching her books. "What will happen to him now?"

"I don't know."

"The telegram." A wildness came into her eyes. "What will they do if they find out the truth?"

He gave her a thin smile. "In the old days they shot deserters."

Her fingers tightened on the books, the knuckles turning white. "They'd *shoot* him?"

"No, you don't need to worry about that. After all, we're living in the modern age now, aren't we?" Once again he smiled in the bitter, mocking way. Then he fell silent, and when he spoke again, his voice was serious. "No, I expect there will be a court martial, followed by a long stint in a military prison."

"That wouldn't be so bad, would it?" There was a wistful, pleading note in her voice. "Afterwards he could pick up his life again."

"If he has a life to go back to."

She grew quiet, and he could see her thinking about it, picturing Eason in prison, as he himself had done so often since his son came home, trying to imagine him overcoming it, and failing. "They will find out what he's done, won't they?" she said, her voice small.

"In time, I expect so, yes. The military might be slow, and they don't always get things right the first time, but in the end they get the job done. You can count on that."

"Then he has to leave." She jumped up, and the books fell from her lap, scattering to the ground with a clatter. "Right now. This minute. He can go to Canada. God knows he won't be the only one."

Cyrus didn't answer. He didn't have to. They both knew Eason wouldn't go to Canada. He wouldn't go anywhere. If there was one thing he'd taught his son, Cyrus thought with a sour feeling of regret, it was the importance of staying on the land. When he'd found himself in trouble, Eason had come home. Now he would never leave.

She sank back onto the swing. "Eason said something to me yesterday about a girl." She pressed a finger to her lip. "A dead girl. He said she had hair like mine." She fingered a hank of her hair, twisting it in knots. "He said—" Her hand flew to her mouth. "He killed her, didn't he?" Her face paled. "Just like Stevenson did to those Indians. He murdered her to prove that he wasn't a coward like the rest of you. To prove he could fire his gun. He killed her and then he deserted—"

Cyrus studied his hands, turning them over and over as if he found it utterly surprising that they were empty, as if he didn't know what to make of them anymore.

Evie put a hand to her throat as if her heart had caught there, a dry pebble. The wildness had come back into her eyes. "I can't talk to you anymore." She stood up, unsteady on her feet. "I can't—" She cast about, as if she had lost all sense of direction. Then her eyes lit on the door, and she fled inside.

Twenty-Two

That night Evie took sick. By the time her father came home, she was lying in bed, wracked with chills and bouts of fever. All night long he sat up with her, plying her with tea and aspirin, and in the morning when she wasn't any better, he bundled her in a blanket and drove her to the doctor. The doctor took her pulse and listened to her lungs, peering with a light into her mouth and eyes. "It's the flu," he said, leaning in close, listening with a stethoscope to her heart. "Although I have to admit, it's awfully late in the season for that." He sat back with a reflective air. "Give her this." He wrote out a prescription on a small sheet of paper. "One teaspoon every eight hours, around the clock."

The medicine was a vile pink liquid that only made Evie feel worse. But she couldn't bear the desperate look in her father's eyes when she refused to take it, so she choked it down. They took turns watching over her, Ruth during the day and her father at night. One night she woke out of a delirium in which it seemed to her that she was lying on the Choke Creek battlefield with Eason bent over her in full cavalry dress, a murderous look in his eyes and a knife in his hand. Her heart pounding, she sat up with a start. Her father was dozing in a chair at the foot of her bed. Taking care not to wake him, she crept to her dresser and took the grey shirt out of her drawer. Then she went down to the kitchen on wobbly legs and shoved it into the trash, burying it deep beneath the rotting potato peels and moldering apple cores.

She felt dirty. Over and over again she went to the bathroom to wash her face and hands, scrubbing her lips with a washcloth until they were chapped and raw. But she couldn't rid herself of Eason's touch—the *murderer's* kiss. One evening as her father sat beside her bed reading, she burst out weeping. Alarmed, he sat down beside her. She threw her arms around him, hiding her head in his lap. "You were right," she said. "I never should have ridden to that ranch."

"Shh," he said. "Don't talk. Just rest."

She was grateful then that he didn't ask her to explain, and even more grateful when he let her cry herself out, holding her until the weeping had stopped.

By the fourth day, she was well enough to sit on the sofa in the living room, sipping spoonfuls of the broth Ruth brought her in a bowl. Outside the sunlight was warm and inviting, and the scent of the blooming irises wafted in through the open window. But Evie had no wish to go out. She felt safe inside, cocooned in the snug blanket Ruth had put around her shoulders. She was still light-headed, and her body felt strange, as if it belonged to somebody else. When her hands moved, they felt odd and disconnected, like curiosities seen from afar.

That afternoon Bobbie stopped by to see her, and the next day the girls sat on the floor together playing cards. The day after that was Sunday, and Evie stayed in bed all day, but by then it felt like a luxury. Her father brought her meals on a tray and sat beside her while she ate, reading through the day's newspapers, the pages fluttering like leaves to the floor beside him.

The next morning when she woke, she still felt weak, but the idea of staying in bed all day seemed boring, like a burden. She dressed, came down to the kitchen, and told her father she was ready to go back to school. He looked at her with worried eyes. "Are you sure?"

She nodded. Just to prove it, she ate the scrambled eggs he prepared for her, and even managed to nibble on the toast. When she was done, she carried her dishes to the sink. "I want you to sell Bird."

Jase was skimming through *The Post*. He dropped the paper and stared at her as if this pronouncement were more shocking than anything she might have uttered in a fever.

"I don't want to ride anymore. I'm done with it. I want—" She was afraid she might cry again, so she turned on the water, pulling herself together as she washed her plate. "I want to work at *The Sun*. I'll take any job I can get."

Jase studied her. "You're sure about this."

She put the plate in the rack to dry. "Yes."

Jase took a thoughtful sip of his coffee. "They might be able to use you in the mailroom. You could start when school gets out."

"All right."

"We won't sell Bird just yet." He pursed his lips. "We'll wait and see how it goes."

"Okay. But I won't ride him anymore." She flung her schoolbooks under her arm and turned to the door. "I mean what I've said."

She was behind in school and the week of illness had only made it worse. She began going to Bobbie's after school for help with her home-work. Sometimes Bobbie's boyfriend, the math whiz, came over and helped, too. Over the next few weeks Evie memorized French verbs, wrote book reports, finished social studies papers, and worked sheet after sheet of algebra problems. She'd always considered herself hope-less at math, but now, to her surprise, the squiggly letters and numbers actually began to make sense. Slowly her grades came up, and while they were still nothing to be proud of, at least she would pass.

Meanwhile she remained true to her word and didn't ride Bird. She still went to the barn each day to check on him, grooming him and turning him out in the paddock behind his stall for exercise. There he trotted back and forth, now and then bucking, just so that she would know he didn't approve of her neglect. After she had put him away, she sank down to the floor outside his stall. The thought of riding still made her feel ill, but secretly she was glad her father hadn't sold Bird yet. There was a comfort in just being in the barn, listening to the snuf-fling sounds his breath made, the meditative chewing of his hay.

Then summer came, school let out, and Evie started work at *The Sun*. Each morning she rose early to drive into work with her father, and she spent her days roaming the hallways of the *Sun* building, going from office to office, pushing a metal cart with the mail. Not everyone knew who she was. She liked it better when they didn't. She handed over their packages and envelopes and received nothing but a curt glance or grunt in reply. The ones who knew her made a point of smiling too broadly at her approach, greeting her and teasing her, forcing her to make conversation in return, expecting her to smile back.

At the end of June, Bobbie left for summer camp. The night before, Evie went to her house to help her pack. She was in the middle of folding Bobbie's sweatshirts, trying to cram just one more into her over-stuffed trunk, when the math whiz arrived. Bobbie asked Evie to stay, but she knew she wasn't wanted. She gave Bobbie a quick hug and said good-bye. As she left the house, she caught sight of Bobbie and her boyfriend already standing together, their arms around each other, locked in a kiss.

When Evie got home, she went upstairs to her window and looked out at the creek. Lately the light had become so faint, it seemed in danger of disappearing forever. She searched for a long time before she finally found it, a pale glimmer beneath the willows. She went to her dresser and pulled out the cigar box, then spilled the contents onto her bed, the seeds, pebbles, and feathers she'd collected on the ranch the summer before, the photograph of her mother, the confusion of notes, and the two hundred dollars Cyrus had given her for training the roan colt—she'd never been able to bring herself to spend them.

She sat down and opened one of the notes she'd written long ago, untwining the tightly folded scrap of paper until she could read what was inside. It was one of the oldest notes in the box, penned when she was six, soon after she'd learned to write. *I had peanut butter for lunch*, the note said in her loopy, uneven scrawl. *They gave out new reading books.* A smile flitted across her face. She opened another note and then another, lining them up in order on her bed, seeing in their progression the maturing of both her handwriting and her spirit, the ever-deepening complexity of the issues she faced each day. Her whole life was contained in this box, she reflected, and her mother would never know it. The thought saddened her, and she put the notes away.

She lifted up the photograph of her mother. In the background stretched a grey streak—the broad expanse of the sea. *Have you ever seen the ocean?* Eason had said to her. *You can't imagine it. It pulls at you, like it's trying to draw you out of yourself. Like it wants you to be greater than you are.* She shook her head and put the photograph aside, drawing her knees up to her chest. Her thoughts drifted to Bobbie and the kiss she'd given the math whiz. Despite herself, she found herself thinking of Eason again and the kisses they'd shared on the battlefield. He had such gentle hands. He'd been so gentle with that roan colt; even when it was wild and out of control, he hadn't resorted to his spurs.

Just like that it came to her. Eason hadn't done it. He hadn't murdered that girl. He was flat out incapable of it. He was a Swale, and the Swales were cowards—even Cyrus admitted it was true. They couldn't even fire their guns. She reached up and took hold of her hair, twirling a long strand tightly around her finger. She should have known—she should have listened to Eason when he told her. He hadn't said he'd *killed* that girl, only that he'd *seen* her. He'd deserted out of cowardice, nothing more. *Isn't it strange the way we believe we can make things turn out differently*, he'd said, *when they always end up being the same?*

The realization surged through her with a rush so joyful, it took her breath away. Her heart pounded, and her head grew so light, she feared she might be getting sick again. All night long, jittery with anticipation, she couldn't sleep. In the morning she brushed out her hair and pulled on her riding boots. When she came down to the kitchen, she told her father she was sorry, but she couldn't work in the mailroom anymore; she was going riding. She left the house, leaving him standing in stunned silence behind her. It was a beautiful summer morning, the air clear and fresh, black-headed grosbeaks singing from the willows, a melody that sounded rich and bright to her, full of promise. Listening to it, she crossed the creek and climbed the bank to Bird's barn.

Twenty-Three

After that Evie rode out daily to the Swale ranch, helping with the horses as she had the summer before. She never forgot the telegram Cyrus had showed her or the things he'd said. One day, he'd warned her, the Army would come for Eason. *You can count on that.* But as the weeks went by and nothing happened, she told herself the rancher was wrong. Why should the Army bother itself with Eason? He was only one soldier, one tiny cog in their vast military machine. Surely they had more important things to worry about. Besides, they thought he was missing in action. Why should they change their minds and come looking for him now?

Still, each morning as she rode up the ridgeline, she had a knot of worry in her stomach, and it didn't dissolve until she caught sight of Eason working around the paddocks or the barn. She didn't see Cyrus much anymore. His hip had taken a turn for the worse, and he spent most of his time indoors. But she didn't mind that. She didn't mind anything as long as Eason was at her side.

She never got used to him. Each day she helped him with his chores, feeding the horses, grooming them, filling their water buckets, turning them out. Together they hauled hay to the outer pastures and mucked out the stalls, strewing powdery fresh lime on the bare earthen floors. From time to time as they worked, their hands touched, or they brushed against each other, passing through a doorway or a gate. Each time felt like an electric shock to her, like plunging her hands into water so cold it took her breath away. Most of all she loved the way he smelled, the clean, musky scent that came from horses and sweat. Whenever she had the chance, she leaned in close to him to catch it, her eyes closed. She discovered that she had become shy again in his presence, perpetually tongue-tied. They spoke little as they worked, confining their conversation to ordinary things: *Could you fetch me that lead line? I could use some help with this mare.* Still she made sure to keep him close to her, in sight if not in reach, as if otherwise she feared he might disappear.

When they were done with their chores, they mounted their horses and rode to the battlefield, where they spent the waning hours of the day sitting side by side on the bluff while their horses grazed. Summer had taken hold of the land, and the heat brought a stillness to the prairie, a feeling of longing and regret. Dust hung heavily on the cattails, while insects droned, the sound rising and falling like a beating heart. Often her thoughts turned to the war Eason had fought in and the terrible things she was sure he had endured. But she was careful not to press him about it, avoiding questions she knew he couldn't answer. As the weeks passed by and June gave way to July, he rewarded her restraint by speaking to her of other things. He talked of horses he'd known in the past, a bay colt that had developed a fondness for oranges, biting straight through the peel to the juicy flesh below. A paint mare that loved so much to roll in the creek, she dropped to her knees even while he was on her back: *She ruined a good saddle that way.* He remembered a winter when the snow fell so hard, they had to tunnel through it from the house to the barn, and a summer when the creek ran so dry, it all but disappeared, and the flow from the well dwindled to a trickle.

Occasionally his thoughts drifted to things she couldn't even begin to imagine, startling and incomprehensible in their strangeness. Rivers so deep they appeared bottomless. Forests so thick they rendered day into night. Rain that went on for days and days. Then she understood he was talking about the war, telling her about it as best as he could, speaking with the same air of wonder and disbelief he'd had when he described the ocean, the bewildering mix of water and light and air.

Other times he fell into a silence so troubled and deep, she feared he might never speak to her again. Then she remembered what he'd told her in the spring: *I'm no good for you. I'm no good for anything anymore.* Afraid of losing him forever, she reached out and drew him close, enveloping herself in his warmth. Eventually he gave a sharp sigh and with a shudder came back to her, a bemused smile on his face as if he had just awoken from a dream and was surprised to find her there. Then she tipped her face up to him until he kissed her, and she felt certain she possessed him once again.

He didn't love her the way she loved him, she knew that, just as she knew that the things that had happened to him had made him incapable of it. He needed her for the brief periods of solace and forgetfulness she gave him, nothing more. But she didn't resent that. She was grateful for it, glad she had at least that much to give.

Usually by the time they returned from the bluff, it was late. They said their good-byes, and Evie headed for home. But one day when they came back, the afternoon feeding still lay before them. Evie tied her horse to the paddock rail and followed Eason up the ladder to the hayloft. Outside the plain was cooling, and a fresh breeze circled in through the wide-open doors. But the loft was still warm from the sun and from the rising heat of the horses' bodies, captured beneath the high, peaked roof.

She took the wire cutters from their nail on the wall and clipped open a hay bale, releasing the summery smell of alfalfa into the air. She worked her side of the loft, tossing the hay flakes through slots in the floor to the mangers below. As she walked, the floorboards creaked, and motes of dust rose before her, so thick and full, she felt like a figure in a watery globe, caught in a shaken snowstorm.

The work with the bales was hard, and she was sweating, her unbound hair clinging to her neck. She grabbed the tail of her blouse to wipe her brow and looked at Eason. He was standing in the doorway, looking over the plain. The sun had sunk behind the mountains, and the light held the fevered brightness of dusk. In the pastures, a breeze was stirring, rippling through the manes of the horses, tucking their tails to their haunches. Eason's back was to her, his shadow lengthening on the floor behind him, the outline of his body sharp and distinct as if chiseled from the light. His knee was bent, his hips off-kilter, his wide shoulders balanced on the flat shoulder blades. With one hand he fingered his collar, the other hand dangling at his side, the fingers curved lightly inward. His hair fell in curves to his collarbone.

"Oh, Eason," she said. "I'm so sorry. I never should have doubted you." She went to him and pressed herself against his back, feeling the knobby ridge of his spine. Then she lay her palms flat on his belly, lifting them to feel the beating of his heart. He turned around and kissed her then led her to the back of the loft where winter blankets lay heaped in a pile. Pulling one from the top, he spread it across the wide-planked floor amid brushy clumps of sweet-smelling hay. Together they lay down, holding each other close, their legs twining together like a braid. She slipped her hands beneath his shirt, feeling the heat of his body and the dampness of his skin. Then she kissed him, long and hard.

In the eaves the barn swallows stirred, a soft, fluttery sound. All at once she realized Eason was crying, shivering, his face lost in her hair. "Shh," she said, stifling her own tears, "shh, Eason, please don't. It will be all right, I promise." And so she comforted him, even though deep in her heart she feared she was lying, and it wouldn't.

They came for him the very next morning, on a day when clouds hung dark over the mountains, threatening rain. Evie saw the soldiers as she rode up to the ranch, two men standing on the porch with Cyrus. Their jeep was parked outside the house, the olive-green Army color gleaming beneath a layer of dust. There was no sign of Eason. She held back while they talked. The first soldier, a beefy man with a squat build, leaned in close to ask Cyrus a question. The rancher shook his head, his eyes directed at the floor in front of his boots. Then the second soldier, a tall man with a face like a blade, took over the questioning, his hands jerking upwards in an impatient way, his eyes darkening with anger. This time Cyrus sought the answer on the distant horizon before once again giving his head the same slow shake. The two soldiers stepped aside to confer. The sharp-faced man turned back to the rancher and issued what appeared to be a warning. Cyrus took it without expression. Then the squat soldier kicked the porch rail, hard enough to crack some of the spindles, and the two men left.

Cyrus was still studying the railing, trying to fit the broken spindles back together when Evie rode down to him. "Where's Eason?" She was breathless, her throat tight.

"I don't know." As he turned to her, he let go of the spindles, and they fell apart, the jagged ends swinging.

Her heart felt cracked now, too, the broken pieces jabbing at her chest. "What did you tell them?"

The rancher kicked the porch rail with all his might, splintering the rest of the spindles, bringing the railing down. He brushed his hands on his pants then cast a pointed look at the chestnut filly's paddock, which lay flat and empty in the sun. "I told them he wasn't here."

She found Eason standing on the bluff, looking out over the creek, the filly hobbled nearby. Even from a distance she could see the serene expression in his eyes. *He's glad they came*, she thought. *It's what he wanted. It means it will all be over soon.* The thought chilled her, and she chased it from her mind. "They're gone now," she said, riding up to him. She jumped down, holding Bird by the reins. "You can come back."

"Can I?" He turned to her with a fond smile. He was dressed in his usual blue jeans and the dusty Army boots, but for some reason he hadn't put on a shirt. Instead he was wearing his great-grandfather's cavalry coat, holding the long rifle in the crook of his arm.

What did he want with that? Did he have some idea of defending himself with that antiquated firing piece, or did he have another purpose in mind? The thought unsettled her, and she pushed it away. She glanced at the sky. The dark clouds were making their way towards them, chased by a cold wind. "Eason." She shivered. "We have to go. Look at the sky."

But he didn't look up. Instead he looked downwards, studying the cavalry coat. It was too small for him, and he seemed confused by that.

He kept trying to fasten it, tugging at the fabric, fiddling with the buttons. At last he let it go, and the coat fell open, revealing his bare chest. He turned back to the creek. "I used to see so much here. I saw it all. The cavalry, the volunteers … " His voice trailed off. "I heard the firing. I felt the snow." His eyes saddened. "I can't see anything anymore."

What was he talking about? If only she could understand what he meant! She shot another glance at the sky. Whatever it was, it would have to wait. They had to get inside. Even the horses had grown nervous at the sight of the coming storm. The filly's tail was swishing, while Bird snorted and stamped the ground. "Listen to me, Eason. You owe me that much." She thought back to the hayloft and the way it had made her feel, raw and vulnerable, sweet and aching all at once. She put her arms around him, resting her head on his shoulder. "Come with me. Please."

At her touch he stiffened and twisted away, stepping back to stare at her, his face tight with anger. "Did you ever think that maybe they had reasons for what they did? Did it ever occur to you they might be *justified*?" With a grave dignity, he straightened the jacket and planted the butt of the rifle in the dirt. Then he relaxed and smiled at her with the fondness from before. "Anyway, it wasn't real. It was only a game we played, cowboys and Indians, like we did when we were kids." He studied her with a curious expression on his face. "You know how to play cowboys and Indians, don't you?"

It made no sense. None of it did. The way he was dressed, the things he said. The storm was about to break, and he wanted to play games. "We have to go."

"C'mon. I'll show you." He took Bird's reins and gave him a smart slap on the rump. Startled, Bird trotted off to join the filly. The two horses turned their faces to the wind, their heads held high, their nostrils wide, scenting the storm. Eason shrugged off the coat and draped it tenderly across her shoulders. "You can be the cowboy." He held the rifle out to her, and when she didn't take it, wrapped her hands around it. "I'll be the Indian." He took a step back and gave her an appraising look. Apparently satisfied, he pulled his hair forward until it fell into his face. Then he began to circle her, his eyes on the ground, his boots stamping a rhythm in the dirt.

The coat hung loosely around her, flapping in the wind. A gust drove her hair into her face, and she blinked, rubbing her eyes. The horses jigged anxiously, the filly testing her hobbles. Eason circled her, his bare skin gleaming. He was so close, she could smell him, but his scent was strange and unfamiliar, feral, frightening her. "Stop it," she said. "We can't stay here. We have to go."

She dropped the rifle and tore off the coat. Eason gave her a look of hurt surprise. "You're not playing." He put the coat back on her shoulders, giving her a light shake so that she would know he meant business. Then he set the rifle back in her hands, making sure she held it properly, her finger on the trigger. "You're the cowboy, remember?" He stepped back to survey his work, then nodded with approval and circled her once more, his feet pounding the earth.

One two three four, *one* two three four. The sky blackened, and the first drops of rain sliced through the air. Eason danced, his boots stamping out the rhythm on the hard brown ground. The wind was whistling, and he added his voice to it, chanting a series of joyful whoops, the flat of his palm beating against his mouth in time to his feet. He was bent over at the waist, half-crouching, his eyes focused on the ground, his bare skin wet with rain. Mesmerized by his dance, Evie spun in place as he circled her, until she grew so dizzy, she feared she would faint. "Eason, don't," she whimpered, but she knew he wouldn't listen. Her voice was too weak to be heard over the storm. She staggered to the side, trying to make a run for her horse, but he was all around her, and there was no escape. "Don't," she said again. Tight with fear, she shouted. "Stop it *right now.*"

A look of cunning flitted across his face, followed by a triumphant smile. At last she was doing what he wanted. She was *playing.* Seized by excitement he danced harder, the tempo of his steps quickening until he was whirling about her, his head thrown back, the low, crooning whoops punctuated by sharp yelps. Circling in closer, he poked and prodded her, feinting like a boxer. "C'mon, cowboy," he said. "Let's go. Let's *play.*"

He was hurting her. "Stop," she pleaded. "Eason, please." It was no use. He wouldn't listen to her. He wouldn't do anything until she gave him what he wanted.

What he wanted.

With a jolt, she realized what Eason wanted—what he had come home for.

She leveled the rifle, swinging it about until it pointed at him like a finger. All at once the rifle jerked in her hands. A loud crack echoed across the bluff, and the smell of burnt gunpowder spilled into the air. Evie screamed, and her hands flinched open, flinging the rifle to the ground. Terrified, the horses spooked and broke into a gallop. Bird stumbled into the creek and came to a halt, staring back at her with wide eyes, but the filly broke through her hobbles and ran towards home, squealing with fear, the empty stirrups flapping.

"Eason." She could hardly bring herself to look at him. When she did, she found him staring at her with disgust in his eyes. The rifle had misfired, and he wouldn't forgive her for it. "How can you be a cowboy," he said, his voice full of contempt, "if you can't even fire your gun?"

Twenty-Four

They rode back to the barn together, sitting double on Bird, with Evie in front, the cavalry coat crumpled on the pommel of her saddle, and Eason behind, the long rifle propped on his thigh, the barrel reaching for heaven. At least the rain had stopped. A great gust of wind blew past, chasing the last of the clouds from the sky. Then the sun came out and shone down on them from a placid sky.

She couldn't bear to look at him. He hated her for failing, but she couldn't forgive herself for what she'd almost done. She was soaking wet, shivering, chilled to the bone. Even the sun didn't help.

They came down to the barn and found Cyrus waiting for them. The arrival of the riderless filly had frightened him, and he looked at them with alarm. "What happened?" Eason didn't answer. He slipped down from the horse and went into the house. That left Evie. But she didn't have any answers either. She just shook her head and headed for home.

Midway there her skin grew cold and clammy. Her face paled, and a foul taste rose into the back of her mouth. She slid off her horse, fell to her knees, and retched into the sand. For a long time she sat back, her eyes closed, her head in her hands. Then she climbed back onto her horse and rode the rest of the way home.

No one was there. Ruth had gone for the day, and her father was not yet home. She shook off her boots, went upstairs, and stripped off her wet clothes. Then she dressed in a clean cotton shirt and a pair of pants.

She put on thick, warm socks and returned to the kitchen, where she fixed herself a cup of tea. She still felt so cold and sick. She sat down and wrapped her fingers around the cup to warm them. Then she lifted the cup to her lips and managed a small sip.

She wanted Eason to live. He wanted to die. At the thought, she felt so sick again, she put down the cup. How could she convince him otherwise? She closed her eyes, and her vision of the massacre came back to her. Her eyes sprang open with despair. She'd tried so hard to understand what had happened that day at Choke Creek, but had found nothing but blank walls and dead ends. Even Cyrus had no explanation for the death of innocents. Everyone else flat out denied it. She remembered the headlines she'd seen in Asa's office the year before: *Great Battle with Indians. The Savages Dispersed!* Her father wanted her to believe in their newspaper. *One day*, he'd told her, you'll see. *Everything you need is in its pages.* But how could she trust something so grievously wrong?

She pushed the teacup away. What if she were mistaken? After all, news traveled slowly in those days, and she'd only read the newspapers written in the immediate aftermath of the battle. What if Asa hadn't found out about the massacre until later? She took a slow, thoughtful sip of her tea. Then she pushed her cup away and padded through the house to the office beneath the stairs.

The sun had begun to go down, and as the light failed, the creek dissolved into shadow. Evie lit the lamp on the desk, went to the filing cabinet, and opened the drawer from 1864. The newspapers were filed in folders, twelve in all, one for each month. She would read from the beginning of the year to get a sense of the whole story, following the events as they unfolded. With some effort she pulled the folders from the drawer and dropped them on the desk. Then she sat down and opened the first one.

The folders were made of thick cardboard, brownish and stiff with age, but the newspapers inside were surprisingly intact, the ink crisp, the paper soft. Well, she'd heard the refrain from her father often enough, every time the newsprint supplier raised his prices. In the old days, *The Sun* had been printed on rag, one hundred percent cotton, good for generations. Newsprint nowadays was worthless, riddled with acids, yellowing within days—at an exorbitant cost.

She pulled out the newspaper from the first of January and held it up to the light. The 1864 edition bore almost no resemblance to the newspaper her father put out each day. It was smaller, only one sheet, with six narrow columns instead of the modern-day three. There was no obvious lead story, only a series of articles with small headlines running into one another. But the logo at the top, a line drawing of the sun setting behind the mountains, had been preserved, along with the motto beneath it, *Rise, shine, for thy light has come.* The motto was biblical. She remembered her father telling her that. Asa had been a religious man, but when the family lost its religious bent, she didn't know. In any case her father had no use for religious institutions, deriding churches as "houses of superstition." His faith was bound up in ink, bundled together with the civilizing effects of the printed word.

She put the newspaper down and rose to her feet. The very first issue of *The Sun*, from the spring of 1859, hung in a frame above the desk. It had been ages since she had paid it any attention, but now she scrutinized it with interest. In the bottom right-hand corner of the page was her great-great-grandfather's first editorial, the inaugural words with which he'd sent his newspaper out to the world: *With our hat in our hand and our best bow we this week make our appearance upon the stage in capacity of Editor.*

Courtly, she thought, momentarily charmed. Like a suitor wooing his beloved. She read on: *We make our debut in the far west, where the snowy mountains look down upon us on the hottest summer day as well as in the winters cold; here where a few months ago the wild beasts and wilder Indians held undisturbed possession—where now surges the advancing wave of Anglo-Saxon enterprise and civilization, where soon we fondly hope will be erected a great and powerful state, another empire in the sisterhood of empires.*

Strange, she thought. *Empires.* What did he mean by that? *Our course is marked out; we will adhere to it with stedfast and fixed determination, to speak, write and publish the truth and nothing but the truth, let it work us weal or woe.*

She nodded. Yes, that was it exactly. *The truth and nothing but the truth.* What she had wanted for so long. Maybe these pages held everything she needed after all. With mounting excitement, she skimmed the last line. *Fondly looking forward to a long and pleasant acquaintance with our readers, hoping well to act our part, we send forth to the world the first number of* The Rocky Mountain Sun.

She sat back down and began to work her way through the newspapers on the desk. At first she found it difficult to keep her mind on the battle; the pages of *The Sun*, she discovered to her surprise, were like a treasure box, full of tiny jewels, odd and unexpected bits of information. She marveled at an article on the opening of Japan, and at another which counseled sailors to avoid Cape Horn. What possible interest could landlocked miners find in *that*? There was a story giving crime statistics for New York City, and another full of information on the sale of shoes. Preachments against the use of tobacco. Commentary on cattle feed. Advertisements for blacksmiths and ironworkers, for dry-goods purveyors and surveyors, and even a physician-surgeon. Asa must have been a music lover. One issue trumpeted with great delight the arrival of the first piano in the territory, and another boasted of a new singing circle. He also loved animals. What else could explain the frequent ads for lost dogs?

Delighted, she read on. *The Sun*, she learned, was not above printing a bit of poetry now and again. One issue exclaimed, *Hurrah for the land where the moor and the mountain/Are sparkling with treasures no language hath told./Where the wave of the river and the spray of the fountain/Are bright with the glitter of genuine gold.* Asa also had a fondness for riddles. *What key is that that opens the gate of misery?* he asked. *Whis-key.* She'd never seen the past laid to her before in such a pure and unadulterated fashion, without the meddling commentary of historians. Just life as it was lived in perfect immediacy, twenty-four hours at a time. If they'd taught history to her like this in school, she would have been a willing student.

Asa offered weekly editorials, and through them a picture of her great-great-grandfather emerged, more vivid than any she'd seen before. He was wildly opinionated and considered himself an expert on just about everything, from the best way to raise beets to how to combat the summer dust which choked the city's streets. He was full of candor, enthusiastically promoting the causes he believed in, and utterly fearless, denigrating with equal enthusiasm the ones he didn't. Again and again he proved himself a relentless campaigner for civic institutions, speaking out in favor of libraries, schools, historical societies, and the one establishment he insisted the city needed above all others: a jail. He showed an almost childlike delight in progress, praising both the telegraph, which had made its way to Danvers, and the railroad, which he hoped would follow soon. The history book she'd read with Bobbie the year before had called her great-great-grandfather Danvers's finest booster. Now she understood why. On the *advancing wave of Anglo-Saxon enterprise and civilization*, Asa was the vanguard.

But her great-great-grandfather, she realized as she read, had more than just the future of Danvers on his mind. He had set his sights on the growth of the entire territory. By 1864 the citizens of Danvers were lobbying Congress to declare their territory a state—the *great and powerful state* Asa had envisioned five years earlier. The key to statehood was population, but in this regard the region was at a disadvantage. Most of Danvers's residents were transients, miners who took their riches from the earth then moved on. If the city were to bulk up the population of the region, it needed *citizens*, people who would set down roots and stay. Farmers, clerks, shopkeepers, tradesmen. Over and over again Asa used his soapbox in *The Sun* to entice potential residents to his new hometown. He praised Danvers's healthful climate, the richness of its soil, its sparkling waters. *From present appearances, our citizens are likely to all be taken off with the Choke Creek Yellow Fever*, he wrote in one instance. *This is all wrong; and our opinion is that farmers who stay at home, will realize more clear profit by so doing, than they will to go to the mines.* Even in its earliest days, Evie knew, *The Sun* made its way back East to eager readers. These were Asa's intended audience, the Easterners whom he hoped would emigrate westwards for new opportunities and new lives—and boost the territory to statehood. If, at the same time, they boosted the subscription rolls of *The Sun*—well, Asa could hardly be blamed for that.

But Asa was worried about more than just the ongoing survival of his newspaper. He had his finger in every one of Danvers's burgeoning pies: real estate, agriculture, civic institutions, even—despite his warnings to the contrary—the mines. Hence his stake in the city's future. All over the front range, mining settlements were already fading into ghost towns, main streets that had once seethed with city halls, post offices, stores, and saloons falling into dusty abandonment as the mines played out. Asa would have known that better than anyone. Just as he knew it was by no means certain Danvers wouldn't share their fate.

Evie rubbed a hand over her eyes. As night came, the wind had begun to blow again, and a pale light wavered in the darkness beneath the willows. She studied it for a moment then turned back to the newspapers. She'd read through most of March and needed to buckle down, ignoring extraneous stories, turning her attention to the battle. Skimming rapidly, she made her way into the beginning of April, where she was rewarded with her first article on the subject. Colonel John Quintius Stevenson, the newspaper reported, had just returned from Washington, where he'd held consultations with the War Department. While the great Civil War hero hadn't received the much hoped for—and in Asa's opinion, *well-deserved*—promotion to brigadier general, he had at least retained cavalry command.

A few days later she found the first mention of Indian depredations: reports of the large theft of cattle on the plains. What was it the history book had said? *All winter long the Indians lay in wait. Then in the spring they rode out, and the depredations began again.* Well, spring had finally come to Danvers, and the conflict was heating up. Sure enough, soon came a headline reading, *Horrible Murder! Two Soldiers Massacred by an Indian.* Evie read through this story with great interest, discovering that the soldiers had been killed when they fell asleep guarding an Indian prisoner—who subsequently escaped. Well, they could hardly blame the Indian for that, could they? Two hundred dollars were offered for his capture.

By the middle of April the newspaper was reporting, *Exciting News! War with the Indians. A Battle Fought.* Just seeing the story made Evie's breath quicken with excitement, too. She plunged into it. It was based on a report by Colonel Stevenson himself, who told of a fight between the cavalry and Indians, in which two cavalrymen and several Indians died. Asa was quick to reassure his readers, *There is not the slightest cause for any general scare.* Still, he urged frequent drills on the part of already-formed militias, especially in the more remote areas: *This is desirable not only for defence, but it may become a policy for every man to shoulder his gun and join in a war of extermination against these miserable wretches.*

Miserable wretches? Evie pressed a hand to her cheek. *A war of extermination?* She flipped through subsequent reports on the Indian War, noting with increasing alarm the epithets Asa used to describe the Indians: *savages, red devils, murderous thieves.* If he wasn't responding to a climate of terror, he was certainly creating one. From time to time he still adopted a note of calm, insisting, *We are not in the slightest apprehension of danger here*, but Evie wasn't fooled. She knew her great-great-grandfather was walking a thin line, serving two competing aims. On the one hand he wanted to downplay the Indian threat in order to stem the tide of terrified settlers fleeing eastwards for their lives. But at the same time he demanded that the threat be taken seriously, so that it could receive the military solution he felt certain it required: *We believe in fighting these red devils, not feeding them.*

By the end of April, stories on the war were easy to find, and, with their sensationalized headlines, impossible to ignore. Most detailed isolated depredations: attacks on the telegraph wires, theft of stock, seizure of wagon trains, fights which led to a smattering of deaths on both sides. In one article, at least, Evie was relieved to see Asa take the Indian side: *Let a single white man lose a steer, and the cry at once is Indian theft, murder, thunder, blood, etc. But let a lot of rowdy teamsters trespass upon the personal rights or livestock of the poor dumb Indians, and it's all right!*

His description of *poor dumb Indians* was hardly commendable, but at least he recognized that Indians, too, had *personal rights*.

By the beginning of May, however, a change had come into his reporting style. For the first time the newspaper mentioned *a general war on the whites*, which the Indians were reported to be planning. Gone now was any talk of Indian rights. Asa was fully for war. *Nothing in the world but the most prompt and exemplary punishment will secure us against the continued depredations of these worthless bands.*

The middle of May brought a break in the Indian stories. Either the territory was experiencing a period of calm or Asa was unable to gather reports from the field. Choke Creek had overflowed its banks and inundated the settlement in a devastating flood. Even *The Sun* had experienced losses, as its printing press was seized by the torrent and transported over a half mile away. But as June dawned, Asa was back on the war beat. Soon the newspaper was trumpeting the event Evie knew so well: the death of the Wyngates. Asa, she discovered with a sickening feeling, held nothing back, giving full descriptions of the *mangled bodies of this cruelly murdered family*, including a baby whose *bowels were ripped open, and its entrails scattered by the sides of its mother*. His conclusion? The savage perpetrators ought to be *burned to the stake alive.*

The murder of the Wyngates was clearly a turning point. Terrified families from nearby ranches and settlements descended on Danvers, taking refuge in hastily constructed stockades. They were, Evie realized, in genuine fear for their lives. And not without reason. As summer progressed, *The Sun* reported how the Indians cut the telegraph wires, isolating the settlement from the rest of the world. They interrupted the mail and disrupted supply trains, leading to shortages of corn, flour, bacon, and other goods. Prices began to rise. From her vantage point in the twentieth century, Evie had always taken it for granted that the Indians would lose the war. But in 1864, the people had no such knowledge. For all they knew, the Indians would descend on Danvers and slaughter them all. It certainly appeared likely.

The settlers had to defend themselves; Asa's voice led the call. But how? The problem was troops. They didn't have enough. They had sent

word back East of their precarious position, but their pleas for rein-
forcements had gone ignored. Washington, embroiled in fighting the
Civil War, had no troops to spare. By early August the governor of the
territory was reporting: *The Indian uprising is general. There is no assur-
ance that troops will be sent here in numbers adequate for our protection.
Self-preservation demands decisive action, and the only way to secure it
is to fight them in their own way.* Earlier in the summer he had issued a
call to all friendly Indians, who wished to avoid chastisement, to come
in and declare themselves, so that they could be escorted to places of
safety where they would be protected and treated peaceably. Now he
authorized the citizens of Danvers to form a regiment of *Hundred Day
Men*—volunteer soldiers empowered to serve in the infantry for one
hundred days. This militia, the *Volunteer Third*, would join forces with
the cavalry already established under Colonel Stevenson's command to
fight the hostiles. Together, Asa reported with satisfaction, *They would
make the red devils howl.*

Through the waning days of August, the militia assembled and
trained. Asa reported almost daily on its activities. *Good Appointments*,
one of his headlines read, followed by a list of the officers appointed to
lead the new regiment—including Lieutenant Thomas Eli Eason. Evie
read the name with a chill. There he was, Eason's namesake, the man
whose coat had rested on her shoulders just that afternoon—the one
whose story still overshadowed the Swales. Was Cyrus right? Had his
grandfather really been a coward? The question remained. How had
Lieutenant Eason conducted himself on the banks of Choke Creek?

By September the militia was ready to be deployed. With all the
pomp and circumstance he could muster, Stevenson marched his forces out of Danvers, ready to engage the hostile foe. But before he could
fight Indians, Evie learned, he had to find them. And while Stevenson
might be good at a great many things, apparently he was terrible at that.
As weeks and then months passed, and summer gave way to fall, the
colonel marched his men back and forth across the plains—encoun-
tering no Indians. At home the people were becoming impatient, then
derisive. The brave volunteers, Evie discovered, had earned a new nick-
name: *The Bloodless Third*. By early November Asa feared that the term

of the *hundredazers* would come to an end before they had a chance to fight. Meanwhile winter was coming and snow was beginning to fall. The Sun devoted great space to a storm which brought snow for thirty-six hours without a break, resulting in drifts up to four feet. Evie could only imagine the deprivations Stevenson's men suffered in the field.

Then just like that, at the end of the month, something happened, and Stevenson found the Indians. A great battle was enjoined—and won. Within days, reports of it began to appear in the pages of *The Sun*. *500 Indians Killed. The Savages Dispersed!* the headlines exclaimed. Asa was ecstatic. *Among the brilliant feats of arms in Indian warfare,* he wrote, *the recent campaign of our Danvers volunteers will stand in history with few rivals and none to exceed it in final results. All acquitted themselves well, and Danvers soldiers have again covered themselves with glory.*

Evie put the newspapers down. Nothing she had read so far even hinted of a massacre. Maybe Asa was lying. After all, if Stevenson and his men had massacred women and children on the creek, wouldn't Asa be the last person to admit it? He'd just spent months calling for the extermination of the *red devils*. He could hardly be expected to be disappointed when his wish came true. And he had too much at stake in Danvers. He would never let anything tarnish the city's name.

She stood up and walked to the window. Beneath the willows the light gleamed with a hopeful air. *The truth and nothing but the truth,* her great-great-grandfather had declared in his very first editorial, *let it work us weal or woe.* Very well. She would grant Asa the chance to exonerate himself. She would continue reading and see what she could learn.

By the middle of December, the men who were now being celebrated as the *Bloody Thirdsters* had returned to Danvers, parading in rank and file behind their commander. A few days later Asa reported an *Unusual Attraction,* which would be presented that night in the town's theater: *A great Indian drama, with new and splendid Indian costumes, and trophies taken in the big battle of Choke Creek. A favorite farce will wind up the big Indian entertainment,* he concluded. *Go and see it.*

Farce? Entertainment? Evie's stomach turned. Even if the battle had been justified, was this the proper way to commemorate it? She paged through the newspaper to the end of the year. Nothing. Not a single, solitary word to lead her to believe that the battle had been anything but as described. Her thoughts turned to Eason, her heart sinking in despair. Once again she had come up empty-handed, with nothing to offer him, not one more word to say.

With a heavy heart, she gathered the newspapers together and returned them to the cabinet. As she put them back in the drawer, she saw the folders for 1865. For a moment she stared at them. Then she swore under her breath. Fine. She would give Asa one last chance. She had come this far, and she would go just a little bit further. She grabbed the stack of newspapers and returned to the desk.

She opened the first folder and began to read into the new year. There it was: what she had been looking for. No, not that. Something else— something entirely unexpected, and yet the answer to her questions just the same. It was a small article, buried at the back of the newspaper at the beginning of January, so inconspicuous, she almost overlooked it. She would have, if not for the fact that it mentioned Thomas Eli Eason by name. *Lieutenant Silas Brem*, the report read, *was found murdered last night on the streets of our city, gunned down by an unknown assailant.* Then came the surprising part. *Immediately following, Lieutenant Thomas Eli Eason left town for parts unknown.*

Brem—she remembered the name from Asa's list. One of Thomas Eli's fellow officers. And something else. She recalled hearing stories about Brem's daughter Ellit, who had maintained until the day she died that her father had been murdered by one of Stevenson's men. Well, apparently Ellit was more right than she knew. Evie could well imagine it, reading easily between the lines. Cyrus was right. Thomas Eli had acted cowardly at Choke Creek. Brem had witnessed his dereliction of duty and threatened to expose it. Alarmed, Lieutenant Eason had murdered Brem and then deserted, leaving his family with a heritage of shame. Just like Eason. *Isn't it strange the way we believe we can make things turn out differently*, he'd said, *when they always end up being the same?*

There was no denying it. Eason had committed murder in Vietnam and deserted in the aftermath. It was time she stopped fooling herself—time she accepted the truth. It was right here in front of her, just like she'd always wanted, in black and white.

She closed the cabinet and returned to the kitchen. A sick feeling had come over her. Her father was right. The pages of *The Sun* did contain everything she needed—only nothing she wanted. She had nothing to offer Eason, no solace, no consolation, and certainly no hope. Only the truth. And what good was that to a man who intended to die?

Twenty-Five

The house was dark. That was odd. Where was Evie? It was late. Shouldn't she be home by now? As Jase pushed open the kitchen door, he felt a twinge of anxiety. "Evie?" No answer. He switched on the light and saw her at the kitchen table, her head buried in her hands. Good God, how long had she been sitting in the dark like that? His anxiety blossomed into alarm. "What's wrong?"

"I—" She had been crying. "Eason—the newspaper—I read it all—I—"

She broke down again, unable to continue. He put a hand on her shoulder. At her elbow was a cup of tea, half-drunk, cold. He put the kettle on and brewed her a fresh cup, pouring a cup for himself as well. He sat down beside her, waiting until her crying slowed, and she was able to speak. "Do you want to tell me about it?"

She did. Finally he had the whole story, beginning with the very first time she rode out to the Swale ranch the year before. It was that boy, Eason. He'd gone to war unexpectedly and then come home equally so. He was a deserter. No one knew why. She had convinced herself the answer lay in the Battle of Choke Creek and so had gone into Asa's office to read about it. There she had discovered that the boy's namesake—the cavalryman Thomas Eli—was a coward. No, not just a coward, a murderer, too. Somehow this all bore on the Swale boy's plight. "Remember when I went to the State Capitol?" She broke into fresh tears. "I was wrong. It wasn't a massacre. Everything I saw last year—

everything I *believed*—was imaginary." Her shoulders shook with sobs. "I'm crazy, just like everybody says."

He put his arms around her. How much she had suffered in the last year! And how much of it was his fault. The thought brought a stab of regret to his heart. "You're not crazy."

Her face turned dark and sullen. "You don't know that."

"Yes, I do." She didn't believe him. He could hardly blame her. He'd lied to her so long, why should she believe him now? "Come on. There's something I want to show you."

He led her to the office beneath the stairs, where he turned on the lamp and retrieved the briefcase from its hidden spot behind the books. She watched him without comment, her eyes still suspicious and wary. He opened the briefcase and pulled out the letters. One from Lieutenant Eason, one from Lieutenant Brem. He hesitated, considering, then chose the one from Thomas Eli and handed it to her first. It was what she'd needed for so long—the one that would mean the most. While she read, he perused the letter from Brem. He didn't want to. He knew what he would find in it, and the events described were too gruesome, too horrifying to bear, even after all these years. But he forced himself to do it for her sake. As a kind of penance. It was the least he could do after all she had suffered in the past year. The letter was dated at the end of December and began:

To Asa Glauber, Editor-in-Chief, The Rocky Mountain Sun,

This is the first opportunity I have had of writing you since the great Indian Massacre, and for a start, I will acknowledge I am ashamed to own I was in it.

Colonel Stevenson led us like a thief in the dark, marched us all night to the big bend in Choke Creek, where we came upon the Indian village, some one hundred lodges, containing not over 500 Indians all told, 350 of which were women and children. They were at peace, and when we came riding up, one of their chiefs came out with a white flag. Well, I got so mad, I swore I would not burn powder, and I did not. Lieutenant Eason did the same. It is no use for me to try to tell you how the fight was managed, only I think Stevenson should be hung, and I know when the truth is known it will cashier him.

We lost 40 men wounded, and 10 killed. Not over 250 Indians, mostly women and children, and not over 75 bucks. After the fight there was a sight I hope I may never see again.

Bucks, women and children, were scalped, fingers cut off to get the rings on them, and this as much with Officers as men. A Lt. Col. cut off Ears, of all he came across, a squaw ripped open and a child taken from her, little children shot, while begging for their lives, and all the indignities shown their bodies that ever was heard of. Women shot while on their knees, with their arms around soldiers a begging for their lives. Things that Indians would be ashamed to do. To give you some little idea, squaws were known to kill their own children, and then themselves, rather than to have them taken prisoners. Most of the Indians yielded 4 or 5 scalps. But enough! for I know you are disgusted already.

After all the pledges made to these Indians and then to take the course he did. I think as comments are necessary from me, only I will say Col. Stevenson has a face for every man he talks to. The action taken by Lt. Eason and myself were under protest. Col. Stevenson was going to have Eason hung for saying they were all cowardly Sons of B—s; if Eason did not take it back, but nary take back with Eason. I told the Col. that I thought it murder to jump them friendly Indians. He says in reply; Damn any man or men who are in sympathy with them. I expect Col. Stevenson will do all in his power to have Eason and I dismissed. Well, let them work for what they damn please, I ask no favors of them. Excuse this for I have been in much of a hurry.

He put the letter down and found his daughter looking at him, shock, horror, and disbelief showing in her face as the truth registered. "It was a massacre, just like I said. And you knew all along." She clutched Lieutenant Eason's letter, her eyes flaring with anger. "You lied to me. How could you do such a thing?"

He winced, accepting the full punishing force of her accusation. "I wanted to tell you about it. I always meant to. I was just waiting until ... " He was about to say *until you were old enough* when he stopped himself. Evie was old enough. He knew that now. She had been for a long time. "You were obsessed with that battle. It was making you ... " His voice trailed off as he searched for the right word. " ... *sick.* I thought if you knew the truth it would only make you worse."

"Worse?" She laughed in a bitter way. "It was *not* knowing that made me that way." She dropped her eyes back to Lieutenant Eason's letter, reading it through a second time. A look of sorrow crossed her face, but she didn't cry. He understood that she was forbidding herself to. She was done being the little girl. She was steeling herself for the future— for what would come.

She put Thomas Eli's letter down and held her hand out for Brem's. While she read, he dropped his eyes to Lieutenant Eason's letter, reading the words he had addressed to Asa:

My dear Sir,

You will be undoubtedly surprised to receive this letter, and perhaps will be inclined to dismiss it, coming as it does from one of my station, but believe me, Sir, when I tell you, that circumstances conspire to give me no choice but to address myself to you, in hopes that some measure of fairness, of Mercy, that may still lodge in your breast, some desire for the Truth that is so often your expressed desire, will lead you to consider the words of a most unfortunate man.

The glorious engagement you have heard so much of was a massacre of friendly Indians camped on Choke Creek. I told them all so, saying, any man who would take part in the murders, knowing the circumstances as we did, was a low lived cowardly son of a bitch. But there was no stopping the colonel. We arrived at the creek at daylight. I refused to fire and swore that none but a coward would for by this time hundreds of women and children were coming towards us and getting on their knees for mercy. Stevenson shouted, "Kill the sons of bitches." The Battery then came up in our rear and opened on them. You can form some idea of the slaughter. When the Indians found that there was no hope for them they went for the Creek, and buried themselves in the Sand and got under the banks and some of the bucks got their Bows and a few rifles and defended themselves as well as they could. By this time there was no organization among our troops, they were a perfect mob—every man on his own hook.

The massacre lasted six or eight hours, and a good many Indians es-

caped. I tell you it was hard to see little children on their knees have their brains beat out by men professing to be civilized. One squaw was wounded and a fellow took a hatchet to finish her, she held her arms up to defend her, and he cut one arm off, and held the other with one hand and dashed the hatchet through her brain. One Squaw with her two children, were on their knees, begging for their lives of a dozen soldiers, within ten of them all firing—when one succeeded in hitting the squaw in the thigh, when she took a knife and cut the throats of both children, and then killed herself. One old Squaw hung herself in the lodge—there was not enough room for her to hang and she held up her knees and choked herself to death. Some tried to escape on the Prairie, but most of them were run down by horsemen. I saw two Indians hold one of anothers hands, chased until they were exhausted, when they kneeled down, and clasped each other around the neck and were both shot together. They were all scalped, and as high as half a dozen taken from one head. They were all horribly mutilated. One woman was cut open and a child taken out of her, and scalped.

Others had Ears and Privates cut off. Squaws snatches were cut out for trophies. You would think it impossible for white men to butcher and mutilate human beings as they did there, but every word I have told you is the truth. It was almost impossible to save any of them. Stevenson will have me cashiered if possible. If they do I want you to help me. I think they will try the same for Brem for he has shot his mouth off a good deal, and did not shoot his pistol off in the Massacre. Brem has behaved first rate during the whole affair. Stevenson reports five or six hundred killed, but there were not more than two hundred, about 140 women and children and 60 Bucks. A good many were out hunting buffalo. When the women were killed the Bucks did not seem to try and get away, but fought desperately.

I suppose Brem has written to you, all the particulars, so I will write half. Give my regards to any friends you come across.

When he finished reading, Evie held out her hand for Eason's letter, and he gave it back to her. "So Thomas Eli wasn't a coward." She looked at both letters with astonishment. "He and Brem were the only ones who weren't." A puzzled look came over her face. "I don't understand. They sent Asa the letters in December. Why didn't he publish them?"

"He couldn't. It was too dangerous. By the time he got the letters, Brem had been killed, and Thomas Eli had fled for his life, fearing he would be next. Asa decided to wait until cooler heads prevailed. In time, he believed, people would be ready for the truth. He would publish the letters then."

"You don't know that." Her voice rose anger. "Asa hated Indians. He called them savages and devils. He was the last person who would care if they died."

Jase sighed. "Asa was a man of his times, Evie. I'm not saying I agree with everything he said. But I do believe he valued the truth. Why else would he keep the letters? Why not just destroy them?"

She was silent for a moment, thinking about it. "It never came, did it, the time Asa was waiting for?"

"No. The story of the glorious battle just became more and more entrenched in people's minds. They didn't want to believe that the men they loved were capable of such atrocities. Besides, the Indian War had been raging for a long time. Atrocities had been committed on both sides. I suppose most people believed the Indians got what they deserved."

Her eyes flared with righteous indignation. "That doesn't justify it."

"No. Of course not."

"Thomas Eli said the Indians on Choke Creek were friendly." Her eyes widened as the realization dawned on her. "That's why they were camped so close to the city. The governor had sent them there. And Stevenson knew it. He knew they were peaceful, but he killed them anyway."

Jase listened with interest. He didn't know this part of the story, but he wasn't surprised to hear it. Stevenson was a scoundrel, capable of any perfidy.

"No one knows the truth anymore," she said. "Not even the Swales. Cyrus thinks his grandfather was a coward. And he won't even talk to Indians. He doesn't want to admit there was a massacre on his land." A fierce light came into her eyes. "You could tell people the truth. You could publish the letters right now—today."

"I'm sorry, Evie." He knew it would eventually come to this, just as he knew what he would have to say. "That kind of thing requires a great deal of courage. More, I'm afraid, than I have."

He was grateful that she didn't press him further. Still, it was a hard thing to see himself diminished in her eyes.

"I thought Eason killed a girl in Vietnam," she said, "but I was wrong. He didn't kill anyone. He *witnessed* a massacre, just like his great-grandfather. He told me so himself. He said he *saw* a dead girl. He didn't understand that his failure to act was a moral choice, so he deserted." A stunned realization came into her eyes. "But now I can show him." She clutched the letters to her chest. "He can go to the authorities. He can tell them what he saw. They'll have to forgive him. After all, he didn't do anything wrong." She was seized by an air of feverish excitement. "I'll show him the letters in the morning." A wistful look came into her eyes. "It will be all right, won't it?"

She turned to him with a hopeful air. It was the last time, he knew, that he would see his daughter like that, wanting him to reassure her, to tell her that the world was a fixable place, and everything would be all right. But he had no such assurances to give. He was done lying to her, and now he had no idea what the morning would bring.

Twenty-Six

After dinner Eason asked his father for the keys to the truck.

"Where are you going?" Cyrus said.

"Nowhere." Then he saw the worried look in his father's eyes, and he relented. "Don't worry. I'll be back."

It was the first time he'd left the ranch since coming home. Crossing the boundary felt like crossing the border between two countries, one familiar, the other entirely unknown. There was a strangeness to it, a feeling that was both dangerous and thrilling. It was just what he wanted. Ever since the MPs had driven up to the ranch that morning, he'd been seized by a restlessness, the conviction that something was about to happen—that something was about to end. He still didn't know what it was, only that he had to make it happen, and that he had to be in motion to do that.

He wrenched the truck onto the county road and turned northwards. The sky was clear, moonlight reflecting on the rainwater that had collected in the ditches on the side of the road. The wind had begun blowing again when night fell, coming in from the west, gusting hard enough to buffet the truck from side to side. He leaned on the accelerator, giving in to the thrill of speed, flying down the empty road, gravel rattling beneath the tires. The thought came to him that he could just keep driving like this all the way to Canada. *Evie would like that*, he thought with a thin smile; ever since he'd come back, all she'd wanted was to save him. But she didn't know the truth, that there was nothing left to save. He felt a pang of sorrow. She would miss him when he was gone. It was almost enough to make him turn around. Then he frowned and shook his head. Hadn't he warned her from the start to stay away? He'd told her he was no good for her. It wasn't his fault if she hadn't listened.

It had been a long time since he'd driven like this, so recklessly and free, letting the road eat away at his anger and grief. The last time, he reflected, was the night Billy died. Then he'd driven to Dane's house, where he'd spoken to Hyde Culbert. It occurred to him that there was something he still needed to tell Hyde. He should have taken care of it a long time ago. He slowed down, and when he came to the turn-off for the feedlot, he took it. Soon cattle appeared beside the road, massing in the darkness along the fence line, their backs turned to the wind. He stopped in front of the Culbert house, where the light still glowed in the upstairs window as it had before. Dane's brother. Curiosity flickered in Eason's eyes. There was a story there; he was sure of it. He should go to Dane's brother and ask. They had something in common now: they'd both come back. Then he shook his head. Not his problem. Besides, if there was one thing he'd learned in Vietnam, it was that the world was full of stories that never got told.

He knocked on the door, and a moment later Dane's mother appeared in the doorway, looking even paler and more gaunt than before, worry eating her up from the inside like a cancer. "Eason?" Her face broke open in a smile. "It is you!" She opened the door wide, but before he could go in, Hyde pushed her aside and positioned himself in the doorway, blocking it with his squat, massive frame. "What d'ya know. Eason Swale. Home from Vietnam." He gave Eason an appraising look, his hand reaching up to scratch his thick, unshaven neck. "Back a little early, aren't you?"

Eason ignored this. It wasn't what he had come for. "I came to tell you something."

Hyde grew cautious, suspicion clouding his eyes. "What's that?"

"I came to thank you."

Hyde's mouth opened, but nothing came out.

"You were the only one who told me the truth."

Eason didn't wait for an answer. He turned and trudged back to the truck. So that was done. What next? He had no idea. He drove away, heading northwards again until the highway appeared before him, a river of bright lights in motion, and he let the current suck him in.

He headed eastwards, the dark plain stretching out on either side of him, the road an unbroken straight line. It was easier driving this way. He didn't have to think; he just let the other cars pull him along. Time passed—he lost track of how much—and when he glanced down, he saw that he needed fuel. In a few minutes a truck stop appeared beside the road, and when the car in front of him took the exit, he followed.

The truck stop loomed on the darkened plain like an oasis of light. Lofty street lamps cast gleaming pools of light on the oily blacktop by the gas pumps, while light spilled in a flickering stream from the windows of the adjacent diner. A row of eighteen-wheelers idled on the parking lot like kneeling camels, their taillights glowing like eyes. Eason pulled up to a pump and stepped outside while the station attendant, a stocky, grey-haired man, pumped diesel into the truck. The wind was still blowing hard, flinging Eason's hair into his face, chasing litter across the ground, crumpled bags and paper cups, torn pages of *The Sun*. The wind was cold, and he shivered. Then all at once he was shaking, huddled with his arms wrapped around himself, his back pressed to his truck. The shaking jarred his bones and made the truck rock, but he couldn't make it stop. The attendant looked at the truck and then at him. "Son, are you okay?"

Eason wanted to answer but couldn't. His teeth were chattering too hard.

The attendant shook his head and flicked the gas cap back on the truck. "You best go inside and get yourself some coffee."

Eason managed to peel some money out of his billfold and hand it over. Then he drove to a parking space and went into the diner. It was larger than he had expected, a long stainless steel counter wrapped around the front of the restaurant, two rows of booths lining the back. In the corner a television, bolted to the wall, played a baseball game.

There were a half-dozen men sitting at the counter before plates of chicken fried steak and potatoes, coffee and pie. They paid little attention to the game. Danvers was too small to merit a major-league team.

Two waitresses in identical pink uniforms worked the room, one behind the counter, the other making trips between the booths and the cook window. Eason found a seat at the end of the counter, and the waitress, a dark-haired woman who looked like she could be the gas attendant's wife, poured him coffee in a thick white cup. He took a sip. At least he'd stopped shaking, now that he was out of the wind.

No one at the counter was talking, but a hum of voices came from the booths. A man and woman arguing in low tones, a little girl demanding ice cream. One of the booths was louder than the others, and Eason found himself glancing at it. It held a trio of young men, college students most likely, just passing through. Their hair was long, they wore tie-dyed shirts, bell-bottom jeans, and sandals, and they looked around with the disdainful arrogance city folk often exhibited on the prairie. Eason shook his head. He'd like to see one of them on the back of a horse sometime.

He finished his coffee and let the waitress pour him a second cup. From time to time the chime on the door sounded, and the gas attendant came in to put money in the register or make change. He never spoke to the waitress, so Eason guessed she wasn't his wife after all. He must have been wrong about that. Well, why not? He'd been wrong about so many things.

He finished the second cup and shook his head when the waitress offered him a third. Nothing left to do now but go. He left a tip on the counter and made his way to the register to pay. As he was reaching into his pocket for the money, the ballgame ended, and the news came on the TV. The men at the counter lifted their heads to watch.

The report opened with news from Vietnam. Images from the war flitted across the screen, followed by a picture of President Johnson making a speech. The men at the counter were silent, listening, and even the couple in the booth put aside their arguing to watch. The waitresses stopped moving, their heads craned towards the television, but the college boys erupted into laughter. "Hey, hey LBJ," one of them chanted, "how many babies did you kill today?"

The other two boys met his words with snickers and loud, appreciative hoots. The men at the counter glanced at the boys then shook their heads and looked away. Eason expected to do the same, but apparently his feet had another idea. They carried him towards the booth. He didn't know what he would do when he reached it, but his hands seemed to have formed a mind of their own, too. They grabbed the boy who had chanted, lifting him out of the booth by his shirt. "You don't know what you're talking about." The boy's feet dangled off the floor. His face was red, his shirt ripped, Eason's grip half-strangling him. "You don't know a damn thing."

Eason expected the other boys to come to their friend's aid. Vaguely he hoped for it; apparently a good, bloodied fistfight was just what he wanted. But fighting, it seemed, was not the college way. The other boys sank deeper into their seats, although one of them muttered "Hey" in weak protest.

Then someone's arms were around Eason, gently prying him loose from the college boy. He let go and fell into the gas attendant's arms. Tears sprang into his eyes, and before he could stop himself, he was sobbing. His face averted, the attendant held him until Eason had gotten himself under control again. Then he let him go and said, "You best get going home now, son."

It was late when Eason got back home, the house dark, his father in bed, although he wasn't sleeping; Eason felt wakefulness in the air as he passed by the room. A moment later he heard a creak in the bed, followed by a sigh. Then steady breathing as his father finally fell asleep.

But sleep was the last thing Eason could hope for, and he lay in bed with his arms behind his head, his eyes staring up at the ceiling. Outside the wind had finally died down, becoming soft and gentle, a murmur whispering in the eaves. He closed his eyes and strained into the darkness, listening, but it was no use. He couldn't hear anything. He opened his eyes. What did he expect? Even Evie said she couldn't hear them anymore.

His thoughts drifted back to the bluff where his namesake, Thomas Eli Eason, had stood without firing his weapon as the great battle unfolded. Then he blinked, and the creek in his imagination was replaced by a river, muddy and torpid and wide. Once more he saw the huts and heard the bawling of the cattle; in the distance the grey body of the water buffalo blended into the misty rain.

He had been the last man to leave the woods—the last one to reach the village—and by the time he'd gotten there, the killing had already started. He had planned to do his part—more than anything, it was what he wanted—but to his great shame, he found himself frozen, unable to fire his weapon, while even Music fired with abandon. In the blink of an eye the villagers were dead; Eason saw a boy of toddler age, a woman, an elderly couple, and the girl with shorn hair. But then he stopped looking because the more he stared at them, the more the bodies, swimming in his sight, threatened to disappear.

They left the bodies where they lay and marched back through the woods, sour and silent. Once again Nye took the lead while Eason brought up the rear. No one said a word about the way he had conducted himself, but already he could feel the gulf that had opened up between himself and the others. It wasn't a question anymore of being as tight as the fingers on one hand; he wasn't even a part of the same body. He knew they were watching him, silently wondering, What will he do now? And what will he say?

Nothing, he wanted to tell them. *I won't say anything. It doesn't matter how bad you think I am. I think I'm worse.* How he missed Liver then! If only Liver were there, everything would be all right, he was sure of it. But then he remembered that Liver had died because of him—and he hadn't done a thing to avenge him.

They returned to Liver's body, and this time Music called it in. They waited until the helicopter came in for the dust-off, and then they watched as they took him away. When they got back to camp, they reported in to the lieutenant. Following Nye's lead, they told him how Liver had died. But they made no mention of the village and offered no explanation for the lost hours. The lieutenant gave them a long look.

Then he shook his head and sent them to their hootches for showers and grub.

Over the next few days they returned to their routines, a fifth man coming in to take Liver's place. The village never came up again. Still Eason knew the others didn't trust him anymore. He saw it in their faces, in the way they looked at him—in the way he caught them looking at him out of the corner of their eyes.

They wanted him gone. No one said it in so many words, but he could tell. He became fearful, began watching his back. He'd heard too many stories about guys who'd had unfortunate "accidents" in the war zone: a grenade going off under one man's bed while he slept, a bullet finding another's back while he was alone on guard duty.

One morning they were sent back out on patrol. After hours trudging through the woods, they stopped to take a break. One by one the men sat down, their rucksacks beside them. Music fiddled with the radio. Page drew circles in the dirt with a stick. Nye stared off into the distance alone. For a while the new guy chattered, trying to strike up a conversation, but when no one answered him, he fell silent, too.

It was a rare, rainless day, the sun shining down from a softly blue sky, casting dappled patterns of shade and light on the forest floor. For a while Eason studied them, turning his head this way and that, watching the patterns shift as his perspective changed. All at once he stood up and took a step into the woods. He paused as if considering a theory. Then he took another step. And then one more. Each one was an experiment, an incremental advancement of a hypothesis, a bit of procedure just to see what would happen next. He felt the eyes of the other men on his back, watching him. They were still watching as the jungle sucked him up, and he disappeared.

He figured he would die now. And why not? It was what they all wanted, wasn't it? Anyway, what were the chances he would survive alone in Indian Country? But Vietnam, as Eason knew quite well, wasn't like that. The things you expected most to happen never did, while the ones you expected least happened all the time. And so he didn't die. Instead he just kept walking without seeing anyone and without anyone seeing him—as if he had already become a ghost.

He was surprised to find how pleasant it was. He'd left his pack on the ground, and without it he felt as light and weightless as a balloon, as if he might just float up and away. He traveled effortlessly through the forest, half-floating already, his mind light and pleasantly empty, too, as if he'd never had a dream or a thought or a fear in his life. As if he'd never been to war. All along the sun kept shining, the dappled light warming his face and hands with a sensation that was so delightful, he stripped off his shirt just to feel it more. He meant to tie the shirt around his waist but instead dropped it, watching with interest as it floated lightly and effortlessly to the ground. Then he took off his pants and watched them float away, too. He thought about leaving his boots off but decided not to. He was so light already, without them he would surely rise untethered into the air, and maybe it was better to stay grounded, at least for a while.

He walked all that day and through the night, skimming naked through the trees, feeling so natural, he wondered why he hadn't thought of doing this before. In the morning he came to a village where a woman was doing her wash, squatting by a stream, wet laundry piled beside her on a rock. He had no idea what she thought when he emerged from the woods, giant and white and ghostly in his nakedness. Nearby clothes were spread out on bushes to dry, and without hesitation he took a shirt from a branch and a pair of pants. They were too small—the sleeves didn't reach his wrists, and the pants hovered far above his boots—but he liked the way they felt, the soft, thin cotton adding to his feeling of effortless lightness. Her eyes wide, the woman held a hand to her mouth and watched without speaking as he took the clothes and walked away.

That day he walked out of the hills. He hadn't eaten anything for over twenty-four hours, and it occurred to him that maybe that was why his head felt so empty and light. If he had known fasting felt this good, he would have stopped eating ages ago. He passed through one village after another, the people staring silently after him, a tall, white-skinned man dressed in the clothes of a stranger, until at last he came to the sea. He crossed the sand and waded into the water, walking until it lapped around his waist. And then he stopped. He had to. He could walk no farther. He turned around, returned to the beach, and sat down on the sand.

The sun was still out, the wind chasing vaporous white clouds across the sky. For a time he watched the water, the white-tipped lines of froth flowing endlessly to the shore, the mystifying ocean light drawing his sight to the curve of the earth. He decided that this was what he had wanted all along: to see the sea one more time before he died. As he looked at it, he found himself thinking of home. He thought of the wind, and the way it sounded as it blew across the plain. He'd never taken the time to listen to it. Maybe he should have. Maybe it had something to tell him. Once, it seemed to him, Evie Glauber had thought so. Maybe if he had listened hard enough, things would have been different, and he wouldn't have had to go to war.

It occurred to him that he wouldn't die in Vietnam. He had to go home for that. Put an end to the story in the place where it began. He stood up, and just as wondrously as everything else that had happened to him since he had stripped himself naked and bare—since he had shed his old self like an insect shedding a husk and had emerged newly born, himself and not himself all at the same time—a man appeared before him with a boat. Eason stepped into it and began his journey home.

Now he lay in bed thinking about it. Outside the wind blew, whispering to him, saying words he couldn't understand. He'd come so close that afternoon on the bluff when he'd played cowboys and Indians with Evie. For a brief moment it had all seemed so clear to him, and then it had fallen apart. Well, maybe he just had to give it one more try. Maybe this time he'd finally get what he needed. He stood up, went to the glass cabinet, and took out the rifle and the coat. He listened carefully, making sure his father was still asleep. Once more he felt a wave of sadness, but he knew better than to give in to it. The story needed to end. He hoped his father would understand. There was some comfort in thinking he was leaving behind somebody who would. He shouldered the rifle and stepped outside.

Twenty-Seven

Evie couldn't sleep. She lay in bed listening to the wind swirl around the house. *Eason, Eason, Eason.* She whispered the name in time to the windy gusts, the letters clutched in her hands. At last she had the truth. Outside the light in the creek burned with a brightness she hadn't seen since the winter. *She could save him.*

She planned on riding to the ranch at first light, but shortly before dawn the wind died down, and as quiet descended on the house, she fell into a deep, dreamless, exhausted, sleep. When she woke, she was surprised to discover the sun was already high in the sky. She threw off her covers and hurried to dress, pulling on her jeans, any old shirt, her tall riding boots. Then she tucked the letters into her pocket and plunged out the door.

The rainstorm from the day before had left a sheen of water on the creek, a dark reflecting pool that contained the far-flung sky. Clouds skimmed through it like shadows. She climbed the far bank and hastened to the barn. *Eason, Eason, Eason.* Her fingers tapped the letters in her pocket in a rhythm tuned to his name. She pulled Bird out of his stall and threw on his tack as quickly as she could, the saddle and bridle, the girth pulled tight. She tugged him outside—he could be such a slowpoke sometimes!—put her foot in the stirrup and leapt into the saddle. Just as she was gathering up the reins, she caught sight of a car pulling up to the barn. Her father's car. She stared in surprise as Jase pulled to a stop and stepped out. There was a grim look to him, his face drained of color, his eyes dark. "I'm sorry, Evie." He looked away, avoiding her eyes. "I'm sorry about everything. I'm—"

He stopped speaking, but he didn't have to say it for her to know what it was. She wanted him to get on with it—get it over. She wanted it behind her instead of looming in front of her, turning her heart to sand.

"I found out this morning when I got to work. He was in the creek. Cyrus called the sheriff out. He had a rifle with him. He—"

"No, no, no." She whispered the words. She couldn't bear to hear it after all. "You're lying." Her voice grew louder. "You always lie."

"Evie, please, listen to me." He held his hand out to her. "It's not your fault. It's the way the world is, it's—"

She shook her head hard enough to startle her horse, and he jigged in place, his tail swishing. "You're a liar. I won't believe you. I won't listen to anything you say." She whirled around so that she wouldn't have to see his lying face. Eason was fine. Her father was wrong. She would ride out to the ranch and prove it to him. She put her heels to her horse and drove him into the creek.

Evie raced Bird down the creek through cottonwood shadows, past the clinging arms of willows and through dry, grasping cattail stands. Here and there rainwater had collected into pools ankle-deep on her horse, and his hooves flung up stinging clods of earth, coating them both with mud and sand. She pushed him blindly on, crouched low to his neck, her face buried in his mane, moaning despite herself, *No, no, no ...*

Bird flung up his head, bloodying her nose. He skidded to a stop then wheeled to the side, so violently he almost threw her. She looked up and saw a tree blocking the trail. It was an old cottonwood, a dead trunk that had stood beside the creek forever, its bark grey and desiccated, its bare limbs as sharp as knives. The wind had brought it down in the night, and now it lay lodged across the creek bed.

Her nose was bleeding, the taste of blood seeping into her mouth. She spit, wiped her face with the back of her hand. Fine. If Bird couldn't get past the tree, she'd make him jump it. She put her leg on him and pushed him forward. *Eason, Eason, Eason.* She would do whatever it took to prove her father wrong.

They galloped towards the trunk, but it was too massive, and the branches stuck out like a screen. At the last second Bird planted his hooves into the earth and skidded to a stop. Then he wheeled on his haunches and spun away.

No. She would get through. She would—she wrenched her horse around and galloped back to the tree. This time Bird reared as he stopped, and she clung to his neck to avoid being thrown. As soon as he had come down she was at him again, digging her heels into his sides, yelping and hollering, beating him forward with the flat of her hand. He swerved then broke for the barn, running flat out, his nostrils flaring, his eyes white. With all her strength she yanked on the reins, sawing on the bit until he threw up his head and came to a jittery stop. Then she was at him again, kicking and yanking, screaming, No, no, no, pummeling him with her fists and her heels. The horse grunted, shuddered, and skittered backwards with a groan, his flanks white with sweat, his mouth tinged with blood.

Evie slid out of the saddle. Her knees buckled, and she crumpled to the ground. Bird took off and ran for the barn. Watching him go, she broke into wails. What had she done? Eason was dead, gone. The blood was like iron in her mouth. What difference did a pair of letters make? It was too late. The thought brought on a fresh wave of sobs. She stood up and through her tears saw the creek lady standing by the fallen cottonwood, clutching her baby, her black hair shining in the morning light.

"Go away," Evie shouted. "Leave me alone."

The ghost came towards her, hovering above the sand, frantically thrusting the baby out in her arms. *Save her*, the creek lady mouthed. *Save my baby.*

"I told you," Evie said. "I can't save anyone. Don't you see?"

The ghost's face was full of anguish, her long white dress streaming. She came closer—close enough to seize Evie in her vaporous grasp. Evie flung up her arms in a last desperate attempt to ward her away.

The phantom loomed over her, fixing her with her pitiful eyes, and as Evie stared into them, she realized she'd been wrong about the ghost all along.

Bird was back at the barn, waiting for her in the aisle outside his stall. Evie was relieved to see that he'd made it back safely. She was also glad to see that her father was gone. At least she would be spared the indignity of telling him what she had done. Gently now, and with great tenderness, she took care of her horse, taking off his tack, cleaning him up, brushing away the sand and mud. She rubbed him with towels until he was dry and doctored his cuts, putting a healing salve on the wounds around his mouth. Then she watered him and put him back in his stall, giving him an extra measure of grain. For a moment she stood outside his stall watching him eat. Things would never be the same between them. All she could hope was that one day he would forgive her.

She went into the washroom and washed the dried blood off her face, touching a tentative finger to her nose. It felt sore and swollen, but she didn't think it was broken. She left the barn and headed for home. As she came in the back door, she heard her father in the kitchen, talking to Ruth. But she didn't want to face them—she didn't want to face anyone—so she slipped back outside to the front door and snuck upstairs to her bedroom. She opened her dresser drawer, took out the cigar box, and put the cavalrymen's letters inside. Then she glanced out the window. The ghost was gone. She scrutinized the creek for a long time just to make sure, then tucked the cigar box under her arm, crept back outside, and took a bus downtown. A short while later she stood at the cashier's window in the bus station, trying to buy a ticket to New York. The man behind the grate—a thin-faced, balding man with a prominent Adam's apple—eyed her suspiciously. "You're too young to be traveling alone."

"I'm not going by myself." Evie pointed to an elderly woman in a hand-knitted caftan who was standing at the far side of the station, searching in a befuddled way through her purse. "That's my aunt. I'm going with her."

The man strained to catch sight of the woman. "Why isn't she buying a ticket, too?"

"She already has hers." Evie waved wildly at the woman. Squinting, a confused look on her face, the woman hesitated then waved back.

"See?" Evie forced herself to smile brightly at the man. He shook his head. Then he took her money and pushed the ticket under the grate.

The journey to New York took three days, the bus traveling both night and day. Evie found a seat in the back where she passed the time alternately sleeping and crying quietly to herself. Often when she woke up, her face was wet, and then she knew she had been crying in her sleep, too. Sometimes when she woke it was day. Sometimes it was night. After a while she couldn't remember how long she'd been on the bus, just as she had no idea where she was. She cried until exhaustion took over, and she fell asleep again.

The bus was old, the seats flattened, the fabric on them stained with a moldy smell. It mingled with the diesel fumes from the engine and the rank odors that emanated from the bathroom cubicle. Most of the time she rode alone, but occasionally someone sat down beside her. Once a spindly man in a black suit took the seat beside her, his skin pale like a specter, his white shirt fastened with a black string tie. He chatted brightly at her until she turned away, feigning sleep until real sleep came. Another time she woke to find a little boy with dimpled cheeks in the seat beside her. He had a GI Joe doll, a plastic soldier that he danced across his knees, all the while making monstrous war noises with his mouth. She ventured a smile at him, but he just stared back at her with wide eyes then took refuge in the lap of his mother, who was sitting on the other side of the aisle. Another time a man in overalls and a ball cap studied the empty seat beside her, but when he saw her crying, he moved away.

She didn't care. She didn't want to talk to anyone. She had no idea what she would say. One time when she woke up with her face wet, she discovered an elderly woman sitting beside her. The woman had a round moon face with deep furrows in her cheeks and wrinkles that radiated from the corners of her eyes. Her dress was belted in the middle of her ample frame, a straw bag held her knees. She was knitting, but she put down her needles to look at Evie. "Child, are you all right?" This act of kindness just brought on a fresh burst of crying, and Evie closed her eyes, crying herself back to sleep. The next time she woke up, the woman was gone.

One night she couldn't sleep. For a long time she stared through the window at the shapes that skimmed through the darkness outside, barns and billboards and looming silos. From time to time sheets of glare flicked over the glass from the headlights of passing cars, and once it seemed to her that she saw Eason's face in that light. But his face was turned away, and she couldn't see his eyes. They were fixed on the blackness outside.

Every few hours the bus stopped in another town. Some of the towns were so small, they didn't even have bus stations, just a designated parking spot in front of a post office or filling station. They picked up new drivers and discharged the old. All the stations looked the same to her, grimy storefronts with grey tile underfoot, fluorescent lights that burned day and night, and a lunch counter in the back. Whenever the driver announced a "long stop"—thirty minutes or so—Evie forced herself off the bus. She used the rest room and tried to buy something to eat at the counter. But she didn't feel hungry, and anyway, she had lost track of the time of day; she didn't know if she should ask for breakfast, lunch, or dinner. Once she asked for scrambled eggs, and the waitress gave her a sour look then pointed to a clock on the wall. "Breakfast was over hours ago." Then Evie didn't know what to ask for, so she gave up and walked away.

Later that day she became dimly aware of the fact that the scenery outside her window was changing, becoming greener, thicker, shaped by small hills. The towns gave way to cities, the rural landscape replaced by long roads studded with traffic lights and bordered by restaurants and shops. When they finally reached New York City, she didn't even realize it. She was asleep as they drove into the city, and when the bus stopped, she woke to what she thought was just another station. The rest of the passengers got off, but she didn't feel like getting up, so she stayed in her seat, the cigar box on her lap. Up front the driver put on his jacket and gathered up his things. She figured they must be changing drivers. "When do we get going again?" she asked.

"We're not going anywhere." The driver gave her a long look. "We're here."

The bus had brought her underground—it took her a few minutes to realize how deep. Evie took one set of stairs after another, climbing the levels of the station until finally she emerged into the daylight. The streets were narrow and crowded, jammed with cars. The sidewalks were crowded, too, full of people hurrying in both directions. Evie was in their way. Apparently she was in *everybody's* way. She backed up and pressed her back against the wall, just to avoid the jostling and dirty looks.

She had no idea where to go. She glanced up and caught a glimpse of the sky, a meager sliver of light lodged between the tall buildings. It was cloudy, a light rain falling. On the corner was a newsstand, and she made her way towards it, waiting for a break in the pedestrian traffic before darting through. She found a copy of *The New York Daily Times*, reached into the cigar box, and gave a bill to the man inside the stand. He glanced up, gave her an indifferent look, and shoved the change back at her. As she was putting away the coins, she realized she was in the way again; a line had built up behind her. Irritably the newspaperman directed her to move to the side, and she did, backing up until she could take refuge against the wall again.

Rain misted her face. She pushed her hair out of her eyes then tucked the cigar box under her arm and shook open the newspaper. She paged through it, searching for the masthead. A foot patrolman, passing by, stopped and looked at her with narrowed eyes. "You lost?"

Evie tried to hide the panic in her eyes, imagining herself—a runaway—arrested and thrown in jail. Worse, her father called, her trip ending when it had only just begun. Then she found what she was looking for. "I'm not lost." She pointed to the address of the newspaper's headquarters. "I want to go there."

A moment later she was walking in the direction the policeman had indicated to her: eight blocks up and two to the right. It was raining harder now, and the sidewalk had become even more unmanageable as umbrellas popped up everywhere. Evie didn't have an umbrella—it never rained enough in Danvers to make owning one worthwhile. But this rain seemed like it could go on for days. She slogged through it, carrying the cigar box wrapped in the newspaper to keep it dry. Was this, she wondered, what it had been like for Eason in Vietnam, tramping through one rainy day after another? She shook her head. There was no use in thinking about that. She would never know what Vietnam was like. She knew that now.

The Daily Times was housed in a tall building built of smooth, polished grey stone. Tall panes of glass banked a revolving glass door. Evie stepped into the stream of people hurrying in and out and pushed herself in. On the far side was a wide lobby with marble floors and a bank of elevators at the back, guarded by a receptionist at a desk. Evie crossed the floor to her. "I want to speak to Agatha Wickham."

"Agatha Wickham?" The receptionist was a middle-aged woman with a brisk, efficient air. Everyone else breezed past her, flashing badges and cards, grinning and tipping their hats. Behind her the brass doors of the elevators gleamed, and lights flickered as the cars went up and down. Only Evie was stuck in front of the desk, feeling as helpless as a stone dropped into a pond, sinking until it disappeared. The receptionist gave Evie an appraising look, and in her eyes Evie finally saw herself the way everyone else must have seen her that day—the bus driver, newspaper seller, even the policeman. She was dirty and dripping wet; for days she hadn't bathed, changed her clothes, or brushed her hair. Her nose was swollen, she had bloodstains on her shirt, and she was wearing riding boots crusted with manure and mud. She had nothing with her but a sodden copy of the newspaper and the old cigar box, clutched to her chest, wrapped protectively in her arms. The receptionist picked up the phone then frowned, considered, and put it back down. Her nails tapped on the desk. "Whom shall I say is calling?"

"Eve Glauber," Evie said, "from *The Rocky Mountain Sun*." The steely look in the receptionist's eyes didn't waver. Being Jase Glauber's daughter, Evie realized, would gain her nothing here. She backed away, withering under the receptionist's icy stare. Then she remembered the ghost in the creek. She stepped forwards, lifted her chin, and looked the receptionist square in the eye. "Forget my name. Tell Agatha her granddaughter is here."

Twenty-Eight

He fed the horses. He fed the horses, didn't he? He must have. There was no one else to do it. Besides, he distinctly remembered doing so. Only when? Cyrus knitted his brow, frowned. Yesterday? Today?

He stirred himself, got up from his chair, decided to go look. He opened the door and stood blinking in the doorway. Outside it was dark, the sky clear, awash with starlight. A low wind feathered the darkness, sweeping the cool night air across his face. Night? Impossible. The sun was shining just a few minutes ago. He looked at his watch. Three-thirty. How could that be? He tapped a finger on the crystal face. Three-thirty in the morning? Surely it was still afternoon?

He grabbed a flashlight, clicked it on, stepped outside. He aimed the beam of light at the watch face, shaking his head again with incomprehension at the time it showed. Eason had stopped the hands on his clock when he returned from Vietnam. At the time Cyrus hadn't understood why, but now he did. His world, his son was telling him, had become timeless, hours and minutes meaningless, the present bleeding into the future and the past. Ever since his son left him, Cyrus had entered into the same timeless place. How long had it been? Three weeks, four? His hip had seized up while he sat, and he could barely walk. He wanted to turn back, but the question still nagged him: he'd fed the horses, hadn't he?

He stumbled to the barn and directed light into the stalls. The horses looked back at him with deadened eyes. Their coats were matted, their stalls filthy, reeking of urine and manure. He shoved a hand into their buckets and found them empty, bone dry. The mangers were empty, too, as were the feed boxes, licked clean.

Dear God, my God, he hadn't been there for days and days.

He lugged a bale of hay into the center of the aisle, cut it open, and threw the flakes into the mangers. Then he filled the buckets. That would have to do. He didn't have the strength to clean the stalls or parcel out the grain.

He hobbled back to the house and sank into his chair. Maybe it was night, but he was awake now and didn't feel like sleeping. Anyway he didn't want to. Every time he dozed off, he was disturbed by nightmares, startled by terrifying images back into wakefulness. Only he never dreamt of Eason. He wished he would. He would do anything to see his son one more time, to hear his voice, even if it meant succumbing to an illusion.

Instead his dreams took him back to another war, his own, the one he had fought in the Pacific twenty-five years ago. He remembered things he hadn't thought of for decades, the guttural whirring of the blowflies, the scraping of the rocky, unforgiving earth, the stench of shit and filth and corpses left to rot on the ground. He came late to the island, a Marine fresh off the boat, horrified to find veterans already fieldstripping the dead Japanese. The men went from body to body, fumbling like lovers through the most intimate places, stealing diaries and letters, cutting loose insignias from uniforms, pocketing weapons, confiscating flags. With their knives they pried gold teeth from stiffened mouths, carved bones from shattered skeletons, and secured entire skulls, which they boiled with lye to remove the flesh, or left out in the sun for the ants to pick clean.

They called these things "souvenirs," and like the postcards and trinkets travelers send home from more innocent places, mailed them to their girlfriends and wives with nary a thought of what kind of reception such atrocities might engender. One of the men in his company even carved a thighbone into a letter opener and sent it to President Roosevelt himself.

He recalled a shriveled, blackened hand that a Marine had slashed from a corpse and left to dry in the heat of the sun. A skull adorning a military vehicle. At first the sight of these things disgusted him, but eventually, like everything else in that weird distortion of the world they called war, they began to appear normal to him. Besides, it wasn't like the Japanese restrained themselves; there were horrifying mutilations of the war dead on both sides. One afternoon without thinking, he stripped a sword from a sniper who'd murdered two of the men in his platoon. The casualness of the act surprised him, as did the thrilling feel of power it gave him. The next morning he plucked a cap from a corpse as easily as once he'd plucked berries from the bushes behind his house. The next day he found himself on the beach, bent over a corpse with grim fascination, sawing a gold tooth from a rigid, blackened gum. The sun was pulsing, burning hot, glare rising from the polished stones on the ground. As he straightened up to wipe the sweat from his brow, he saw the other men of his platoon crouched over the beach the same way, like round-backed beetles scavenging the dead. Unexpectedly his mind turned to Choke Creek. Is that what the battlefield had looked like then, after Stevenson was done? The thought sickened him, and after that he didn't touch the corpses anymore.

A few days later he was hugging the ground in a foxhole, pinned down in a firefight, when a voice came to him, saying, "Stand up." Without giving it a moment's thought, he did. As he raised himself to his feet, it seemed to him that everything came to a stop—the firing and the fighting and even the endless shelling. There was a moment of complete silence, and in that silence he was shot, never once hearing the bullet that hit him.

Afterwards he was ashamed of what he had done and never spoke of what he had heard. He told himself the voice was a delusion, brought on by the shock of the shelling, by the intense, unbearable heat, and the sight of men falling all around him. But the shame persisted. He knew he didn't deserve the Purple Heart they gave him and was hounded by a lingering stain of cowardice. He had let his buddies down; he had been spared, but at their expense.

They sent him home, but home brought no relief. Instead he found his thoughts turning over and over again to the voice he'd heard. What if he had been wrong? What if it hadn't been a delusion? What if somehow—no matter how improbable it seemed—it had been real? He wondered why it had spoken to him. Did it want him to die—to stand up and be killed? Or had it spoken to save him? It never occurred to him that the voice might come from God. He'd never believed in the existence of supernatural beings, never once had faith in angels or the heavens. Besides, he wasn't foolish enough to think that if God wanted to speak to someone, it would be him. Why should he be chosen?

The most likely scenario, he knew, was that the voice had been the product of his own diseased yearnings, a secret expression of his wish to kill himself, as once his father had done. But he rejected that idea. He didn't want to die. He didn't cling to much, but he couldn't help it; he clung to life.

Still he couldn't help feeling awed and grateful. Miraculous or not, his survival was a gift, and it was up to him to treat it with reverence. He'd never considered doing anything more with his life than run the ranch his mother had left him, but now he wondered if he shouldn't do more. Before the war he'd gone to agricultural college, but now he went back to school at night, studying law. When he got his degree, he opened a part-time practice in the county. He did his best to conduct himself in a fair and impartial fashion, and in time gained a reputation for it. When a seat opened up on the county bench, he was elected to it—the youngest judge ever to serve in that capacity. The day he heard his first case, he thought this must be the reason he had been spared on the battlefield: he had been judged, and now it was his job to dispense justice in return.

In the flush of those times he married his wife—the only decision he still did not regret. A few years later he saw his son born. He was proud of himself then, sure he was making something of himself, fulfilling the obligation the voice had burdened him with in the war. Then his wife took sick, and the past began to haunt him. He saw it in the eyes of people like Hyde Culbert, who'd served with him in the Pacific. Hyde had fought to the end, whereas Cyrus had been sent home with his "million dollar wound." Whenever Cyrus saw him, he read the unspoken accusation in Hyde's eyes: other men had bled and died in his place.

Then his wife died. The day after he buried her, an Indian drove up to the ranch. It was only an elderly man, seeking permission to go to the battlefield, but Cyrus was convinced he had come there to mock him. Driven by rage, he seized his grandfather's rifle and chased the Indian away. That night he ended up in jail, and a few months later he was disbarred.

He turned his back on everything then, on good works and the law, devoting himself solely to the horses. They, at least, looked on him with unjudging eyes, keeping their opinions to themselves. From time to time as he worked the ranch, he found himself stopping in his tracks to listen to the wind as it sheeted across the tin roof of the old bunkhouse or rustled through the straw leavings by the haystack. But he never heard the voice again.

One day, overcome by curiosity, he drove to the library and opened an encyclopedia to the entry on "scalping." The practice, he discovered to his surprise, dated back to ancient times, and had been brought to the "New World" by the English. The Indians learned it from them. The English paid a bounty for Indian scalps, the price determined by the age and sex of the victim, whether man, woman, or child. It was a crucial pin in the extermination campaign that they quickly determined was necessary to ensure their domination of the new world. Soon they were vilifying the Indians for the same behavior they had practiced so ardently themselves, pointing to the taking of scalps as proof of the Indians' inherent savagery, rendering them primitive, soulless creatures, beyond redemption. Did these Englishmen, Cyrus wondered, really have so little awareness that they had taken the worst of themselves and ascribed it to their enemies? The only savages they needed to fear were themselves.

The same thing had happened in the Pacific, where the Japanese— a darker-skinned, alien race—were vilified as diabolic and barbaric.

Cyrus remembered once overhearing a group of Marines debate the relative merits of Indians and Japanese. One Marine had a father who had fought in the Philippines, and before the boy left for the war, his father told him, "Watch out for those Japs. They're just as bad as the goo-goos we fought in the Philippines—as treacherous as Indians." The second Marine agreed, "They're every bit as savage." But the third argued in favor of the Indians, "At least they had an honor of a sort."

These judgments, Cyrus understood, were necessary to the forging of a national consciousness: acts of remembering and forgetting, the creation of myths and distortions, the telling of lies. He hadn't expected them to affect him so personally. He'd gone to the Pacific believing he was fighting a new war, only to discover he was fighting an old one, or rather the same war, happening over and over again. The same fate, he knew now, had befallen his son, who had gone to Vietnam to fight the enemy of his generation, only to discover the "goo-goos" of years past, transmogrified conveniently for the new crop of soldiers into "gooks."

Cyrus sat in his chair, waiting out the night. In time the darkness softened, and as dawn came, a pale grey light glowed on the distant horizon. In the pastures the horses stirred, and the trumpeting call of a stallion sounded over the paddocks. On such a morning he had risen to find his son's bed empty, the chestnut filly standing riderless outside her stall. His heart in his throat, he'd pulled himself into the saddle and ridden eastwards across the plain to what he'd long feared he'd find.

A vision of his son came back to him now with sudden, undeniable clarity, and he shuddered. He'd found his son lying half-naked in the creek beside the crumpled cavalry coat of his namesake. Eason had maneuvered the long rifle into his mouth so that it blew away the back of his head, but his face was still blessedly intact. As Cyrus fell to his knees beside his son, he found himself giving thanks for this small measure of grace. With blundering fingers he traced the cold streaks of mud Eason had smeared on his cheeks like war paint before he died.

He'd cradled his son in his arms, his grief rising in a keening wail. At last he understood what the voice that had spoken to him so many years ago on the war-torn Pacific island had wanted of him. He'd taken it literally, believing it wanted him to stand up and raise his body into the line of fire, when all it wanted was for him to stand up in a metaphorical sense: to take a moral stance in the world. He'd gotten a glimpse of that when he realized that the mutilation of the Japanese war dead mimicked the atrocities at Choke Creek. But he'd failed to take the realization any farther. He'd spent his life judging others, when the only person who needed judging was himself. He'd sent his son to war, believing Eason would finally succeed where he had failed. But the truth was, he'd sent him to his death, as surely as if he'd ordered it himself. And that was what he would have to live with now, every day for the rest of his natural life.

Twenty-Nine

The first thing Agatha did to Eve was feed her.

She took her to her Park Avenue apartment and fixed her a supper of oatmeal, scrambled eggs, juice, and toast. While she cooked, she sent Eve for a bath, shoving an old bathrobe into her hands to put on afterwards. Just as the food was ready, the girl emerged in the robe, barefoot, a towel coiled around her wet hair like a turban. She still looked like she'd been in a fight—her face was bruised and swollen, her eyes rimmed by dark circles, her skin unnaturally pale—but at least she was clean. Agatha sat her down at the glass table in her dining room, where she looked distinctly out of place amid the Warhol and Lichtenstein prints Agatha had hung on the walls, the Red Grooms sculpture she kept on a pedestal in the corner. Agatha had a million questions, but they would have to wait; even she could tell the girl was in no shape to talk. She appeared to be in no shape to eat, either, although she picked at her food to be polite. After a suitable interval Agatha released her from the table and sent her into the living room. She cleared the dishes, and when she next checked on her, Eve was fast asleep, her head lolling against the back of the couch.

Agatha left her there. She'd meant to put her up in the library on the day bed that doubled in a pinch as a guest bed, but didn't have the heart to wake her. The girl looked like she hadn't had a decent night's sleep in days. Maybe longer.

While Eve slept, Agatha went back into the kitchen to wash up the pots and pans. From time to time she glanced at the phone. She really should call Jase, but she'd promised Eve not to. It was the first thing the girl had made her do when they'd met that afternoon in the lobby of *The Daily Times*. "You have to tell your father where you are," Agatha had protested as soon as she could think straight—as soon as she'd re-covered from the shock of discovering that her granddaughter, by all accounts a runaway, had come all the way to New York City to see her, by bus, and alone. "He'll be worried sick!"

Eve hadn't budged. "He's kept secrets from me my whole life," she'd said, tightening her grip on an old cigar box which, as far as Agatha could tell, was the only thing she'd brought with her—not a stitch of luggage in sight. "It's time he learns what it's like to be kept in the dark."

"I don't understand," Agatha had said.

That was when Eve had loosened her grip on the cigar box just long enough to reach inside, through what appeared to be a mass of paper scraps, to a photograph nestled in the bottom. She held the photo-graph out to Agatha. Agatha squinted at it. The light in the lobby was flat and grey from the rain, and the picture was hard to make out, the image old and grainy. Her breath caught in her throat. "Oh," she said, "I see." Because at last she did.

The next day she took her shopping. They began the morning at a near-by coffee shop, where Eve picked at the French toast Agatha ordered for her, until finally in frustration Agatha pulled the plate over and ate it herself. Nerves. She never had more than coffee in the morning, black. Afterwards they took a taxi to Saks. Fifteen minutes later they were on the street again, Eve still expressing her outrage over the New York styles, which she found ludicrous, and the prices, which she said were inflated beyond belief. Agatha thought hard then took her to Ma-cy's, where Eve managed to find some clothing she deemed acceptable: a pair of shorts, two matching shirts, some sneakers, underwear, and socks. She tried to pay for the clothes herself, pulling handfuls of dol-lars out of the old cigar box, which she still insisted on toting with her everywhere, clutched to her chest in a death grip; what other mysteries did that box contain? But when Agatha insisted, Eve finally relented, and let her grandmother pick up the tab.

Agatha sent Eve to the dressing room to change, and she returned in the shorts and one of the new shirts. She had tucked her old clothes into a brown paper Macy's bag, and Agatha flirted with the notion of burning them, or at least dropping them into the nearest trash bin. But she had a feeling Eve wouldn't take well to that, so she left the bag alone. As she flagged down a taxi, she detected the pungent odor of horses emanating from the top.

Once back at the apartment building, Agatha swung into high gear. She directed the doorman to bring her car around, and told Eve to wait for her in the lobby. Then she took an elevator upstairs and packed herself an overnight bag. Before leaving, she made two phone calls. The first was to her editor, telling her she wouldn't be in for a few days; she'd be at her cottage at the shore. The second was to Boo. There was no answer. Agatha glanced at her watch. Well, of course not. It was only ten-thirty, and no one who was anyone, at least in Boo's eyes, rose before noon.

The drive took them eastwards, out of the confines of the city and into the leafy suburbs. When the traffic lightened enough so that Agatha could glance at her granddaughter, she found her staring out the window, her eyes dark and maddeningly inscrutable, the cigar box still tucked firmly in her arms. Once again Agatha checked the impulse to pepper her with questions. Eve had such a fragile air, watchful, and waiting. It would be best, Agatha decided, to let her granddaughter reveal herself in her own time. She'd been through a lot; anyone could see that, but in the end, by her own calculation and of her own free will, she'd come to her grandmother for help. There was a measure of trust in that which Agatha was determined not to abuse.

In time they crossed the Connecticut state line, and the landscape changed again, becoming decidedly rural, a mixture of woods, farm-lands, and seaport towns. This was a drive Agatha took at least once each month, and it never failed to raise in her the most painful emotions, a mixture of hope, regret, and despair. Today, with Eve beside her, the inner turmoil was even worse. She left the parkway for a county road, which led them to a small village of white clapboard cottages and tidy brick homes. She idled at the sole stoplight in the center of town, while Eve took it all in without comment beside her. On the far side of the village, she turned onto an unpaved road that led into the woods. Eve pressed her lips together as they emerged from the woods, driving into a clearing that contained a cluster of neat brick cottages amid long, sloping lawns. Agatha pulled the car to a stop in front of the largest of the buildings, a two-story brick house fronted by a portico of white columns. Space had been left there for visitor parking, alongside a discreet sign reading, "Chestnut Ridge Psychiatric Facility."

Agatha shut the motor and turned to her granddaughter. They'd come to the moment she'd been dreading with increasing anxiety all morning, the one where words and explanations would have to be given, meanings determined and judgments rendered. Eve was only a child, but already Agatha feared that any judgment that came from her would be particularly hard to take. She cleared her throat. "It's a hospital," she said, "a place for people with a certain kind of illness, for patients who—"

Eve put a hand on her arm. "It's okay. You don't have to tell me. I know."

"You know?" Agatha looked at her in surprise. "But how—?"

"That doesn't matter." She left her hand a moment longer on Agatha's arm, then turned and got out of the car. Agatha was too stunned to follow. Tears came to her eyes, and she felt blindly with her fingers for the place her granddaughter had touched. It was such a simple gesture, and Agatha didn't even know why it should be so, but for the first time in her life, she felt forgiven.

She needed to tell the staff. Irene was used to her visits, but the doctors liked to be informed of any change in their patients' routines, and surely Eve's visit, Agatha thought wryly to herself, would qualify as that. She followed Eve outside the car. It was a beautiful day, the sun shining softly down from a pale blue sky, shadows thrown invitingly from the trees across the lawn. Here and there residents of the facility were visible, taking walks or sitting in one of the chairs that were scattered conveniently across the grass. When she got to the office, she would ask about Irene, too. She never knew where her daughter might be on a day like this, whether inside or out. She was on her way up the steps when she realized it was too late. Eve had already found her. Irene was on the far side of the lawn, sitting in the dappled shade of an oak tree, and Eve was trudging towards her across the grass.

Agatha hurried after her, catching up to her just as she reached Irene's chair. "I've brought someone to see you," she said brightly to her daughter. It was the one habit she could never seem to shake, no matter how much she despised it: this tendency to speak to Irene in bright, chirruping tones, the way one would to a child or a pet. Today, with Eve there, it was even worse. "It's Eve, love. You remember Eve, don't you?"

The answer to this question was something Irene chose to keep to herself. Her eyes swept across Eve without expression then returned to the spot she had been staring at before: a bit of nowhere on the far side of the lawn, in the distant trees.

"Well," Agatha chirruped to her granddaughter. My God, she was doing it to Eve now, too. "I'll just pull up some chairs for us, and we can sit down, too."

She found two lawn chairs and dragged them over, positioning them on either side of Irene. As they sat down, she began to chatter, filling the air with nonsense, with anything to break the silence: news from *The Daily Times* and the art world—things she knew, even as she said them, held no possible interest for either Irene or Eve. Neither of them answered her, and after a while she gave in and stopped talking. Maybe they were right. Maybe silence was the better course today after all.

Anyway it gave her a chance to study the two of them, her daughter and her granddaughter, brought together in a way she never would have dreamed possible. Irene was a beautiful woman. Well, she had always been a beautiful girl. But that she should be so still … It was something Agatha never could quite get used to. In many ways her daughter still looked exactly like the girl in Eve's photograph, taken when she was—what—seventeen, eighteen? The summer before she left for college in any case, going to that godforsaken school out West—going, Agatha supposed, as far away from home as she possibly could.

It was the illness, Agatha thought, that had made life pass her daughter by, and as a result Irene's skin showed none of usual signs of aging that characterized the faces of other people, the smile and frown lines, the clouded eyes and furrowed brows. Even her hair was the same color as when she was a girl, brilliantly dark and long, falling straight down from her prominent widow's peak. Just now she was sitting demurely in her chair like she used to when she was a schoolgirl, her hands folded neatly in her lap, her ankles crossed beneath her. She was dressed like a child, too, in a flowered skirt with flounces and a bright blue sweater. Agatha had chosen the clothes for her herself, thinking they would bring some color into what she felt was her daughter's drab and endlessly repetitive life. But now she realized what a mistake that had been. Irene deserved the dignity simple clothes provided, dark colors and straight lines. Especially on a day like this one.

She glanced at Eve. What had her granddaughter hoped to get out of this meeting? What was she feeling now? She hoped Eve was getting at least some measure of the solace she so clearly sought. There was no way of telling. Like Irene, Eve kept her thoughts to herself. She sat silently in her chair, now and then stealing glances at her mother, her hands clinging tightly to the cigar box. There was no doubting the relationship between them; anyone could see the similarities in their faces, in the dark, penetrating look in their eyes. Agatha clasped her hands together. Is that why Eve had come here? Did she suffer the incipient signs as Irene had at her age? Agatha shook her head. There was no point in asking. Eve would tell her when she was ready. Until then, she would just have to wait.

From the distance came the whine of a mower, and the smell of cut grass floated into the air. Wind rustled through the leaves of the trees, and in the woods squirrels exchanged high, chattering calls. The daytime shift must have been ending; a bevy of nurses hurried down the steps to the main building, passing another group on their way in. Shadows lengthened over the lawn, and soon Agatha noticed the other residents preparing to go into their cottages. Visiting hours were over. A nurse appeared, seemingly out of nowhere, and hovered at a discreet distance. Irene still hadn't spoken or acknowledged Eve's presence. "I'm sorry," Agatha said. "Sometimes she can be so talkative. Other days ... " Her hands described a futile circle in the air.

"It's okay," Eve said. If she was disappointed, she didn't let it show.

Agatha nodded. "Well, then." She stood up, her voice chirruping again. "Shall we go?"

"Just a minute." Eve opened the cigar box and rummaged through the bits and pieces of paper inside, pulling out the photograph, the dollars, and a pair of old letters, which Agatha hadn't noticed before. She tucked these into her pocket then closed the box. For a moment she gazed down at it, her hands resting on the top. Then she took a deep breath and placed it in her mother's lap. "This is for you."

Irene hands parted, and she accepted the box, her fingers closing tightly around it, gripping it as firmly as Eve had before.

"Okay." Eve stood up and turned to Agatha. "We can go now."

"Wait—" This was the final straw—too much for Agatha to take. "What's in that box? Why—?"

It was no use. Eve had no intention of answering. She just headed towards the car, leading the way as before. Agatha sighed and shook her head. Then she bent over and kissed Irene lightly on the forehead. "Bye, love."

Irene stood up. At first Agatha didn't understand. She thought Irene was just preparing to go with the nurse, who already was approaching, back to her cottage. Then she realized Irene was looking at Eve, her eyes focused on her for the first time that day.

"Did you save her?" Irene clutched the box to her heart. "Did you save the baby?"

Eve stopped. She turned around and walked back to Irene. Agatha's mouth flew open, but Eve didn't seem at all surprised by her mother's words. "Yes." Her eyes shining, she encased Irene in her arms. "I did."

Eve was starving. Now, after all that, the girl wanted to eat, while Agatha was in such a state, she was convinced she would never allow a morsel of food to cross her lips again. She drove them to a diner in the village where Eve consumed an entire burger, a plate of fries, a milkshake, and an enormous slice of apple pie. While she ate, Agatha excused herself to make a phone call. The pay phone was in the back, by the restrooms. This time Boo answered. "I'll be out of town for a few days," she told him, "at the shore." She had planned on telling him about Eve, but at the last moment decided not to. "I'll explain later." She hung up the phone and returned to the table to pay the bill.

Night came as they drove towards the ocean, and Eve fell asleep. Agatha glanced at her. Even in sleep the girl looked different. There was an air of resolution about her, a sense of completion. Without the cigar box, her hands rested peacefully in her lap. When they arrived at Agatha's beach house, Agatha showed Eve her room. Afterwards the girl joined her in the living room, a wide space with a slate floor, wicker furniture, and white woodwork walls. Maybe Agatha still couldn't eat, but she discovered she could drink just fine. She poured herself a stiff dose of whiskey, neat, and threw open the shades, revealing her favorite view in the world, a wall of windows overlooking the sea. Eve sat beside her on the couch, and for a time the two looked past the low stone wall of the terrace to the water, where the froth-tipped lines of the waves rolled towards them in the darkness.

"I've always wanted to see the ocean," Eve said.

"Your mother loved it here." Agatha took a sip of her drink and began telling her granddaughter about Irene, beginning when she had been a little girl, so bright and full of promise. Of course she had always been a fragile child, overly sensitive, subject to mood swings, adversely affected by change. "I wasn't the best mother for her," Agatha admitted. "Your father's right about that." She smiled ruefully. "I suppose I wouldn't have been the best mother for *anyone*." There were the divorces, the first one from Irene's father when Irene was only four, and then from her stepfather when the girl was thirteen. She left her third husband, Norman, whom Irene adored, when Irene was seventeen. Six months later Irene retaliated by leaving herself, driving off to college in Kansas City.

"Kansas City!" Agatha exclaimed, the shock still registering in her voice. "Can you imagine?" The only things Kansas had, as far as Agatha was concerned, were cattle and tornadoes. But the West, it turned out, suited Irene just fine. She loved the open spaces and wide skies. For the first time in her life, she confided in her letters, she felt as if she could *breathe*. Agatha sniffed. As if there were no air in New York. "She majored in journalism and art history, and then she moved to Danvers and got her first job, working as the art critic for *The Rocky Mountain Sun*."

For a time they sat in silence, and when Agatha picked up the story again, Irene was married and pregnant. "I went out to see her that summer," she said, brightening. "I'd never seen anyone so happy in my life. Both of them were, your father and your mother. It was all they could talk about, the new baby, and what it meant."

Agatha had hoped her daughter's happiness would be real and abiding, that Irene had finally managed to achieve everything her mother had never been able to provide her with: a loving family, a stable home. But she knew how difficult change was for her daughter, and having a baby was the biggest transition, physically and emotionally, a woman could undergo. Irene fell ill after Eve was born—she fell *apart*—the highs of the previous summer plummeting into a winter of black despair.

"I tried to warn your father," Agatha said, her fingers tightening on the whiskey glass as she recalled the late night phone calls to Jase. "But he wouldn't listen. He said she would get over it. He kept talking about how happy she'd been during the summer—as if that mattered now. He said all she needed was more time."

But time, it turned out, was the one thing that didn't help Irene. As the winter progressed, bringing with it snow and cold and long, dark nights, she got worse. She no longer had the healing power of the bright, summery sunshine to help her. One night, when Jase came home from work, he found his wife in the creek behind their house, stumbling through the snow with their baby in her arms. Irene was crying, incoherent. Everyone knew the best hospitals were in the East. Two weeks later, when Irene still hadn't recovered, Jase brought her to Chestnut Ridge for what both he and Agatha hoped would be a short curative stay—a few months at the most. She turned in sadness to Eve. "That was sixteen years ago."

There was a troubled look in Eve's eyes. "It's all my fault."

"Your fault?"

"She wouldn't have gotten sick if it weren't for me."

"Don't say that—don't *ever* say that. Irene wanted you. I've never seen anyone want anything so much in my life. The happiness she felt the summer she was pregnant was the happiness of knowing you were on the way. Everything that happened afterwards ... " Agatha's voice trailed off. "Even the doctors can't say."

"My father should have listened to you." Eve's eyes flashed with anger. "He should have gotten her help right away."

"Jase?" Agatha shook her head. "Your father is a good man, Eve, don't you ever forget it. He did what he thought was best for Irene. He loved her. He couldn't bear to part with her. And he couldn't bear to see his family broken up, his daughter without a mother."

"He never remarried. He never even tried."

Agatha took a long pull of her drink. "No, I'm afraid your father is still waiting for Irene to come home."

Eve fell silent, and when she spoke again, her voice was full of bitterness. "He never told me the truth about her. He never said a thing."

Agatha walked to the window and put her hand on the glass, looking out at the waves. She'd always found the beach restorative; now she could only hope Eve would, too. "I understand how angry you are. And you have every right to be. But consider your father's position." She paused, choosing her words with care. "Irene's illness frightened your father in ways I believe he still can't admit. He's used to being in charge, to tackling crises as they come up and solving them. Irene was the one problem he never could resolve, no matter how hard he tried. I don't believe he's ever forgiven himself for that. And sickness scares people, they fear contagion—even the power of suggestion." She sat back down on the couch. "I can't say I agree with your father, Eve, but I do believe he was trying to protect you. He loves you. You're all he has left."

Agatha's glass was empty. She stood up, refilled it, and returned to her seat. "At the hospital today—Irene said something to you." She hesitated. "Something about a baby."

Eve nodded. "Last winter I saw some things." She turned and looked out at the ocean, avoiding her grandmother's eyes. "I didn't know what they were. I thought they were phantoms, or ghosts." Her voice dropped. "I was afraid I was getting sick—like *her*." She turned back to Agatha. "But I wasn't sick. I know that now. They weren't visions. They were memories."

"So the baby—the one Irene asked you about—" Agatha breathed in hard as the realization dawned on her. "The one you saved—"

"Yes." Eve nodded. "It was me."

Agatha had planned on spending only a few nights with Eve at the shore, but one day turned into another, and soon several weeks had passed, with neither of them showing any inclination to leave. Eve spent most of her time looking out at the ocean, often standing by the low stone wall at the edge of the terrace. The sight of her there never failed to startle Agatha; Eve looked uncannily like Irene in the photograph. From time to time she took walks on the beach, and while she never swam, she often bent down to put a hand in the water. Once, when Agatha asked her why, she just shook her head and said, "I like the way it feels."

She didn't talk much, and Agatha grew used to the fact that much about her granddaughter, like the cigar box, would remain a mystery, perhaps forever. But Eve didn't complain either. She ate heartily whatever Agatha put in front of her, and was reasonably helpful, keeping her room neat, her bed made. Gradually the bruising on her face faded and her skin took on a healthy glow from the sun. She was healing, and Agatha had no desire to rush her. She let her be.

Late at night when her granddaughter was asleep, she called Boo. He was impatient—she'd never stayed away so long before—and he wanted her back home. He had managed to get a show at a gallery—his first one. The opening was in September, and he couldn't decide which photographs to show. He needed her help. But the more Agatha heard Boo agonizing over his pictures, the more annoyed with him she became. Boo could be such a baby sometimes. She didn't know why she'd never noticed it before.

One morning, when she came back from the market, she found Eve sitting at the kitchen table, the old letters she'd guarded in her pocket spread out before her. Without saying a word, Agatha put the groceries away, fixed herself a cup of coffee, and sat down beside her. To her surprise, Eve handed her the letters.

Agatha read through them and then, despite her horror, read them again. When she was done, she looked at her granddaughter with questioning eyes. Hesitantly at first, but picking up speed as she went, Eve told her the whole story, beginning with the first time she rode out to the Swale ranch, ending with the suicide of Eason, the rancher's boy.

Agatha was quiet for a moment. "Your father's right," she said at last. "Eason's death wasn't your fault. You have to understand that. No one can make that kind of choice for another person."

"I loved him." Eve's eyes filled with tears. "He was the one."

Agatha put her arms around her and let her cry. "Shh," she said. "I know."

The ocean air was good for Eve, but it had the oddest effect on Agatha. The strangest thoughts coursed through her mind—the most irrational hopes and dreams. She wouldn't go back to New York after all. She'd stay here, in Connecticut, at her beach house. They'd move in together, she and Eve, and make a proper home of it. She'd never been able to do that before, but there was no reason, was there, that she couldn't do so now? In the fall she'd find a school for Eve, a new job for herself. One of the local papers. Maybe this was what Eve's trip had meant for Agatha after all—a second chance.

She was sitting in the living room one night thinking about it, when all at once she heard a noise at the door. Then the door opened, and Boo tumbled in.

He was cranky and irritable. A true New Yorker, he'd never learned how to drive, and so had taken the train north and then searched for a cab to take him to the house. It had taken him over an hour to find one. There was only one taxi in town, and it was out on a call. He'd had to wait until it came back in.

He would have telephoned, but he'd wanted to surprise her. He didn't seem at all interested in the fact that Eve was there; he gave her a cursory glance then returned to complaining about the things that evidently were far more important—things that concerned him. He'd brought boxes of photographs with him, which he immediately began ferrying inside and dumping on the floor. Agatha wouldn't come to New York to help him organize them for his show, and so he'd decided to bring them to her. Out of the corner of her eye, as Boo talked, Agatha saw Eve steal softly to her room and close the door. Boo gave Agatha a sour look as he dropped the last box to the floor. Apparently everything—including the taxi—was all her fault.

The next day Boo slept late, and Agatha and Eve had their morning together, with its usual quiet routine. But shortly after lunch Boo appeared, demanding to be fed. Agatha complied and afterwards sat with him on the living room couch while he went through the photographs, holding them out to her, talking endlessly about each one, about why he had taken it, and what it was supposed to mean.

Agatha tried to listen, but she couldn't. Boo was so loud. Didn't he ever stop talking? At one time, it seemed to her, Boo had been so pleasantly quiet. Her gaze kept drifting outside to the terrace, where Eve was standing by the stone wall. Boo noticed and grew irritable. Well, he said, if Agatha had no interest at all in what was probably *the most important show in his entire life*, he would go outside himself, and take shots of the beach.

A moment later Agatha saw him on the terrace with his camera under his arm, talking to Eve. Boo, Agatha thought with a start, was actually closer in age to Eve than he was to her. A picture came to her mind of Boo as he'd been when she first met him. He'd been working at a tawdry lingerie magazine, shooting photos of the models while he tried to break into the newspaper business. Every once in a while, he'd bragged to Agatha, he'd managed to talk one of the models into coming home with him for nude "artistic shots."

As Agatha watched in horror, Boo turned his camera on Eve, focusing on her from one angle after another. She saw Eve shake her head, avert her eyes, and turn away. She came inside and looked at Agatha. "I'm going to call my father now." She put her arms around her, hugging her tight. "Thanks for everything," she whispered. She stepped back and smiled. The smile lit up her face and took Agatha's breath away; once again she saw Irene before her, looking just like she had before she'd taken ill. "It's time I went home."

Thirty

Her father came as soon as Evie called for him, arriving the very next day on Agatha's doorstep. "Good God, what you put me through," he scolded Evie as she opened the door. His voice broke, and he stifled a sob as he enveloped her in his arms. "Thank God you're safe."

Safe. Yes. That was it. Evie closed her eyes and pressed her cheek against her father's shoulder. Exactly what she felt in his arms.

He'd flown to New York then rented a car for the drive to the shore. His arrival irritated Boo, who left mercifully soon afterwards, packing up his photographs in a huff. Even Agatha seemed relieved to see him go. Jase and Evie spent the day on the beach, then joined Agatha after dinner in her living room. Long after Evie had gone to bed, she heard the two of them talking, far into the night.

The next morning they bid Agatha good-bye and began their journey home. On their way to the airport, they stopped to see Irene. It was a grey day, a light rain sifting down from a murky sky. Irene was inside, in her cottage, sitting in a chair by the window. Her mother's room, Evie noticed, was small and Spartan, furnished simply with an iron-framed bed, a tall wardrobe with curving doors, and a small round table flanked by a pair of ladder back chairs. Like a nun or monk's chamber, she thought, meant for quiet repose and spiritual healing. But she was also glad to see that it was bright and cheerful, with a beautiful view of the woods and decorative touches in which she saw Agatha's hand at work: colorful abstract prints on the walls, a soft throw rug on the floor, a pottery bowl filled with bangle bracelets and beaded necklaces on the table.

Irene was in a talkative mood and spoke at length to both of them, a monologue delivered in rapid, earnest tones. Evie perched on the bed and tried to understand her mother's words, but they made little sense to her; Irene's thoughts were jumbled and jumped in a seemingly random fashion from place to place. Jase pulled his chair over to her as she spoke, his head bent to hers, his elbows on his knees, as if just being close to her were enough. It broke Evie's heart to see them together. How much they had both suffered over the years! But it also brought her a measure of consolation. For the first time she understood why her father had kept his secret for so long—how much he had wanted to spare her the pain he felt. His mistake—if she could call it that—was in loving his wife too much; he'd never once wavered in his loyalty to her. And Irene, Evie had to believe, loved him back. She saw signs of it in the way her mother drew close to her father as she spoke, now and then placing a trusting hand on his arm. Evie knew she would never doubt her mother's love for her again. Despite everything, they were still a family. The proof was in the cigar box which, she saw with satisfaction, Irene had put in a place of honor on her wardrobe, saved like a treasure.

On their way out, Jase asked Evie to wait while he spoke to the hospital director. She followed him up the steps to the main building then sat outside on a bench beneath the portico, listening as rain pattered on the roof. Clouds scudded through a windy sky, but the air in the woods was still, and a watery sheen gleamed like glass on the grass. She was still waiting for her father to return when the door opened and a nurse came out, hurrying down the steps. She glanced at Evie then stopped and looked again. "You're Irene Glauber's daughter, aren't you?"

"Yes." Evie was surprised at how good it felt to say so. "I am."

"I thought so." The nurse nodded to herself. "You look just like her." Evie smiled. "I know."

They were quiet as they drove to the airport, Jase maneuvering the car on the county roads past the village.

"She won't get any better, will she?" Evie said at last.

"No one knows." He lifted a hand from the wheel in a helpless way. "We can only hope."

"You have to stop blaming yourself." Evie rested a hand on his arm as her mother had done before. "And you have to stop worrying about me. I'm not like her. I mean I am in a lot of ways, but not like *that*."

Jase gave her a wary nod. She knew it would be a long time before he believed her. In the meantime, he would be watching her. But next time—if there was a next time—he wouldn't deny her feelings. He wouldn't pretend not to see what he saw.

"Tell me about her," Evie said, settling herself in for the story as they reached the highway, and the car took on speed. "Tell me what she was like when you met her. Tell me *everything*."

The end of summer had come. The trickle of water in the creek was nothing more than a whisper now, the chokecherry bushes clinging to the banks with brittle, dry limbs, the willows huddling close to the sandy soil. Only the cottonwoods still thrived, thick and leafy. Cottonwoods, Evie had heard once, had deep taproots, making them uniquely suited to the harsh climate of the plains. They burrowed far past the dusty topsoil to the bedrock deep below, seeking out hidden reserves of water. Perhaps she, too, was like the cottonwoods, rooted in place. Despite everything, in the end she had come back.

Soon school would start, and she wouldn't have much time left for riding. She would need to apply herself if she were going to bring her grades up and learn to drive by the winter. But in the meantime she took advantage of the warm weather and languid blue skies to take Bird for long rides in the creek. Like summer, she sensed, her childhood was ending, and she wanted to hold on to the vestiges while she still could.

Most days she rode to the Swale ranch. The first time she came there, she was shocked to discover how much it had changed, how neglected and run-down it had become. The horses had untrimmed hooves and raggedy coats; the yearlings ran wild in their pasture. A rail had come down on the riding ring and lay splintered in the dirt; a loose patch of tin on the old bunkhouse flapped in the wind. The rancher had been transformed by Eason's death. Once he had seemed like a giant to her, towering in both presence and will, but now he was shrunken and bent, hobbling in pain between the house and the barn. She helped him as much as she could, currying the horses, filling the mangers in the barn, bringing fresh water to the stalls. When he drove the pickup to the outer pastures, she sat on the tailgate as she had the year before, flaking bales of hay and filling the feed trays with grain.

"You can't give up," she said to him one morning as they stood by the mares' pasture, watching the foals at play. She almost added, *Eason wouldn't want you to*, but she knew she didn't have to. He knew that.

The foals were weaning, and they looked comical as they tested out mouthfuls of hay, still keeping a wary eye on their mothers. She reached into her pocket and pulled out the cavalrymen's letters. "I want you to have these. As far as I can tell, they belong to you."

She handed the letters to Cyrus, and he tipped his hat back so that he could see better as he read. A look of astonishment crossed his face, followed by a deep wave of sorrow. "So it's true."

"Yes." She ran her hand over the rail top, feeling the coarse grain of the wood. "I'm sorry. I should have known. In a way I did. If only I'd trusted myself—" What had she seen in the rotunda? Had her father been right? Had her obsession with Choke Creek driven her dangerously close to the edge? Or had it brought her a glimpse of the truth? She found herself thinking back to the first day she'd come to the Swale ranch—to the day she'd ridden the wild roan colt. She'd wanted to conquer him with her mind and her will, but it wasn't until she gave herself over to her instincts and her imagination—despite how dangerous it felt—that she'd succeeded in taming him. "I'm sorry," she said again. "I should have said something to Eason. If I had—"

"Don't blame yourself." He pulled his hat down and wiped his eyes with the back of his hand. He blamed himself for Eason. She knew that, just as she knew nothing she said would ever make him change his mind.

One of the foals was eying them. Feeling courageous it pranced over to the rail, and she stuck her hand out, letting it lick the salty sweat from the palm of her hand. "I'm going to take over *The Sun* when my time comes." She nodded towards the letters. "If it's all right with you, I'd like to publish those."

"People won't like it." Cyrus rubbed the forelock between the foal's ears, and it lowered its head in pleasure. "It'll ruin you."

"It'll ruin me even more if I don't."

Cyrus shook his head. "You never let anything stop you, do you?"

"Not when I know I'm right."

"Then I guess you best keep these." He handed the letters back.

The foal had had enough. It lifted its head with a snort and cantered with jerky strides back to its mother. They both watched it go. When she turned around, she saw a plume of dust rising in the distance on the drive. She followed Cyrus to the front of the barn just as a car came to a stop by the riding ring. An elderly man in a cowboy hat got out, followed by a woman in a long denim dress and a young boy. The boy hung back like the foal had done, peeking at them from behind his mother's skirt.

Evie turned to Cyrus. "Let them go."

They stood by the pump and watched as the three Indians headed eastwards down the creek, the elderly man talking as they went, gesturing broadly, pointing things out to the boy.

Maybe, Evie thought, when they came back, she would talk to them. She would like to hear their stories, the ones that had been passed down to them through the generations. She was eager to know more about what had happened at Choke Creek—she was eager to know *everything*. History, she knew now, was nothing like the dry, dead topic she'd come to dread in school. It was vibrant, colorful, alive. The past was like a prism, full of glowing facets of light, each one a story, illuminating another angle. Only by listening to them all could she begin to approach the truth.

The Indians were just disappearing now, fading into the distance. One day soon she would ride out to the battlefield. She needed to see the place where Eason had ended his life, the latest—and she hoped last—of Stevenson's victims. She'd always felt closest to him when she was there. He was a part of that place now, his story connected to the others, joined in blood and water, in earth and wind and sky. But first Cyrus would need her help, bringing the horses in.

Afterword

This book is based on an historical event, the Sand Creek Massacre. On a cold November morning in 1864, in what is now southeastern Colorado, a mixed band of federal and volunteer troops led by Colonel John M. Chivington descended on a sleeping village of Cheyenne and Arapaho Indians camped on the banks of the Big Sandy. At the end of the day over one hundred and fifty Indians, mostly women and children, had been killed. Afterwards the troops remained at the site, scalping, mutilating, and desecrating the bodies. Two soldiers, Captain Silas Soule and Lieutenant Joseph Cramer, refused to participate in the massacre. Horrified by what they had seen, they wrote letters about it to Major Edward Wynkoop in Washington. A federal investigation followed, but the perpetrators were never punished, and a few months later Soule was dead, gunned down in the streets of Denver.

The incident was dogged by controversy from the beginning. In the east it became known as the Sand Creek Massacre, but in the west many people, including William Byers of *The Rocky Mountain News*, insisted it was a justifiable battle. When a monument to Civil War soldiers was erected in front of the Colorado State Capitol building, Sand Creek was named on the battle list.

Then in September of 2000, in one of those fortuitous accidents that sometimes influence the course of history, the letters—which had been lost—were rediscovered. A few years earlier, in December of 1995, *The Rocky Mountain News* had issued an editorial acknowledging its role in the incident. Finally at the end of 2000, in what is surely one of its most belated acts, Congress designated Sand Creek a National Historic Site.

A few months ago I went back to Sand Creek. The first time I was there, in the early stages of researching this book, the land was still privately owned, and I was warned not to step onto it. I stood on the dirt road that crosses the creek and looked northward towards the killing ground. Then, as now, it seemed serenely peaceful. The creek was mostly dry, its course marked by thick green grasses, scattered dark pools of water, and cottonwood trees. On one side rose the bluff where Chivington's men had gathered to fire their howitzers. The wind was blowing, but I was unable to hear the plaintive voices of the murdered victims so many other people have reported hearing there.

I grew up in Denver, about one hundred and fifty miles from Sand Creek. At school I learned the history they taught me, which meant I knew virtually nothing about the Indian Wars. I certainly never heard anything about Sand Creek. When I became a writer, I became interested in the place I had come from, and began reading about it. I was horrified to discover that one of the worst atrocities in U.S. history had taken place in Colorado—and I was filled with outrage when I realized I had been told nothing about it.

I decided to write about Sand Creek, not just what had happened there, but how such a significant event could become distorted—or ignored—in the historical record. I created two families, both of whom traced their roots to the Indian Wars. For the purposes of my story, I made two major changes to what I called "Choke Creek." The first was locating the massacre site in the outskirts of "Danvers" so that Evie could ride her horse to the Swale ranch, just as I once rode my horse from Denver to the outlying prairie. The second was having the soldiers send their letters directly to Asa Glauber, Evie's great-great-grandfather. Otherwise I adhered as closely as possible to the truth. The letters and newspaper reports that Evie discovers in her family's archives are, with minor changes, word for word actual documents from 1864.

I am not the first person to notice the parallels between the Indian

Wars and Vietnam. The Native American writer Simon J. Ortiz has written about it in his poetry collection *From Sand Creek*: "Remember My Lai .../Remember Sand Creek." More recently, the historian Patricia Limerick, commenting on the war in Iraq, wrote, "Much of what we have taken to calling 'the lessons of Vietnam' ... could just as easily have been learned as 'the lessons of the Indian Wars.'" As George Santayana noted, "Those who cannot remember the past are condemned to repeat it."

Much has been written about Sand Creek. The historian who first brought the massacre to my attention was Elliott West. His books *The Way to the West* and *The Contested Plains* are well worth reading for anyone interested in the history of the region. A good place to start for further reading on the massacre itself is Stan Hoig's *The Sand Creek Massacre*. For the opposing view, try William R. Dunn's *"I Stand by Sand Creek"*. Newspaper reports from the era have been compiled by Scott C. Williams in *Colorado History Through the News: The Indian Wars of 1864 through The Sand Creek Massacre*. Soule's and Cramer's letters are available through the archives of *The Rocky Mountain News*. For the Vietnam chapters in this book I relied on material from many sources, including Philip Caputo's powerful memoir, *A Rumor of War*, the journalist Michael Herr's *Dispatches*, Michael Bilton and Kevin Sim's *Four Hours in My Lai*, and Jonathan Shay's *Achilles in Vietnam*. Above all I am indebted to Tim O'Brien's many books on the war, especially *The Things They Carried*.

As for the Indian Wars—there is much that still needs to be said. It is my hope that this book will become one voice in the conversation.

Acknowledgments

The saying goes, It takes a village to raise a child. The same is true for books, especially when the writer, as in this case, is the publisher, too. Each step of the way, I have had the good fortune to encounter people who supported me in the most generous, dedicated, and patient ways possible. I will forever be grateful.

Kathy Hudson and Greg Otto assured me that if I wrote a book, there would be an audience to read it. Lavinia Edmunds and Leslie Goetsch read through early drafts with unflagging enthusiasm. I was fortunate to study with Mark Mirsky, Gerald Duff, Sandra Scofield, and John Dufresne. With insight and wisdom, Nina Romano and the other gals of Screw Iowa! fame—Mariana Damon, Marnette Graff, and Melissa Westemeier—provided the skillful editing that enabled me to finish the book. Working with them has made living the writing life not only possible but also enjoyable.

Thanks to David Halaas, who showed me the way to Sand Creek, to Margie Simon for her help with the afterword, and to Melissa Rosati, who provided essential publishing advice. The keen eye of Amy Eward combined with the artistic talents of Professor Bert Smith and his graduate student Giordana Segneri in the School of Communications Design at the University of Baltimore to produce a book that is delightful both to look at and to read. My children, Adam, Sara, and Benjamin, shared their mother with her work with cheerful grace.

The publication of this book is, quite simply, the realization of a dream I have had for a long time. Without my husband, Don, I wouldn't even have known to dream it.

About the Author

A native of Denver, Colorado, Lauren Small earned a Ph.D. in Comparative Literature from the Johns Hopkins University. She has published in academic journals such as *MLN* and *German Quarterly*, and her work has been anthologized in *Exile in Culture*. She co-translated an essay in *Kafka's Contextuality*.

Small's fiction has appeared in literary magazines such as *Fiction*, *The Monocacy Valley Review*, *Partisan Review*, and *StoryQuarterly*. Her short story "Livia" was nominated for a Pushcart Prize. She has published essays in *Driftwood* and *Finding Change* and has presented her work at readings in New York and in Colorado. She lives in Baltimore, Maryland, where she is an adjunct professor of creative writing at the Community College of Baltimore County.